A Rose in Amber

Between the Rifle and the Spear,
Book Three

by

Roberta C. M. DeCaprio

A Rose in Amber: Between the Rifle and the Spear, Book Three

COPYRIGHT © 2011 by Roberta C. M. DeCaprio

Cover Art by *Angela Anderson*

The Wild Rose Press
PO Box 708
Adams Basin, NY 14410-0706
Visit us at www.thewildrosepress.com

Publishing History
First English Tea Rose Edition, 2011
Print ISBN 1-60154-926-1

Published in the United States of America

Dedication

My sincere thanks to my friend Paul Rex Steers
and his lady, Cath, of Arbroath, Scotland,
for the advice and help in researching
the train travel sequence of this novel.
Also to
my beloved dog Kitty and calico cat Ginger,
who sat beside me while I wrote.
And lastly to my editor, Patricia Tanner.
Working with her on this series
has been my complete honor and enjoyment.

True Love, Like a Rose In Amber, Lasts Forever

Chapter One

Fall, 1892
Aboard an England-bound vessel, the Entrenous

Sunny Elizabeth Eagle paced the small cabin's floor, the worn wooden planks creaking with each step. With hands fisted at her sides, fearful images triggered frightening thoughts.

Where were Raven and Gabriel? Why had they not returned to the ship?

"Good heavens, will I end up traveling to England alone?" Her stomach clenched, and she paced a little faster.

She wished she were back in the Apache village she called home, in spite of the, *indah*, white agents taking over her tribe. They destroyed her people's way of life and compromised the women, thus the very reason she and her siblings were sent to live with her mother's aunt in Brighton.

"Good heavens," she groaned again, as the ship jerked and swayed. "It appears I *am* going to England all alone."

Another lurch of the ship knocked her off balance. She reached for the post of the bunk to steady her stand and slowly made her way to the edge of the bed. Her stomach churned, this time the meal she had eaten that morning threatened to make its appearance. She swallowed hard, the bile rising to the back of her throat, and lay down upon the bunk. Closing her eyes, she took deep breaths to calm the nausea, practicing the warrior's way of detaching your mind from whatever pain and discomforts your body was experiencing.

As soon as her stomach calmed, she drifted off to sleep.

****

Sunny awakened to the gruff tone of her brother's voice. "Where is Raven?"

She wiped the sleep from her eyes and blinked them into focus upon his worried face. With bushy brows furrowed and his jaw clenched, Gabriel Golden Eagle was visibly upset. It was something not at all pleasant to experience but even less appealing to wake to. "Is she not with you?"

His frown deepened. "My last words were for the two of you to remain locked in this cabin, so *hat'ugha*, why the *hell* would she be with me?"

With a swipe of her tongue she moistened dry lips. "*Bigha,* because she went to look for you."

He crossed his arms over his muscular chest. "Again, I ask, *hat'ugha*?"

Her stomach soured, this time with anxiety. Getting Gabriel angry was never a good thing to do. "You took so long to check on your luggage, that we grew worried. Then Raven entered your cabin and saw the bags upon your bunk and—"

He bellowed his interruption. "What right did you have to go snooping around in my room?"

Inside, she cringed. "We did not snoop, just glanced around and spotted the bags sitting on the bunk." She lifted a defiant chin. "Besides, did you not just barge into our room?"

His lips thinned. "I called out several times, both of your names, and did not receive an answer."

She cleared her throat. "Then you can understand how we felt when we did the same. That is when Raven decided to leave the cabin. She had a good feeling where to find you."

His frown deepened. "Oh, she did, did she? And where would that be?"

He stiffened beneath the gentle finger that traced the scar across his back.

"How did you get this?" a voice laced with concern came from behind.

Rafe spun around to find Sunny standing with a flask of water in her hand, and a most endearing look upon her beautiful face. "Don't look at me like that."

She neared him. "Like what?"

Frustration coursed through his body. "Like that...the way you are now, as if I were an injured animal in need of rescue."

She gasped. "How do you know about my animals?"

"It doesn't matter how." He scowled. "I'd also advise you not to go sneaking up behind a man wielding an axe. It could be disastrous."

"I did not sneak up, in fact I called out your name twice," she defended.

Frustration mounted to rage. "And so you thought touching me would be better?"

She ignored his anger. "How did you get that scar?"

He frowned at her audacity. "That's none of your business."

"Why?"

He wiped the sweat from his brow with an arm. "Why, what?"

"Why is it not my business?"

"Because it isn't," he retorted. "Nothing I do has any bearing on you at all."

"How can you say that?" she argued. "We are friends, are we not? You are staying in my aunt's home, helping my brother, you have saved me from my doom twice already...and you even know about my rescued animals. Why am I not part of your life as you are of mine...why can I not ask you a simple question?"

Praise for Roberta C. M. DeCaprio

A ROSE IN AMBER is the third installment in Roberta C. M. DeCaprio's Between the Rifle and the Spear series, carrying on the saga begun in *THE GOLDEN LADY* and *ONE PERFECT FLOWER*. Both previous books have been given four-star reviews.

"At the cantina we passed on our way to the ship."

Gabriel ran his hand through his hair, the one pale strand splashing from his crown to his temple, curling forward. Annoyed, he brushed the lock aside. "Well, *dayden*, that was a very unwise thing for Raven to do."

She sat forward, now also frowning. When her father called her *dayden*, the Apache word for little girl, it sounded way more endearing. "And I told her so in those exact words."

"Not forceful enough, it seems," he snapped.

Her heart raced. Swinging her legs off the bunk, she stood to face her brother—a whole head-and-a-half taller than she. "If Raven never found you, and she is not here, then where can she be?"

He threw his hands in the air. "Still in the cantina, wandering the streets, or perhaps she boarded the wrong ship? There were two others docked beside this one. Your guess is as good as mine, Sunny."

She reached out for her brother's arm, gripping tight with fear. "Good heavens, Gabriel, what do we do now?"

She watched the play of emotions wash across his face, a mixture of fear and rage combined. Gabriel was sent along on this journey to guard and keep her and Raven safe. Now, not even gone long from America's shores, one of them was already lost. She knew her brother was blaming himself far more than he deserved—although in truth, if he had not left to go drinking in the cantina none of this would have happened. But she was not about to point that fact out to him for fear of causing a worse upset.

What would Father say if he knew?

Inside she shuddered at the thought. Proud Eagle, when angered, was not any better than Gabriel.

"The captain, the one that runs the ship," Gabriel said, breaking through her thoughts. "We must go to see him, tell him to turn the ship around—go back to shore so we can find out what happened to Raven."

She gasped. "And what if he refuses?"

Gabriel's deep blue eyes flashed with anger. "I will not allow him to refuse." He reached for her hand. "Come," he grunted, leading her to the door. "From this time on you are not to be out of my sight."

She pulled free from his grasp. "Stop it! Stop pulling me along like I was a child."

He narrowed his eyes. "But that is exactly what you are, Sunny…a child who could not obey."

His insult cut her deep, and she blinked back the tears welling in her eyes. "I am *not* the one who left the cabin, Gabriel."

He took an audible breath and leaned against the oak portal. "I am sorry, Sunny. What you say is true." Closing his eyes he rested his head back against the door. "It is just I…I was supposed to…"

She went to him, wrapping her arms around his waist and placing a cheek against his hard chest. The beat of his *biijii*, heart, echoed in her ears. She took pity for her brother's agony over losing Raven. The obligation to keep his sisters safe had not been met, and for this he suffered greatly. She sighed and tightened the embrace, instantly forgiving him for his outburst to her. "All will be fine, my brother."

Gabriel placed his hands on her shoulders. "I pray you are right, Sunny."

She lifted her head to look deep into the worrisome glance that met her gaze. Gabriel, at times, could look and sound like a bear, but deep within his heart the loyalty he had for his family was genuine and strong. He loved fiercely, as well, grieving still for the loss of his wife and baby boy, though three years had passed since their death.

And now, this situation with Raven gave him great torment.

He tweaked her nose. "Ah, *dayden*, you are so much like our mother, with the golden hair and the large blue eyes. And both of you have a way of being a comfort during difficult times." He chuckled and added. "As well as getting everything you want."

"Right now the only thing I want is to find Raven."

He nodded and reached gently for her hand. "Come then, let us find the captain."

She forced a smile in agreement as he opened the door and led her out into the corridor. The floor pitched beneath her feet, and she stepped carefully, so as not to lose her balance. The shaking ground made it difficult to keep up with Gabriel's long strides.

Up until that point the queasiness had subsided, or was forgotten because she feared so for her sister. But now, coming out onto the open deck and seeing where the choppy sea met the sky, the nausea returned. Clapping a hand over her mouth, she broke free from her brother's hold and ran to the rail. There, off the side of the ship, she spilled the contents of her stomach.

Her head spun and she groaned. "Oh, Gabriel, I am so dizzy."

He turned her to face him, his own flesh appearing a faint shade of green. He swallowed hard and cleared his throat. "It does not help to look at the water, it will make matters worse."

"I do not know how matters can be any worse." No sooner had the words left her lips, than her arms and legs grew weak and she collapsed. Her brother's strong embrace was all that kept her from hitting the deck before her world darkened.

****

Sunny had only lost consciousness one other

5

time in her life. She was seven and playing with a friend by the river while her mother did the wash. The other girl fell and hit her lip on a rock. The wound bled, and bled, and bled. The sight of so much blood caused Sunny to faint. It was the same now as it was then. She could feel and hear everything, but could not move or speak...imprisoned in her own body.

She knew Gabriel carried her away from the rail, felt him lay her down, and then heard voices chattering around her. First her brother's familiar tone, then the high-pitched one of a woman's. Repeatedly they called out her name.

A strong odor, placed beneath her nose brought her back to her senses. She jerked away from the potent aroma and coughed, then blinked open her eyes.

"There she is, coming around now," the woman said, dabbing a handkerchief across Sunny's brow. "You just stay put, you poor mite, till you've fully recovered your bearings."

She blinked again, taking in her surroundings. The bunk she lay upon was much larger than her own, as was the cabin. "Where am I?"

"You're in my cabin, mite," the woman answered. "You collapsed right outside my door, and it was faster and more convenient to bring you in here instead of back to your own quarters." She sat her stocky frame down upon the edge of the bunk and gave Sunny an affectionate pat on the shoulder. "I'm Lady Eugenia Abbott. My husband, Lord Stanley, and I were just coming out for a stroll on deck when we saw you collapse." Her thin lips spread over uneven teeth. "I do hope you don't mind my coming to your aid?"

"No, not at all. *Ashoge*, thank you."

Gabriel knelt down beside the bunk and took her hand. "Are you feeling better, *dayden*?"

6

She cleared her throat, dragging her gaze from the elder woman to her brother's. "Yes, much better."

"That's so wonderful to hear, my dear," the woman preened. "I have a daughter around your age. Annabella's her name. In fact, we're returning from a visit with her. She just had her first born, a son, named Thomas Matthew. A good Christian name, don't you think? My daughter married a missionary, and the two are spreading the word of the Lord in Texas."

"That's probably enough, my lady," a voice drawled from across the room. A tall, thin man with a balding head made his way into view and after introducing himself as Lord Abbott, he turned his attention on his wife. "Let's give her some room to breathe, shall we?"

Lady Abbott giggled. "Oh my, so sorry, I do tend to rattle on. I believe I just got carried away. My motherly nature, you see. And with my own precious daughter gone, I do miss being needed."

Sunny cast her brother a silent plea, one he caught instantly.

Gabriel stood. "I thank you both kindly for your help, but my sister and I were on our way to discuss an urgent matter with the captain. So if you will excuse us?" He extended a hand to help her stand.

Again the room spun. "Good heavens," she gasped, quickly sitting back upon the bunk.

"Oh, dear, dear," Lady Abbott fussed. "This will never do."

"Hmm, it appears you're correct, my love," her husband added.

"It might be wise to wait here, mite. Let your brother talk with the captain," Lady Abbott advised.

Gabriel extended a hand to Lord Abbott. "I am sorry for not introducing myself properly, but with all the commotion—"

"That's quite understandable," Lord Abbott interrupted, accepting Gabriel's greeting.

"I am Gabriel Golden Eagle, and this is my sister, Sunny."

She gave the elderly couple a nod and forced a smile. "I am ashamed for being such a bother."

"Nonsense," Lady Abbott said, helping Sunny to lie back upon the bed. "I think you just need time to adjust...get your sea legs, as the sailors would say. My first voyage found me flat on my back, in bed throughout the first few days of the trip."

Sunny frowned, hoping that did not happen to her.

"Then a kind woman traveling in the next cabin put me on to ginger tea and sucking on peppermint sticks. It helped considerably, so I never travel aboard without either."

Again she glanced at Gabriel. He was growing impatient, and rightly so. With each moment Raven was being left farther and farther behind.

Sunny took an audible breath. For fear Gabriel would lose his temper, she did not like the idea of him going to see the captain without her along. But a decision had to be made, and quickly. Since she was in no condition at this point to walk the distance to the captain's cabin, there was no other choice. "Perhaps you should see to the matter with the captain while I rest a bit more."

"A capital idea," Lady Abbott said. "And after I get a bit of ginger tea into you, Stanley and I will escort you back to your own cabin."

"Thank you, Lady Abbott," Gabriel said.

"I will pray the captain complies with our wishes," Sunny said.

"Captain Rafe Cavendish will do everything in his power to straighten out whatever problem you're having. Isn't that right, Stanley?"

"Aye, my wife speaks the truth," Lord Abbott

vouched.

"He comes from a family of stellar quality. Though at times he's a bit too fond of the ladies, several I hear, all in all, I believe he's a fair chap. If you've a problem, and he can be in accord, he will." Lady Abbott giggled. "We're practically like family, well by marriage that is. The captain's brother, Simon, is engaged to my niece, Fiona Wade."

Lady Abbott, though she meant well, was making Sunny's head hurt worse. She cast another silent plea to Gabriel, who again picked up on the meaning. Kneeling down beside the bunk, he placed a warm hand upon her brow.

"Do not lose your temper," she whispered.

He tweaked her nose. "Stop acting like Mother."

She frowned. *That is exactly what Raven had said just before she left the ship.*

Chapter Two

The knock on the portal disturbed Rafe Cavendish from the heavy realm of paperwork, and he motioned for Aaron, his cabin boy, to see who it was.

The passenger list showed two hundred travelers were on the voyage. In the years he'd captained the *Entrenous*, he'd prided himself on learning the names of each commuter that came aboard and their destinations. Sadly, this would be the tiny ship's last run. Though the *Entrenous* was still quite capable of making a trip across the ocean, newer luxury liners were the preference of the day. They had more sophisticated bathroom facilities and lamps that used mineral oil to light the cabins instead of whale blubber oil. At one time, the whaling industry was a business that had traders cashing in on both sides of the Atlantic; everything from catching the whale, to the rendering, and distribution of the final product. Now with mineral oil and petroleum available the whale industry was slowly collapsing.

The new ships had triple decks, smoking rooms with tiled floors, red leather chairs; even libraries. And the dining rooms, at the top of grand, spiral staircases, were as elegant as any posh restaurant. Stabilizers at the base of the new ships also made for smoother ocean travel.

Aaron broke through his thoughts. "Beggin' ye pardon, Cap'n, there's a bloke at the portal needin' to speak with ye. He said 'twas o' an urgent matter."

Rafe nodded. "Very well, show him in." He set

aside the register and stood, straightening his waistcoat.

A tall, solid built gent, tanned and broad shouldered, entered the cabin. The tensing of his jaw betrayed his deep frustration. He extended a large, calloused hand and introduced himself. "I am Gabriel Golden Eagle."

Rafe accepted the greeting. "Welcome aboard the *Entrenous*, Mr. Eagle. I am Captain Rafe Cavendish." He smiled, hoping Mr. Eagle would do the same. "Are you and your two sisters comfortable in your accommodations?"

The other man raked a hand through his hair. "My sister, Sunny, is unable to leave the bed, at the moment, or she too would be here with me."

"Aye, many first time sea goers have trouble adjusting to the rock of the ship. In a matter of days she'll feel better."

"And my sister, Raven, has been left behind."

Rafe frowned. "I'm afraid I don't follow, sir. Left behind where?"

Mr. Eagle took an audible breath. "She was left in America, Captain."

His heart sank to his toes. "Are you sure of this, Mr. Eagle?"

The man nodded and crossed his arms over his chest. "You need to turn this ship around immediately."

Rafe didn't mean to laugh sardonically at the man's absurd demand. "A vessel this large is not that easy to turn around."

Mr. Eagle shrugged. "I do not see why it would be a problem; there is more than enough room to do so."

"Well, that's not the only factor here."

The other man frowned, his eyes narrowing. "What else is there to be concerned with?"

He stroked his beard, responding with calm

emphasis. "I have a schedule to keep, Mr. Eagle. I am obligated to my employer and the passengers aboard this ship to arrive at England's docks in a timely fashion."

There was a distinct hardness to Gabriel's tone. "I do not care about your schedule or your obligations. My sister is all alone, and she is either stuck on shore or has boarded another ship by mistake." His jaw muscles throbbed. "And I need to find her."

Rafe's annoyance with the bugger increased. "And if she did get on another ship, we'd be turning back for naught. Both ships boarded beside the *Entrenous* departed before us."

Mr. Eagle stiffened as though he'd been struck. "What were the other ships?"

"One was an oil barge, and even at first glance it looks nothing like the *Entrenous*. I highly doubt your sister would mistake that sea-going vessel for this one."

"And what of the second ship?"

"The *Sweet Maureen* is a cargo ship." He arched a brow. "I have to admit she could be mistaken, especially to an untrained eye, for this one in the fog. And I do remember it being a bit foggy."

The other man's voice was completely emotionless, and it chilled Rafe. "What is the similar ship's destination?"

"Ireland, Mr. Eagle. Limerick, Ireland."

Rafe didn't expect what happened next. One minute he was discussing the problem with Mr. Eagle about his sister and the next the other man's temper flared out of control, forcing Rafe to wrestle him to the floor. Never, in all the years at his command, had he ever dealt with a paying passenger in such a way. He was just grateful the incident didn't come to hard blows or bloodshed of any sort. Injuring a passenger, or suffering an injury himself, would result in paperwork and questions by the authorities when he docked in England. Rafe wanted neither.

Aaron ran for backup at some point during the skirmish, and Rafe ordered his men to lock Mr. Eagle in the galley storage room. He hoped this would give the chap a chance to cool down and listen to reason. Mr. Eagle's confinement would also give Rafe a chance to talk with the sister who remained on board. Perhaps he could get her to reason with her brother, if she herself didn't take to hysterics.

He could never stand to see a woman cry. He survived the Royal Army, weathered many storms at sea, and could handle his weight in a fight. But a woman's tears totally crushed him, undid him to the very core, and were the very reason he would forever be branded with an ugly scar across his back.

Aye, all because of a woman.

A certain woman, to be exact, by the name of Deandra, whom he foolishly fell in love with in spite of the fact she was engaged to another man. She had come to him late one night with woeful tears, bloodied and bruised by the hands of an abusive fiancé. He swore then and there to defend her. That was a mistake he'd never repeat. After fighting a duel on her behalf and winning, Deandra returned to the bloke. He sighed, secretly chastising himself for his stupidity. But there was no time for rehashing old wounds when he had a difficult task at hand.

Why did leaving a passenger behind have to happen on my watch?

By rights this last voyage was suppose to be under his brother, Simon's, command. The two of them were equally employed by Henderson and Company, the owners of the *Entrenous*. The engagement party his parents were throwing Simon and his betrothed, Fiona Wade, this very evening was the reason he'd agreed to take his brother's place instead.

Marriage, what travesty. Though his brother's fiancée was a wonderful person, striking, with long amber curls and large brown eyes, how Simon could think of staying tied to land for the sake of being at a woman's side was a mystery to him. It wasn't something he ever planned on doing, especially after seeing how fickle women can be. Nay, he neither wanted nor needed a permanent relationship.

The sea was his love instead, and the only one he'd have in his life now. Her vast blue waters set him free and there was never a dull moment to be had. The salt spray on his face, even the winds of stormy weather, captivated him. The sea spoke to him with a crash of a wave, her voice a familiar comfort to his ears. And he'd not be bound by the confines of matrimony. Besides, he had his pick of women. After he bedded them, had his fill, there were nay an obligation or strings attached. He was a free agent—free like the wind and the sea.

He stroked his beard as he approached Miss Eagle's portal and braced himself for one very distraught woman. And she had every right to be upset. Only the good Lord knew where her sister was, and her brother was being detained below. If Rafe were in her place he wouldn't exactly be pleased.

Taking a deep breath, he hesitated to knock on the door. His beloved grand mamma's words came to him, *"Stop your lollygaggin', mite, and get a move on."*

He let out the breath he'd been holding and prepared himself for another confrontation.

Chapter Three

After a bit of ginger tea and sucking on a peppermint stick, Sunny felt much better. Lady Abbott, in spite of her constant chatter, was really the reason her health returned. Though still a bit queasy in the stomach, her dizziness subsided, making it possible for her to return to her own cabin and change into something more comfortable. She removed the traveling suit and cumbersome petticoat and replaced it with a simple day dress. The longer sleeves would help to combat the evening chill. She loved how the white woman's clothing made her appear older, but she had to agree with Raven. The garments were not as comfortable as a buckskin tunic and skirt. The footwear did little soothing as well. At the moment her toes screamed out for a pair of moccasins.

A knock on the cabin's portal startled her. The Abbotts knew she wanted to sleep and promised they would not look in on her till morning. And her brother would have used the adjoining door. A bit apprehensive, she made her way on shaky limbs to the portal. "Who is it?"

A rich, deep voice answered. "Captain Rafe Cavendish."

Her heart raced. If Gabriel was not still speaking with the captain, then why had he not returned to his cabin? Panic welled in her throat.

What now has happened to Gabriel?

She opened the portal and stared silently at the man standing before her. His cornflower-blue gaze met hers, a buttery smile as soft as a caress curling his full lips. "I hope you're feeling better, Miss Eagle?"

She nodded; a vaguely sensuous light passing between them. Then a curious *swoop*—and not of the ill kind—pulled at her innards as she searched his ruggedly handsome face, bronzed by wind and sun. His beard gave him an even manlier aura.

She forced a smile in return. "I am much better, thank you."

His thick, dark hair tapered neatly to his collar, curling upon the confident set of his powerful shoulders. "Welcome aboard the *Entrenous*."

The muscles straining against the crisp, white shirt he wore quickened her pulse, momentarily robbing her of a voice. All she could manage was a nod.

He then took the liberty to enter her cabin and shut the door behind him. She stepped back, his boldness for a moment frightening her. But then, with a gentle hand he led her to a chair, went to the pitcher set upon the table and poured her a glass of water. When he handed her the drink, their fingers touched, sending a rush of warmth throughout her body.

"Where is my brother?" she whispered.

His smile fell. "Ah, well, Miss Eagle that is why I am here."

She closed her eyes. "Has he lost his temper?"

"Aye, miss, he has."

She opened her eyes, catching the strain and fatigue upon his face. It seemed this day had been a long one for them all. "Where is he now?"

"Below, in the galley." He met her gaze boldly. "I'm afraid, for his own sake and that of the rest aboard, I had to detain him."

Tears burned the back of her throat. She took a sip of the water, swallowing it hard. "You could think of no other way?"

16

"Nay, miss. Your brother was quite...well, let's say, beside himself, for a lack of a better word."

She came to Gabriel's defense. "And would you not be the same in his situation, Captain?"

"Aye, Miss Eagle, I would. But the way your brother reacted was something I cannot abide on this ship. It is my duty to protect him and the others from harm while aboard."

Her heart hammered. "You cannot believe my brother would do anyone harm?"

"I cannot...will not take that chance, Miss Eagle."

The captain's attitude infuriated her. "My brother's *reaction* would never be directed to another aboard this ship. Obviously, his outburst was due to your refusal to turn the ship around and go back for my sister." She raised a defiant chin. "Am I correct in assuming that is what happened?"

His eyes roamed her facial features, a glint of what appeared like admiration flickering in his eyes. "It was not a feasible task to accomplish, and your brother refused to accept my decision." He pulled a second chair beside her and sat down. "Could you tell me how it is your sister came to be separated from the two of you?"

"Gabriel did not tell you?"

"Nay, we never made it as far as an explanation."

Her breath seemed to solidify in her throat, sorrow and fear building beyond anything she could endure. Placing the glass she had been holding on a nearby table, she covered her face with her hands, and wept.

The deep tone of his voice broke with emotion. "Please, Miss Eagle, don't do that."

"Do what?" she choked out hoarsely.

He stammered. "Get so...get so..."

She raised her gaze and finished his refrain.

"Upset?"

He nodded, the raw emotion in his eyes struggling to stay in check. "Though you have every right, it will not help the situation."

She nodded in agreement, wiping her eyes with the backs of her hands. "You are right, of course."

He handed her a handkerchief. "I need to know what transpired."

The handkerchief smelled of his citrus and musky scent. She blew her nose on the hanky and cleared her throat. "You see, Captain, my brother takes his comfort from drinking the harsh spirits, ever since his wife and infant son died," she began, then went on to explain why Raven left the ship.

"Ah, it becomes clear now." He arched a brow. "Your brother blames himself for your sister's plight."

She nodded again. "So you can see why he needs to set things right again."

"Aye, I understand."

She handed him back the handkerchief.

He smiled, a lopsided grin that for some reason she thought endearing. "Keep it, Miss Eagle."

She stuffed the hanky in her skirt pocket. "*Ashoge*, thank you."

He stood and extended an elbow. "I will take you to your brother now."

She looked into his cornflower blue eyes. "Please, Captain, keep what I have told you about my brother between us."

He nodded. "You have my word, Miss Eagle."

And for some strange reason she believed he was a man who kept his word.

Still weak and desperate to keep down the ginger tea Lady Abbott insisted she drink, Sunny leaned on his arm as they made their way to the galley.

The captain unlocked the storage room door, and

she glanced around. The small quarters had no windows and wooden crates were stacked against the walls. A lantern, hung on a hook, was the only light available. She spotted her brother sitting on one of the crates, and she ran to him, flinging her arms around his neck and burying her face beneath his chin.

He embraced her with strong arms. "I hope you are happy, Captain. Look how you have upset my sister, after she has been so ill."

"Happy is the last thing I am, Mr. Eagle." The captain sighed. "I've brought her here so we could all come to terms with this problem."

"The only term I will agree to would be the one where you go back to America for my other sister," Gabriel snapped.

She pushed out of his arms. "Stop, Gabriel."

He frowned. "Silence, Sunny. This is between us men."

"No, it is not, my brother. Raven is my sister as well, and fighting is not going to help a thing."

"You might try listening to her, Mr. Eagle."

Gabriel's face reddened. "And you might try understanding how horrible this whole thing is for her...for us both."

"I do, Mr. Eagle," the captain countered, his own face now turning a shade of crimson as well.

Sunny realized the two men again using their fists on one another would not help Raven a bit, and it may leave Gabriel locked in the cramped storage room throughout the night.

"Gabriel, I am begging you to remain calm." She cast a glance at the captain and sharpened her tone. "And you might try doing the same."

Rafe blinked, bewildered at her snappy retort.

She stepped away from Gabriel and placed hands on hips. "We will settle nothing with anger."

The captain cleared his throat and inclined his

head politely. "You're right, Miss Eagle."

She could not help but think his apology cost him dearly a measure of pride. "Please, explain *hat'ugha*, why you cannot turn this ship around."

The captain took an audible breath. "First, I would like to ask Mr. Eagle what is his livelihood?"

"I fail to see what my work has to do with this situation," Gabriel spat.

Sunny turned on him with a sharp look.

Gabriel read her meaning and reluctantly offered an answer. "I am a scout. I lead wagon trains to their destination by way of a safe route."

"Are you in a position to follow a schedule, to be responsible for others?"

"Yes," Gabriel grumbled.

"Are there several trains going to several destinations at the same time?" the captain probed.

"Yes, at least three bands depart at one time," her brother explained.

"And if one of those wagons left with the wrong party, what would you tell their family in your care?"

"I would tell them when the lost family got to a destination, someone would send word to where we were going."

"And then the lost family would be escorted to the proper destination?"

"Yes," Gabriel said.

She frowned, casting her gaze again at Rafe Cavendish. "Where are you going with all this, Captain?"

"I am merely trying to prove the responsibility to my job is not all that different than Mr. Eagle's. Even if it was possible to turn the ship around, and it isn't, as I told your brother when we first spoke," the captain added, "there is no guarantee your sister stayed ashore. If she boarded another ship, our efforts would be for naught."

"But I am not certain she boarded one of the other ships," Gabriel protested, his forehead vein swelling with annoyance.

"I am," Sunny said, turning to look at her brother.

"How can you be sure of this, Sunny?" Gabriel demanded.

"Raven knew when we sailed. She made a point of asking the cabin boy. If she could not find you in the cantina, she would return to the ship. She would have to, because she would not leave me to travel alone. We gave each other our word we would never be apart." She turned to look deep into the captain's eyes. "Were the other two ships very similar to this one, Captain?"

"Just the one, as I told your brother earlier. The *Sweet Maureen*, a cargo ship bound for Limerick, Ireland would look similar to the *Entrenous*. I know of Captain Kirby and the owner of the vessel, Lord Braiton Shannon, who always travels with his cargo. If your sister landed on that ship, and I can make a safe bet she did because the other was just an oil barge, then she'd be well cared for. After the *Sweet Maureen* docks in Ireland, your family will be contacted and your sister will be placed on a ship bound for England. Her passage will be paid by Lord Shannon. He is not only a rich man, but a kind and generous person. He will do what is right by your sister."

The captain glared at Gabriel. "And staying locked up in this storage room isn't doing right by this sister," he said, gesturing to Sunny. "So I will forget about your indiscretion tonight and allow you to return to your cabin." His brows furrowed. "But should this ever happen again, you have my oath this storage room will be your quarters for the remainder of the voyage." And with that said, he left them alone to worry about Raven together.

Chapter Four

Sunny slept fitfully. The thought of Raven on a strange ship, without benefit of her own clothes and family, tormented her.

Lady Abbott, true to her word, came by early, followed by a steward carrying a tray of tea and biscuits. "The breakfast bell will ring at 8:30," he announced and placed the tray on the table before leaving the cabin.

"So then you must hurry to get washed, dressed, and join us downstairs in the dining hall," Lady Abbott coaxed.

Sunny looked at the food tray. "Is this not breakfast?"

"Oh, heavens no, mite," Lady Abbott shrieked. "This is just the beginning, you'll see." She giggled and left the cabin, giving Sunny a playful wink.

She glanced down at the tray of food, her stomach rumbling. The only nourishment she'd had since boarding the ship was ginger tea and peppermint candy. The delicious aroma of biscuits heaped with apple jam filled the room, and she could not resist the temptation any longer. She ate as she dressed and when the bell rang she was ready to leave her quarters.

Gabriel, appearing tired and unusually quiet, escorted her to the dining hall. They sat with Lord and Lady Abbott, and a young German count by the name of Ivan Sontag.

"I do not understand the formalities before all of your names," Sunny confessed. "Why do you use lord, lady, and count?"

Ivan's huge azure eyes locked with hers, his complexion as fair as his hair. Over oatmeal porridge, salmon strips, bread with jam or butter, tea and coffee, Count Sontag explained the titles of society and the various class systems.

She frowned. "It is the same in my country, with my father's people." *The white men look down upon the Apache.*

Ivan's chiseled features brightened. "*Fraulein*, I should very much vish to hear all about your father's people, as I am intrigued vith other cultures."

"You speak in a similar tongue as a friend back home, Reverend Ben. He is from Sweden," she said.

The count made no comment in regard to her statement, just inclined his head politely and smiled.

"And what is your reason for traveling from America to England?" Gabriel probed, his eyes fixed on the count.

Ivan waved a hand over his head. "I never speak of my *arbeit*, vork vhile I take my pleasure."

She caught Gabriel's frown. Her brother did not like the count being so evasive.

"I must beg you to reconsider for this one time, Count," Lady Abbott urged. "I find the reasons for travel so interesting."

Ivan cleared his throat. "Ve vill talk more at dinner, then, *ja*?"

"Oh, that would be lovely for us all to share a table at dinner," Lady Abbott said.

Ivan stood. "But for now I must take my leave. I have promised to play a game of *Karten*, cards with a *freund* staying in the cabin across from mine." He bowed politely in Sunny's direction. "If you vill *entschuldigen sie*, excuse me, *Fraulein*?"

She smiled. "Of course, sir."

He looked around to each one at the table. "*Herr* Eagle, Lord and Lady Abbott, *Haben Sie einen guten Morgen*, good morning to you all."

Gabriel frowned and chewed his bread in silence.

****

Sunny did not know how she would be able to eat again when the bell summoning every passenger to the dining hall rang. It seemed to her all one did on a ship was eat. At half past the hour of one, they were called to eat mutton, vegetables, fruits, and nuts. At four, again, a steward came to her cabin with tea and biscuits. At half past the hour of six in the evening, she would be called to dinner. If she kept this up throughout the entire seven days of the voyage, she would not be able to fit into any of her beautiful dresses. Perhaps this was the reason the other women aboard hardly touched the food on their plates. All of them just picked at a potato here, a slab of beef there. How wonderful it would be if she could share all this food with the starving members of her tribe. Her people would not leave a morsel untouched. "I will not either, in honor of them," she whispered aloud.

Rummaging through her trunk for something different to wear at dinner, due to Lady Abbott's tutoring that evening attire needed to be more elegant then daytime wear; Sunny found her mother's wedding dress. She fingered the delicate lace and then held it close to her heart. How she missed her parents. Raven's clothes were also in the trunk. *My dear sister, what are you wearing throughout your journey?*

With sorrow in her heart for their separation, she pushed Raven's clothes aside and reached for a blue and white dress she thought the most fancy of the lot. With pearled buttons at the front of the outfit, it was easy to dress in it without the help of another.

She fashioned her waist-length hair into a long braid. She had seen white women wearing their braid to hang down one shoulder, so she arranged her hair to fall in such a way. By the time the bell rang she was ready for Gabriel to escort her for a third time to the dining hall.

He wore a dark waistcoat and trousers. His white shirt was buttoned to the neck, a dark cravat adorning the collar. "I agree with Raven," he mumbled. "This fancy way of dressing is most uncomfortable."

She cast him a smile. "But you are so handsome, my brother."

"Humph," he grunted.

Lady Abbott waved them to the table she and her husband occupied, and again they were joined by the count. This time his friend, Armond Preston, was along. Mr. Preston was of large build, his rounded belly hanging over his trousers. He only inclined his head politely to her and Gabriel when he sat down, and seemed uninterested in whom he dined with, spending the rest of the evening quietly enjoying his meal.

Ivan's smile, however, brightened at her presence. He wore a royal blue suit, enhancing the color of his eyes to even more brilliance than before. A white shirt, with a tier of ruffles down the front and at each cuff, accentuated the tight-fitting jacket.

Though the count was an exceptionally attractive man, he lacked the rugged good looks of the captain. Rafe Cavendish's striking appearance was the kind that made heads turn. Tall, broadly built, and well-proportioned, his strong body added to his charm.

The wine flowed, and with each sip she took, Gabriel's scowl deepened. Her head felt light, her spirits lifted.

After dinner an entertainer played music on a piano. Beneath the table her feet kept time to the rhythm. Other folks around her rose from their seats to dance.

Count Sontag's eyes shimmered from across the table, a smile curving his lips. "Vill you valtz vith me, *Fraulein*?"

"Sunny does not know how to waltz," Gabriel snapped.

Her cheeks heated with her brother's remark, and she swallowed hard her embarrassment. Actually she was a very good dancer, just not knowledgeable in the sort done here tonight.

"Then *Ich werde ihre lernen*, I vill teach her," the count said, standing and making his way to her side of the table. Dipping his head slightly, he held out a hand.

Her pulse raced as she accepted his gesture. When their fingers entwined she cast a glance at her brother, who by now had the face of a thunder cloud ready to burst. She forced a reassuring smile and allowed the count to lead her onto the dance floor.

He put a hand on her back, the musky scent of his cologne filling her senses with an overly sweet fragrance, and not the manly scent of the captain's. Slowly, she followed his steps, moving as he instructed.

When the music stopped he smiled, lowered his mouth and whispered. "Shall ve get a breath of fresh air?"

His warm breath tickled her ear; the nearness of him causing her insides to clench. Would he try to kiss her? She inhaled sharply at the thought, moving to put a distance between them.

"Are you all right, *Fraulein* Eagle?"

She nodded. "Please, call me Sunny."

He offered her his elbow and smiled. "If you vill call me Ivan."

Together they walked to the door.

Gabriel rushed to her side. His sharp eyes bore into the Ivan's. "Where are you taking my sister?"

Ivan's voice was courteous but patronizing. "Ve are only going out for a breath of air, *Herr* Eagle."

"Then I will join you," Gabriel said, holding the door for them both.

The three of them took a stroll along the deck in silence, her steps awkward, but she was relieved she would not be alone with the count. Coming upon the rail, she made sure to face away from the water. Though she could not see the sea for the pitch of night, she was not taking a chance of getting sick again; especially in front of Ivan.

Ivan leveled a confident glare at Gabriel. "I vould like a private moment vith Sunny."

Gabriel gave a sardonic chuckle. "Oh, I am sure you would, but I cannot allow that to happen, not now, or anytime on this trip."

"Gabriel," she gasped, her face heating with humiliation. "Your tone need not be so harsh."

Ivan arched a brow. "I understand your concern, *Herr* Eagle, having already lost one sister."

Gabriel's stare drilled into Ivan's. "How do you know about that?"

Ivan shrugged "Passengers have a habit of listening vhen the cabin boys talk, *ja*?" With an air of command Ivan continued, "Though you might doubt me, I understand the torment you must be going through."

"It has been terrible to think of Raven all alone. But we are hoping she boarded the cargo ship docked beside ours, rather than stayed ashore. The captain assured us the owner of the ship, Lord Shannon, would send her to England as soon as they landed in Ireland," she said

Ivan arched a brow. "Then the *Kapitän* has not told you of the grave danger she vould be in if she vere on the ship?"

Sunny shook her head. "What grave danger?"

"Ah, I see he has kept the truth from you."

Her heart froze. "What truth?"

"Cargo ships are sometimes stopped and examined by the Sea Patrol."

"How do you know this?" Gabriel said, the muscles at his jaw throbbing.

"It is something everyone knows who travels by sea," Ivan said.

"And what does the Sea Patrol examine?" she asked.

"The cargo, *Fraulein,* to see if vhat the ship carries matches the receipts of sale," Ivan explained.

Gabriel's voice began to rise with his frustration. "And what has this to do with my sister, should she be on board?"

Ivan looked over at Gabriel. "I don't know how to delicately put this into vords, for the sake of the lady present."

"Ivan, I have left my home because of conditions I will not go into now, traveled many days in a small coach and on a stuffy train, wearing cumbersome clothes I am still trying to get used to being on my body. Now my beloved sister has been separated from me, might be in grave danger, my stomach has not felt right since we have left the shore, and you are worried how I will react over a few indelicately put words?"

"Not the vords so much as the implications, *Fraulein.*"

"Speak them, sir," she demanded. "I have a right to know what will happen to my sister."

"Like I said, the Sea Patrol looks for merchandise that is not accounted for."

She neared him. "But my sister is not merchandise."

"Sweet Jesus," Gabriel snarled.

She turned to glare at her brother. "Why did you call upon mother's God?"

"Because Raven will need His help," was his

whispered response.

She turned back to look at Ivan. "Why will my sister need God's help?"

He arched a brow. "Vould you care to explain it to her?"

"No," Gabriel said.

Ivan gave a taut nod. "Very vell then, you see, *Fraulein*, sometimes ships at sea take aboard, illegally, vomen for carnal pleasures."

She frowned. "Carnal? You mean to...to..."

He nodded.

Her mouth thinned. "Raven is not *that* sort of woman."

"They von't believe that or care. If there is not a document giving a valid reason she has a right to be aboard a cargo ship, then that is the conclusion they'll come to."

Her brother's tone was low, agonized. "Obviously she has no document to be aboard that ship, so what will the Sea Patrol do?"

"They vill remove her from the cargo ship and take her to prison."

Sunny gasped. "Please tell me there is something the captain of that ship or the owner, Lord Shannon, can do?"

"There vould be only one solution, and it's hard to say if the parties involved vould be villing to take it."

She moved closer to Ivan, her whole body shaking, growing weak again. "What would that solution be?"

"Lord Shannon vould have to ask the *Kapitän* to perform a certain ceremony, then your sister could remain safely on board."

"What sort of a ceremony do you speak of?" Gabriel snapped.

"Marriage, *Herr* Eagle. To save your sister from going to prison, Lord Shannon vould have to marry

29

her."

A stricken cry escaped her lips. "Good heavens."

This time it was Ivan who caught her before she hit the floor.

****

Sunny opened her eyes to find herself back in her own cabin, and thankfully not the Abbotts' this time.

Though the elderly couple were nice enough folks and she appreciated their help and friendship, Lady Abbott's steady chatter was something she had no patience to deal with right now. And the high-pitched tone of the woman's voice, which made her teeth ache, would just cause her head to pound even harder than it already did.

She glanced around the room and discovered Gabriel sitting in an arm chair at the foot of the bunk. He was wrapped in a blanket, head resting back and eyes closed. With long legs sprawled awkwardly out in front of him and his feet still clad in boots, he looked too tired to care much about comfort.

"Gabriel, my *chickasaw*, brother," she called out to him, sitting forward in the bed.

He stirred and opened one eye.

"Why did you not go to your own room to sleep comfortably?"

He leaned forward in his chair. "I did not want you to find yourself alone when you woke."

She held her pounding head between her hands. "How long have I been asleep?"

"Only a few hours at the most."

"What happened?"

He came to sit at the edge of her bunk. "How much do you remember?"

"I remember collapsing on deck." She groaned miserably. "And in front of Ivan, no less."

"You do not remember coming around, crying in

30

my arms, and then falling asleep?"

She shook her head.

"After the count caught you from falling to the floor, I took you from his arms," Gabriel explained. "Then I brought you here."

It all came flooding back to her. "Oh Gabriel, if what Ivan said is true, then Raven is lost to us forever."

Her brother's lips thinned. "In the morning I will talk again with the captain."

She sighed. "What good can that do?"

"He did not tell us all there was to tell."

She reached for his hand. "Promise me you will say nothing to the captain, and let me talk to him instead."

He shook his head. "I am sorry, Sunny, but I cannot do that."

"All that you will manage to do is cause another fight, and then you will be locked in the storage room again. Do you want that?"

He raised his gaze to meet hers. "The last thing I want is to have you walking about the ship alone, beneath the hungry eyes of that Ivan Sontag."

It was the last thing she wanted as well.

"I do not trust the man; I sense he hides something." His expression stilled, grew serious. "But you are right about one thing, *dayden*. There is nothing that can be done for Raven now." He took an audible breath. "Maybe it is best you do speak to the captain."

She nodded. "*Ashoge,* this time for seeing things my way."

"Now all I can do is hope the Lord of Limerick does what is right and marries our dear sister."

She gave her brother a sidelong glance of disbelief. "I cannot imagine why you would want that to happen."

He arched a brow. "You would want instead for

31

her to go to prison?"

"No, of course not." She swung her legs off the bed and moved to sit close to her brother. "But think of it, Gabriel. Lord Braiton Shannon might be old and ghastly, demanding from his wife things Raven would not want to give."

Once already her sister had been taken against her will. How would she react enduring the violence a second time, with not one of her family around to help her get through it?

Of course Gabriel knew nothing of the first injustice, and to tell him now would just be like pouring fuel on a smoldering fire.

"The captain said the Lord of Limerick was a kind and generous man, would do right by Raven. And as soon as they landed in Ireland, the lord would send her to England."

"He will not let her leave for England if she is his wife."

He frowned. "It is not like he would care, Sunny. They did not choose each other at a mating ceremony and agree to marry."

"But they would have to take vows, Gabriel. Vows are not made so they can easily be broken." *Raven married, how can this be?* She thought of her mother's wedding dress she held just that afternoon close to her heart. Her sister would never wear it now.

He stood and paced the room. "Either way, Raven is in a situation, but at least with the Lord of Limerick she will be cared for. In prison there would not ever be a chance we would see her again. She would be cold and hungry, be beaten and..."

She interrupted his words, blocking her ears with her hands. "Please, say no more, say no more." Sunny could not bear to hear the rest. She curled back onto the bunk and pulled a blanket over her head. "Go to your cabin and sleep, Gabriel."

"You will be all right here alone?"

"I will be fine," she lied, tears spilling from her eyes and wetting the pillow covering.

Far better off than poor Raven.

Chapter Five

It seemed confrontations on this voyage had become a constant annoyance for Rafe Cavendish. First, there was the one with Gabriel Eagle yesterday over his misplaced sister. He'd been forced to sequester the man for a time, for his own good and that of others aboard the ship. Then, another with Sunny Eagle, a woman he found more beautiful than any he'd known. Now, another following dinner with Count Ivan Sontag, after he overheard a conversation the German had with Mr. Eagle and his sister. The count made the poor woman swoon. He forced himself not to run to her aid, as the brother had the situation under control. After Gabriel Eagle had gathered Sunny into his arms and carried her away with a possessive expression upon his face, Rafe took the opportunity to speak his mind to the count.

"I find you quite malicious for telling Miss Eagle about the Sea Patrol's activities."

Sontag's smug look irritated Rafe. "The voman deserved the truth, *Kapitän*."

He arched a brow. "There's nothing that can be done to rectify the problem, why worry her further?"

The count's lips curled in a snarl. "Sooner or later both of them vould have discovered their sister vould never be returned, vhat is the difference if they learned the truth now or vhen they docked in England?"

Rafe frowned, clenching his fists to his side to keep them from striking the arrogant bastard. "I kept silent to keep the peace while aboard the ship,

Count. It's a pity you can't understand that."

Sontag cast him a black layered look. "It's a pity you cannot keep the peace aboard your ship any other vay than to lie to the passengers."

"Stay away from Sunny Eagle," Rafe demanded, the thought of the other man touching her raised a streak of rage down his spine the likes he couldn't explain.

The count laughed. "You have no right to demand this of me." He waved a hand in the air. "*Gehen Sie*, go...*lassen Sie mich allein*, leave me alone. Vhat I do, the people I speak to, is none of your concern."

He squared his shoulders. "Well, I'm making it my concern while she's aboard this ship."

Sontag's laugh was sardonic. "And vhat then, *Kapitän*? She isn't the usual kind of voman you're interested in."

Rafe leveled his gaze to meet the German's. "What do you know of my business?"

"Your reputation has preceded you. I don't know of anyone in England who isn't aware of your liaisons." The count straightened his collar. "I think ve're done here, *Kapitän*." He clicked the heels of his polished boots together and inclined his head in mock respect. "*Guten Abend,* good evening. Sleep well."

Now Rafe looked out over the rail, the dark of night blanketing the sea, and puffed on his pipe. He'd have the fourth confrontation when he returned to his cabin to talk with his cabin boy about spreading gossip. He'd only taken a switch one other time to the lad's bared backside, for fighting with another male passenger his age. Unlike other ship captains, he was truly troubled to dole out such chastisement, remembering well his own days of angry superiors. He had endured his share of harsh punishments, strict discipline, and cruel pranks. The humiliating tricks played on him by higher ranking seamen were the fabric of many nightmares. But such tactics went with the territory. And now that he had paid his dues, made it to the top of his career, he couldn't allow disrespect from his own cabin boy. Aaron was the steward who knew about the Eagle's plight, so it stood to reason he was the one guilty of starting the talk. Rafe would have to make an example of the boy, whether he wanted to or not.

He sighed and emptied out the tobacco from his pipe before placing it in his pocket. *I might as well get this over with. Bad enough having your naked bum beat, but even worse to be awakened from a sound sleep to boot.*

As he rounded the corridor to his quarters, he spotted Sunny sitting on a bench. The skirt of her gown was wrinkled; thick golden tresses hung in long curls to her waist, and a shawl wrapped around graceful shoulders. With her head resting back, and eyes closed, she took a deep breath.

Rafe looked around for the brother and when he was nowhere in sight, he approached with concern. "You shouldn't be out and about at this late hour, unescorted, Miss Eagle."

Her lids opened slowly, large sapphire eyes regarding him with a speculative gaze. "My brother is exhausted, sir. It would have been cruel of me to wake him from his much needed rest just *bigha*, because I needed a breath of air."

"Ah, aye, the nausea again. Well, it will pass soon enough."

"One can only hope." She pushed back a wayward strand of pale hair. "But right now it is not my stomach that is sick, Captain, as much as my heart."

He gave her a taut nod. "I know this whole situation with your sister has been difficult on you and your brother."

A tremor touched her full lips. "Is that why you failed to tell us about the Sea Patrol?"

"I didn't *fail,* Miss Eagle, I *chose* not to tell you." He searched her upturned face, which was a perfect oval, arresting, well-modeled and feminine. Her smooth skin glowed in gold undertones from the light of a nearby hanging lantern. And she was now nervously biting the bottom lip of a temptingly curved mouth. "Believe me when I say, it wasn't to trick you or to be deceiving. I just felt there was no reason to add to your grief and sorrow. Especially considering there was nothing any of us could do." He inclined his head politely. "But I apologize for my actions; you had every right to know the full extent of the situation."

Her golden hair, like strands of lustrous glass, framed her exotic yet delicate cheekbones. "You mentioned before Lord Shannon was a generous and kind man who would do right by Raven."

He nodded. "Every word of that statement is true."

The corners of her mouth turned down. "I do not want to see my sister imprisoned by the Sea Patrol, but I also do not want her to be captive to a horrible marriage. It troubles me greatly to think of Raven at the mercy of some ghastly old man who would expect her to...to..." She broke off, her cheeks heightening with color.

"Lord Shannon is not ghastly, nor is he old," he reassured her. "I am not inclined normally to take heed of another man's visage, Miss Eagle. However, in this case I will make an exception." He cast a quick smirk and stroked his beard. "If I recall, Lord Shannon is a man that most definitely turns the heads of the female persuasion."

She raised a defiant chin. "Then why has he not taken a wife by now?"

He shrugged. "There are some men who are not

interested in marriage. Perhaps this is Lord Shannon's case."

Her eyes widened. "Do you think he will resent awfully much then, having to marry Raven?"

"I believe he will do what is right...what needs to be done with a clear mind and honorable heart."

Her silky voice held a challenge. "If you were the one in Lord Shannon's position, would you let the Sea Patrol take my sister?"

He hesitated with an answer. Already he'd come to the aid of one damsel in distress and been kicked in the gut for his efforts. Never would he be so foolish again.

"You would marry; spend a lifetime with someone you did not love just to save her?" she probed.

He took an audible breath and lied. "If need be." Then another thought struck him and he added, "But in truth I would not have to, and neither will your sister, for there's a way marriage vows can later be dissolved."

She frowned. "I am afraid I do not understand."

"The legal term for the process is *annulment*. If the marriage has not been consummated, the parties involved have the right to cancel out their first decision to wed, and granted by law an annulment."

A strange, faintly eager look flashed in her eyes. "Are you saying if Raven and Lord Shannon do not allow their bodies to come together as one, they do not have to stay joined in marriage?"

He had to smile at her terminology for a good ole romp between the bed linens. "Aye, that is exactly what I'm saying."

Her excitement added to the shine in her eyes and put a polish to her cheeks. "So then Raven would really be able to leave Ireland, and come to live with me and Gabriel in England?"

"Aye, within a matter of time I expect that will

happen."

She stood and unexpectedly wrapped her arms around his waist, placing a cheek against his chest. "Oh, Captain, I am so relieved to hear this."

He inhaled the light floral scent of her hair, drinking in the nearness of her. Caught in her enthusiasm, he placed a hand on each of her shoulders, drawing her to him.

Abruptly she stepped back, her tone apologetic. "I beg your pardon, Captain." She forced a smile. "I meant not to appear so bold. I was just so happy to learn my sister can come home...to England, I mean, that I...I..." she stammered.

The very air around him seemed charged, his heart aglow, his innards actually jangling, and if he were to speak at that very moment, there is no doubt he too would've been tongue-tied. He crammed his hands into his pockets, his fingers playing nervously with the pipe he cast there, and returned the smile.

She straightened herself with dignity. "I hope you can understand."

"I do completely, Miss Eagle."

Her sapphire eyes caught and held his. "When will you decide to call me Sunny?"

She totally enthralled him, her innocence was refreshing. "I should be pleased to decide that on the spot." He turned up his smile a notch. "If you think you could choose to call me Rafe, that is."

"Rafe," she whispered, trying out his name. "It is most unusual."

He masked the inner turmoil the mere whisper of his name caused him. "It is short for Raphael...Raphael Joshua Cavendish."

She rewarded him with a larger smile of her own. "Ah, then you are named after an archangel, just like my brother Gabriel. I believe there are seven of them." She used her fingers to count them off. "There is Michael, Gabriel, Raphael, Uriel,

Raguel, Sariel, and Jarahmeel. Raphael was the healer."

He arched a brow; his escapades hardly classified him in such an honorable light. "You are of the Christian faith?"

She nodded. "On my mother's side, my father believes the Apache ways, though he prays to Jesus often. My name is Sunny Elizabeth Eagle. Sunny is of Apache origin, Elizabeth is Christian. She was John the Baptist's mother."

"Sunny Beth, it is, then," he teased.

The lilt of her laugh was almost like a melody to his ears. "That is what my mother often calls me."

He joined her mirth. "And what does your father call you?"

"*Dayden*." Her eyes grew tender. "It is the Apache word meaning *little girl*."

His gaze dropped from her eyes, to her shoulders, then to her full breasts. *Clearly, you're not a little girl any longer*. When he raised his eyes again to catch hers, her face was flushed. Such innocence again captured his heart. With just a slight incline of his head, his lips could easily rest upon hers. But in the instant it took him to decide, she cast a demure glance at her hands, made her way to the rail and gazed out to sea.

"I am not dizzy when I look out at night."

He joined her. "By day the trick is to look beyond the horizon, and not turn around quickly."

"Everything is so frighteningly dark." She sighed, turning his way. "Just like every moment since Raven has been gone."

"But every dark moment has its bright side. Even the darkness of the night sky is only the previous side of a waiting horizon and a new day dawning."

She wet her full lips with a swipe of her tongue. "I pray you are right, Captain."

Again his focus was on her luscious, moist mouth. "Rafe, remember?"

She nodded. "I will remember."

His heart jolted as he became extremely conscious of her womanly charms, but such an attraction would be perilous. He mentally shook his head to clear it and offered her his arm. "It grows late, Sunny Beth. And I have no doubt in my mind that if your brother woke from his much needed rest to find you anywhere but in your cabin, there'd be hell to pay."

She rolled her eyes. "Paying hell would be putting it mildly."

He laughed. "Then let me escort you promptly to your quarters."

She nodded in agreement. "*Ashoge*, thank you. Your words have meant much. I am only sorry to have kept you away so long from your other duties."

"I assure you, the pleasure was mine." And he was certain Aaron would agree with him, for now the lad's adolescent hide would not suffer his wrath until the morning.

Chapter Six

Sunny remembered her mother sharing a wish she had as a child, whereby a message to one person from another could somehow be transported through the air in a matter of moments. Right now she wished the same, as she needed desperately to talk with her parents, tell them what happened to Raven and store away whatever encouragement they would offer. How wonderful it would also be if she were able to contact her sister, and know all was well with her...if indeed it was.

She took an audible breath and squared her shoulders before knocking on her brother's door. One never knew the mood Gabriel was in. He was not always so angry; in fact before he lost his wife and child, he had a winning sense of humor.

"Enter," was his sharp reply.

She sighed, realizing fully his grumpy tone meant he had not slept well and would be in a foul mood. He was lying on his bunk, hands beneath his head, dark pockets beneath his eyes. She knew her brother was blaming and punishing himself for Raven's absence.

She forced a cheery tone. "Good morning."

He grunted.

"Are you not going to breakfast?"

"The early tray of tea and biscuits are enough this morning for me. I am not in any mood to be surrounded by people, anyway." He yawned and sat forward. "But if you give me a moment to put on my boots, I will escort you."

She raised a hand to stall him. "No need for you

to bother. Last night at dinner Lady Abbott promised to come by for me this morning. She wishes for me to accompany her to an acquaintance's cabin for breakfast."

He frowned. "Who is this *acquaintance*?"

"A Mrs. Halston, I believe she said. Lady Abbott met her a few days ago while she was taking her usual stroll on deck."

His frown deepened. "Why have we not met this woman before?"

She shrugged. "Maybe she is much like you and does not wish to be surrounded by people."

He arched a brow. "You are not very amusing right now."

"And you are not very nice."

"I am being cautious," he countered.

She gave him a sideways glance. "Do you not trust Lady Abbott to be my chaperone?"

"I trust no one to be your chaperone but me."

"You cannot be my shadow, Gabriel. I am in need of and deserve to have a measure of privacy."

"That is your opinion, not mine," he muttered.

She gasped. "I am certainly not going to inform you every time I need to relieve myself. And the last thing I want is my brother standing in line with me as I wait at the door for my turn."

"Then you had better ask a cabin boy to bring you a bucket, and use it to do your business in, because I am not letting you walk about on this ship alone."

"Well, I will not be alone this morning," she argued. "Lady Abbott will be with me, and I do not believe she will bid me goodbye until she has brought me safely back to my cabin."

He sighed and stretched back upon the bed. "Very well, then, as long as you give me your word you will stay with her at all times."

"I have no reason to do otherwise. And if I

should see the captain at all, I will do as we agreed and speak to him about the Sea Patrol matter." Better to let Gabriel think she would connect with the captain under the watchful eye of Lady Abbott, than to learn of her late night conversation. She did not need her brother to argue further with her or to be a bother to Rafe Cavendish. He went out of his way last night to talk with her, even apologized and tried to put her mind at peace. Then he politely escorted her back to her cabin. The last thing she wanted was for Gabriel to misunderstand the gesture and start something new with the captain.

He nodded and rolled onto his side. "Now go."

"Did you not sleep well?"

"I slept as well as I could, considering all that is running through my mind," he mumbled. "Now go," he repeated. "Enjoy your breakfast."

****

Sunny could sum up Collette Halston in one word...*impressive*. From her long, dark lashes that matched curly tresses, to round ebony eyes, slim fingers with nails painted red, right down to the many strands of pearls draped over a plunging neckline, Collette Halston was extremely impressive. She appeared to be a bit older then Gabriel and held herself with confidence. Full bowed lips were painted to match her nails, making her already even, white teeth look whiter. She was slim framed, her waist hardly in need of a bodice cinching, and delicate features added to her charm. Smiling, she poured Sunny and Lady Abbott tea into white china cups rimmed with yellow roses. A white linen tablecloth and pale pink linen napkins adorned the table, as well as silver utensils with roses carved into the handles.

"Your table is exquisite, Collette," Lady Abbott complemented.

"Thank you, my lady." Collette cast a demure

smile. "I prefer to travel with my own tableware, adds a notion of home. And I love yellow roses." She turned her attention toward Sunny. "You, my dear, with all those golden curls, remind me of a yellow rose encased forever into a piece of amber jewelry I own."

She frowned. "What is amber?"

Collette's brows arched. "You have never seen amber?"

Sunny shook her head.

"Ah, then let me show you, for a picture is worth a thousand words," Collette said, rising from her seat and making her way to a large black trunk standing in the corner of her stately cabin. She opened a drawer and from it pulled something out. She returned to the table and reached for Sunny's hand, turning it palm-side up. Placing a brooch in the center, Collette smiled. "This is amber."

Sunny gasped. The beautiful cut and polished stone was framed in gold, and the rich orange-brown gem encased what looked like, but could not be…"Is that a rose?"

"Aye, that it is, and I like to believe it was once a yellow one, since they are my favorite. But now it is a fossil and it's tens of millions of years old," Collette explained further.

She cast Collette a strange glance. "How did it get there?"

"Millions of years ago there were huge forests that covered vast tracks of the earth. Some trees within the forests exuded a resin from their trunks and branches; these were the ancient amber trees. A number of theories have been proposed about why the trees secreted so much resin. One main theory amongst many was the resin was a defense mechanism against insect attacks." She pointed to the brooch Sunny held. "This rose probably bloomed on the ground beside the fresh seeping sap of a tree.

45

The sap then must have oozed over the rose, trapping it, and then perhaps it was eventually covered by dirt and debris. The sap later hardened and became a fossil. Fossils are mostly insects such as flies and bees. Occasionally more exotic insects are trapped in the amber such as beetles and butterflies. But what is most rare are those chunks of amber with plant remains encased, including flowers, pine needles, and pine cones. That's why this piece is very rare. The rarity of the trapped fossils control the value of the amber more so than the quality of the amber."

"Why is that?" she asked, awed by the brooch she held in her hand.

"Because these fossils are not the same species that are alive today," Collette said. "But amber had many uses other than to wear as jewelry. The ancient Greeks used amber to assist in the healing process. When they rubbed amber with a cloth, it warmed. Around the year 1835, in some European countries, there was a widespread belief that amber, if worn as a necklace, would ease a baby's teething pain."

"My, my, amber is magnificent, much like true love," Lady Abbott mused.

Collette frowned. "How is it you are able to compare the two, Eugenia?"

"Well, the warmth of true love can heal a broken heart and lasts an eternity, as does the fossils when wrapped in the amber."

"I certainly encountered anything but true love from my now deceased husband. And I have yet to hear any married women speak of it. How is it you know what true love is?" Collette challenged.

Lady Abbott folded her hands neatly in her lap. "How do you know that amber is not just glass someone pressed a rose into?"

"Because I have given it the ultimate test before

I framed it in the gold," Collette said. "Amber is much lighter than glass and can float in salt water. What test can you give love to know it is true, my dear Eugenia?"

"Time, Collette, the test of time, patience, and loyalty," Lady Abbott said, smugly taking a sip of her tea. "Stanley has given me all three and much, much more."

Collette arched a brow. "Then you are luckier than most."

Sunny caressed the smooth texture of the stone with a tip of a finger and changed the subject, before the discussion of love turned into a heated debate. "Where is amber found?"

Collette turned her attention toward Sunny. "In Southern England near the Cheddar/Creswell crags. But it can also be found on the beaches and fields of Denmark and on the shores of the Baltic region."

"How do you know so much about amber?"

"I married when I was only sixteen, to a man thirty years my senior. After three years of marriage he passed, leaving me a very rich woman. I decided marriage wasn't something I particularly liked, nor did I want to ever do again. So," Collette continued, "I hired a tutor and learned all I could about many different subjects. And then I traveled all over the world and saw firsthand many of those that interested me. I simply adore learning about the past and how it has affected present day situations and even the future to come."

"My heavens," Sunny muttered. "A piece of amber is like looking at a picture from the past."

Collette smiled. "Aye, that's exactly what it's like, and the reason I am so fascinated with every piece I own. Each one tells a different story, shows me another picture of what once was."

Sunny's eyes widened. "How many other pieces do you have?"

"Many, perhaps five or six," Collette admitted.

Sunny held the brooch up to the candle's light. "I would be pleased to just have this one."

"Then today I shall please you with it," Collette said.

She gasped. "Oh, no Mrs. Halston, I could not possibly accept such generosity."

"Please, call me Collette, and you not only can, but you must," Collette insisted. "And I always get my way." She leaned forward in her seat and pressed Sunny's hand. "Take it, my dear. Let it bring you a measure of comfort and happiness." She frowned. "If what I have been hearing is true, about your sister, then you could use all the comfort and happiness allowed."

Sunny sighed. "I suppose I should explain that situation."

"Only if you have the heart to, mite," Lady Abbott said.

She nodded. "Strangely enough, I do. I have needed someone to talk to. My brother, though he shares my troubled heart, is not very...very..."

"Sympathetic," Collette supplied.

"Yes, he looks at things differently than I do, and has another way of dealing with it all."

"I've found most men don't deal with much, other than money and politics that is," Collette said, pouring them each another cup of tea. "And even that they do with a ferocious vengeance."

Sunny did not think of Gabriel as ferocious, but his attitude was not at all pleasant.

Lady Abbott gave her an affectionate pat on the hand. "Suppose you start from the beginning, mite."

She munched on warm blueberry scones and sipped more cups of tea while spilling out her heart. All she kept silent was the real reason her brother left the ship, she refused to paint him in a bad light. Both of these women were English matrons and probably knew many of the same folks her Aunt Kaylena did. She would not want any of them to get the wrong idea about Gabriel and the *firewater* he liked to drink. So, as far as anyone else knew, except for her, Captain Rafe Cavendish—and she was confident he would keep silent—and Gabriel, her brother left the ship because he was just searching for his luggage. She told them how she believed Raven boarded the *Sweet Maureen* and about Lord Braiton Shannon.

She concluded with what she had learned last night from Count Sontag. "So, you see how frightened I have been for Raven. Though I do not want her in the hands of the Sea Patrol, to be married to a man she does not know or love is not really the greatest solution."

"Why, my dear, that's done all the time in England," Lady Abbott said. "My own Stanley was a man my parents picked, and I've been extremely happy all these years we've been together."

"Huh, you are a fortunate one, Eugenia," Collette snapped. "My Alistair couldn't make a frog happy." Catching the crest-fallen look on Sunny's face the other woman added. "Then again, he was as old as dirt, and I was young and vibrant." She shrugged. "Perhaps if we were equally paired things might have been different."

She knew from her conversation with Rafe last night that Lord Shannon was young and desirable to the ladies, and that once in Ireland the marriage could be annulled, but she could not divulge that news to either of these women lest it get back to Gabriel.

"All will be fine," Lady Abbott assured her. "These things sometimes have a wonderful way of working out for the best."

"But it is not our custom," she said.

"Tell us about your custom," Collette inquired.

"My father, Proud Eagle, is chief of the Western Apache tribe and my mother, Golden Lady, is a white woman who cared for him when he showed up wounded by hostiles at her back door. My mother's father had been recently murdered by a hostile tribe, so she was not sure at first if she should help my father. But as a good Christian woman she decided to care for his wounds. He thrived with her care, so when warriors from the hostile tribe attacked her farm, my father helped her to escape. By that time they had fallen in love, and she returned to his village with him to become his wife." She took a sip of tea before continuing. "Apache custom allows the woman to pick her mate at a dance ceremony. All unmarried men and women sit cross-legged in a circle. One by one each woman rises from her seat and dances to the beat of the drums, making her way to the man she chooses for a husband. With a light slap upon his cheek she will let him know she is interested."

"How unusual," Collette whispered. "What happens then?"

"A few days after the dance ceremony he goes to the place where she draws water or washes her clothes, and he lines a path with stones. If she walks down the path he has provided, she has accepted his proposal. He then takes her back to his home, and she washes his clothes, makes his meals, and saddles his horse for him."

Lady Abbott gasped. "And do they...do they..."

Sunny giggled. "No, they do not. This is a time of much honor and trust. To start a life together built on deceit would not be wise. But that is a question all of us unmarried women ask."

"Please, go on," Collette urged.

"After the woman does these chores a while for the man, he brings her family gifts...beads, a pony, and blankets. If the family accepts the gifts then the woman is his wife."

Lady Abbott arched a delicate brow. "Just like that...with no vows said?"

She nodded.

"And your mother, being a white woman and accustomed to another way of courtship, didn't mind marrying your father in this manner?"

"No, she loves him dearly and accepted his ways." She raised a finger. "But later they were married by her law and vows *were* taken with a clergyman present."

"How strange all of this must have been for her," Lady Abbott reflected. "Yet the two of them worked it all out, and I trust are happy to this day?"

"Very happy," Sunny confirmed.

Lady Abbott smiled. "Then perhaps the same will be true for your sister?"

"But my parents fell in love, Raven did not."

Lady Abbott again gave her an affectionate pat. "Love happens in many different ways, in many different forms, mite. I believe all will be well with your sister. Thank the good Lord for Braiton Shannon."

And for annulments. But she would keep that bit of information as a consolation to herself. "I am sure you are right, Lady Abbott," she agreed with a smile and took another sip of her tea.

Chapter Seven

Sunny did not see Rafe Cavendish while out and about with Lady Abbott and therefore could not report a conversation of any sort to Gabriel. She hoped at dinner she might have a private moment with the captain, whereby she could use that as the time she spoke with him about the Sea Patrol.

She bit her bottom lip. If her brother would not even let her use the *privy*, as she learned from the cabin boy the private facilities was called, without accompanying her to the door, how would she manage to get a private moment with Rafe? Sighing, she sat at the edge of her bunk. "I will think of something."

Still holding the brooch Collette Halston gifted her with, she again admired the rose fossil nestled in the amber. The rich color of the stone reminded her of one of Raven's dresses she saw in the trunk. It was of the same deep orange shade, trimmed with cream-colored lace at the neckline, sleeve cuffs, and hemline. Since the two sisters were the same size, the dress would be a perfect fit. And what harm would it do, just this once, if she were to wear it to dinner?

"It is not like Raven has a use for it now," she justified to herself. As sad and disturbing as that fact was, Sunny knew she had to make do with the situation for the time being. Besides, seeing her visibly upset was not a good thing for Gabriel. His guilt and worry was getting the best of him, and Sunny feared for his health and frame of mind. She had to remain strong in order to help her brother through this difficult time.

She sighed again, and made her way to the trunk to search for Raven's dress. Thankfully, the one she desired to wear had buttons up the front and would be easy to get into without assistance. Her Apache clothes were simple buckskin dresses or a tunic and skirt, neither needing another's help to put on. But the white woman's clothing, though fancier and more fashionable, was quite a different story. And there was so much that went on underneath. She thought back to the first time she and Raven were garbed in them, and how much her sister hated all the material. Sunny wanted so much to like the new dresses, and did at first in spite of all the fuss, because they made her look older, more attractive. But as of late she found herself agreeing with Raven.

She pulled from the trunk a pair of bloomers, a chemise, a petticoat, and a bodice and laid them all out on the bunk, beside the dress. Then she searched for clean garters and stockings. By the time she found pairs to match, an hour had already gone by. This could be the reason white women began dressing for dinner hours ahead of time.

Holding up the corset she winced. There was no way she would be able to get into this garment by herself, and she certainly was not asking Gabriel to help her. She had worn the corset only once before, when she and Raven first left Arizona. Sitting on the stagecoach with the binds squeezing her waist nearly choked her. Now she understood why the women garbed so cruelly could only pick at their food.

She arched a brow. "Fashion or not, I will never wear this torturous thing again," she vowed, tossing the corset back into the trunk. Sunny figured, by the time she wrestled herself into all the clothes and fixed her hair, she would be darned hungry...and she wanted the freedom to eat everything on her plate.

****

It pleased Sunny to see Collette Halston sitting at the dinner table with the Abbotts. She had told Gabriel all about the fascinating woman and was so happy with the brooch. Gabriel smiled politely through introductions and actually appeared at ease for the first time since they left America.

"Your sister has intrigued me with your people's courting ritual," Collette said, buttering a biscuit.

Sunny thought Gabriel looked a bit intrigued with Collette as well.

"Ah, yes, the marriage ritual." Gabriel chuckled. "Many cannot understand the Apache way, but it has served my people well all these years."

"I for one think it's marvelous," Collette said, flashing Gabriel a smile that made his cheeks flush. "Think of all the women who wouldn't have to put up with some cheeky bore her parents picked to spend the rest of her life with." She turned to Lady Abbott. "I mean no offense to you and Stanley, Eugenia."

Lady Abbott, her mouth stuffed with a biscuit, just inclined her head politely.

"I am fascinated with different ideas, and the traditions of other cultures," Collette went on. "It's why I travel all over the world, soaking it all up."

"And were you able to soak up much in America?" Gabriel probed.

"Aye, this trip was one of the most informative yet," Collette said.

"Care to share your findings with us?" Lady Abbott challenged.

Collette hesitated when Count Sontag and his friend, Armond Preston, joined the table. Collette leaned over and whispered to Sunny. "Speaking of cheeky bores, these two are prime examples." Then she pasted a fake smile upon her ruby lips and extended a hand to the count. "Count Sontag, again we meet."

"At your service, *Frau*," he said, kissing Collette's hand before taking a seat opposite Sunny. "I see you are getting along vell, though unescorted."

Collette shot a glance at Gabriel and smiled. "Sometimes being alone has its rewards."

Even though she did not know the exact meaning of *cheeky bore*, she was sure Collette's reference regarding Ivan as one was not meant as a pleasantry. She also glanced over at her brother, who obviously overheard the comment because he was stifling a smile. Controlling her own mirth, she turned her attention to the fish on her plate.

After dinner, they were entertained by a pianist and violin player. The accomplished duo filled the room with beautiful music.

Collette offered her hand to Gabriel. "Since you're accustomed to a woman making the first move, would you care to dance?"

Gabriel inclined his head in a gesture of agreement and led Collette onto the dance floor.

Sunny breathed a sigh of relief. With Gabriel occupied by Collette's attention, perhaps she would have a chance to talk again with the captain. She wanted to set Gabriel's mind at peace, like Rafe had done the previous night for her. And the only way she could relay what she had learned was to make it appear their conversation took place tonight.

She hoped Rafe would ask her to dance, but Ivan requested the honor instead. She glanced around for her brother, and when she spotted him enjoying a dance with Collette, she decided to accept Ivan's invitation.

"You look lovely tonight, *Fraulein*," he said, whisking her around the dance floor. His steps, so smooth and quick in contrast to her own awkward movements, had her straining to keep from tripping.

By the time the music stopped she was quite out of breath.

Another glance at Gabriel found him on the opposite side of the dining hall, engrossed in conversation with Collette as they sipped wine. She was glad to see him finally relaxing a bit and having some fun, but she needed his presence to reprieve her from the count.

The next tune was a waltz and, before she could protest, Ivan led her again to the dance floor. One hand possessed her waist, and the other claimed her hand, his fingers entwining with hers. "I cannot think of any place I'd rather be," he said, drawing her closer.

"May I cut in?" came a deep voice.

She turned to find Rafe standing behind her, his blue eyes boring into Ivan's. She welcomed the intrusion with a smile, but then quickly stifled her relief so as not to hurt the count's feelings.

"Have you not something important to tend to, *Kapitän?*" Ivan said, with an icy glare.

A slow, sardonic smile spread Rafe's lips. "I'm doing it, Count."

The silence that followed between them was deadly, and it brought chills down her spine. "I think I have danced enough for tonight."

"But, my dear, an evening is not complete vithout dancing a valtz," Ivan said, gripping her hand tighter, yet keeping his gaze locked with Rafe's.

Rafe stepped forward. "Then this last dance shall be mine." He clapped a hand on Ivan's shoulder. "I trust you don't mind, ole boy?"

Ivan's lips thinned as his glare turned to hatred. "Ah, but I do, *Kapitän.*"

"Then you will get over it," Rafe countered, his tone cool and sharp.

Ivan's eyes darkened with rage. "This is not over

between us."

The Captain's confident gaze intensified. "Have a nice evening, Count."

Ivan released her, clicked his heels together, and gave her a polite bow before departing.

Rafe stepped into his place. He smiled down at her and offered her his hand. "May I, Sunny Beth?"

She moved toward him, excitement welling in her chest at the thought of being totally embraced by his muscular arms. "Maybe you should not call me that in front of my brother."

Rafe chuckled. "It is your name, isn't it?"

She frowned. "Yes, but...but..."

"Such familiarity might upset him," he finished for her.

"Yes," she admitted. Her mouth was only inches away from his full lips.

"Ah, then, I will be careful," he promised.

Rafe's large hand rested at the base of her spine, his touch warming the flesh there. Another large hand covered her own, the connection sending jolts of excitement through her. His scent caused a heady thrill to envelope her. Clean and masculine, it was a pleasant arousal.

His eyes shifted from her upturned gaze to the brooch she wore at the neckline of her dress. "That's a magnificent piece of jewelry you've got there."

She smiled. "Collette Halston gifted me with it this morning."

He arched a brow. "Most definitely you've found favor with the woman, because that piece is extremely rare."

"Yes, I know, Collette explained the reason to me, and I am so grateful she wanted me to have it."

His voice was low and smooth. "It reminds me of you, Sunny Beth."

Her cheeks warmed. "How is that so, Captain?"

"With your pale curls and honey hued dress, you

are just like a rose in amber...and a yellow rose at that." He searched her face. "My mother always said the yellow rose is a symbol of joy and friendship. I can see such qualities in you."

She was strangely flattered by his interest. "I am pleased that you do."

"There are a few myths about the amber. Care to hear them?"

She loved listening to folklore. It was something she truly enjoyed doing while sitting around the fire-pit with her family. For an instant a pang of homesickness stabbed at her heart. "Yes, please."

"Some say the honey-colored stone is the tear of the goddess Freya, fallen into the sea. And yet others say it is likened to the blood of the dragon; every golden drop the essence of courage."

She gasped. "How purely beautiful."

His eyes appeared to memorize her features. "Aye, truly so."

"I think the fossils caught within give a glimpse of the past, painting a picture only the imagination can create."

His deep cornflower-blue eyes held concern. "Aye, scenes we would otherwise never be privileged to see."

"A grand thought, do you not agree?"

He smiled. "That I do, Sunny Beth. That I do."

****

While Gabriel escorted Sunny back to her cabin, he talked about Collette. "I have never heard such stories from a woman."

She giggled. "I think she has had the adventures of a man."

He nodded. "And I admire her for that, Sunny."

She playfully narrowed her eyes. "Of course, the fact she is extremely beautiful has nothing to do with some of that admiration?"

He blushed and shrugged. "Perhaps some."

She giggled. "It is allowed, you know."

He arched a brow. "What is?"

"For you to be attracted to a woman."

"I did not think I ever wanted to be again...after..."

"Life does go on, my brother," she interrupted using Collette's words. "And we must go on with it." Their conversation left her an opening to tell Gabriel about her talk with Rafe. "I believe Raven has."

He frowned. "I saw you dancing with the captain and did not like the way he held you so close. I would have interrupted, but we agreed you would talk to him about the Sea Patrol matter, so I kept at a safe distance."

Though she hated lies or lying, she had no choice. In order to keep the peace, one small lie would not hurt. In her own defense, she did not really think it was an out and out fib, anyway. She was just leading her brother to believe the talk took place at a different time than it actually had. Taking an audible breath to calm her guilt, she relayed the entire conversation, including what she had learned about marriage annulments.

A satisfied glint filled Gabriel's eyes. "Then Raven will be well cared for, and will be able to return to us."

She nodded. "So, rest easy now, my brother. All has turned out fine."

He arched a brow. "That is if Raven was not left on shore."

"I feel deep within my heart she would return to the ship." She frowned, "Unfortunately, it was the wrong ship."

They were at her cabin door now, and Gabriel reached for the portal knob to unlock it. "I pray you are right."

She gave him a quick hug, feeling his heart beating against her cheek. She loved her brother deeply. He was the only family she had left, and she did not want him to blame himself further for what happened to Raven. "Sleep well, Gabriel."

He sighed, returning the embrace. "I think finally...tonight I will."

Chapter Eight

Rafe traced Sunny's full lips with a tip of his finger. They were warm and soft, just as he knew they'd be. He moved closer, cupping her chin with the palms of his hands. There was delicacy and strength emanating from her face, as her sapphire eyes held his. Desire mounted, passion swelled his loins. He moved his hands to her shoulders and lowered his lips to hers, tasting the sweetness, exploring the soft folds of her mouth with his tongue. Her body melted against his, lush firm breasts pressed to his chest. He deepened the kiss, looping a finger through each strap of her chemise and sliding it off her shoulders. Stepping back he surveyed her beauty, then reached out to caress...

"Cap'n, Cap'n," a frantic voice called through the portal.

His eyes flew open, struggling for a moment to reconnect to his surroundings. With a swipe of his tongue, he moistened his lips, the warmth of her still quite real upon them, and sat forward in his chair. In his hands he held the docking manifest, the one he'd been reading, no doubt, before he fell asleep.

"Cap'n, Cap'n," Beeker, his first mate's raspy voice came again from the other side of the portal. "Yer needed, sir, on deck."

He frowned—annoyed his dream had been interrupted. Or was he disturbed by its content? *Why the bloody hell am I dreaming about Sunny Eagle?* She was the sort of woman a man married, had a family with...definitely not his sort, for sure.

He stood and with a few quick strides made his

way to the portal, pulling it open. Arnold Beeker, a thin, tall man in his late twenties, took a step back. Annoyed more with himself than with his first mate, he muttered, "There better be a damn good reason for this intrusion, Beeker."

Beeker removed his cap, a mop of blond curls falling over his forehead. "Aye, Cap'n, there is."

He cleared his mind with a shake of his head and set his focus on the worried face of his first mate. "Well, speak what you've come here to say, my good man." And Arnold Beeker was a good man, standing by Rafe in all circumstances, proving to be a reliable and loyal first mate.

Beeker gave a taut nod. "I've spotted a storm comin' this way, sir. She looks like a nasty one, she does. Thought we'd better get everythin' and everyone locked down before she strikes."

He reached for his coat and gestured ahead. "Lead on, mate."

"Aye, Cap'n," Beeker said and hurried along the corridor.

Aaron came upon them as he rounded the corner. "What can I be doin', Cap'n to 'elp?"

He stifled a smile. His cabin boy, no doubt, was doing everything to remain in his good graces. The belt he was forced to take to the lad's bum a day ago for spreading gossip was something he hated to do. But the discipline was necessary. The boy needed to be taught respect for his captain and those aboard the ship.

"Gather the other cabin boys and have them go around to each guest's quarters. Tell them to make sure everyone puts away their breakable valuables somewhere safe, and bring each a bucket." He ran his fingers through his hair. "We're going to have a lot of sick folks on our hands."

Aaron nodded and took off to perform his duties.

Already the waves crashed against the ship's

side. In no time the sea would make it over the rails, cover the deck, and rock the vessel like a cradle. The *Entrenous* wasn't exactly in her prime, but she was solid, well-made, and he had no doubt she'd get them through. However, he could not take the chance. His utmost concern was for those aboard. He hated going off course. His employers wouldn't be fond of the idea either. Time was money, but there'd be hell to pay if he made the wrong decision. He wasn't taking any unnecessary chances with the passenger's lives. If the *Entrenous* was late pulling into Liverpool's harbor, then so be it.

As he turned onto the causeway connected to the dining hall, he smelled smoke and heard frantic shouts. Upon entering, he found the far side of the room engulfed in flames. Several of the dining room staff, Lord Abbott, Gabriel Eagle, and Sunny were beating the blaze with the linen coverings they'd taken off the tables. She was on the opposite side of the fire, clear to his view but not to the others. So no one noticed when the hem of her dress swayed closer and closer to the inferno with each move she made to squash the flames. He was just about to shout a warning to her when his worst fears happened. Without her knowledge the back hemline of her garment caught fire. In no time it would burn away the material and into her flesh.

He reached for a covering from a nearby table and in one fluid motion was beside her. Her eyebrows shot up in surprise when he pulled her away from the flames and pushed her to the floor. He smothered the burning skirt with the tablecloth and his weight, rolling with her from side to side, until the fire died. Fear, stark and vivid rioted within him as he ripped away the singed material, prepared to find her bronzed flesh burnt and peeling. He tore through the petticoat and down to the bloomers, ripping until her shapely limbs lay naked before his eyes. With trembling hands he turned them from side to side for evidence of burns, but there were none. The tanned flesh was smooth, healthy, not a mark on them.

He stood, looking down at her. Only a thin strip of material remained to keep him from knowing what she was all about. Neither of them spoke, but her sapphire gaze, round, frightened, and humiliated, locked with his. She modestly crossed her legs and covered her frontage with her hands.

He grabbed a cloth from another table and cloaked it over her nakedness, then gathered her into his arms. Her brother, still occupied with battling the blaze, saw none of what happened. Rafe didn't stick around to inform him. Instead, he carried Sunny to her cabin, kicked open the portal, and gently set her upon the bunk.

The awkward silence between them enveloped the room as she arranged the cloth in a modest fashion, then clearing her throat she was the first to speak.

"I would say it is a darn good thing I wear several layers now."

He burst into laughter, the tension and panic drifting from his bones. "It's a darn good thing indeed." He sat at the edge of the bunk, his mirth sobering. "I apologize for having to...to..."

"Rip away my clothes," she finished for him, her cheeks turning crimson.

He nodded and frowned. *Why does she have the uncanny knack of finishing my sentences?*

She sat up on her elbows. "I would say *my* thanks are in order for your quick thinking and the action you took." She shivered. "I hate to think of the consequences if you had not come by the dining hall when you did."

His frown deepened. "What happened in there?"

"A lantern came free from its hook and crashed

down onto a table. Thankfully the folks sitting there had already left. Gabriel, the Abbotts, and I were enjoying a conversation over tea, and so we decided to linger on a bit. When the lantern fell, it immediately caught fire and...well, I guess you saw the rest."

"Aye, and I should return to see if all is under control, that is if you're all right?"

"I am fine, *ashoge*, thank you again."

"I will send by a cabin boy to help you secure the room, and now the portal, since I have broken the lock. He'll also bring you a bucket."

She frowned. "I do not understand."

"A storm approaches, and although I have hopes in navigating around it, the waters will still be quite choppy." He gave her a sardonic smile. "If you think you were sick before, riding out a storm is a whole new experience."

Her frown deepened. "And that's why I will need the bucket?"

"Aye."

"Will we sink, Captain?"

He chuckled. "I don't anticipate so, Miss Eagle."

"Still," she said, moistening her lips with the tip of a pink tongue. "There is always a chance."

"Aye, there is always a chance. But I have learned it is best not to worry over something that hasn't happened yet. The *Entrenous* is a strong, solid ship that has weathered a few storms throughout her voyages, and I have no doubt she'll survive again." He stood. "Secure your breakables and stay in the bunk." He made his way to the portal, then turned her way before leaving. "What did you mean about wearing layers now?"

"Do you remember the night we talked on deck, and I told you my father was an Apache?"

He nodded. "But I did not think you were brought up as one, with your mother white."

"She loved my father very much and went to live with his people, embraced his customs. And so I wore the clothing of an Apache as well, which was not as cumbersome as the white women wear. A buckskin tunic and skirt, or dress is all that is needed. And the garments only cover to below the knee. Such a way allows easier movement to work and is cooler during the hot day. So you see I am not used to wearing so many layers now."

He arched a brow, picturing her in the Apache wear. He'd seen riding garments made from leather. The material hugged the body's form. How might she have looked in her buckskin clothes, molding to her nakedness, shapely legs exposed?

She broke through his thoughts. "I would say you certainly earned the right to call me Sunny Beth now."

All he could manage was a taut nod before he left the cabin in a hurry.

****

Sunny secured the door with a chair while she changed into another day dress, something simple and more comfortable to wear while curled up in the bunk. A cabin boy, the one called Jackson, arrived with a rope and a bucket for her and Gabriel. He helped her pack away the delicate and breakable items in her cabin, then lent a hand to secure Gabriel's belongings. With the rope, he showed her how to secure the portal so no one on the opposite side could enter her cabin.

"Someone will be by to fix it properly, Miss, when the storm settles. For now, the rope will keep away intruders."

Gabriel arrived a while later, his clothes and flesh blackened from fighting the blaze. She turned his hands over to inspect them, searching for burns, but there were none. After she explained her mishap, he frowned and pulled her close to him in a brotherly embrace. "You are damn fortunate, Sunny."

"With a storm approaching, I pray our fortune continues," she said, pulling her brother with her to sit on the bunk. Already the floor pitched from side to side, and the queasiness returned. She reached for the peppermint sticks wrapped in a handkerchief Lady Abbott brought her and handed one to Gabriel.

He arched a brow. "This really helps?"

She nodded. "I just hope I have enough to get us through the storm."

He eyed the bucket. "I see you took my advice."

"Oh no, that is not for...for..." she clipped her tongue, knowing full well if she was too sick to move off the bunk she would have to use the bucket for a few reasons. "You have one too," she concluded.

Gabriel's gaze took in the roped door. "I will stay in this room, you take mine."

"But your bunk is much bigger."

He shrugged. "It will not matter much where we lay while we get through the storm, and I would feel better if you were in a room with a door that properly locks."

Gabriel's logic proved so true. As the storm worsened, the *Entrenous* tossed from side to side. It did not matter if she were on a bed the size of the cabin or a plank, nor did it matter if she had a basket filled with peppermint sticks and sucked on them continuously...there was no appeasing her stomach. Besides the room pitching from the storm, it also spun out of control every time she opened her eyes to reach for the bucket. Its stench added to her illness, as well as the sound of Gabriel retching in the next cabin.

With deep breaths, she rubbed her raw and quivering abdomen and set her thoughts on a nurturing time...back to when she was a little girl and her mother held and rocked her to sleep. Golden

Lady was as natural as the day was long, and Sunny could almost smell the clean scent of her flesh, a mixture of sun and rain and fresh cut flowers.

Her father's strong hands engulfed hers, as they walked to the river. He taught her to fish and hunt, use a bow, arrow, and spear, and to fight like a warrior. Strong and smart, Proud Eagle always made her feel safe in spite of the white agents that intruded upon the village. Now she wished she could once again climb on his lap and snuggle her face beneath his chin.

The ship squeaked and groaned, bounced and pitched. Sunny cringed and clamped her eyes shut. She had to fight with herself to keep from picturing the *Entrenous* sinking to the depths of the cold dark sea, her body floating lifeless to the roof of her cabin, eyes staring blankly.

Gabriel retched again.

She cupped her hands over her ears and sung her mother's lullaby. Then she prayed she would one day see her parents again...that she would see Raven again—*Oh God, let both our ships survive this storm.*

****

Rafe's eyes burned from lack of sleep. He and Beeker battled the storm all night, but they'd gotten around it, and now there were smooth waters ahead. Aaron and the other cabin boys made the rounds, knocking on cabin doors, emptying buckets and bringing the passengers fresh pitchers of water. He accompanied Jackson to Sunny's door, wanting to reassure her personally that all was well.

When he knocked he was surprised to hear Gabriel's voice. "Whoever you are, go away."

"Mr. Eagle," he called through the portal. "I have a cabin boy along to bring you fresh water and empty the buckets."

Something hit the floor with a *thump*, then the sound of footsteps, slow and dragging, made it to the portal. When the door opened he looked into Gabriel's bloodshot eyes. "You look like hell, man."

"That is because I have been there and back," Gabriel muttered, crawling back to the bunk.

He frowned, glancing around the room. "And where is Miss Eagle?"

"In my cabin. I did not want her sleeping in a room without a lock." Gabriel said, taking a sip of the water Jackson offered him.

"Don't drink too much too fast," he warned.

Gabriel gave a taut nod and lay back upon the bunk. "Please bring my sister water before you leave."

He and Jackson made their way into the adjoining room. Rafe found her lying in the center of the large bunk, her perfectly oval face pale. The aqua dress clung to her sweaty flesh, beads of moisture glistening on the curve of her neck. Her neckline, partly unbuttoned, revealed a glimpse of her swelling bosom. With each breath, her breasts strained against the material, the nipples small, hard globes. Her golden curls clung to her cheeks and fanned out over her shoulders.

Rafe's loins swelled as the dream he had earlier enveloped his thoughts. He longed to reach down and touch her, pull her against his burning flesh and quench the aching desire for her now consuming his body.

Apparently similar desires were also consuming Jackson's young body, because he cleared his throat and whispered. "Holy mother o' God."

He turned to face the boy. "What the bloody hell are you gaping at?"

Jackson's face mortified. "Nothin' Cap'n."

He frowned, taking from the lad the glass and pitcher of water. "Get to them buckets, the stench in here is enough to kill an elephant."

"Aye, Cap'n," Jackson said and hurried to the task.

He set the pitcher on the bedside table and reached into his jacket pocket for a hanky. After moistening the cloth, he got down on one knee beside the bunk and swabbed her face, pushing aside the golden strands of hair. He cooled her neck and then abruptly stood. He dared not touch her further, his control at a thin thread now.

She stirred and opened her eyes. "Rafe."

The way she whispered his name sent chills of delight down his spine; so natural for her velvety tone, like she'd been saying it for years. "I've come to see how you're doing."

She licked her peppermint stained lips with a matching tongue. "A bit better I think."

He poured water into a glass, then placing one hand behind her head, brought it to her lips. "Drink slowly."

She obeyed, her sapphire eyes never leaving his.

He returned the glass to the bedside table. "What ails you will pass soon."

"Then we made it through and all is well?"

He smiled and reached for a blanket to shield her from his eyes. "Aye, Sunny Beth, the danger is gone. All is fine."

She returned the smile before closing her eyes again.

He lingered a moment, feasting on her splendor. *Ah, beautiful rose in amber; even a bit wilted you are still a vision of loveliness.*

"I thank you for all you have done for us, Captain," a voice came from behind, startling Rafe from his disturbing yet intriguing thoughts. He turned to find Gabriel leaning against the adjoining door's frame, arms crossed. "But I will care for my sister now."

Rafe gave a polite nod. "As you wish, sir," he said and made his way to the broken portal. "I will send a crew man to fix the door and a cabin boy with tea and crackers."

Gabriel's glare hardened. "I ask you to keep in mind, Captain, she is only a child."

He arched a brow. "Nay, Mr. Eagle, a mite she isn't...not now, not any longer."

Chapter Nine

The dining hall, because of the fire, was rendered unusable for the remainder of the voyage. It was the main source of socializing while aboard, and Sunny soon grew tired of eating and working on her sketches in her cabin. So when the Abbotts invited her and Gabriel to their stately cabin for dinner, she was excited and thrilled, spending most of the day planning what she would wear and doing up her hair.

"This is turning out to be a disaster," she commented to herself in the mirror. Not knowledgeable in arranging her hair in anything but a *nah-leen*, the traditional head garb worn by the maidens in her tribe, her attempts at sweeping curls atop her head became fruitless. The golden mass looked like a tangled, messy blob. Sitting down on the bunk, she sighed, exasperated, and swallowed the tears of frustration burning the back of her throat.

Gabriel knocked on the adjoining door and waited for her to grant him entrance. Usually he did not wait for her permission, instead calling her name through the portal and announcing his entry. Since the storm, he had been more respectful of her privacy. She did not understand the change but was grateful for it.

Taking an audible breath, she bid him access.

He stifled a smile when he took in the golden disarray capping her crown. "Looks like a rat has made a nest on top of your head," he teased.

Blinking back tears Sunny folded her arms in

front of her. "It is not one bit funny, my brother."

"It is from where I am standing."

"Then go stand somewhere else," she snapped.

He left the room without further comment, to her relief, but returned some moments later with Collette Halston.

Gabriel pointed to Sunny's hair. "Can you see what you can do about *that*?"

She gasped. "Gabriel, how dare you."

He arched a brow. "How dare you leave this room looking as you do," he said before he exited her cabin.

"You poor dear, this is worse than I expected," Collette cooed while gently tackling the snarled splotch of curls. "This is why a genteel lady always has the help of a good handmaiden." She frowned. "I myself miss my Veronica and cannot wait to get home to her expert administrations."

"What does a handmaiden do?" she asked, surrendering her head to Collette's hands.

"All sorts of conveniences, like doing up one's hair, dressing, and bathing," Collette explained.

She gasped. "Even bathing?"

"Aye, especially bathing. And my Veronica gives me the most delicious massage after, using warm, scented oils." She sighed. "Such heaven."

"Are you not...well...shamed to let someone wash you, stroke your flesh when you are undressed?"

Collette laughed. "Why should I be? Veronica has all the same parts as I, only mine are younger and better kept," she added.

She shrugged. "It just seems odd, is all. I mean, when I was a little girl my mother bathed me, but she is my mother. I do not think I would feel comfortable having someone else do for me what I can do for myself."

"You will change your mind," Collette warned,

as she properly pinned up an unsnarled curl and reached for another long lock to untangle. "Otherwise you will spend half of your day trying to fasten the back buttons of a dress and arrange your own hair. With so many social events to attend, sometimes two and three within a day, you will welcome the help of another."

Sunny frowned. "Two or three in a day?"

"Aye, sometimes more if you're in fashion, which I have no doubt you'll be."

Her frown deepened. "What is meant by *in fashion?*"

"The fresh gossip, the new face in society, and with such a face as yours, I know you'll be the talk of the town."

"And how will I become the talk of the town if I am just going to live with my aunt?"

"Tell me about your aunt," Collette probed.

"I have never set eyes on her, I only know of her from what my mother has said."

Collette finished arranging the second curl and started on the third as she spoke. "And that is?"

"Aunt Kaylena Bentley owns Bentwood, a manor house in Brighton. Mother said she dresses elegantly and has the means to care for us properly. Our passage to England was by her generosity."

"Then your aunt is a genteel lady, a lady of means and education. She, no doubt, has a handmaiden to help her, as well as several more servants in her charge. She is a woman who socializes, entertains company regularly, and is invited to attend functions. Her week and weekend card is always filled and dressing in several outfits throughout the day and then into evening is very possible. She knows you'll need an attendant, Gabriel as well, and she's probably interviewing servants to care for you both as we speak. "

Her eyes widened. "Gabriel will have a

handmaiden to dress and wash him as well?"

Collette laughed again. "Though I'm sure he would mind that a lot less then you, nay, he will not have a handmaiden but a manservant or a gentleman's gent."

"Do you think my sister Raven will have servants?"

"As a lord's wife, most definitely," Collette said. "She will be extremely pampered. There's nothing she will have to do but sit and look pretty."

"Raven will not like that. She is a willful girl, curious and headstrong." She frowned. "I feel sorry for Lord Shannon if he expects my sister to act differently."

"How fabulous," Collette purred. "I would love to meet her."

"I am anxious for her to join us as well. I just hope..." her voice trailed off.

"What do you hope, Sunny?"

"I will feel at home in Brighton." She sighed. "It would have been so much easier to do with Raven along."

"You'll be fine, especially after you settle in and have an attendant to serve you. After she learns what you want her to do, and does things just the way you like them, you'll be very much at home. As I said, I miss my Veronica immensely."

"Why is Veronica not with you now?"

Collette sighed. "The old twit has some strange fear of the ocean and refuses to step foot upon a ship."

"Why not hire another girl then, just for your travels?"

Collette captured and performed her magic on yet another curl. "I have tried and halfway out to sea I am stuck with someone who is either seasick or homesick for her family. So now I travel alone and hire an attendant at my destination. At times it is a most efficient thing to do because locals know of the best sites to see, especially if I am exploring ruins or on safari."

"You are so interesting, Collette," she mused.

"Now, if we can just get your brother to believe the same, I'll be very pleased."

She turned in her seat to face the other woman. "You have eyes for Gabriel?"

Collette arched a brow. "Doesn't every woman?"

She shrugged. "There have been a few, but since his wife and child died three years ago he has not cared much for such things."

Collette turned Sunny back around so she could continue to work on her hair. "Well then, I'll have to do something to change that."

Sunny found out at dinner just how Collette planned on going forward with those changes. Dressed in a teal blue gown sporting a tempting and tantalizing neckline was just the start. Her seductive glances, with round, exotic eyes were added throughout the evening, drawing a man like a spider's web would to a fly. The combination was potent. Even Lord Abbott looked flushed a time or two throughout the meal. And Gabriel flourished beneath the fussing and fawning, his own glances sparkling for the first time in ages. His laughter vibrated with heartfelt joy and his appetite diminished. All these ways were definitely not how her brother was prone to acting.

But she was not about to complain. Besides being thrilled for her brother's new found happiness, she was also no longer the full focus of his thoughts. When he asked Lord Abbott to see Sunny safely back to her cabin so he could accompany Collette to hers, she saw the opportunity to grab a bit of happiness for herself.

Lord Abbott's duty ended at the portal, with a polite bow, instructions to bolt the lock, and a curt goodnight. As soon as the elder man was out of site, she went for an evening stroll along the deck. In her entire time on the *Entrenous*, she had been saddled with Gabriel's concern and watchful eye. Not even a moment of privacy walking to the *privy* was granted to her. Now she walked alone along the rail, gazing out onto the dark sea. The gentle breeze played with the thin strands of hair escaping her up-do of curls and cooled her flesh. She shivered, sorry she had forgotten to grab her shawl.

"Allow me, *Fraulein* Eagle," Count Ivan Sontag said, doffing his waist coat and placing it about her shoulders. "I vould not vant you to catch your death." He smiled, large blue eyes roaming the length of her. "*Nein*, death would cheat us all of such a vision."

Her cheeks warmed. "I thank you for your concern."

He inclined his head politely. "It's my pleasure, *Fraulein*."

"Call me Sunny, if you please," she reminded him.

"I do please and vould have you remember to call me Ivan," he countered.

"I will remember," she said, turning her gaze once more to the darkness enveloping the ship. Placing a hand on the rail, she took an audible breath. "I wonder when we will arrive in England?"

"My calculations predict another day or so. Ve vill be docking in Liverpool." He cleared his throat and moved closer, his shoulder touching hers. "And the thought of never setting my eyes on yours again saddens me greatly."

His nearness disturbed and confused her, and she took a moment to catch her breath. At home Night Wolf, a warrior her age in the tribe, followed her to the river when she did the wash with her mother. He smiled, and she smiled in return. Her heart danced at this mere attention. Throughout her journey to England she often wondered if she had stayed on the Reservation, would she and Night Wolf be together now? Would she have chosen him at a mating ceremony? Would he have accepted?

Ivan's fingers cupped hers. "I vould be honored for the chance to keep your company, know you better."

"I'm sure you would," a deep familiar voice came from behind.

She pulled her hand free from Ivan's grasp and spun around. The captain stood leaning against a post, muscular arms crossed over a broad chest. His hat, pushed back upon his brow, revealed dark curls gracing his forehead. His unshaven chin lent a rugged, handsome look to the already perfect features.

Rafe frowned. "Does your brother know you are out and about alone, Sunny Beth?"

Ivan answered for her. "She is not alone, *Kapitän*. She is vith me." Ivan placed a possessive arm around her shoulders.

His boldness surprised her and for some strange reason angered Rafe. "It would be wise if I escorted Miss Eagle to her cabin now."

"If anyone escorts her, it vill be me," Ivan protested, drawing her closer to him.

Rafe glared at the Count's hold upon her.

She'd had about enough. First she was smothered by her brother and now these two. Did they even realize she was still standing there?

"Stop it, both of you."

They turned to gaze at her, blinking and baffled at her outburst.

First she turned her attention on Rafe. "I do not need my brother's permission to take a walk on deck, nor *your* consent to speak to another passenger. I am a grown woman, and I will make my own decisions, is that clear?"

He nodded, the muscles at his jaw tightening. "Perfectly."

She looked over at Ivan. The smug look on his face annoyed her to the very marrow of her bones. She shrugged off his arm from around her shoulders and proceeded to set him straight. "You, on the other hand, *do* need my permission to touch me. I am no one's possession, is that clear?"

"*Ja, Fraulein,*" was all the reply Ivan managed, his pale complexion coloring.

She removed Ivan's jacket from around her shoulders and handed it to him. "And I am perfectly capable of walking *alone* to my cabin." She forced a smile. "Good evening, gentlemen." With that said she turned on her heels and made for the companionway leading to her room, leaving both men speechless behind her.

Once in her quarters, she secured the lock and went to knock on the adjoining door.

Gabriel did not answer.

Turning the knob, she opened the door a crack and called out his name.

There was still no answer.

Pushing the door wider, she peeked into the room, his bed was empty.

At first she was relieved she had made it back before him, but then she frowned.

Could Gabriel still be with Collette? She had not run into them, fortunately, on deck. So, they had to be in Collette's cabin. What could they be doing all this time?

The heat rose to her cheeks, and she clamped a hand over her mouth. She knew exactly what they were doing. And she also knew Collette's intentions would not be long-lasting. She herself admitted marriage was not for her, nor would it be something she would ever do again.

Gabriel, on the other hand, loved being married and grieved long and hard when he lost his family. It had taken him years to even think of moving on, because marriage was a serious commitment to him. The steps he made tonight, being with Collette, she fully realized were not easy ones. That was why she was so pleased for her brother. Finally, he was having a measure of joy in his life. She hoped they would seek each other's company while aboard. But now would Gabriel want to say his goodbyes to Collette after they docked?

She knew her brother went to the cantina to meet women. She and Raven talked often about such things. Men had certain needs, and there were certain women who fulfilled those needs. But Collette was not that sort of woman, and she knew Gabriel realized this as well. This was a woman he would expect to court, to fall in love with, to marry. And right now he was probably mistaking Collette's intentions for something more than the woman's actual purpose. Sunny did not want to see her brother hurt again.

"Oh, Gabriel," she moaned. "You have done an unwise thing."

She made her way back to her own quarters, sitting upon the bunk. There was no choice but for her to tell him Collette's true feelings. Perhaps there was still a chance to save him the pain, the heartbreak.

She sighed. *But will you even believe me?*

For now all she could do was pray that he would.

Chapter Ten

"You were always a willful child, and now you are a willful and jealous woman," Gabriel shouted.

Sunny cringed at his harsh words, although she was pleased for the fact he called her a woman. "I am not trying to be willful, nor am I jealous. I am just telling you the truth. Collette Halston told me herself she has no thoughts of marriage and a family. She wants to remain free and is quite happy with being able to go on all her adventures...accounting to no one but herself. She is not the sort you are looking for, my brother."

"And how do you know the sort I am looking for?"

She sighed. "I know it is not Collette."

"Do you think of me as some sort of monster...an ugly ogre no one could stand to set their eyes on, Sunny?" he snapped, his gaze glaring into hers.

She remembered the ogre that came into her family's wickiup when she was a child. It happened a few times to her and Raven, and quite a number of times to Gabriel. The ogre threatened to take her to the underground if she continued to misbehave. It was a custom her people used on bad children. An elder would dress up as an ogre, painting his face to look horrible and scary, and then creep into the bad child's wickiup. Any child would promise to be good after waking to see such a frightful thing lurking over them.

"You are handsome and strong, Gabriel. I would never think of you any differently," she said. "It has nothing to do with your looks."

He frowned. "Then do you not think I could, perhaps, in time change Collette's mind?"

"And what if you cannot?" she countered. "You will hurt again, and I do not want that to happen."

His eyes saddened, his voice softened. "I do not think I could be anymore hurt than what I have been these last three years." He combed fingers through his hair. "Losing my wife, the love of my life, and our tiny son has to be the most horrible hurt there is. There is nothing Collette, or anyone else for that matter, could do to me that would be as bad."

"I am afraid for you, Gabriel," she said, making her way to where he stood and wrapping her arms around his waist.

He embraced her in return. "I am afraid as well, *dayden*, but I am almost more fearful of not taking the chance to see how all this with Collette plays out." He sighed. "I am not getting any younger, and I have come to the conclusion I do not want to spend my life alone any longer. The heavens know I miss my wife, *Nahdaste*, Fire Star, lost to me in childbirth three years ago. I will grieve her loss and that of my baby, forever. But as you said, life does go on and on and on...and I want to spend mine with someone, have children and grandchildren."

She leaned back to gaze up into his large blue eyes. "But Collette does not share your way of life."

"Neither did mother share our father's ways, yet once she fell in love with him, there was no doubt in her mind that she would be with him, wherever that took her." He forced a smile. "Perhaps, if I am patient, Collette will come around to my way of thinking as well."

She nodded, though she still had some doubts. He was right about their parents, though. Mother came around to her father's way of living, in spite of the difficulties their people shared. It would be a lot easier for Collette to conform to Gabriel's ways then it was for Golden Lady, and yet, she made a life and had a family with Proud Eagle. Would the two coming together be an impossible task? No, perhaps not impossible, just improbable. But Gabriel was not a child, and although she wished to spare her brother further pain, the choice was his to make.

Gabriel shared his lunch with Collette, in her cabin, while Sunny joined Lady Abbott. The conversation she had earlier with her brother remained on her mind as she chewed a slice of ham.

"You look rather preoccupied this afternoon, mite," Lady Abbott commented. "Is there anything upsetting you?"

She met Lady Abbott's gaze. "How well do you know Collette Halston?"

Lady Abbott waved a hand casually in the air. "Oh, not very well, I admit. We've only become acquainted on this voyage. Why do you ask?"

"I have reason to believe my brother has become smitten with her," she said.

Lady Abbott leaned closer. "Do tell me everything."

And she did, swearing the elder woman to secrecy. She concluded with, "Do you think things can work out between them?"

Lady Abbott frowned. "If Collette falls in love, aye. A woman in love goes to great lengths to make a relationship thrive. And your brother is quite charming."

"And what of a man in love?"

Lady Abbott narrowed her eyes with reflection. "I believe it's different for them. A man has so many other outlets in life to choose from. And since the standards for a man are far more relaxed and accepted then those for a woman, they aren't scrutinized by society." She shrugged. "Besides, a woman's main goal is to marry and have a family."

"It should not be that way," Sunny said. "We

should have the same rights and wishes for our lives as do the men."

"It's been this way for years, mite."

"Then it is time for a change."

Lady Abbott gave a sardonic laugh. "I give anyone my heartfelt best wishes in trying." She placed a hot, buttered almond biscuit on Sunny's plate. "Now, eat your lunch before it grows cold."

When Sunny returned to her cabin, she opened her sketch book. There she found a drawing of Raven she had done just before they left home. Her sister, hair tied back with the *nah-leen*, was dressed in traditional Apache garb. With one hand on her hip, another on a spear, and a moccasin clad foot upon a rock, Raven struck a regal pose. In the background was the flowing river, the very one where the two of them played. She sighed, tears welling in her eyes and whispered to herself, "I have so much I need to talk with you about."

Turning to a fresh sheet, she reached for a lead stick and began to draw Night Wolf, wondering as she sketched what he was doing now. But something peculiar happened as she moved the lead implement over the paper. Instead of Night Wolf's image, she was compelled to draw Rafe's. His lopsided smile, that was so endearing to her for an unexplained reason, now grinned up at her from the paper.

She frowned, angrily crossing out her work with a swipe of the lead stick. Why on earth was she compelled to draw the captain?

She threw aside the sketch book and climbed upon the bunk, covering her head with a blanket. *Why compelled, indeed?*

****

The day the *Entrenous* docked in Liverpool, England, Sunny could not have been happier. The time was a chaotic one though, with passengers gathering their belongings and scurrying about to secure personal information from those they met aboard.

Ivan caught up with her, pressing for further contact, while she and Lady Abbott watched land approach from their stand on deck. As handsome and charming as the man was, she hesitated as to whether she would want to see him again. For a reason unbeknown to her, the captain did not approve. Why Rafe's opinion should matter to her, was another unbeknown reason, but it did.

In fact, she found her disappointment growing when the captain appeared too busy to speak with her throughout the remainder of the voyage. Perhaps he resented her haughty remark and the way she stomped off to her cabin the last time they spoke.

Ivan broke through her thoughts by bestowing a gentle kiss across her knuckles. "I vill be unable to sleep vithout knowing how to find you."

She frowned. Far be it from her to keep him from his sleep. "But I know not the exact whereabouts of my aunt's home," she admitted.

"Give me her name, and I vill find you," he said, keeping a hold on her hand.

In order to break free from his grasp, she complied. "Her name is Kaylena Bentley, and she lives at Bentwood Manor in Brighton."

He released her hand, bowed, and clicked his heels together. "I vill find you," he repeated and hurried off toward his own destination.

"Well, now, how exciting," Lady Abbott mused. "Already you have a gentleman caller."

Casting a last glance at the approaching shore, she sighed. "But he is not the right one."

Lady Abbott arched a brow. "And how can you know this so soon?"

She shrugged. "I just have a feeling."

Lady Abbott laughed. "Give it time."

"That is what my mother always tells me."

"Then she is a very wise woman." Lady Abbott looped an arm through hers. "Now, come, mite. It's time to go home."

Chapter Eleven

"Liverpool...what a strange and funny name for a town," Sunny commented, climbing into a horse-drawn cab with Lord and Lady Abbott. They waited as Gabriel said his farewell to Collette, who would be staying on in Liverpool to visit with friends and would not be journeying to her home in London for several weeks.

Looking out the cab's window at the hustle and bustle of the odd-named city, Sunny was grateful she had become acquainted with and was befriended by the Lord and Lady Abbott. If not for them, she and Gabriel would be wandering around Liverpool, trying to find the train that would take them to London, where Reverend Joshua Holmes was to meet them.

As they arrived at the Lime Street station, within an hour after disembarking from the *Entrenous*, Lady Abbott informed her, the ride to London's Euston station would be an eight hour trek. The train stopped at the town of Crew, Birmingham, Coventry, and Rugby along the way.

This did not please her in the least. For the last month all she had done was ride in coaches, on trains, and aboard a ship...and now still another train waited for her to embark. Her body was tired of sitting motionless in uncomfortable clothing. With a drained spirit, she followed Eugenia Abbott to the *Ladies Only* compartment of the large steam train. Gabriel and Lord Abbott entered another compartment strictly for the men.

Men and women were not the only separate

compartments. The train also consisted of other composites called first, second, and third class, seating folks according to the amount they paid for a ticket. Even the luggage had a separate compartment. Fortunately Aunt Kaylena provided enough funds to purchase first class tickets, allowing her and Gabriel to join Lord and Lady Abbott.

Each compartment had two doors, one on each side opening onto the platform. The first class compartment seated six people in relative comfort on padded upholstered seats complete with arm rests and privy facilities.

"There aren't arm rests in second class, and third class has bare wooden seats and no privy," Lady Abbott explained.

She frowned. "Where are the folks expected to relieve themselves?"

"At a stop along the way, if they're quick enough at it," Lady Abbott said, settling her plump frame comfortably into a seat opposite hers.

Two other ladies entered the compartment and after introductions and pleasantries were exchanged, they conversed mostly with Lady Abbott about London's turmoil, the streets being dug up for the building of an extension to the sewage system and the electrification of the underground railway network.

"Why, we'll be riding in a tube, I hear, with scarce a window to look out from," the elder woman of the two complained.

Lady Abbott inhaled sharply, placing a hand upon her chest. "My breath is labored just with the thought."

Sunny found her own breath ragged as she pictured herself enveloped in a dark tube beneath the ground, burrowing along like the moles that ravaged the garden her mother had planted by the river, hidden from the white agents. *Buried alive,* came to mind. She shuddered and turned her attention to the scenery flashing by the train's window, as they headed for the first stop.

The two women rode with them as far as Birmingham. She stretched her gaze to get a glimpse of that station, but from her seat not much could be seen. Another woman boarded the train at that stop, accompanied by a child around the age of four or five years old. The little girl had large green eyes and fiery red curls that sprung out from beneath a yellow, lacy bonnet. The mother, a thin woman who appeared somewhat frazzled, introduced herself as Harriett Jones and the little girl as Clarissa. It was a name Sunny would always remember because Mrs. Jones said it every few seconds.

"Clarissa, stop fidgeting, Clarissa, stop swinging your legs. Clarissa, leave your bonnet alone. Clarissa, wait till I tell your father how naughty you're being," the mother chastised, eyes narrowing and thin lips pursing with aggravation.

In spite of Sunny's love for children, she grew just as irritated. Being hemmed into such close quarters with an unruly child, wore on her nerves. A glance in Lady Abbott's direction proved the elder woman shared the same feeling, her plump face twisted with silent annoyance. It was not until Mrs. Jones, obviously her own patience stretched to the limits, decided to take drastic measures to remedy the problem before any of them finally got a moment of peace.

Reaching for Clarissa, Harriett pulled the child across her knees. What happened next totally shocked Sunny. Mrs. Jones then yanked the hem of Clarissa's yellow brocade dress to her waist, lowered ruffled white bloomers to the ankles, and with a few sharp slaps to a much bared bottom, disciplined her daughter before their eyes.

Shocked and shamed, Clarissa sat quietly the

rest of the way to Coventry, where the pair disembarked, her face a shade of crimson and tear-filled eyes fixed on her shoes.

Lady Abbott sighed with relief after they left the compartment. "I was about to thrash that mite myself," she admitted, straightening her collar with a huff. "Why, I never allowed such behavior from my own daughter."

"Did you discipline her like that?"

"Aye, whenever there was the need, which wasn't often. After she learned a few times the consequences she'd receive for bad behavior, she acted accordingly with only a stern warning," Lady Abbott said.

"Strange as this might sound, I felt sorry for Clarissa and even shared her shame. I certainly would not have liked my mother correcting me in front of strangers that way."

"If Harriet Jones had previously punished her daughter, she would have only needed to threaten. Unruly children aren't only an upheaval to their parents, but a rude awakening to those around them, as Clarissa was. I never wanted anyone to think of my daughter as anything other than a perfect lady." Sighing, Lady Abbott leaned back in her seat. "It was the only fitting measure to take, and you can't tell me parents across the pond don't use the same punishment."

"I do not know of the people across the pond that you speak of," Sunny said, feeling completely lost.

Her reply made Lady Abbot giggle.

"But my people use the ogre," she continued.

Lady Abbott arched curious brow. "The ogre?"

Now it was Sunny's turn to giggle. "It is how Apache parents make a child behave."

Lady Abbott leaned forward in her seat. "Do tell."

Since no other passengers entered their

compartment for the rest of the ride, Sunny was able to explain about the ogre and a few other Apache customs.

Lady Abbott sat spellbound, listening like an eager child herself all the way to London.

****

The train arrived at the London Bridge station around eight that evening. Sunny ached from sitting so long. After indulging herself in a quick stretch, she followed Lady Abbott onto the platform. There they were met by Lord Abbott and Gabriel. The swollen flesh around her brother's eyes revealed he most likely slept through the journey.

He certainly would not have liked traveling with Clarissa Jones. Again a pang of shame for the girl's embarrassment snared her heart. She hoped if and when she became a parent, her children behaved without her taking such measures.

Lady Abbott looked at the others milling around the station. "I hope we spot your connection soon, if not the two of you are more than welcome to spend the night at our home. There's ample room."

"I thank you kindly," Gabriel said, reaching for their baggage. "But the Reverend Holmes would have no way of finding us if we accepted your offer."

Lady Abbott's eyes rounded, and her high-pitched voice rose to another octave. "Reverend Joshua Holmes is who you're meeting?"

Gabriel nodded. "He is an old friend of my mother. In fact, his chaplain position at a church in Brighton, was offered to him by our aunt, Kaylena Bentley."

Lady Abbott's chubby hand went to her throat. "Good heavens, Stanley, they know Joshua Holmes and are related to Kaylena Bentley."

"Aye, I heard, love," was all Stanley commented, in his usual calm demeanor.

"And how do you know the reverend and my

aunt?" Sunny probed.

"He is Simon's uncle...as you know, I've spoken of Simon. He's the young man betrothed to my niece, Fiona Wade," Lady Abbott reminded them. "And I know Kaylena through Josh, though I've only had the pleasure of meeting her twice."

She gasped. "And if I am not mistaken, Simon is Captain Cavendish's brother?"

"Aye, that's the way of it," Lady Abbott agreed with a smile.

"Then it looks as though we have not seen the last of the man," Gabriel muttered.

"Nay, not in the least," Lady Abbott said. Giggling, she added. "I hope you two left the ship on good terms."

Sunny remembered how Gabriel and Rafe clashed, and her own last remark to him.

Taking an audible breath she shifted her gaze a moment Gabriel's way. "So do I, Lady Abbott...so do I."

Chapter Twelve

"With all those golden curls, aye, I'd know you anywhere," a deep voice came from behind.

Sunny turned to lock eyes with a distinguished looking gentleman. He was tall, well-framed, and near to her parents' age. His hair, grayed around the temples, fell in thick waves above the *holy man's* collar that he wore.

"Reverend Holmes," Lady Abbott said, moving nearer to the man and placing a hand upon his arm. "Can you imagine how surprised I was to just now learn my traveling companions are friends of yours?"

"I shan't begin to envision it, my lady," the reverend replied, his gaze still locked on Sunny. It was as if he savored every feature upon her face. "I trust your accommodations aboard were acceptable?"

Heat rose to her cheeks with his bold assessment. "They were more than comfortable. *Ashoge*, thank you."

"You are the image of your mother," he said, taking her hand and bestowing a gentle kiss across her knuckles.

His bold gesture caused her to flush. "Is my Aunt Kaylena with you?"

"Nay," he said, raising his gaze to lock with hers. "She was feeling a bit under the weather and asked that I come without her."

She frowned. "Nothing serious, I trust?"

"Nay, she'll be fine, just needs to rest." He smiled. "Tell me then, how is your mother?"

"She is well, sends you her best."

His smile brightened. "Does she now?"

"I am Gabriel," her brother interrupted, extending a hand in greeting.

The reverend pried his gaze from her to accept Gabriel's hospitality. "Ah, and you are definitely Proud Eagle's son." He glanced around. "And where is your other sister?"

Sunny sighed. "Right now I would say she is probably setting foot on Ireland's shores."

The reverend frowned. "Ireland? I'm afraid I don't understand."

"It's getting late, Joshua, and we're all so exhausted from our travels," Lady Abbott said. "Perhaps explanations can wait?"

"Of course," the reverend agreed. "And it would please me to offer you a ride home. I have a carriage waiting to take us to Cavenworth, my sister's mansion, which is only blocks away from yours."

"Oh, nay, we couldn't trouble you," Lady Abbott said. "I'm sure we can catch a public conveyance, since Hemsley, our own carriage driver, had no clue as to when we'd arrive."

"It's not a bother, really. There is more than enough room for us all. I insist."

"Capital idea," Lord Abbott said. Not allowing room for any further protests by his wife, he quickly picked up his baggage and headed for the street.

During the thirty-minute ride to the Abbot's home, Gabriel explained Raven's predicament. Of course, he left out the real reason she left the ship, which is what they both agreed upon. While hearing the details, Sunny relived the horrible situation. The emptiness of Raven's absence pained her still and would continually leave a void in her heart until they were reunited.

"I'm confident my nephew will see to contacting Lord Shannon," the reverend said, lines of concern creasing his brow. "In no time we'll have Raven with us, where she belongs." He turned to look at her with a reassuring smile. "On that you have my word."

****

Rafe went over the paperwork one last time, organizing the roster and other documents in a file. He added his version of the dining hall fire, for his employers benefit, and a note to himself to contact Lord Braiton Shannon. After putting everything into an envelope, he sat back in his seat and ran his hands over burning eyes. The last seventeen days had been exhausting, both emotionally and physically.

Perhaps it was best this was his last voyage upon the *Entrenous*. Maybe the lost passenger and the fire were warnings to him to travel the sea leisurely for a time. He had enough savings. Perhaps he could buy a small vessel of his own, travel to the Orient? His brother had recognized the need for change and was carving out a new life. Was it time for him to do the same?

For years the *Entrenous* was all he needed, the special element and driving force of his life. Her name, the French word for *confidential*, rang true to form. There was an actual bond just between them, the way she steered beneath his guide, the storms they'd weathered together. He owed her his success and wealth and the opportunity for a new life after his dueling incident. At her helm, the nightmarish memories were put behind him.

He sighed and pushed his seat away from the desk. Standing, he stretched his spine and made his way to the portal. Although he loved the sounds of the sea, lately the voyages held little adventure for him. In the early days of his career passengers weren't as rude and demanding as they were lately. Friendships acquired aboard lasted. But times had changed. Once travelers left the ship, they were gone forever—back to the people they loved...to a world that meant something to them.

But what would my world be without the sea?
And in that instant Sunny Beth, with the golden
curls and large sapphire eyes, popped into his mind.
In the weeks past, her courage and stamina
impressed him. She was bound for a new land,
withstood the frightening loss of her sister, saw her
brother locked in a storage room, endured a storm,
and helped to fight a fire. A brave and hearty
woman, she was—yet tender and beautiful.
Watching her stroll the deck of the ship became a
favorite pastime. He longed to join her, take her
hand in his, and feel its warmth.

He shook his head to rid himself of such
musings. Thoughts like that usually led to trouble,
like it did with Deandra. He returned to his seat and
propped booted feet upon the edge of the desk, his
heart quickening with mixed emotions. He'd have to
see her again, in order to bring her news of her
sister, and for that he was somewhat pleased. And
yet, setting eyes on her beauty would only bring
back a strange disturbance. Hopefully, he'll bring
her good news. If Lord Shannon indeed married
Raven Eagle, she would soon join Sunny in Brighton.
His obligation to her would be fulfilled, and he could
go about his life as usual.

But what would he do if the news were bad?
What if, for whatever reason, things didn't go as
they all hoped, how would he tell her? He shuddered
at the thought of Raven being taken by the Sea
Patrol, imprisoned as a prostitute. Once, he'd played
cards with a drunken patrol captain. The wretched
bloke spilled his thoughts to everyone at the table,
laughing and bragging about the way the women
were treated before reaching the prison. If Rafe had
not been outnumbered at the time by the bloody
bugger's friends, he'd have put a bullet between the
bastard's eyes.

The treatment was unmerciful and disgusting. If

crude conditions didn't kill the women, the brutality surely would. Often the women bled internally from the harsh physical abuse, objects inserted into them the men thought sport to use. If they were lucky enough to live through such violation, they were mentally scarred, permanently in a state of shock or driven insane. With no other way to escape the humiliation and torture of their bodies, their minds broke. Never would they know reality again, walking around like the dead among the living, dwelling safely in a world of their own. It's how their minds coped, but what of their bodies?

He frowned, remembering the patrol captain's detailed account. Naked and gaunt, the women defecated in their cells like an animal locked in a cage. Caked with dirt, their own excrement, vermin crawling in their hair and upon the stench of their flesh, they begged for a morsel of food. The jailers would throw trash upon the cell's floor and watch as the women desperately fought amongst one another to reach it, only to see a rat snare the food first and victoriously run off to eat it himself.

Again he shuddered. If Sunny Beth's sister was taken to prison, she must never know. Better for him to lie and say he couldn't reach his contact, than for her to learn the truth. Though he hadn't known Sunny long, Rafe realized such news would morally kill her. And Gabriel Eagle would probably tear apart his surroundings, wherever he was at the time.

Nay, whatever I know about the Sea Patrol, I must keep to myself.

After mumbling a quick prayer on Raven Eagle's behalf, he swung his legs off the desk, reached for his travel satchel, stuck the envelope inside, and made his way to shore. Unfortunately, his employers were closed, so he'd have to wait till morning to file his report and send word to Ireland. Even if he'd been able to finish his business on time, the last train to London had already gone. He sighed, missing his family and Lydia's roast beef. His mother's cook made the most delicious gravy, smooth, rich, and a bit spicy. He licked his lips, hunger rumbling deep within his stomach. Foremost in his mind now was to appease his appetite and quench his thirst. He would have dinner and a mug of ale at the Bayside Inn, then head to the small apartment he kept here in Liverpool. He smiled, thinking of how he'd end the evening, with Felicity's expert hands pleasing his every desire.

****

Sunny's weariness reached well into her bones, the true meaning of *bone tired* now completely clear. Reverend Holmes knocked upon Cavenworth's door, to have it opened by a man introduced to her as Kendall Jones. Tall and lean, the man was obviously employed by the family.

"The Cavendish's have retired for the evening, sir," Kendall said, beady little eyes glancing with annoyance at the watch he pulled from his vest pocket. "It is rather late, you understand."

"Aye, Kendall, and I apologize for the disturbance at such an unfair hour, but our guests from America have just arrived. I expected them much earlier myself, but a storm at sea set things at a different pace, and we're all trying to work accordingly."

Kendall's audible sigh made her feel anything but welcome. "I understand then, sir, come in and have a seat in the parlor. I shall call for Margaret, so she can see the guests to their rooms."

Reverend Holmes gave a taut nod. "Thank you, Kendall. Fletcher will be bringing in the bags from the carriage, please see to them as well."

Kendall bowed. "Very good, sir," was his remark before turning to leave.

"Your last name is Jones?" she said, halting his departure.

"Aye miss," Kendall replied, his eyes narrowing. "Do you know the name?"

"I do, but only recently. A woman by the name of Harriet Jones traveled a way with me on the train today."

Kendall arched a brow. "And was she toting along with her a mite she called Clarissa?"

"Yes, truth be told, she was," she said, remembering the child's name being called by the woman throughout the entire time they shared the train.

"The woman is my brother's wife and the mite his daughter." Kendall frowned. "And a rather difficult one at that, but I'm sure you noticed this for yourself."

She noticed all too well but refrained from relaying Clarissa's embarrassing punishment. "Yes, I did."

"Humph," was his response while stalking away.

"Friendly fellow," Gabriel said sarcastically as they followed the reverend into the parlor.

"Ah, well, he's on a schedule and doesn't like his routine compromised." The reverend motioned for them to take a seat on one of the upholstered chairs. "I believe that's exactly why my sister keeps him around." He chuckled. "Marietta's always been a bit of a free spirit, doesn't adhere well to organization. Kendall has been a godsend to both her and my brother-in-law."

Sunny sunk down into the plush comfort of the chair. "Mama always said we are all individuals, having our own strengths and weaknesses."

"Tell me now, how does Amanda really fare?" the reverend probed.

She smiled with the thought of her mother; always busy running their household, trying to protect her family. If it were not for that, they would not be here in England. "She is well, still handsome in her bones and on top of things at all times. Truly she is the backbone of the family, sometimes even the entire tribe."

Gabriel added with a chuckle. "She usually manages to have things her way."

The reverend arched a brow. "Then not much has changed."

Gabriel frowned. "It is by her request—"

"You mean strong urging," she interrupted.

Gabriel's frown deepened, and he cleared his throat before he continued, "That I am standing here before you."

The reverend smiled. "Then you are more like your father then I thought."

She rested her head back and closed her eyes. "Neither of them can say no to mother."

"You are just as willful," Gabriel accused.

Her eyes flashed open. "I am not."

Gabriel cast a teasing smile. "Oh, but you are, *dayden*." Turning to the reverend he added. "There before you is a younger version of my mother."

"Just as I remember her," the reverend said, searching the features of her face as he had done at the train station.

Sunny was relieved when the awkward moment was disturbed by Margaret's entrance. The elder woman took one look at Sunny's face and clicked her tongue. "Poor mite, ye must be bloody tired from yer travels." She motioned for the two of them to follow her. "Coom 'ere now, just this way to yer rooms."

Margaret left Gabriel off at his door, but led Sunny into the room she would occupy.

"Let me 'elp ye, miss," Margaret offered, removing the cape from her shoulders and placing it across a nearby chair. "See 'ere, Fletcher's brought up yer bags," she said, pointing to the luggage placed on the floor at the foot of the bed. "I'll find ye a nightie, then get the grime washed from yer flesh, and see ye on yer way to yer rest."

Her cheeks warmed with the thought of another washing and dressing her. She remembered the conversation she had with Collette one evening aboard the ship. They discussed the duties of those who attended others who were wealthier. But she was not a wealthy person, and Margaret was not a young one. In her village, it was the elders who were taken care of by the young. How strange the roles should be reversed here in England. Feeling awkward and uncomfortable accepting Margaret's help she politely declined the offer. "You need not bother, Margaret. I am fine doing things for myself."

"It's nay a bother, miss."

"It is late, and I am perfectly able," she protested further, reaching for one of the bags and placing it upon the bed. "Please, go and get your own rest."

Margaret frowned. "Are ye sure, miss?"

She smiled. "Very sure."

"As ye say then, but mind ye I'll be 'ere coom the morn to 'elp ye greet the day."

"I am sure you will."

"The privy's just through those doors there, if ye have a need to use it."

After Margaret left, Sunny stripped off her day clothes and made her way to the *relief room*, as she chose to call it. A flush toilet, similar to the kind she used on the ship, but much cleaner, furnished the small area. She took her time, not having to worry about other ladies standing in wait outside the door, and surveyed her surroundings. A white clawed foot tub was set in another corner and beside it a table with a pitcher full of water, a basin and several clean white towels folded atop it. A round mirror hung on the wall just above the table, as well as a shelving unit lined with soap, bottles of bath oil, and cologne neatly in a row.

The first time she pulled the chain the toilet did not flush. She frowned. "*Aco'tndn'nil'gon'ye,* what is the trouble," she muttered to herself and tried a second time, pulling the chain harder. To her horror all the water and everything that floated around in it, rose higher and higher. "No, oh no," she gasped as the entire mess spilt over the toilet's rim and onto the floor.

She reached for a towel and sopped up the mess, wringing it all out into the toilet's basin. A second and even a third towel dried the floor. After everything was wiped clean, she hung the wet towels over the tub then poured fresh water from the pitcher atop the wash table into the basin provided. She then scrubbed her feet and hands with a fragrant bar of soap and used a fourth towel to dry her own flesh. As she placed that towel over the tub to dry along with the others, she could not help but think the nice clean privy she entered, thanks to her, was not so clean anymore.

Glancing at her reflection in the mirror, hair in disarray, pockets of weariness settled beneath her eyes, she sighed and whispered, "Welcome to England," before heading off to bed.

Chapter Thirteen

The night had not exactly gone as Rafe hoped.

"Yer just out o' sorts, pet," Felicity said when he failed to rise to the occasion. "These things 'appen sometimes. Just might be the weariness catchin' up with ye." She stroked his chest and curled her thin, shapely form around his. "A good night's sleep'll 'elp ye."

Felicity, with dark hair and eyes complimenting a fair complexion, turned heads. But her beauty was no match for the lovely Sunny Beth. He squeezed his eyes shut, willing the blonde curls and sapphire eyes to leave his thoughts.

Felicity's arm went about him, her slim fingers splayed across his abdomen. "All will be fine in the mornin'," she whispered.

But the situation was the same and it gave him cause to worry. He had always prided himself at being able to *do the deed* in the midst of battle, if need be.

"Mayhap if ye get yer mind off whatever 'tis on, pet, things will turn up for ye," Felicity suggested, giggling over the pun she'd made.

He found none of it amusing. "How do you know my mind's on anything but you?"

She snickered. "Cause if it were ye'd be feckin' the life out o' me."

He frowned, her terminology annoying him as he remembered Sunny's referral. *Coming together as one*, she had said. It sounded so much better. "Must you use such brazen language to describe what we do?"

Roberta C. M. DeCaprio

"'ey, pet, I call it as I see it. What we do is feck, simple as that. No strings attached, no obligations, just as ye like it."

She was right, that's what he wanted. In all the time Felicity had been pleasing his manly desires he never once asked her anything about her life—did she have siblings, where she lived, her interests—because he didn't want to know or be involved in a woman's personal life ever again. And she never inquired about his, her words were only said to arouse him. Up until now, the arrangement suited him just fine, as it did in other ports with other women he encountered.

She slipped naked from his bed and went to the basin, lifting a leg to rest a foot on a nearby chair. In plain view she boldly scrubbed those parts he, for the first time ever, was unable to enjoy. While she washed herself, he couldn't control the urge to compare her to Sunny Beth.

Felicity's legs were long and lean...nicely shaped but bony around the knees. Sunny's were perfect. He'd gotten a glimpse when he stripped away her burning skirt. Her limbs were well muscled, evenly proportioned. She'd said her Apache garments only hung to the knees, allowing all her smooth flesh to become bronzed by the sun. He thought darker skin looked healthier than the pasty, white shade most women had.

Felicity's breasts were perky and round, but small, whereas Sunny filled her necklines to capacity. The rounded mounds were lush, ample to caress.

Felicity turned, and misunderstanding his surveillance, she gave her bared bottom a playful slap and smiled. "Ye like what ye see, pet?"

"Aye," he lied. In truth, what he saw no longer pleased him at all.

She meandered over to the bed and sat with legs

askew, all she was about open to his gaze. Her hand moved to caress her inner thigh. "I've still a bit o' time, should ye want another crack at it."

Disgusted, with her...with himself, he cast a glance to the window.

"Ah, now, there 'tis." She sighed. "Knew it would 'appen one day."

He turned her way, frowning. "I haven't the foggiest idea what you're talking about."

She arched a brow. "Don't ye now?"

"Nay, care to enlighten me?"

"All's I can say, is I 'ope she's worth it, pet." She stood and reached for her clothes.

He rubbed a hand over his face in frustration. Why the bloody hell was Sunny Beth Eagle popping into his mind anyway? He was perfectly content before he met her. He'd moved on from his heartaches and troubles and liked his life now. "How do you know it's a woman?" he snapped annoyed.

"I've been around long enough, pet, to know these things," Felicity remarked, slipping into her clothes.

"Well, you're dead wrong," he said, wishing he'd sounded more convincing.

Felicity reached for her shawl and purse, then made her way the door. Before turning the knob, she halted. "If she's what ye want, pet, don't let 'er slip through yer fingers."

He combed a hand through his hair. "Nothing has changed."

She shook her head, gave a little snicker, and left the apartment.

Now, in a foul mood, he headed for his employer's office. Getting word to Ireland was paramount to Rafe, and the reason he believed Sunny troubled his thoughts. As soon as he could settle the situation with her and the lost sister, he could move on with his own life.

The familiar aroma of ink and paper filled his senses as he stepped into the office of Henderson and Company. Old man Henderson sat at a desk, bent over a ledger. With the sound of the bell above the door ringing to indicate a client, Maury Henderson raised his glance.

Rafe smiled and approached the desk. "Good morning, sir."

Maury nodded, specs slipping down a bulky nose. "And a good morn to you as well, Captain." He motioned to the open ledger. "I was just about to enter your report, when I realized I hadn't received one."

Rafe pulled the file from his satchel and placed the envelope on the desk. "I decided going around the storm was best for the safety of the passengers, therefore didn't arrive in Liverpool until late last night."

"A wise choice," Maury said while he looked the report over. A small frown creased the already wrinkled brow. "Well, you've had some adventures on this run."

"More than I would have liked," he said.

Maury sighed. "This explains the telegram I received from Ireland a few days ago, then."

His heart leapt in his chest as he calculated the *Sweet Maureen*, a cargo ship with no passengers to consider, must have gone head to head with the storm. She could afford to stay on course and within scheduled time, making it to destination and port ahead of the *Entrenous*. "My missing passenger is with him, then?"

"Aye, the Lord of Limerick has taken Miss Raven Eagle for a wife, and she's safely abiding at Shannonbrook."

"Lord be praised," he whispered.

"Aye, for sure," Maury agreed. "Fortunate she was to find herself in the right hands." He rummaged through the stack of papers on his desk, and when he found the one he searched for, handed it to Rafe. "I suppose her family would appreciate having confirmation."

He smiled; glad to soon be rid of the whole situation. "Aye, and I will take it to them as soon as I make a stop in London to see my folks."

"Then you'll want your pay." Maury handed him another envelope. "Thank you, Captain, for a job well done."

He arched a brow. "Even in spite of a burned dining hall?"

Maury shrugged. "She's going to be scrapped anyway, so nay a difference."

Hearing this saddened him. He'd piloted the *Entrenous* for over ten years now, and her pending demise hurt as much as losing a friend. He accepted the envelope and stuck it in his satchel. "If you've nay a further use for my services, I'll be on my way."

"Actually, I do, but I'm not sure you'd accept," Maury said, sitting back in his seat. "It's an entirely new venture, and one I've done extensive research on."

"I'll have a listen," he said, throwing the satchel over a shoulder.

"I've chosen Peter Smiley and Randall Holloway to captain the new passenger ship, which will take its maiden voyage to America in two weeks time. But I figured, since you and Simon co-captained the *Entrenous* so well, perhaps you'd like to continue working together on this new project." He ran a hand over his flabby jowls. "But when I presented the new position to Simon, he declined the offer, said his father-in-law-to-be offered him a better proposition." He waved a chubby hand in the air. "Something about the import, export business."

Rafe arched a brow. "Sounds interesting."

"Aye, well, if you like that sort of sea travel. I

prefer something unique," Maury added.

"And what was your offer?"

"Tour boats, along the coast of France," Maury blurted.

"And how long will the tours last?"

"Only four hours, two going out and two coming back, then the evening will be your own," Maury explained. "There are a lot of pretty women in France. I expect you'll find something to occupy your time."

Four hours is hardly a trek at sea. For a sea lover that bit of a taste would be torture, not to mention monotonous in spite of all the pretty women. Now he understood why his brother declined.

"Would you like to think it over, mayhap convince Simon to change his mind?"

"Nay, sir," he said, positioning the satchel higher upon his shoulder. "Simon is to be wed after the holidays and would not want to rip his new bride away from her family." He smiled. "Nor would Fiona appreciate the pretty women. And I have no desire to travel up and down the coast with tourists. Passengers and all their problems have been quite enough."

"Then what will you do, Captain?"

He shrugged. "Invest my savings in a vessel of my own, perhaps. I've always wanted to see the Orient." He chuckled. "Or mayhap Simon's father-in-law needs another hand."

Maury nodded. "Both of you are fine men. Henderson and Company is sad to see you go, but will give the pair of you high recommendations to your new employers."

"I thank you, sir," Rafe said, making his way to the door.

"Give my regards to those in London," Maury called after him.

"Aye sir, I shall," he agreed. "Then I am off to Brighton, to give a certain young woman some good news." *And rid her once and for all from my thoughts.*

****

Margaret, true to her word, returned in the morning.

Sunny stretched, blinking her eyes into focus as Margaret opened the drapery. The sun shone bright through the large window, casting its ray across the bed. In the light, the room took on a different sense. Flowered wallpaper lined the walls, raised roses of yellow and pink complimented the pink and cream hues of the drapes and matching bedcover.

"I trust ye slept well, miss," Margaret inquired while rummaging through the luggage for clean clothes.

"I did, thank you, Margaret," she said with a smile, somewhat surprised herself at how sound she slept in a new place. She wondered if Gabriel slept as well.

Margaret laid out undergarments and a violet day dress trimmed in white, then made her way to the privy. Remembering the mess made the night before, Sunny hopped out of bed and rushed ahead of her. "There was a bit of a problem, Margaret."

The elder woman glanced at the towels drying on the tub's rim. "Aye, I see ye 'ad some trouble 'ere with old 'enry."

She frowned. "Henry? Henry who?"

Margaret pointed to the flush toilet. "That there's 'enry, as I call the contraption." She clicked her tongue. "Bloody nuisance if ye ask me, always floodin' and makin' a mess." She turned her gaze to Sunny. "Sorry miss, I didn't warn ye about the bugger. If ye pull the chain too 'ard, 'enry doesn't like it much and spits out everythin' he's got in the basin." Margaret waved a hand in the air. "I'll have

Flecther tighten a few bolts. That usually takes care o' the problem for a bit." She smiled a toothless grin. "Coom 'ere now then and let me wash and dress ye for the mornin' meal. Mum is waitin' to meet ye."

She frowned. "Mum?"

"Aye, miss, the lady o' the 'ouse, Marietta Cavendish," Margaret explained. "Yer brother's already downstairs, enjoyin' a good talk with both mum and the mister, seems the three are gettin' along rather well."

Her stomach clenched. She was about to have breakfast with Captain Rafe's parents.

"Get yerself outta that nightie now, miss and 'op in the tub," Margaret instructed as she poured water from the pitcher onto a washcloth.

Her cheeks warmed. "I can wash and dress myself, Margaret."

"It's my duty to serve ye miss," she said, taking Sunny by the arm and leading her over to the tub. "Now off with the bedclothes."

Before she could further protest her nightwear lay in a heap upon the floor, and she stood naked in the tub, Margaret pouring water from the pitcher over her head and scrubbed every part of her clean.

Never was she more humiliated, and cooperated only to have the task over with quickly. Margaret then handed her a cup of buttermilk, but when she tried to drink it, the elder woman stopped her. "Nay, miss, the buttermilk's for ye hands, to keep them nice and soft."

It seemed a waste to Sunny pouring the liquid over her hands just to preserve their softness, especially when she thought of all those starving in her village. But again, she complied. She was also given a small glass of white wine, again, not to drink, but for cleaning her teeth. Along with using a fine piece of linen and a paste made of mint and salt, her mouth felt refreshed.

The next challenge came when Margaret insisted on helping her on with the corset. "It's customary to wear the cincher, miss, though I admit with yer tiny waist there isn't much to cinch."

"I do not mind the chemise or the bloomers, even the petticoat, but I refuse to wear that horrible garment. It is nothing but torture and hinders digestion."

Margaret frowned, her toothless mouth puckering into a bow. "Aye, it does at that. Seen women swoon myself from lack o' air. But ye'll be improperly dressed, miss without it."

She placed hands on hips. "Who will know I am not wearing it?"

Margaret's frown deepened. "Well, ye are tiny on yer own, but…"

She placed a hand on Margaret's arm. "It will be our secret."

The elder woman's wrinkled face broke into a toothless grin. "Oh, aye, miss. My lips are sealed."

With a sigh of relief, she did not protest Margaret's further administrations, allowing the elder woman to finish helping her dress and fix her hair. In no time at all she was presentable enough to meet her hosts.

Making her way down the corridor to the dining room, she lingered at the family portrait upon the wall. In her weary state last night, and led to her room only by candlelight, she had not noticed the lovely painting. She was awed by the artist's use of color, the way shadows and light graced the subjects of the portrait. All of her creations were done only using the lead stick. To add color and dimension, as the work before her had, would be such an interesting challenge. Upon further observation it was clear to see Rafe had his mother's blue eyes and dark hair. But his lopsided smile was that of his father, as well as the strong chin and high cheekbones.

"Do you like it?" a man's voice came from behind.

She turned to face the elder gent seen in the portrait. "Yes, the likeness is amazing."

The man arched a brow. "And, my dear, how would you know that?"

"Rafe...Captain Cavendish was in charge of the *Entrenous*."

The elder man frowned. "Hmm, I've spoken with your brother all morning, and he never said a word."

She was not surprised to hear of Gabriel's silence. He and Rafe were not exactly friendly toward each other while aboard the ship. Her guess was Gabriel hoped to be well on the way to Brighton before the truth was discovered.

"What a coincidence, aye?" Mr. Cavendish went on. "Did you happen to tell my son the connection you shared?"

"No, sir, I did not know we shared a connection until I arrived in London, and if the captain knew he never mentioned it to me." *Nor did he mention the Sea Patrol; I had to find that out from Count Ivan Sontag. It seems my dear brother and Captain Cavendish have more in common than they realize. Both keep silent to save their own hides.*

"My son's been away at sea for a number of months. He would have no way of knowing about the letter your father sent to Joshua, my wife's brother." He cleared his throat. "Where are my manners?" He bowed and took her hand, bestowing across her knuckles a brief kiss. "I am Jerome Cavendish, Captain Raphael Cavendish's father, at your service." The familiar lopsided grin returned. "But you already know that."

Her cheeks warmed from his gesture. "The portrait made it clear." She curtsied, the way Reverend Newcomb's wife Sylvie taught her, and nearly fell to her knees. "I am Sunny Eagle."

Jerome chuckled and steadied her upon her feet. "Aye, I am clear on that as well." He glanced in admiration at the painting. "The artist, a young man by the name of Elwood Hunter, is quite talented, don't you agree?"

"Yes, his work is wonderful." She sighed. "I draw with the lead stick, but how I would love to learn to paint with all the colors."

Jerome turned his gaze to hers. "Perhaps that could be arranged. I know Elwood has a small art school in Brighton, and gives private lessons."

Her face brightened. "My aunt lives in Brighton."

Jerome smiled. "Well, so I've heard. Another coincidence, wouldn't you say? But I'm sure Elwood would want to see your work."

Her heart leapt. "I have brought with me my sketch book and several of my drawings are in it."

"Then you are off to a good start." He offered her his arm. "Shall I escort you to breakfast? My wife is anxious to meet you."

She nodded and accepted his arm. "But you need not serve me, sir. I feel strange enough accepting Margaret's help."

Jerome frowned. "Serve you?"

"Yes, when you introduced yourself you said you would be at my service. And there is no need, I am quite self-sufficient."

The elder man threw his head back and laughed. "I am sure you are, my dear girl but that is just something a gentleman says to a lady, to be polite."

She frowned. "Then if he has no intention of helping her, why offer?"

Jerome Cavendish's dark bushy brows furrowed. "Well, I'm positive he would help her if his assistance was needed, he just wouldn't serve her.

The term is only used as a measure of respect, something expected to be said."

She was more confused now than before. "Why not just say, please to meet you, then?"

Jerome cleared his throat. "Aye, well, it's simply that way and will remain so, I imagine." He gave her hand an affectionate pat. "Perhaps my wife can explain it to you better." He smiled down at her. "She's quite good at that sort of thing. Now come along, my dear, before the morning meal grows cold."

Marietta Cavendish, beautiful in her bones and sprouting a well-oiled spirit, welcomed Sunny with open arms and a kiss upon each cheek. "I am told you are the image of your mother." She searched her face and smiled. "Now it's clear to me why my brother was so taken with her."

Reverend Holmes, who politely stood when she entered the room, now reclaimed his seat. "That was a long time ago, Marietta."

From all the years her mother spoke of Joshua Holmes, she knew he was a dear friend, almost considered family. But hearing this inclination gave her new insight into his close scrutiny of her on two occasions. Feeling awkward she glanced at her brother, his furrowed brows a silent indication he felt the same.

The reverend cleared his throat. "Sometimes, in her excitement, my sister tends to exaggerate."

She merely nodded, somehow believing Marietta Cavendish spoke the truth.

"You're right, of course, Josh," Marietta said, showing Sunny to a seat beside her.

"Did you know, my love, Sunny and Gabriel were on Raphael's ship?" Jerome said, taking a seat at the other end of the table.

"How simply wonderful," she purred, passing Sunny a plate of toast. "And how did he look? A mother always worries about such things no matter how old her children are."

"He looked well, in control and in command of the ship at all times," she said, spreading preserves on her toast before taking a bite.

"Did he look like he'd been eating right, sleeping well?" Marietta probed.

"I'm sure he's fine, my love," Jerome said.

"Oh, how I wish he'd known who you were," Marietta mused.

"Do you think he would have agreed then to go back for my sister?" Gabriel retorted.

"Such a shame about your sister," Marietta said. "But I'm sure my son did all he could."

Sunny flashed her brother an angry stare. How could he be so rude to the folks who opened their home to them? "I am positive he did."

Marietta took a sip of tea from a flowered china cup. "And I know my son will find out where your sister is."

She sighed. "I hope so."

Marietta gave her hand an affectionate pat. "I have a feeling all is well, my dear. Now, let me ring for Trudi," she said, reaching for a small bell beside her plate. "I'm sure you're famished, and I know you'll just love Lydia's hotcakes."

To *love* Lydia's hotcakes was an understatement. The round, syrup-slathered cakes melted in her mouth. And the sausage, sweet and juicy, left her pallet singing. And she was extremely happy she had the good sense to forfeit the cincher, as she would have never enjoyed such a meal if she were wearing it.

"I have sent word to your Aunt Kaylena that we will be arriving in Brighton within two days time," Josh announced.

Gabriel frowned. "Why not today?"

She caught his gaze and again a silent response echoed between them. Her brother hoped to be long gone from London before Rafe returned. Whatever was holding him up would not last much longer, Sunny was sure. And truth be told, she shared her brother's anticipation.

"It will give Sunny time to recuperate; besides the two of you have other engagements here in London."

Sunny frowned. "What other engagements do you speak of?"

"You've both been invited this evening to dine with Lady Lucinda Collins. Her father, Lord Sherman Collins was a good friend of your great grandfather, Wilson Bentley."

"And where does Lady Collins live?" she asked, accepting a second cup of tea from Trudi with a nod and a thankful smile.

"Lucinda's estate is in the rural county of Glenshire Sussex, not more than a thirty minute carriage ride from here," Josh explained. "Beautiful mansion, exquisite gardens, used to be horses there till a fire swept through the stables. Thank the good Lord none of the workers were killed, but unfortunately three championship stallions perished."

"That is a great loss and a pity," Gabriel remarked.

"Do you ride, Gabriel?" Jerome said.

"It is what I do for a living, scouting for wagon trains. I am in a saddle more than I am not," Gabriel said.

"My son, Simon, loves to ride, and does so frequently at Spring Meadows, where he's a member," Marietta offered. "He has his own flat in the city, but will be by this afternoon. What a pity there is no time before you leave for Brighton for the two of you to have a chance to enjoy a few hours *in the saddle,* as you say."

Gabriel inclined his head politely, yet refrained

from giving an answer.

"Why must we wait two days till we meet our Aunt Kaylena?" she asked Josh. "We are dining with Lady Collins tonight, but why can we not leave in the morning?"

"Lady Abbott has invited you both to have tea with her tomorrow afternoon. She is most anxious for you to meet her brother, Lord Wade and his daughter, Fiona."

"She's a lovely young woman," Marietta countered. "I'm sure you'll enjoy her company, Sunny." She smiled. "Though I am a bit biased." She giggled like a school girl. "After the holidays I will have a daughter." Again Marietta reached over to pat Sunny's hand. "And of course you, Gabriel, and your aunt are all invited to the wedding."

"I have heard a lot about both Fiona and Lord Wade as Lady Abbott mentioned the two of them often while we were aboard the ship," she said.

"That's right. They were on the *Entrenous* as well, coming back from seeing their daughter in America," Marietta said.

"Another coincidence," Jerome said with a smile. "But I still have one more."

Marietta, who seemed to hang on every word her husband uttered, leaned forward in her chair. "Do tell, my dearest."

"I have learned from a brief conversation with Sunny on the way to breakfast that she draws."

Gabriel nodded, smiling over at her like a proud Papa. "And she is quite good at it as well, especially considering she has had no education or formal training."

"I suggest, once you're both settled in Brighton, that you look up an artist by the name of Elwood Hunter. He's done a family portrait of us, but I know he also gives private lessons. And his small art school just happens to be located in Brighton,"

Jerome said.

"My, you're right, Jerome," Marietta said. "I'd say all these coincidences are positively wonderful."

"Yes, positively," Gabriel muttered before gulping down the rest of his tea.

Chapter Fourteen

Sunny pulled her cape tighter around her shoulders and snuggled down into the carriage seat to keep warm. The dampness of London's evening seeped clear through to her bones, chilling her from the inside out. Even the coldest Arizona night did not bring such a shiver to her flesh.

Gabriel, the ever-ready protector, noticed her situation and moved closer, placing an arm around her shoulders. She leaned against him, soaking up his warmth.

In the seat across from her sat Josh Holmes. He smiled at Gabriel's attempt to keep her warm. "There is nothing greater than family love and loyalty. I see you have it as fierce as your parents."

Gabriel gave him a taut nod. "This is true, and for that reason I am anxious to know what has happened to Raven."

Josh's azure gaze softened. "I have been praying that all is well with your sister, and I am sure when Raphael returns to London he will have good news for you."

"Do you have a family, Reverend?" she asked.

"Aye, you've met them...my sister, her husband and nephew Raphael. So sorry Simon never made it to the house today, but you'll meet him at Lady Abbott's tea tomorrow."

"No, I mean a wife, children," she probed.

His gaze saddened. "Nay, I was never able to find the right woman." He forced a smile. "But I serve an awesome God and have a wonderful life being an instrument of His love." She searched his

119

face, and this time he broke the connection, peering out the carriage window. "It won't be long now till we arrive at Collins Stead."

She could not help but ponder the thought it was a good possibility the reverend hoped Golden Lady was the right woman for him at one time. Or, did he still harbor that idea, thus the reason he never took another woman into his heart? Sunny knew, as well as the others in the tribe, of her father's protective nature toward her mother. Proud Eagle was always at Golden Lady's side, to console her, make her laugh, and to love her. He was even possessive at times. Yet he spoke fondly and respectfully of the reverend. Did Proud Eagle know of Josh's feelings? If indeed her father did, Sunny would be interested to know how the three handled the situation. Or, perhaps they did not handle it well at all, and that was the reason Josh left America?

"We've arrived at Collins Stead," Josh said, breaking through her thoughts.

She peeked out the carriage window and gasped. The gracious and stately manor home of Lady Lucinda Collins sat back from the Glenshire Sussex's main county road. Silhouetted against the night sky were gargoyles perched upon the roof. The sounds of crickets and night birds filled the evening with their melodies as they traveled down the long, dark path to the mansion.

A striking young woman with large green eyes and hair the color of ginger greeted them at the door. Her smile was warm and radiant. "I am Riley Flanders, Lady Collins's ward." She took Sunny's cape and the men's jackets and ushered them into a large sitting room. "My lady will be with you momentarily."

She noticed Riley's gaze favoring the sight of Gabriel. And his eyes returned the interest, resting on the sway of Riley's hips as she strode from the room. Sunny could not help observe a spark for life awakened in her brother that had been stilled for a long time. She was sure Collette's affection aboard the ship had a lot to do with the revival.

The large parlor was tastefully decorated in soft blues and rich lavenders. Three large windows complete with window seats graced one whole side of the room.

"They look out upon the garden," Josh explained. "In the daylight this chamber is ablaze with natural light."

"It must be beautiful," she mused, walking over to a window seat and sitting on a plush pillow. Slowly she scanned the parlor's size. "Do you realize, my brother, we could probably fit three wickiups easily in here."

"And what the bloody hell is a wickiup?" came a voice from the archway.

She turned to find a thin woman, dressed completely in black, with thick, silvery-white hair piled high atop her head, standing in the door frame.

"Lady Collins, such a pleasure to see you again," Josh said, making his way to the elder woman and taking her hand. "Your servant, my lady," he added, bestowing a light kiss across her knuckles.

"And how does Kaylena fare?" Lady Collins inquired.

"A tad under the weather at the moment," was Josh's reply.

"Humph," was Lady Collins' response. "Why does that not come as a surprise to me?"

The reverend was quick to change the topic. "Let me introduce to you her great nephew and niece, Gabriel and Sunny Eagle."

Sunny stood in direct line to Lady Collin's view. She gave the elder woman a polite curtsey and a smile. "It is a pleasure, my lady."

Lady Collins returned the smile. "Well now, you

are the image of Amelia, your grandmother. She and I, and another girl by the name of Anita Noble were inseparable at one time. Rarely did you see one without the other tagging along." She sighed. "Those were wonderful days, and setting eyes on you this evening has brought them all to mind." Her smile deepened. "You are quite a beauty."

She inclined her head politely. "*Ashoge*, thank you, my lady."

When Gabriel approached, Lady Collins's gaze froze on the streak of gold hair that swept from his temple to his crown. "Lord have mercy," she whispered.

The elder woman's already porcelain complexion paled, and she reached for the back of a winged chair to steady herself.

"What is it, my lady?" Josh asked, taking Lady Collins's arm and helping her to claim a seat.

Her gaze, still riveted upon Gabriel, widened. "Mr. Eagle, the gold streak through your hair is most unusual. Might I inquire whereby you inherited such an oddity?"

"I believe from my great-grandfather, who was a fur trader that happened upon our village. I am told he had eyes the color of mine, and hair as black as a moonless night, with a streak of the *holos*, sun sweeping across one side of his head. The Apache people said he had been kissed by lightning. And because he was a man of small stature, yet a fearless hunter, they called him *Ittindi Maba*, Little Lightning Bear. But his people called him—"

"Silas," Lady Collins finished the sentence.

Gabriel's eyes widened now. "Yes, but how could you know that?"

Lady Collins stood and took Gabriel by the hand. "Come, young man, I've something to show you in the library."

Sunny and the reverend followed the two into

another large room; its walls covered with shelves housing rows and rows of books. Above the fireplace there hung a portrait of two men.

"The man on the left is my father, Lord Sherman Collins. The man standing to his right is his brother, Lord Silas Collins. This portrait was done just before Silas left for America."

Sunny gasped. Silas Collins had a sweep of gold through his dark hair. "My brother, his hair is like yours."

Gabriel frowned. "I do not understand."

Lady Collins found a seat nearby and motioned for them to sit in the chairs remaining. "My father, Lord Sherman Collins, was a close and dear friend of your maternal great-grandfather, Wilson Bentley. The two went to the university together, but stayed in contact long into their lives...through business ventures, marriage, and raising their families. As I said, your grandmother, Amelia Bentley, and I grew up together. I missed her so when she left on her own journey to the States." She paused, pulling a handkerchief from a dress pocket to wipe the perspiration forming on her delicate brow.

"Would you like a beverage, my lady?" Josh offered.

She pointed to a bell beside the reverend's chair. "Ring for tea, Josh."

He nodded and complied.

Within a few moments Riley appeared, carrying a tray with cups, saucers, and a teapot, all patterned in lovely and romantic hues of eye popping colors. Sunny held the tea cup up to eye level, admiring the painted earthenware.

"The china is called Chintzware," Riley supplied. "It was created here in England at the Staffordshire factory. The pattern is called *Summertime*."

"It is charming," she said. "So bright and cheery."

Riley nodded in agreement and continued to serve them in silence, a warm smile lifting the edges of her full lips, and directed mainly Gabriel's way. He was eager to return the smile, his eyes never wavering from hers.

Lady Collins cleared her throat and dismissed Riley with a wave of her hand. For a few moments all sipped their tea in silence.

With curiosity growing, Sunny broke the stillness. "Please, continue your story, my lady."

Lady Collins frowned. "Now where was I?"

"You were telling us of your friendship with Amelia," she offered.

"Ah, aye, Amelia...beautiful, golden-haired Amelia," she said, thin lips curving into a smile. "She was a stubborn and willful mite, always getting her bum strapped for her antics. She definitely was her own person, wanted more in life than to marry, raise a family, and sew samplers." Lady Collins sighed. "I envied her spirit and determination, her sense of adventure and curiosity."

"Now we know where you and mother get it from," Gabriel mused.

She ignored her brother's comment. "Please, go on, my lady."

Lady Collins gestured to the man standing to the right of the painting. "My Uncle Silas never married and was also the restless sort, always looking for an escapade or quest. As I said, he ventured to America, and I dare say found the ideal exploit in such travels. I was only three when he left to pursue his dreams, so all I remember of him is what my father would read from the letters Silas sent, which only numbered a few. On my eighteenth birthday, my father held a large dinner party in my honor. After dessert my father entertained us all with a letter Silas sent. None of us had heard from him in over fifteen years, in fact, we all believed he was dead. So, you see, receiving this bit of correspondence and listening to my father read from it aloud, became the highlight of the evening. In his post, Silas wrote he'd been living all these years in an Indian village he'd come upon and decided to settle his bones there. He'd fallen in love with one of the tribe's maidens and took her for a wife. They had a daughter at this point, grown and wed herself. We were all shocked, of course. My father swore us all to secrecy, least there be a scandal cast upon the family name. But Amelia was awed, hanging on every word with those large blue eyes of hers sparkling. It was on that night, she later confessed to me, her decision to go to America. Of course her father protested, beat her and did everything short of locking Amelia in her room, to still her desire. But she couldn't be silenced and finally Wilson Bentley agreed." Lady Collins took another sip of her tea before continuing. "She left a month later, promising to write. And she did, for several years. Her letters read like a novel, and I savored each and every one, reading and rereading them until they crumpled from age. In the last letter I received from Amelia, she wrote of her marriage to Ethan Gregory and her mission to travel to a place called Arizona. Once there she planned on opening a school and teaching the children of a tiny settlement in Willow Creek."

"And she did just that," Sunny said, remembering the stories her mother told about Amelia Gregory.

"Was she happy with the life she chose?" Lady Collins probed.

"Yes, very. Ethan was her one true love and Amelia was delighted when my mother was born," she explained. "Sadly enough Amelia died of a fever when my mother was only nine, and would never see her as a grown woman or enjoy her grandchildren."

Lady Collins nodded. "Aye, I heard as much

from Kaylena, when she returned from her own travels to the States."

"And did you ever hear again from your uncle?" Gabriel said.

"Aye, a letter arrived about two years later. By then his daughter had given birth to a son. Silas gave the boy the Christian name of Peter. But the Indians called him Proud Eagle."

Gabriel's mouth dropped open. "Are you saying Lord Silas Collins is my great-grandfather?"

Lady Collins narrowed her eyes at Gabriel and cocked her head sideways. "I am, and I can prove whether I'm right or wrong with just one question. Do you have a crescent shaped birth mark anywhere upon your person?"

Gabriel nodded. "I do, my lady, on my right ankle. My father has one on his right thigh, and his mother, White Dove, had the same such mark on the top of her right foot."

"I have one on my...my..." Sunny cleared her throat. "Over my heart," she offered, the flush heating her face. "And my sister, Raven has one on her...her..."

"Backside," Gabriel interrupted, stifling a smile.

Lady Collins rolled up the left sleeve of her dress to reveal an identical mark on her forearm. "My father had one on the back of his left shoulder and Uncle Silas had the same on his abdomen. We call it the Collins Crest. Did you notice the coat-of-arms above the entrance door?"

"No, sorry, we did not," Gabriel said.

Sunny stifled a smile now. All Gabriel had eyes for was Riley Flanders.

"Well, it's there...has been since as long as I can remember...a red shield with a gold crescent in its center, flanked by two swords."

"Good God in heaven," the reverend said. "Then Amanda's children are your relations?"

126

Lady Collins nodded. "It appears so, and a blessing I've prayed for nightly. You see, I was an only child, and Uncle Silas's offspring was in America."

"He only had one, and my grandmother passed away several years ago," Sunny said.

"Well, there you have it. I am the sole heir to the Collins fortune and estate, and I'm not getting any younger."

"What of Riley, your ward?" Josh said.

"Riley's mother, Anita Noble Flanders was a close and dear friend, almost like a sister to me," Lady Collins explained. "Anita's parents didn't approve of the man she chose to wed, so Anita eloped one summer night. Of course, for her defiance she was disinherited. Unfortunately, not long after Riley was born, Anita's husband disappeared, leaving Anita destitute to care for Riley alone. By then both her parents had passed, leaving their riches to charity. With little funds and a child to care for, the hardships took a toll on Anita, and by the time Riley turned eleven, Anita had become very ill. A year later Anita passed away, leaving me as Riley's guardian. Since I never married and had no children of my own, I took Riley to my heart like a daughter. When I pass from this life, Riley will be completely compensated for and will want for nothing; however the responsibilities of running the Collins estate far exceed her duties or desire. And it saddens me to think Collins Stead would be owned by anyone other than a Collins or of the same blood." She glanced at Sunny then Gabriel. "Until now, that is."

Gabriel arched a brow. "You cannot mean that...that we are—"

"I do mean," Lady Collins interrupted. "You, Sunny, and Raven are now rightful heirs to the Collins estate. And I shall contact my barrister come the morning to have your names added to my will."

Sunny remembered her conversation aboard the ship with Count Sontag about titles. "Does this mean Gabriel, Raven, and I will be a lord and ladies?"

"Nay, a title can only be given to one British born and in direct line from father to son, father to son, and so on. Uncle Silas's first born was a daughter. But nevertheless, when I pass all this," she said, waving a hand in the air "belongs to the three of you." Suddenly realizing Raven was missing from the group, she frowned. "Where is the other sister?"

"We hope she's in Ireland," Josh offered.

"What do you mean, you hope?" Lady Collins snapped.

Josh cleared his throat, but before he could explain, Gabriel muttered, "Well, I'll be damned." With a trembling hand he reached for his cup of tea.

"Think you could use something a tad stronger?" Lady Collins's said, a slow smile curving her thin lips.

Gabriel nodded, swallowing hard.

"Ring for some brandy, Josh."

Again, he complied.

Lady Collins sat back in her seat. "Now, maybe one of you would be so kind as to tell me why you *hope* your sister is in Ireland." She arched a brow. "And what the bloody hell is a wickiup?"

****

Once back at the Cavendish's manor, the evening's events skittered like frightened rabbits through Sunny's mind. She found sleep difficult to come, in spite of her weary body. Learning this evening she would inherit property from her father's side of the family, as well as her mother's, was a lot to consume.

She sighed, covering her eyes with her hands and willed her thoughts to be still, but they raced on and on. After tossing and turning in the large bed, she finally decided a breath of fresh air might help. But as hard as she tried to raise the window, the pane would not budge. So she threw on a robe, grabbed the lantern and made her way downstairs on tip-toe, so as not to awaken the rest of the household.

Through the den's double doors she found a stone veranda. From this vantage point she could look out onto a small garden. The water fountain standing in its center was void of water and stood silent in the night. A cool breeze played with the loose tendrils of hair that framed her face, and she shivered. With a quick intake of breath, she inhaled London's night air, pulled the collar of her robe tight against her neck, and made her way to the doors.

He surprised her, the size of him blocking the archway with hands on hips, broad shoulders filling out his jacket, and a stern expression upon his handsome face.

He arched a brow. "What the bloody hell are you doing in my house?" he snapped, his gaze roaming the length of her. "And half-dressed at that," he added.

His harsh tone for a moment rendered her speechless. She stepped back with a sigh, searching his face. The very handsome, and at present very perturbed, Captain Raphael Cavendish had finally arrived in London.

Chapter Fifteen

The heat surged through Rafe's flesh, in spite of the cool night air. She looked like an angel standing before him, pale curls dancing in the breeze, the lantern's light shining upon her perfect features. The white robe and matching nightgown she wore circled around her delicate ankles, small bared toes curling against the veranda's stone floor.

Oh, aye, he scanned her but once, and only quick at that, yet summed her entirety to memory. And how could he not? The woman had been circling his thoughts for what seemed like an eternity.

Sunny raised a defiant chin. "Your parents' home, you mean."

He arched a brow. "You quibble with semantics, Sunny Beth."

She moved closer. "I am wondering why we quibble at all, Captain?"

Because you have taken over my every thought and I want...nay, I need you gone, he wanted to shout. But instead, he crossed his arms over his chest and glared down at her. "You haven't answered my question."

She pushed passed him, into the warmth of the den, and placed the lantern upon the desk. Pulling her robe tightly around her, she shivered. "Perhaps you could close the door first?"

He complied, returning to her with the same glare.

"Well, obviously I have been invited here," she began.

He raised both brows at her retort. "Have you,

now."

She placed hands on hips. "Certainly you cannot believe otherwise."

"I don't know what to believe." He narrowed his eyes. "Mayhap I should count the silver."

She gasped. "You are making no sense at all."

He took a calming breath. She was completely correct; all sense had fled from him. His private torment angered him to the point of unfairness. He inclined his head politely and motioned to a chair. "Then explain it all to me."

As she spoke his insides clenched like the fists of a fighting man. There'd be no way now he could just deliver the news about her sister and walk away. She was incorporated into the family through his Uncle Josh's friendship with Kaylena Bentley.

When she finished her explanation, she stood and reached for the lantern. "And there you have the truth, so you can stop thinking I have broken into your parents' home to steal the silver."

"I apologize for that remark," he said, reaching for the paper he had tucked away in his jacket pocket. "Mayhap this will smooth the waters a bit."

She set the lantern back upon the desk and took the paper he handed her. As their fingers brushed together the blood stampeded in his veins. She was the first to pull back, bringing the paper closer to the light in order to read its contents.

Her enchanting visage brightened, sapphire eyes welling with tears. "Then Raven is safe," she whispered.

"Aye," he said.

In one fluid motion, her arms were around his neck. Her cheek nestled beneath his chin, and full breasts pressed against his chest. "Oh thank you, Rafe. I have been out of my head with worry."

He swallowed hard, placing his arms around her, pulling her closer. All that separated their flesh was the scant material of her nightwear and his shirt. His voice came out shakier than he liked and hoarse with frustration. "There's nay a reason to worry further."

She pulled back, gazing deep into his eyes. Every facet of his being fought for restraint, cautioned him to pull away. But her lips, full and inviting, beckoned to him. They were so close, so very tempting. His pulse raced to enormous proportions as he drank in her splendor. All he needed to do was incline his head but a fraction, and his mouth could cover hers. Dare he?

Nay, it would be poor judgment. He shook the idea from his thoughts and put more distance between them. "Rest assured, your sister is well cared for and is now the Lady of Limerick."

She giggled with relief for her sister's safety. It was a marvelous and catching sound of pure joy that floated in the air. The anger he'd welcomed her with faded now, his own spirits lifting. He searched her face, peace and contentment washing over her beautiful features. "I'm glad everything turned out as it did."

"I am as well, and I have some news myself."

He arched a brow. "And what might that be?"

"I promise to tell you in the morning." She reached for the lantern. "*Ashoge*, thank you for everything, captain," she said, hurrying for the stairway.

Void of her energy, the room turned empty in seconds. But her scent lingered and it filled his senses as he stood in the dark, collecting his wits. *Tomorrow, I will see her tomorrow.* He was both pleased and disturbed she slept only a corridor away from his own door.

"I knew I 'eard someone in 'ere," Lydia said, breaking through his thoughts.

He turned to find her standing in the door

frame, candlestick in hand. The dim light cast an eerie glow on her aged countenance. How old would she be now? One could only guess as the woman kept her private matters to herself. All he knew was Lydia had cooked for the Cavendish household for as long as he could remember.

"Welcome 'ome, sir. 'Tis nice to see ye back."

He gave her a polite nod. "It's nice to see you as well, Lydia."

"I've a bit o' the mutton stew left; think ye'd like to feast on some o' that?" She didn't wait for an answer, just motioned for him to follow her to the kitchen. "Coom now for yer repast."

"I thank you, my dear woman, but I shall pass on your generosity."

"Now what sort o' rubbish is this?" She frowned. "Ye ain't ailin' or nothin' like that, are ye?"

He forced a smile. "I am quite well, thank you." *In truth my insides are knotted so tight I fear they'll snap.*

She shook her head and clicked her tongue. "Just ain't like ye to turn down food, is all."

"Aye, well it's late, and it's been a long day. I'm just going to take to my chamber for a bit of rest." *But I sincerely doubt I will be able to even do that with Sunny sleeping just down the next corridor.* "And I advise you to do the same."

She nodded. "Save yer appetite for the mornin', then. I'm makin' blueberry muffins, sausage, and poached eggs."

"I shall do that," he said.

Once again alone, he made his way to the window, glancing up at the moonlit sky. Lydia was right, he never turned down food, especially something she prepared.

"Little witch," he whispered. Sunny Beth's bewitching smile came to mind. "Not only have you infiltrated my thoughts, played havoc with my body, and undoubtedly will keep me from my slumber, but you've also spoiled my appetite as well."

****

Sunny lay in her bed, upon her back and stared at the parted drapes adorning the window she previously tried to open. The moon's ray cast a sliver of light across the bed, the only illumination in the room. In the quiet privacy, Rafe began to dwell in her romantic thoughts. Tonight his lips were so close to hers, all she needed to do was stand on tiptoe, adjust her head slightly, and they would have touched. His strong arms enveloped her, totally engulfing her in his muscular embrace. Chest to chest they stood; her nipples hardening with his nearness.

She remembered hearing the other young married women in her tribe speak of the pleasant sensations brought on by their husbands suckling their breasts. The thought of her baring her bosom to Rafe, and allowing his lips to tease and tantalize her tiny pink summits, brought a flush to her whole body.

"You are a wicked and shameful girl," she admonished herself with a whisper and turned onto her side. Thoroughly disgusted with such scandalous thoughts, she yanked the quilt over her head, squeezed shut her eyes, and willed herself to sleep.

Chapter Sixteen

Gabriel, the reverend, and the rest of the Cavendish household were sitting at the table eating the scrumptious smelling breakfast Lydia prepared, when Sunny entered the dining room the following morning. She stifled a yawn and forced a smile, taking a seat at the opposite end of the large oak wood table; as far away from Rafe Cavendish as she could possibly get. Images of him doing things she had no business imagining ravaged her throughout the night. So vivid and intense were these unspeakable visions, she was almost shamed to look at anyone seated around her for fear they would read her thoughts. Most definitely, if she glanced in Rafe's direction, the heat would steal its way to her face and give her private affair away.

"Did you sleep well, Sunny?" Josh inquired.

"Yes, *ashoge*, thank you for asking," she mumbled. To stay grounded she kept her eyes from wandering, staying her gaze upon her plate as she ate. Though she had already experienced Lydia's delicious food, now she ate it without really tasting, chewing each morsel more than needed and swallowing hard past the lump forming in her throat. Quickly, she took the next bite, and the next, then the next. Her mother, if she were present, would surely scold her for shoveling the food into her mouth.

"And might I then ask what it is you've been about while in London?" Rafe probed.

Her toes curled within the confines of what people had a nerve to refer to as shoes. The ankle high and tightly tied restraints tortured her feet. And now Rafe Cavendish tortured her spirit. For a reason she could not explain, the man had some sort of deep-seeded anger toward her...last night accusing her of stealing the silver, and now interrogating her at the breakfast table. Certainly the words she snapped at him the last time they spoke aboard the ship could not have offended him so thoroughly that he should remain out of sorts forever.

"Have you nothing to say?" he goaded.

She could not continue to cower under the pretext of being so intent upon her food. Such behavior was not what she was all about. Born of proud blood, the Eagle clan did not shrink from confrontation or their duty to one another. She had seen her father stand up to the white agents many times for the sake of his family and the tribe, but in a way where it did not render repercussions upon either or compromise his own reputation. Respect within control.

She sighed, gathering her courage to look Rafe straight in the eye. She would best this man at his own game. "I assume you have sat a while at this table with the good reverend and my brother, have you not?"

"Aye, I have," he said, laying aside his fork and challenging her with a strong gaze of his own.

She would not relax her own stand. Raising a brow she sharpened her tone. "Then certainly you have already heard the details you now badger me for."

Gabriel came to her aid. "The entire situation we had at Collins Stead has been explained."

A faint blush crept into Rafe's cheeks. "I'd like to hear what Sunny has to say," he said in answer to Gabriel's remark, but kept his eyes locked with hers.

She threw out a word she heard him use last

night. "Semantics, Captain?"

"More a principality, I'd say. I expected an explanation from you," he said.

"And do you always get what you expect?"

His lips thinned. "When I am promised as much, aye."

Gabriel broke in again. "And when did my sister promise you anything?"

This was the dilemma. In order to explain his words, Rafe would have to tell of their meeting last night, void of a proper chaperone? Would he dare to tarnish her respectability just to make a point? Even worse, would he chance Gabriel's wrath and the disapproval of his family?

She thought now she would take a bit of a chance herself. She raised a defiant chin. "My brother patiently waits for an answer, Captain."

Rafe hesitated, searching her face. "Come to think of it, I don't believe she ever did, right Sunny Beth?" he finally concluded.

From the corner of her eye she caught Gabriel's frown at the familiar way Rafe addressed her. She knew she would have to deal with her brother's questions later, which was probably just what the captain wanted...her consequences for baiting him, no doubt. But for now she was thankful for Rafe's discretion and the fact she won the first round of whatever game he played. For his gentlemanly performance, however, she conceded a bit herself. "But I should be glad to tell you about yesterday's events, again, if it pleases you."

Gabriel took control at this point. "Why repeat what he already knows? Besides, he has word from Lord Braiton Shannon about Raven."

She feigned excitement, acting as though this moment was the first she had heard the news. "Then she is with him, and she is safe?"

Rafe cast a devilish smile, and played along.

"Aye, quite safe and now married. In fact, she has inherited a whole new life, just like you."

"Now that I know Raven is safe," Josh interjected. "I will send word to Willow Creek that all is well."

"Will you explain about Ireland?" Gabriel probed, a frown creasing his brow. Sunny knew Gabriel had been placed in charge of both his sisters' care. If her parents learned of Raven's circumstances, obviously it meant he had not done his job right.

"Nay, not at this point," Josh said. "It's best to keep the situation quiet until it has been totally resolved."

Gabriel sighed with relief. "You are a very wise man, Reverend."

****

It did not take Gabriel long to find a time to interrogate Sunny. He took her by the arm, soon after breakfast, much as he did when he was sent out to fetch her as a child for the evening meal. He would find her playing by the river with the other children in the tribe and demand she come with him. If she dallied or objected, he would take her by the arm and lead her home, shaming her in front of all her friends.

Leading her onto the same stone veranda she visited the previous night, he questioned her. "Why does he call you Sunny Beth?"

She sighed. "It is my name, is it not?"

"The way it so easily rolled off his tongue, worries me," he said.

She gazed out at the stilled fountain. "Why, Gabriel?"

"Because I got the impression the familiar use of your name was not just boldness on his part, but something agreed upon by the two of you."

She turned his way with a frown. "So what if it

138

was?"

He arched a brow. "Then I would like to hear when and how that agreement took place. If I remember right, it was not done in my presence."

"Perhaps it was when he saved me from burning during the dining hall fire. A person tends to get familiar when someone saves their life. Or maybe it happened while we danced, or when I confronted him about Count Sontag's knowledge of the Sea Patrol." Her frown deepened. "And you were not present then because you were interested in wooing Collette Halston, if I remember right."

He narrowed his eyes. "Do not dare to turn this around to be my fault."

"Why does anything have to be anyone's fault? A mistake or a crime has not been committed here, Gabriel. Someone just called me by name."

"And in time that could turn into something very wrong, Sunny, especially by the captain."

"Why so?"

"The *why* of it does not matter, just that you stay clear of the man."

She folded her arms in front of her, waiting for a better explanation.

"You listen to me," he began. "I am responsible for the good of your well-being, and Rafe Cavendish is not good for any woman's interests. Trust me on this."

For the second time today, she gathered her courage. Sick to death of being treated like a child, she sharpened her tone and yanked free from his grasp. "Well, I am not just *any* woman, and I am certainly not interested in Captain Cavendish."

"That is good to hear, because the man has not a sincere bone in his body," Gabriel said.

"And how do you know this?"

"I heard the men aboard the ship talking one night. It seems Captain Cavendish has a female interest in several seaports and is pure about none of them."

"You would base a man's character on what a few drunken shipmates have to say?"

"A drunk speaks the truth, Sunny," he said.

"And how sincere have you been with the women you have been with since your wife's death?"

As soon as she spoke the words, she wished she could take them back. Gabriel's expression clouded into a mixture of hurt and shame. "I am not happy for those times, and will regret them for the rest of my life."

"Gabriel, I am so sorry. I did not mean..."

"No, you speak the truth, my sister," he interrupted. "What I did was not honorable, I can see that now. All those times, with those women, I tried to fill the emptiness left in my heart. But that was not the way to do it."

"Maybe Rafe is doing the same as you did?"

He sneered. "I find that idea hard to believe. He appears to me to be a man who treats a woman as a conquest." He searched her face. "And that was not how it was for me, Sunny. The women I saw were not maidens, as you are. I did not compromise their virtue. After offering themselves to me, they would visit another man's bed. If they were innocent, I would have never taken them, because I knew I could not offer them the proper commitment."

At that moment, her sister's circumstance popped into her mind. The Lord of Limerick married Raven to keep her from the hands of the Sea Patrol, not out of the proper commitment. Would he control himself so Raven could have the union annulled and join her family in England? Or consummate the marriage and forever bind Raven against her will? And once Braiton Shannon discovered Raven had already been compromised by a white agent, would he understand or would he treat her with disrespect?

"If Captain Cavendish cannot see the wrong in using his charms on you, then I will make sure he does," Gabriel said, breaking through her thoughts.

She shook her head to clear it. "You need not do a thing because the man has not tried his charms on me...in fact; I doubt he has any charms. So rest assured there is nothing between Captain Cavendish and myself, and never will be. He is not the sort of man I fancy," she said with conviction, in spite of the unexplained annoyance gnawing at her upon learning of Rafe's many women.

He chuckled sardonically. "And what would you know about what sort of man you fancy. You are just a child."

She squared her shoulders. "Stop saying that. I am not a child any longer."

He sighed. "No, I guess you are not, but you are not worldly either."

"Maybe I am not as worldly as some, but I am certainly not foolish, Gabriel. I have seen the good men of our tribe—like our own father. I know what honor is. Do you not think I want that kind of love and respect from the man I choose to be my mate?"

He pushed a wayward curl from her forehead. "Yes, I know you would. It is in your nature."

"Then trust my nature to make the right choices," she said in a soft tone.

He sighed. "I will try." Then he added with a frown. "But it is not in the captain's nature, so I will still be watching."

****

Sunny was not at all pleased to learn Rafe was to accompany her and Gabriel to Abbotsford, the Abbott's mansion for tea. His reason for going, or so he claimed, was in the hope of meeting up with Lord Wade, Lady Abbott's brother. He wanted to talk a bit of business with him and his brother Simon, should either man be present.

They traveled in two carriages. The first vehicle carried Marietta and Jerome Cavendish and Reverend Holmes; the second, Sunny, Gabriel and Rafe. Gabriel took a seat beside her, his presence protective and his eyes observant. Rafe took a seat opposite from her, gazing out the carriage window in silence throughout the short ride to the Abbott's. However, their knees touched now and then, as the carriage jolted and rumbled over the cobblestone streets. Disturbed by the warmth the mere touch caused throughout her body, Sunny grew annoyed with herself. But her foul mood changed when she set eyes upon her friend, Lady Abbott, and immediately walked into the warm embrace the elder woman greeted her with. She was introduced to Simon, who resembled Rafe but was not quite as handsome, along with Lord Morgan Wade and his beautiful daughter, Fiona. The young woman's dark eyes and auburn hair complemented the fair complexion and pleasant smile. It was not hard to see why Simon Cavendish chose her for his bride.

Lord Wade's deep brown eyes twinkled as he took her hand, brushing a light kiss across her knuckles. "Your servant, miss."

She stifled a giggle, knowing full well the claim was anything but true, and still could not imagine why it needed to be said at all. But she inclined her head politely and said, "My pleasure, my lord."

He was a pleasant looking man, of middle age, tall, slender, and of good bone structure. His brown hair grayed at the temples, and his smile was genuine. "My sister, Eugenia has told me so much about you; I feel we are already good friends."

"I do as well," Fiona chimed in, stepping closer.

"I hope we can be," she said, and truly meant every word.

Gabriel shook hands with Simon and Lord Wade, and when the men retreated to the den, she moved to the parlor with the women.

"Tell me how you're enjoying your stay in London," Lady Abbott inquired, pouring tea into a china cup decorated with blue and yellow birds perched on tree branches, a much different pattern from Lady Collins' earthenware, yet still beautiful.

Marietta spoke for her. "Our Sunny now is in line for the Collins fortune."

She forced a smile and nodded in agreement, not quite knowing when she had become *Marietta's Sunny*.

Lady Abbott leaned forward in her seat. "Ah, do tell."

Marietta sat back in her seat, refraining from saying another word, and Sunny commenced to explain the whole situation about her great-grandfather and Lady Collins being related.

Fiona sighed. "The whole thing is simply fascinating and so romantic. I mean, what are the odds of something like that happening, and being discovered after so many years?" She placed a dainty hand over her heart. "Doesn't it stop and make you believe there was some divine purpose, a definite reason you were to come to England?"

She had not thought of it in that way before, but now that Fiona brought the notion into the light, her own imagination ignited. "Like it was my destiny to be here, you mean?"

"Aye, a plan already written out for you to achieve," Fiona added.

"By the very hand of God," Marietta added, her warm smile growing upon her serene face. "I can think of no other explanation for it."

"And what does your Aunt Kaylena think of all of this?" Fiona probed.

"She does not know as of yet," she said.

Fiona arched a brow. "How could she not?"

"Kaylena Bentley is not in London," Marietta

explained.

"Ah, aye, I remember Josh saying she did not come on this trip, was under the weather, so to speak," Lady Abbott reflected.

"Then you have yet to meet her?" Fiona said.

Sunny nodded. "And I am quite anxious. Have you ever met her?"

"Aye, once or twice, and she's a nice enough woman." Fiona sighed. "I find it such a pity—" she clipped her words and reached for her cup of tea.

She frowned. "What is a pity?"

Lady Abbott stood. "Come now, ladies," she said, ushering them all into the dining room for lunch.

Sunny wished Fiona would have continued to explain her comment, but at the moment such a hope was not possible. Her thoughts then turned to the dining table, set in a lovely table setting of even more exquisite china and crystal goblets filled with wine. She gasped. "This is all so beautiful, Lady Abbott."

"I agree," Marietta said. "But I thought it was just tea we'd be having, else I would have had Lydia prepare something for dessert."

"Though that's so thoughtful, Marietta, I would not hear of it," Lady Abbott said, motioning for them all to take a seat. "And I wanted something more than just an afternoon tea to serve in honor of my new friends," she said, smiling over at Sunny.

"I am honored, Lady Abbott," she said, sitting in a chair beside Fiona.

The men soon joined them, talking business and politics as they entered the room.

Rafe sat across from her again, thankfully this time there was a distance between their knees, and she would not have to endure the disturbing sensations his nearness caused during the carriage ride.

Lord Wade took a seat beside his daughter, and

gave her hand an affectionate squeeze. Thoughts of Proud Eagle filled Sunny's mind. He, too, was a loving father, always there for her. How many times when she was a child did he wipe her tears, kiss her hurts, hold her upon his lap, and tell her stories before bed? Such reminders of her family filled her heart with a mixture of happiness and loneliness.

"Did my daughter tell you my surprise?" Lord Wade said, bringing her back to the present.

Suddenly aware of everyone looking her way, she blushed and cleared her throat. "A surprise?"

"I said nothing, father," Fiona said. "I thought it best you tell them."

Gabriel frowned, his tone protective. "What is there for you to tell us?"

"I have a small import business," Lord Wade began. "In fact, while you ladies were off having your tea time, I have talked to both Simon and Rafe about joining me," he added.

Marietta's brows rose. "Really, how delightful."

"My travels take me a few times a year to Ireland to do business with Lord Braiton Shannon of Limerick," Lord Wade continued.

Sunny's heart raced. She glanced at Gabriel and his eyes met hers.

"I am due to leave in a matter of days for one of my voyages," Lord Wade said, turning to look at his daughter and giving her a warm smile. "And of course I will be back in ample time for the wedding."

"So my brother will be able to find out if your sister is in Ireland," Lady Abbott chimed in.

"Actually, that won't be necessary," Rafe said. "I got news from Lord Shannon that Raven Eagle is in Ireland. And I've relayed such to Gabriel and Sunny Beth just this morning."

The condescending tone he used irritated her. Gabriel's frown deepened along with his own voice. "Yes, we are all relieved my sister is safe and now

145

wed to Lord Shannon."

"But we thank you, Lord Wade for your kind offer," she added, then sighed. "However, I still miss my sister something fierce, and no doubt she misses us as well."

"Then perhaps, Father, you can deliver a letter to Raven from Sunny?" Fiona suggested.

She gasped. "Do you think you could, Lord Wade?"

"Aye, I'd be glad to," Lord Wade said, a larger smile spreading across his kind face.

"Oh, what a splendid idea," Lady Abbott said. "And I have the perfect stationery for you to use." She stood and extended a hand. "Come, mite, and follow me to my sitting room, where you can sit at my writing table and compose a beautiful piece of correspondence to your sister."

"My dear, what of lunch?" grumbled Lord Abbott.

"This won't take long, Stanley, and I do believe Sunny won't be able to eat a bite until this is settled."

Lady Abbott's private chamber was done in soft blues, the furniture delicate and of light wood. The writing table, with its ornate designs of cherubs along the curved legs, stood by the window. The sun's light cast its ray across the fine paper, quill, and ink bottle set out for her use. Once left alone, Sunny reached for the quill, dipped it into the ink, and then hesitated. Should she begin with the news of their recent inheritance to the Collins fortune? Or perhaps it would be beneficial for her to explain about an annulment, in case Lord Shannon kept that bit of truth to himself. When she did finally put pen to paper, Sunny decided instead to pour out her relief in learning Raven was safe. She briefly wrote about the journey aboard the ship and Captain Cavendish. She mentioned Lord and Lady Abbott,

Lord Wade and Fiona. Then she added her hopes of learning to paint in colors at an art school. Raven would be thrilled to hear this, as she was a great supporter of Sunny's art work. She also added that Josh offered to send word to Willow Creek that all was well, so her sister need not worry for her parents when she had so much to already cope with. Sunny believed keeping her words light would be less overwhelming for Raven and not bring her such loneliness. All other news could wait. After she admitted how much she missed her, Sunny signed it, *with all my love, your sister Sunny*, before placing it in the envelope.

Lady Abbott entered the sitting room shortly after, sealed the envelope with her personal stamp using the hot wax and handed it to Sunny with a smile. "Now, let's have a bite of lunch, the men grow restless."

She nodded, pressing the letter to her heart as she followed Lady Abbott out the door.

Chapter Seventeen

Rafe stayed on at Abbottsford after the others left, to talk about a business deal with Lord Morgan Wade.

"I do a profitable business with Lord Shannon, importing wine and other goods from Ireland," Lord Wade explained further. "In turn, I sell the goods here in England. But come the summer I plan on traveling to Australia, try my hand at selling goods there."

Rafe frowned. "Is that not cutting out Lord Shannon?"

"Nay, he travels to America and the Orient only, bringing goods back to Ireland, England, and Scotland's buyers. He has no desire to venture into Australia, nor do I wish to travel to America and the Orient. That's what makes our partnership work. No one is stepping on anyone else's toes, in fact it will be quite the opposite. By opening up a venue to Australia, I am lining Lord Shannon's pockets as well as my own. At the present time my one vessel, the *Fiona* is only capable of making a trip to Ireland and back, but no further. So, twice a year I make the trip as England's main buyer. However, in the last year, I've become interested in *down under*, as I've heard Australia called. I am having another vessel, larger and stronger, built now. She's half completed, and I'm calling her the *Filigree*. I shall need a captain for her helm."

He glanced over at his brother, Simon. "Should I wish to try for this position would I be stepping on your toes?"

"Nay," Simon said. "I am interested in manning the *Fiona*. Her present captain is retiring after this next voyage, and I very much wish to take his place. Ireland is a quick voyage. I do not relish being separated from my bride for too long."

"And as the father of his soon to be wife, I agree," Lord Wade added.

Rafe chuckled. "Ah, you've got it bad. Better you than me, is all I've to say about that."

Simon moved closer and gave Rafe a playful slap upon the back. "Be careful, little brother what you say. I've learned never to say never about anything." Narrowing his eyes, Simon teased. "In fact, you might eat your words sooner than you realize. This afternoon I caught you a few times eyeing Miss Eagle."

He gave a sardonic laugh. "Then your eyes are playing tricks on you."

"Are they now?" Simon sneered. "Perhaps it is you who are deceived?"

"I am definitely not interested in Sunny Eagle, nor would I ever be," he objected.

"Hmm, me thinks thee doth protest overly much," Simon teased.

"And me thinks thou art an ass," he countered.

Simon laughed and slapped him on the back again. "Good to have you around, too."

Lord Wade cleared his throat, bringing the banter to an end and the conversation back to business. "Gentlemen, please. Let's keep to the matter at hand," He turned his full attention toward Rafe. "Are you on board with this, Captain Cavendish?"

He smiled. "Aye, my lord."

"Splendid, splendid," Lord Wade said. "But until the ship sailing for Australia is ready for her voyage, I will need you to help manage my business from my London office. When I return from Ireland we can meet, talk further on the matter." He frowned. "I know you rent a flat in Liverpool, but..."

"I haven't a problem letting the flat go and moving here. I could stay for a time with my parents, just until I secure a place of my own."

"Why not take my flat?" Simon offered. "Fiona would never be comfortable in something so small, so we've decided to move into Lord Wade's mansion until I build a home of our own." He sighed. "Which, I fear, won't be for quite sometime."

"Wade's Landing has more than enough room and ample privacy for the three of us, as well as the offspring to come," Lord Wade said. "I've already agreed to give you and Fiona the entire east wing, and I will stay to the west side."

"I thank you, my lord," Simon said. "I'm sure such an arrangement will be sufficient enough for quite some time."

Lord Wade turned again to Rafe. "After I explain your duties, do you think you would be able to begin at your new position within a month, Captain?"

Having something other than Sunny Beth to think about was what he needed to do, and fast. He inclined his head politely. "I can be at your service even sooner, my lord."

****

Sunny joined her brother and the reverend in the carriage. Marietta and Jerome Cavendish boarded the second carriage. Rafe, deciding to stay on at the Abbott's home a while longer, would catch a ride back to the Cavendish mansion with Simon. She was both relieved and disappointed to hear this, and harboring these mixed feelings annoyed her even further.

Gabriel sat beside her, Josh Holmes across from her, as the carriage made its way through several London streets.

"How have you enjoyed your stay in London so far?" the reverend asked.

"It has certainly been interesting," she said.

"Aye, that it has, especially now that you are in line for yet another inheritance," Josh said. "I can only imagine what your aunt will do when she hears the news." He arched a brow. "That is, if Lady Collins hasn't already sent her word."

"What is wrong with Aunt Kaylena?" she blurted out.

The reverend frowned. "Nothing's wrong with her, why do you ask?"

"You said she did not come to meet us because she was under the weather. And whenever anyone else speaks of her, they are either annoyed or pity her. So, I want to know what made her under the weather." She leaned forward in her seat. "What is wrong with my aunt, reverend?"

His frown deepened. "It is not my place to say, Sunny." He sighed. "Besides, you will find out for yourself soon enough."

****

Rafe returned to his parent's home quite late, he and Simon deciding to take Lord Wade out for a mug of ale at the local pub after they closed their deal. He could tell by her silence on the ride to Wade's Landing that Fiona was anything but pleased with the idea of being escorted to her home by the three of them, and then left to her own devices. How Simon handled the smothering was beyond him. Shan't a man do as he pleases, allowed to stay out at the pub with his mates for whatever time he chooses?

Strangely enough Fiona gave no time limit, nor a protest or quarrel issued forth; she just simply drew her cute little bowed mouth into a pout and batted those long dark lashes. That was all it took, and Simon melted, literally commenced to eat out of her hand. With a promise not to be too long and back at his own flat at a decent hour, he gave her a long kiss to prove his devotion before he left her, then worried away the time from that mark on. The whole display nearly sickened Rafe, and deliberately, he took his sweet time downing his first mug of ale, then ordered another to nurse in the same fashion.

"You are bent on seeing me shunned for the next few days," Simon complained.

Lord Wade chuckled. "Aye, she is much like her mother, that one. With no words she says quite a lot, striking a man to the core." His face saddened. "But I would move heaven and earth if it were in my power to have one more day with my beautiful Regina." He sighed. "She was everything in my life and more, and I'm proud to admit that."

"I feel the same sentiments toward my dear Fiona," Simon added.

"And to think it's only taken a few ales to loosen your tongues in a melancholy way," Rafe teased.

"You won't be so cocky when it happens to you," Simon warned.

He laughed. "It will never happen to me, because I won't allow it to."

"You will have no say," Simon went on. "One glance of her eyes, the way she holds her head or tosses her hair, a smile, the way she says your name, something will grab you and won't let go no matter how you struggle. And then you discover you don't want to struggle, and—"

"It's all over," he interrupted.

Simon smiled. "Nay, little brother, it just begins."

"Sheer hell on earth," he countered.

"Nay, it is anything but hell. When you've the right one, it can be heaven," Simon said.

Lord Wade raised his mug in a salute. "I say God save the Queen to that."

"And how do you know when the right one

comes along?" he asked, refusing to take part in their salutation.

"She'll infiltrate your dreams, upset your appetite, and take your thoughts down a totally different path," Simon explained.

"Nothing that you did or enjoyed before will be enough," Lord Wade added.

"Bloody hell, it all sounds like a horrible plot to rob a man of his dignity and self worth," he bitterly reflected.

"Aye, it is, yet it's absolutely wonderful and well worth it, if you've read all the signs correctly and gotten the right one, that is," Simon said.

He frowned, a chill running down his spine. "I'd sooner risk a storm on the high seas," he admitted and ordered another mug of ale.

Now he made his way up to his bedchamber, passing the one occupied by Sunny Beth along the way.

From the room he heard her shouts. "No, no, not again, not now. Please stop doing this to me."

His heart raced as he reached for the small dirk he kept fastened to his belt. Pulling it from its sheath, he charged through the door and into the room. Who dared to intrude upon his home, and bother Sunny? He'd waste the man where he stood. He'd waste any man who touched her.

"Oh no, no," her cries continued, coming from the privy. "Please stop!"

Casting all protocol to the wind, he barged into the next room with dirk drawn, ready to defend her.

She screeched when she saw him. "Rafe!"

"What goes on here?" he bellowed.

Clad only in a chemise, she sat upon the tub's edge, knees drawn to her chest. Her feet and legs, bronzed and bared, were fully exposed for his view. He hesitated to remove his gaze, taking in her magnificence. The chemise rose high upon her thigh, a tease to the naked splendor barely hidden beneath.

Her cheeks colored fiercely. "It is Henry, he is acting up again."

"Where the devil is the rogue?" He raised his dirk and glanced around the room. "He has this to meet." Then he frowned. "How do you know the man?"

"Henry is not a man," she corrected, a tinge of humor in her tone.

His frown deepened. "I don't understand."

"That is Henry," she said, pointing to the toilet, now gushing water from its bowl. "Margaret calls that horrible contraption, Henry. And every time I pull the chain too hard, this is what happens," she said, gazing down at the soaked floorboards. "There were not enough towels to continue wiping away the water that keeps coming. So I climbed onto the tub's edge to stay dry, and I got myself trapped."

He stifled a smile, replaced his dirk, and neared her. With one effortless swoop, for she weighed next to nothing, he gathered her into his embrace. When she wrapped her arms around his neck, her full breasts pressed against his chest. His hands, now holding the smooth flesh of her thighs, seared—the heat making its way down through his abdomen.

He carried her into the adjoining bedchamber and set her down. She scurried to fetch the robe draped across the foot of the bed, and donned it with haste, tying the cord tight around her slender waist. Making a quick retreat back to the privy, he tugged on the toilet's chain and ceased the flow of water. Looking around the room, he made a survey of the damage.

"I am sorry I have made such a mess of things."

He turned to find her standing in the door's frame, her feet now clad in slippers. "It's not your fault. This bloody thing's been a problem from the start." He looked around the room for a second time.

"I'll call for Margaret; have her bring up more towels to dry the floor."

She backed away as he came through the door, large sapphire eyes growing concerned. "I hate for the poor woman to be awakened from her sleep, can it not wait till morning?"

He arched a brow. "You tell me?"

She bit her bottom lip...a very full and tempting lip, then sighed. "You make a good point."

God help me for wanting to kiss you where you stand, then gather you again into my arms and place you upon this very bed. God save me...God stop me!

Annoyed with his thoughts, he shook his head to clear it. "See if you can stay out of trouble long enough for Margaret to arrive," he snapped. Turning on his heels, he strode to the door.

Her voice was like velvet, smooth and soft. "Why are you so angry with me all the time, Rafe?"

He hesitated, his pulse quickening. How could he answer that question? He couldn't very well admit she took over his thoughts. Nor could he go on to explain her voice, scent, or very presence tarnished his ability to enjoy other women. He couldn't confess she spoiled his appetite or left him tossing in his bed. He ran fingers through his hair, annoyed with himself for having such ideas. It was just as Simon had said it would be when the right one came along. *Except I don't want her to be the right one...I don't want anyone to be the right one, so I refuse to give into it...I won't allow it to take over.*

With great reluctance he faced her. Taking a calming breath he lied. "The hour is late, and I am tired. It's been a long day." He bowed politely. "Forgive me if I've acted out of sorts."

"There is nothing to forgive," she said with a smile. "We all have those moments." She sighed. "I thank you for your help."

His gaze traveled over the sculpted beauty of

her face, searched the deep blue of her eyes, and settled upon her ripe mouth.

Leave her now, before you do something you'll regret.

"I shall go for Margaret now," he said and rushed from the room. *Just get through tonight, and then you can be off early come morning, before she wakes.*

Taking the steps two at a time he hurried to find Margaret and ran smack into his uncle.

"Just the person I want to see," Josh said.

"What is it you need, Uncle?"

"Your help on the morrow to take Sunny and Gabriel to the train bound for Brighton, and then deposit them safely to Bentwood Manor," Josh said.

He frowned. "I was to leave for Liverpool early. I've some affairs to attend to there."

His uncle's tone turned stern, "Are they urgent, Raphael?"

He cringed at the use of his Christian name. This would not be so easy to get out of. "Aye, in a sense."

"But not in every sense?"

"Nay," he said.

"I intended to go myself, however, Lady Collins's friend has taken seriously to her bed and is asking for clergy."

He nodded. "Aye, that is far more pressing than my own affairs."

Josh gave Rafe an affectionate pat on the shoulders and smiled. "I thank you for your help. Now, where are you off to in such a hurry?"

"To fetch Margaret. The privy's pot in Sunny Beth's chamber has overflowed."

Josh's smile broadened. "I am pleased you're making an effort to make our new guests feel comfortable. They don't know many people here in England, and it was my hope you would take the time to get to know them. Now, on the train ride to Brighton you'll have the perfect opportunity."

His insides stiffened, but he managed to force a smile in return. "Aye, that I do."

Chapter Eighteen

It turned out to be a morning of surprises for Sunny. The first was learning Rafe would be escorting her and Gabriel to Brighton instead of the Reverend Holmes. The second surprise came only an hour before they were all ready to leave for the train station.

Fiona Wade, big brown eyes red and teary, stood at the door holding a dress the shade of a forest tree.

"My dearest friend, Lady Valerie Riggs has run away with the stable boy who cares for the horses at the Spring Meadows Country Club, her parents are heartbroken and mortified, no one knows where she's gone, and in three month's time I am to be married without a maid of honor."

"You poor dear," Marietta chided, taking the weeping Fiona into her arms.

Sunny followed them into the parlor, where Fiona's wails increased.

"There, there, we'll think of something," Marietta comforted.

"What is there to do at this late date?" Fiona worried, biting her bottom lip.

Sunny sat down beside the crying young woman and placed an arm about her shoulders. "Do you not have another friend to ask in place of the one who ran away?"

"Not that would fit in Valerie's dress," she said, holding up the dark green gown.

"Let me see the gown," Marietta said. Taking the garment from Fiona, she held it up, narrowing her eyes as she surveyed it, then her brows rose. "I think I have a remedy here."

Fiona wiped her nose on the lacy hanky she held. "Oh, do tell."

"The gown looks like it might fit Sunny," Marietta said.

She gasped. "Me?"

"Aye, Valerie is about your size," Fiona agreed. Her face brightened. "Would you have time to try it on?"

"Well, I am about ready to leave for the train station but—" Fiona's wishful expression cut her words, and she nodded taking the gown from Marietta. "I think I can at least try it on."

The three rushed to the bedchamber Sunny had occupied and with everyone working together, she was able to slip into the gown and twirl a few times before the mirror. In their hurried state; neither woman realized she was not wearing a corset. If they did, it was not mentioned, and for this she was grateful.

"The color is striking against the shade of your hair and the length is perfect," Fiona said.

"But it's a bit tight in the bosom area," Marietta said.

"Aye," Fiona agreed. "Sunny has much more spilling out of the neckline than Valerie did."

"Well, this will never do," Marietta said.

Marietta was right about that, the gown was hideous with its long waist, puffy sleeves and a slight train to a skirt ballooning out at the hips. The garment made her backside appear to be swollen.

"But it wouldn't take much to alter, only a seam taken out here and there," Marietta continued.

"I could do the alterations myself, in one night, if Sunny weren't leaving," Fiona said, biting her bottom lip with worry again.

"Then come to Brighton with me," she offered. "I think there is a lot more to do than just the neckline." She pulled lightly at the extra material trailing behind. "The backside is way too large."

Marietta laughed. "Nonsense, it is perfect...all the style."

"Any other time I'd love visiting Brighton, but at the present I'm not packed for travel, and I dare not leave London with so much to do before the wedding," Fiona said. "And it wouldn't be fair to ask you to stay on; when you're so anxious to meet your aunt and all." Fiona sighed. "It is just hopeless."

"Nay, not in the least, my dear," Marietta comforted. "I've heard one of Kaylena's servants, Cirie is an excellent seamstress," Marietta smiled. "My idea is to let Sunny take the gown with her and have Cirie work her wonders."

Fiona's face brightened again. "Oh, would you? Could you, Sunny?" She took Sunny's hands. "Just instruct Cirie that everything is perfect, except for the bodice."

And the entire backend of the dress as well.

Fiona giggled. "This will be so much fun. Thank you so much for saying you'll be my attendant." Then she frowned again. "I'm afraid in all the excitement you never said you would, I just assumed when you agreed to try on the gown. And I haven't even asked you properly if you'd consider being my maid of honor."

She knew declining would break Fiona's heart. And if it were not for Fiona suggesting she write a letter for Lord Wade to bring to Raven, Sunny would not have been able to let her sister know all was fine and how much she was missed.

"I would love to be your maid of honor." Then she arched a brow. "But what does a maid of honor do?"

It was then she got a rushed version of her duties, hugs and kisses from a grateful Fiona, and the gown neatly packed into her luggage.

"I'll see you after the holidays," Fiona said. "You need to arrive at least a week before the wedding for rehearsal and pictures, and shopping for matching shoes." She hugged Sunny again. "Oh, thank you for this."

And just as quickly as Fiona arrived, she left, but minus the tears.

Margaret would be her chaperone aboard the train. Since men were not allowed to sit in the women's compartment, she would be traveling unescorted. She did not see the problem, all she would do was sit in a seat for a few hours and glance out a window, but those were the rules. Some rules, she decided, definitely needed to be broken...like wearing a corset and the cumbersome material women toted on the backsides of their dresses like a small wagon. Bustles, she was told they were called.

The carriage ride to the train station only took thirty minutes. It was not the Euston Station this time, but the London Bridge Station's train that would travel the two hours to Brighton. In the carriage she sat beside Margaret. Gabriel and Rafe sat opposite them.

"I'm sure gonna miss ye," Margaret said. "Bet ye ain't gonna miss ole 'enry though," she said with a giggle.

"No, that I will not," she agreed, glancing over at Rafe.

The tensing of his jaw betrayed his frustration, and his memory of the previous night. Burning eyes held her gaze until an unwelcome blush heated her cheeks.

She cast a glance out the window, remembering how his hands felt against her bared thighs and the feel of his muscular chest against hers. He had seen her scantily clad, wearing only a chemise. The way his eyes roamed the length of her caused her stomach to flutter like it was filled with a hoard of tiny butterflies.

"But I 'ear yer coomin' back after Christmas 'cause yer Lady Wade's attendee now," Margaret said.

"Yes, she asked me this morning to be her maid of honor," she said, keeping her eyes fixed out the window.

"And what happened to Lady Riggs?" Rafe's tone was sharp, as it was the night before. Obviously he still was tired or else just a permanently angry person.

She turned to glare at him, trying to keep her own anger in control. What right did he have to constantly be gruff with her and why was he so disagreeable? "It seems she decided to run off with the Spring Meadows Country Club stable boy."

He arched a brow. "Bloody hell, you say."

"Bloody hell, I speak the truth," she retorted, finding satisfaction in the surprised expression upon his face at hearing her own gruff reply. From a quick side glance, she caught Gabriel stifling a smile. She knew there was no love lost there between the two men.

"Well now, ain't that nice, Master Rafe, ye bein' the best man for yer brother and all." Margaret giggled again. "Look's like yer gonna be walkin' Miss Eagle down the aisle."

Rafe's grunt was proof he thought it was anything but nice. She did not know what she had done to gain such an unfavorable attitude from the captain, but at this point she no longer cared. If he wanted to be at odds with her, it was his problem. She would not let it get to her, nor would she remain passive. He would soon see he had met his match in wits and temper. She had thrown a few tantrums of her own in her day, although she now prided herself with keeping her control. But if made mad enough, she could pull out the fire once again.

At the train station platform, she was relieved the women were separated from the men, and she would be free for a time from Rafe's scrutiny. Taking responsibility for the luggage, the two men made their way to their section of the train bound for Brighton as did she and Margaret. Just as she took a seat by the window, the whistle blew and the train lurched forward, its engine belching a jet of steam. The wheels ground against the metal tracks, slowly picking up speed. Those left behind waved their goodbyes to loved ones as the train parted company from the platform, and London disappeared in the swamp of white smoke.

Soon the train's swaying motion calmed her spirit and with eyelids growing heavy she was lulled to sleep.

****

Taking a seat opposite Gabriel, Rafe settled in for the two hour journey, and to do what his uncle expected...get to know the new guests better. Already he'd had an opportunity with Sunny Beth. Rescuing her from the privy pot flood brought him in close proximity to more than just the woman's presence. He remembered now the feel of her, the warmth, and the memory gave him an exhilarating shock through his body. The thin chemise she wore covered little. Draped over her shapely form, the undergarment hugged the best parts of her; tiny waist, rounded hips, and full breasts. The hardened nipples, pressed against the silky material, filled him with desire. He took an audible breath and quickly cleared the image from his mind.

"Does something trouble you, Captain," Gabriel said, his large eyes, as blue as Sunny's bore into him.

The Indian man cut a sharp presence, the sort that would turn a woman's head. Broad shouldered with strong hands, Gabriel Eagle could be a formidable foe. He experienced firsthand the other man's strength when they wrestled each other to the floor of the *Entrenous*. The truth was Rafe didn't know if he'd have been able to hold his own for too long. Thankfully, with the help of his fellow shipmates, he didn't have to find out.

Gabriel Eagle wasn't a person he particularly liked, nor was he someone Rafe saw himself befriending, but he respected him. If the situation was reversed, and Rafe had left a family member behind, he couldn't say he'd react any differently. So, in view of that, and the fact his uncle was a friend of their folks, he'd let bygones be bygones and make the effort. After his brother's wedding the chances of seeing either of them again was slim, as they wouldn't be socializing in the same circles.

"I'm not troubled," he said, forcing a smile. "Just thinking ahead of all I must do in the next week."

"Ah, yes, with your new business venture," Gabriel said.

"Aye," he said.

"And escorting us to my aunt's home was not something you really had the time to do," Gabriel said.

"Aye, but I'm resigned to it and hope on this ride we'll come to know each other in a different light," he offered.

Gabriel nodded. "I hold no bad feelings for you, Captain. Now, as I have had time to think things over, I see you did what you had to do aboard the ship."

"That's the truth, and if there were any other way I would have gladly taken it," he said.

Gabriel smirked. "Of course, should Raven have fallen into the hands of the Sea Patrol instead of the Lord of Limerick I cannot say we would so easily be coming to terms like this."

He gave a taut nod. "That's understandable."

Gabriel glanced out the train window. "It will be late when we arrive in Brighton." He turned to meet Rafe's gaze. "I expect you and Margaret will be spending the night?"

"I will, Margaret will return to London, where she's needed by my mother," he said.

"She is not a young woman, and the tiredness shows in her eyes. Could she not have this night to rest?" Gabriel said.

"I will give her the choice," he said, then searched Gabriel's face. "Why are you so concerned?"

"I am concerned for all those treated unfairly," Gabriel said.

He arched a brow. "Margaret is hardly treated unfairly. The woman is paid for all of her services, plus given decent clothes to wear, lodging, and meals."

"But does she not have a life of her own, with family and friends?" Gabriel pressed.

"I think she has a brother." He shrugged. "For all I know the bloke might be dead by now." Frowning he continued. "You have to understand something, Gabriel. Most people of Margaret's station live in the harsh shadows of the London streets. They are either Toshers or Mud-Larks."

"And what are Toshers and Mud-Larks?"

"A Tosher is a person who scours the sewers for pieces of tin, rags, bones, teeth, whatever they can find of any value to sell."

"It is how these poor ones buy their food?" Gabriel said.

He chuckled sardonically, "More how they can purchase a mug of ale."

Gabriel shook his head. "Firewater, it is the downfall of all men."

"Aye," he said, remembering Gabriel left the ship to visit an ale house himself. Undoubtedly, the other man's remark stemmed from his own experiences with drinking spirits. "But ironically most of them, because they are daily exposed to such filth, have somehow managed to build a resistance to typhus and other ghetto diseases."

"And what are the Mud-Larks?" Gabriel probed.

"A Mud-Lark is a person who wades into the Thames hoping to fish from the river iron, brick, canvas, bone, or a chunk of coal from a passing ship. Perhaps even a coin purse that floated away from the body of someone who has met with a deadly outcome. Then they sell their finds to dealers. This is how they survive," he explained. "So you see, securing a position with a family of means is salvation for many of these unfortunates. A young woman on the streets would only resort to unscrupulous means to make a wage. It's much better she clean and cook, assist a lady of good standing, and then reap the benefits of a clean, safe place to live, and regular meals to eat."

Gabriel arched a brow. "And do all those that employ these people treat them as well as your family does?"

He sighed. "Nay, some are beaten. But even that is not as harsh a life as trying to fend upon the streets."

"And so they are to be grateful for whatever they receive at the hands of the rich because they are unworthy of anything better," Gabriel snapped.

"We are all worthy of better, Gabriel. And within all of us there is the power to rise above our lot in life."

"Do they rise above themselves, Captain or are they forever bound to do the bidding of others?" Gabriel said.

"Aye, they do and can," he said. "I have seen for myself many boys, who steward aboard a ship, serving the passengers and their captain; grow to be men who have a decent means of supporting themselves. A chance they would not have had if they stayed upon the streets. The same applies to the stable boys and butlers."

Gabriel leaned forward in his seat. "And what about the women, like Margaret?"

Rafe sat speechless, staring into the other man's eyes.

Gabriel smirked. "I thought as much."

"This land is hard for women."

"For the white man's woman, that is the truth. But Apache men hold much respect for their women and give them a say in tribal matters. They sit in on council meetings as well, their opinions hold substance, and they have the complete run of their household. Apache women are precious, the very foundation of the family, and we do not abuse them or think them less a person than a man," Gabriel said.

"I want you to know here and now, I don't agree with the way the system works against the rights of women," he said. "I agree with you, women are just as intelligent and deserving of a good life as the men."

Leaning back in his seat Gabriel's stare hardened. "And what are you doing to change things?"

"What can any one man do against many?" he said.

"I can tell you what I have done," Gabriel said. "I scout for the *indah*, white agents, who have infiltrated my village, not because I have given up my heritage and beliefs or because I fear them or do not think I deserve better, but because it affords my family more food. These agents want to keep the Apache people dependent upon them, so twenty people are expected to live on one small shoulder of beef and twenty cups of flour. I do not want my sisters or my mother to beg, lower their pride or submit their virtue to these intruders so the family can eat." He turned his gaze out the window. "And so I ride until my back breaks, until the muscles in my legs cramp. I sleep at night with no blanket upon the hard ground, shivering from the cold and suffer the bites of insects." Gabriel hesitated, his strong, chiseled profile becoming vulnerable for a moment as he swallowed hard. "But one day, I will stop the madness, the abuse my tribe suffers." Gabriel turned again to look at Rafe. "I have come to England for two reasons. The first to make sure my sisters are safe; have the chance to live in peace. As women now with financial means they have a better chance at that here than in America. But once I know they are settled and doing well, I will return to my country and my people with enough influence to stop the injustices they suffer. I will change the way they live, I will make a difference."

"You take a lot upon yourself. You're only one man," he said.

Gabriel arched a brow. "But it has to begin somewhere, why not with the first man...why not with me?"

"Aye, why not indeed?" he said.

The two men sat silent the rest of the way to Brighton, Rafe respecting Gabriel more than he did when the journey began. In fact, now he even admired the man. But befriend him? That was still only a possibility.

****

Sunny awoke with a start, rubbing her eyes with the backs of her hand.

Margaret chuckled. "The wheels sing a sweet lullaby."

"I am so sorry to be such poor company."

"Nay a problem, miss. I caught a few winks myself," Margaret confessed.

She sighed. "I wonder if I'll like Brighton?"

"Nay a reason ye shouldn't," Margaret said. "I 'ear it's a beautiful place. Day-trippers and 'olidaymakers are always takin' the train there to enjoy the clean air and the sea." Margaret pointed to the train steward just entering the women's car. "Pay attention now, miss. This chap is gonna tell ye all about where yer goin'."

As she directed her full concentration to the man, Sunny wondered how many times a day he repeated his speech.

After clearing his throat, the train steward started his monologue, pronouncing Brighton as *Braiton*, like her sister's new husband. For a quick instant, she wondered if Raven was happy in her new home.

"Brighton lies in East Sussex on the south coast of Great Britain and has emerged during the 18th century as a health resort; especially after the arrival of the railway in 1841." The train steward cleared his throat a second time before he continued speaking. "Some of the sites you'll want to see are the Royal Pavilion, once the home of the Prince Regent, Preston Park, the museum, aquarium, library, and many ballrooms. There is even a general hospital also at your disposal, but pray tell none of you lovely ladies will need its services."

Several women in the car reacted to that remark with shy gasps and giggles.

The train steward waited until the noise settled before he explained further. "The oldest quarter of the town is known as *The Lanes*. If you venture there you will see it is made up of a myriad of narrow passages lined with fishermen's cottages from the 17th century. Brighton's churches feature stunning architecture, carvings, and exquisite stained glass windows, so be sure to take the time to visit St. Bartholomew's Church, the tallest church in the country, and St. Helen's Church, another lavishly decorated structure dating back over 600 years. And," he concluded, "you shouldn't miss the view from the curve of Brighton Bay toward New Haven and Worthing, as it's quite spectacular." He smiled, finishing off with, "Thank you for your kind attention. Enjoy the rest of your journey and your stay in Brighton."

"Ah, miss, yer finally goin' 'ome, and Brighton sounds like such a wonderful place to live," Margaret said.

"Yes, it does at that," she said, gazing out the window once again. But she wondered if it could ever really be her home.

****

It was quite late in the afternoon when the train pulled to a stop at the Brighton station. Sunny stood and stretched. Looking over at Margaret, she caught the elder woman doing the same.

"I'm not used to stayin' this still for so long a time," Margaret commented as her hand massaged the area along the base of her spine. "Strange but I feel stiffer than I do after I've washed the floor and scrubbed the sheets."

The two women met Gabriel and Rafe on the platform, their groggy faces and tousled hair sure indicators they too slept a bit through the journey.

"It's too late for you to return to London, Margaret," Rafe said, pulling a small purse from his pocket. As he handed Margaret a few coins his large blue eyes softened. "Secure yourself a room and some dinner, and I shall meet you back here in the morning for the return trip to London."

Margaret gasped. "Nay, sir. Yer sweet mother'll be needin' my services coom mornin'."

"You are way too stiff and tired to return home this evening," Sunny interrupted. "And I do not think Aunt Kaylena would mind in the least if you stayed the night at Bentwood."

"I agree," Gabriel chimed in.

Margaret's already wrinkled brow puckered further. "Oh, I don't know, sir."

"Not to worry, Margaret," she said, giving the elder woman's arm a reassuring pat. "All will be fine. Besides, Marietta Cavendish instructed you to chaperone me to my aunt's door, did she not?"

"Aye, miss, those were her words," Margaret agreed.

"Then if my mother wished for you to do as Miss Eagle said, she fully realized you'd not be returning to London tonight and most definitely made other provisions for her morning care," Rafe added.

"Aye, I suppose yer right, Master Rafe," Margaret said, handing him back the coins. "But still and all—"

"But still and all, it grows late, and we have quite a ride yet to Bentwood," Rafe interrupted. He turned to Gabriel. "You stay with the women while I rent a public conveyance so we can be on our way."

As they rode through the town, they passed the New Brighton Pier and Aquarium, as well as several little shops that lined the street situated along the seaside.

"This area of St. James Street is known as the *Bond Street District* of Brighton, visited by tourists and holiday makers," Rafe explained.

Brighton's air, unlike London, smelt cleaner. The streets were not as crowded, the shops and homes were painted in brighter colors. With a sigh, she sat back to enjoy the rows of sparrows perched upon the red roofs of those houses dotting the picturesque hills. Perhaps she would feel comfortable living here after all.

Roberta C. M. DeCaprio

Chapter Nineteen

About twenty minutes after they left the train station, the carriage driver made a right turn onto a dirt road, whereby a marker read: *County of Bentley: Established in 1723.*

Sunny's eyes widened. "The Bentley's own an entire county?"

"Aye, at one time they did, at least that's what I hear from my Uncle Josh. Being a clergyman for Bentwood's chapel, he knows quite a lot about the family history," Rafe said.

"I should be interested to hear it then," Gabriel said.

Rafe stroked his beard. "If my memory serves me correct, your great grandfather; Wilson Bentley was not the first upon these shores. Hiram Bentley, his grandfather, was a wealthy young barrister from Wales who arrived in this region around 1720. By 1723 he had bought a vast amount of land in Brighton, hoping to develop it into a resort. However, as I remember the story told, Hiram fell into debt several years later due to a gambling vice and was never able to set his plans into motion. After a fatal accident took his life unexpectedly, his young wife, Hannah, was forced to sell all but the section of land your family continues to own, in order to pay the bills and feed her three children. Jacob, being the eldest son, took full responsibility for the property as the years passed. When he married Anna, the two inherited the few remaining acres and the mansion known as Bentwood."

"Then Anna and Jacob were Wilson Bentley's

172

parents?" Sunny asked.

"Aye," he said.

She arched a brow. "Your uncle has taught you a great amount about my family."

"I can tribute this to his love of storytelling, fiction or otherwise," he said. "He'd come to London once a month for a visit and a home-cooked meal and explain Brighton's history and the Bentleys." He chuckled. "On a cold winter's night there isn't much to do but sit around the fire and listen."

Gabriel grunted. "My people are the same."

"Well, now. I'd say we're not so very different from one another after all," Margaret reflected.

Gabriel grunted again.

A sudden cloudburst deluged the earth with a heavy downpour and slowed their travel. A few feet down the dirt road the driver pulled over to the side, climbed down from his seat and rapped upon the window.

Rafe opened the door and met the man where he stood. In a matter of seconds, the two became drenched as their discussion heated. Just as Gabriel was about to join the group, Rafe stalked back to the carriage with an angry frown upon his face.

"What is the trouble?" Gabriel inquired.

"This buffoon refuses to travel further," Rafe said, smoothing back his wet hair and shaking out his jacket the best he could before climbing back into the carriage. The water dripping from him accumulated in a puddle between his feet, soaking the coach floor.

Sunny frowned. "I do not understand."

"This dirt road to Bentwood is narrow and winding, with a cliff along the shoreline. In such a rainstorm as this, the road becomes muddy and unsafe. The driver fears the horse will lose his footing, and we'll plunge to our death."

She looked out the window and up at the gray

sky. "From the looks of things, we will be sitting here for a while, then."

"Nay, he wishes to drop us here and be on his way back to town before the storm worsens," Rafe explained.

Margaret gasped. "And leave us 'ere to do what...walk the rest o' the way with all the baggage in 'and?"

"Aye, that's his plan," Rafe said. His jaw tensed. "But it isn't mine, and so we have a problem."

"The two o' ye are much bigger and stronger than this bloke," Margaret rationed. "Why not just whip his mangy bum and drive the carriage yourselves."

Gabriel's lips thinned. "We cannot take that chance. If the road is unsafe for horse travel we could all be killed." He looked over at Sunny. "I will not put my sister's life in danger."

"A little rain will not hurt me," she said. "I say we walk the distance."

Rafe arched a brow. "Surely you jest."

She shook her head. "I have walked in the rain many times, Captain. It will not melt me."

"Might 'ave ye catchin' yer death o' cold, though," Margaret added.

"I do not worry for myself, Margaret, but I am concerned for you," she said.

"Humpf, nay a need for that, miss. I've been through worse in my years. A bit o' a drenchin' won't melt me none either," the elder woman declared, pulling her cape tight around her shoulders.

Gabriel gave her a nod and buttoned his jacket to the chin.

"Let us be on our way, then," she said, raising the hood of her own cape.

Rafe sat back in his seat, surveying her with a smirk upon his face. "I am truly astounded. Never did I think I'd live to hear a woman make such a statement and mean it."

"Then I would say this is a day you will remember," she quipped, removing her shoes. Then she reached beneath her skirt to release her stockings. His eyes were fixed fully on her, watching as she rolled each stocking down her leg and stuffed them into her shoes. She felt herself coloring beneath his scrutiny, but continued to prepare herself for the hike to Bentwood. She tied the shoes together by their laces and threw them across her shoulder, then opened the carriage door. "Ready?" she called back over her shoulder. Upon hearing an affirmative from each occupant, she glanced at Rafe. He donned his already wet jacket and motioned her to proceed. She hiked her skirt to her knees, tucked it between her legs and stepped down onto the wet ground.

Bared feet met sodden earth, cold mud seeping between her toes. With each step she took, Sunny soon discovered Rafe would not be the only one to remember this day. Chilled drops of rain pelted her face as she kept a hold on her skirt with one hand, and secured the hood of her cape tighter around her face with the other. Briefly she looked back at her traveling companions. Rafe was carrying most of the bags, because Gabriel was holding on to Margaret, who was just a slip of a woman. Her tiny stature made walking against the sharp winds difficult. The sudden gale in all its fierceness rocked the treetops, surrounding them all with the damp air it breathed.

Her bared hands and ankles froze to the bone as her toes sunk deeper into the muddy path, yet she kept on the long and winding road. To the left tall, willowy trees lined the narrow lane, looking like sentries guarding Bentwood's entrance. They seemed to watch her as she passed, standing strong against the elements.

To the right the road was lined with jagged

rocks and thistles. Beyond the bushes an embankment jutted off to a cliff. Looking down she could see the white crests of foam rippling atop each wave. The ivory caps floated like lace before meeting their demise against the rocks below.

Not only did she shiver from the cold, but from the thought of them all plunging to their death. And even though she hated walking the distance in such foul weather, the driver was right to deny them a ride. Just as she was secretly thanking him for standing his ground with Rafe, her foot slipped out from under her, and she found herself sliding to the edge.

She tried to scream, but the sound caught in her throat. Her heart raced as she clawed the ground with her hands, reaching out for anything to stop her from careening over the side. A large tree branch halted her descent. Desperately, she clung to it for dear life, trying to wrap her legs around its base. Her shoes and cape slipped off her shoulders and fell to the ground below, and her skirt, wet and heavy, caught around the thistles. This posed a problem when she tried to free herself from the brush's confines. The movement and her weight upon the branch caused the large limb to come loose and slide down the embankment even further.

Flashes of her life with her parents and friends passed through her thoughts. Had she come all this way to fall off a cliff and die? Just inches from the edge, the limb caught in an overgrown thistle patch, becoming entwined amongst the briars. Her skirt was also caught, making it impossible for her to move from harm's way.

"Give me your hand," Rafe called.

She looked up to find the captain reaching down to her with an outstretched arm, one foot braced against a rock, a hand holding onto a thick vine. How long would either hold him?

Every bone and muscle in her body was frozen solid. She glanced down at the raging waters below, and her vision swam. Squeezing her eyes shut she dared not to move an inch.

"Don't look down," he demanded. "Set your sight on me."

She swallowed the nausea threatening to come and remained still.

"Did you hear what I said, Sunny Beth," he persisted in an angry tone. "Look up at me."

Slowly, she brought her gaze to lock with his, but his eyes did not hold the anger that was in his voice, just a fright mirroring her own. It was then the fearful images of them both going over the side struck her countenance, and she bit back the tears. His alternate bravery thrilled her with a surge of affection, and the thought of him risking his own life to save hers suddenly frightened her the most.

He reached further. "Take my hand, now," he commanded.

She managed to speak passed the lump in her throat. "No, step back," she warned, visions of his death sending a stabbing pain to her heart. "You will not be able to pull me up; my skirt is caught amongst the branches."

His moves were slow, cautious, as he managed to reach for the dirk hidden in his boot. Lowering himself to his belly, he extended his hand to her again. "Now, take hold."

She let go of the limb and stretched out a hand to meet his, their fingers entwining. The incredible strength of his grip fused with her own as he pulled her toward him. When she was close enough for him to reach the waistband of her skirt, he cut away the material hampering her release. The garment, now hacked to shreds, fell to the ground below, joining her cape and shoes.

With a long, loud grunt, his face red and eyes

bulging, Rafe pulled her up and away from the danger. She landed on top of him, clad in only a blouse and bloomers, soaked and pasted now to her flesh.

His arms moved to embrace her around the waist, holding her tight against him. She buried her face beneath his chin, feeling the throbbing pulse at his throat, his heart echoing through her own chest. For a long moment they both laid still—shivering in each other's arms.

Only when she heard her brother screaming her name did she pull back. Their eyes locked; lips inches apart. His breath was warm upon her mouth; his hands remained tight around her waist.

"*Ashoge*, thank you," she whispered.

He arched a brow. "I'd say this is becoming a bit of a habit."

"What is, Captain?"

"Me disrobing you of your skirt in order to save your life," he countered.

She had no time to respond to such a remark, because Gabriel was upon them, helping them both to their feet and farther from the cliff's edge.

"Good heaven, miss, you're 'alf dressed," Margaret said, removing her own cloak to wrap it about Sunny. "And yer shiverin' like a kitten in an ice chest."

"Can you walk, Sunny," Gabriel inquired, looking down at her bared, purple-colored feet.

Rafe did not wait for an answer. He swept her up into his arms and carried her the rest of the way to Bentwood Manor.

"I am fine," she protested. "You can put me down."

"Not a chance. If carrying you is the only way I can see you safely home, then carry you I will," he said.

He brought her right to the stone steps of

Bentwood's front entrance, set her down before the large oak door, and rang the bell. Stepping back a bit, she gazed up in awe at the three story mansion. With its turrets and gables it appeared to her both romantic and gothic.

The door flew open and a fair-haired woman stood, curls in disarray, eyes wide with terror. But it was what she held in her hands that made Sunny gasp.

Kaylena Bentley had a gun, and she was pointing it at Rafe's head.

Chapter Twenty

This wasn't the first time Rafe found himself facing the barrel of a gun. Being in the military and dealing with some of the scum he had, put him in such a position periodically throughout his life. But those pointing a weapon at him were always men, his enemies, not a woman he'd known since he was a child.

He stepped back, raising his hands in surrender and kept his voice calm. "No need for this, Miss Bentley."

Kaylena frowned. "Who are you, what do you want?" Her gaze shifted for a brief moment to what was taking place behind him, no doubt catching a glimpse of Gabriel and Margaret approaching from the rear.

"We are Amelia's grandchildren, Aunt Kaylena," Sunny began to explain, moving ahead of him. He put his arm out to shield her, pushing her to stand behind him. The gesture was so automatic it surprised even him. For a reason he couldn't explain and didn't have time now to understand, he had appointed himself Sunny Beth Eagle's savior and protector, more than once now. And it was not the role, after his experience with Deandra, that by any means he wanted.

"We have come from America," Sunny went on, peeking at the elder woman from around his shoulder. "I am Amanda's daughter, Sunny Beth. You sent money for me, my brother and sister, to come to England."

The frown creasing Kaylena's brow softened.

"Aye, Amanda, the Indian's woman."

"Wife," Sunny corrected, raising a defiant chin. "And he is an Apache."

Recognition flashed across Kaylena's features. "And you are much like her in his defense, if my memory serves me right." A slow smile brought forth the splendor hidden by the years. At one time her beauty was astounding. Even as a youngster Rafe was pulled into her large blue eyes and soft voice. She mesmerized him, fascinated him, and fueled his boyish fantasies. But now, she looked haggard and worn, dark pockets settled beneath her eyes, and she reeked of brandy.

"Aye, Amanda's children," she said, lowering the gun. Then as fast as the frown disappeared, it resurfaced, and she leveled the gun again. "And who are you?"

"Rafe, Rafe Cavendish, Joshua Holmes's nephew," he reminded her. "It's been a while, Miss Bentley. I haven't seen you since before I left for the military."

"Ah, the military," she said, in a sardonic tone. "My Wesley was in the military, the Royal Navy...doing his part for the crown. And he never returned." Her eyes welled with tears. "We were to be married, but he never returned." With the back of a hand, she swiped away the tear trickling down her pale cheek "I'd say you're a fortunate one, then to be standing here."

"Aye, mum, that I am," he said, bowing his head respectfully. "And I'm sorry for your loss."

Kaylena sighed and lowered the gun to her side. "So am I."

Sunny stepped from behind him, into Kaylena's view. Shivering and wet, wearing nothing more than a blouse that was now pasted to her ample bosom, bloomers reaching only to her shapely knees, and Margaret's cape wrapped around her waist, she gave

181

her aunt a comforting smile. "I am so happy to meet you, Aunt Kaylena."

Kaylena made a welcoming gesture with her hand. "Enter, all of you. Come in out of the rain. I would have sent Fritz and the carriage for you, but I had no idea when you'd arrive." She stumbled backward when allowing them access.

Sunny immediately reached for her aunt's arm, Margaret's cape slipping from her grasp and falling to the floor. "Let me help you, Aunt Kaylena."

The sincerity in Sunny's voice and the tenderness in her eyes warmed his heart. He suddenly admired her for more than a beautiful woman. She too reacted automatically to a role of concern, that of being responsible for her aunt. He knew from this time on Sunny would be the one to care for Kaylena, have compassion for the troubled woman. And a small part of him wondered if Kaylena would appreciate the effort. But in reflection this wasn't the first time he'd witnessed Sunny's kindness, her fierce loyalty for family. Aboard the *Entrenous* her concern for her sister's plight and brother, who spent a time locked in a storeroom, was her main focus.

Kaylena frowned as she surveyed Sunny's appearance. "Sunny Beth, what in heaven's name happened to your clothes?"

"It's quite a story to tell," he said, picking the cape up from the floor and replacing it around Sunny's shoulders. She reached to adjust the wet garment in place, causing their hands to touch. Again there was a tingling in the pit of his stomach, the same sensation he experienced every time he came in contact with her...whether to dance, save her from catching fire, rescue her from a flooded privy, or holding her close after nearly losing her over a cliff and into the English Channel. He cleared his throat and stepped away. "Perhaps all can be explained after we've cleaned up and put on dry clothes."

"Of course, of course," Kaylena said, leading them through the foyer and into the main parlor. "Fritz, Cirie," she called. "They've arrive...my family has arrived and is in need of certain comforts."

****

Sunny followed Cirie up a winding flight of stairs and down a long hallway, lit by lanterns that hung from wall sconces. Along the way to a bedchamber situated at the back of the mansion, she passed portraits of the grand relations, their faces void of emotion and frozen in time. Their stiff images lined the walls in ornate frames. She never understood why people, when having a portrait done or a photograph taken, opted for a strict appearance instead of a smile. Did looking mean make them think they would capture a more regal facade?

Her gaze wandered to the bottom of each portrait, where a copper plate was inscribed with the name of the family member; Wilson and Cornelia, Jacob and Anna, Hiram and Hannah. There was one of Amelia and Kaylena as well. Amelia had a glint in her eye, like she had just been told a funny story or shared a secret and could barely contain her excitement. Amelia's features; high cheekbones, large round blue eyes, full lips and golden hair, was a striking resemblance to Golden Lady, Sunny's mother.

And to me as well.

How strange to think at one time Amelia walked this hallway, played and grew up in this very mansion, then left all she knew and loved to pursue an adventure.

Much like me again.

And if Amelia had not followed her dreams, went with her heart, Sunny would not be standing here today. What was even more mind boggling, was that within the last two days, between discovering the Bentley and Collins history, she had really learned a great deal about both her paternal and maternal roots. She was made up of all those who came before her, their blood ran through her veins.

She smiled to herself. *I am born of proud blood.*

Immediately upon entering the room she would occupy, she made her way to the large windows curtained in blue and white linen drapery, and looked out onto the big waters. A set of stone steps led to the beach.

A far better access than that darn cliff.

And one she knew she would be using often, as the weather warmed, because she loved to swim. The English Channel, however, with its crashing waves and jagged rocks spiking up from the ground like the teeth of a vicious animal, appeared much meaner than the Gila River.

The room was of a generous size and made up of refreshing hues of blue and white. It was a classic palette to please the eye and quite fitting for a dwelling so near to the big waters. The drapes matched and complemented the bed coverlet and dressing table skirt, the combination soft and airy, like a summer afternoon breeze in spite of the angry winds that now rattled the encasements. Everything, decorated in hints of white with a ribbon of blue trim, was clean, crisp, and inviting.

A thick octagon-shaped rug covered most of the polished hardwood floors, and she rolled her eyes heavenward as her cold feet sunk into its plush fibers.

A canopied oak wood bed with a matching bedside table and armoire furnished the room. In the far corner a soft-cushioned chair sat beside a fireplace and along the wall, was a full-length mirror.

Cirie, just a few years older than she, was

assigned her care. Gabriel and Rafe were sent off with Fritz, and Margaret went to find someone named Bertha, who manned the kitchen.

With large brown eyes, ebony curls, and freckles dotting her small, upturned nose, Cirie's efficient administrations soon had Sunny's wet garments removed and her basking in a tub of warm water.

"I'll unpack yer bags, miss, while ye soak a bit," she offered.

Sunny nodded, pleased to have the warm water caressing her shoulders. Laying her head back against the tub, she surveyed the privy, which folks in England called the water closet. Done in whispers of blue, to match the bedroom, the bath area brought an element of softness to the large claw-footed tub that took up most of the room. Other furnishings included a wash table with a pitcher and basin atop, and a toilet, which to her relief was not the flush type but instead just a chair with a hole in its seat and a pot beneath.

She smiled with satisfaction. *That is a lot easier to clean.*

When Cirie came in to wash her back and assist her into a skirt and blouse for dinner, she did not protest. Though she still felt somewhat awkward for accepting help in doing personal things, it was the way a lady was cared for in England, and it was best she try to oblige in such ways. Some aspects she had to adjust to were not all that horrible, she supposed. But she still drew the line at wearing the corset, which stopped the air from filling her lungs. Or the bustle, which looked like a small wagon trailing from behind. It reminded her of a storage place, packed and prepared for the winter months, like the squirrels who stored a supply of nuts in their cheeks.

"I noticed such a grand ball gown in yer trunk, miss," Cirie said, as she finished lacing Sunny's shoes. Fortunately Kaylena had loaned her a pair after her own went over the cliff.

"I am to be in a wedding, Cirie, and the gown needs to be adjusted a bit in the neckline."

"Aye, I figured as much." Cirie said, eyeing Sunny's bosom. "As a seamstress by trade I 'ave an eye for measurements."

Her cheeks warmed at the other woman's scrutiny. "I need the repairs done by Christmas, as the wedding is after the New Year, and I am expected back in London one week before."

Cirie bowed her head respectfully. "I will measure ye in the gown before breakfast on the morrow, and 'ave it back to ye within the week."

She nodded and smiled. "I cannot ask for anything more."

"Oh, but you must, miss, as that is my position here," Cirie said, her dark eyes growing concerned.

"Do you not have enough to do caring for my aunt?"

"Nay, miss. Yer aunt's care falls upon Greta," Cirie explained.

"I have not met Greta," she said.

Cirie led her over to the dressing table and began to brush Sunny's hair. "She is away, visitin' her brother till later this evenin'." She sighed. "Sometimes the poor girl just needs to get away from...from—" Cirie halted her words.

"From my aunt?" she supplied.

"Aye, miss," Cirie said.

She frowned and turned to face Cirie. "Is my aunt a difficult person to get along with?"

"She isn't if she stays away from—" again Cirie clipped her tongue.

Her frown deepened. "What is it...what ails my aunt, Cirie?"

"I've said too much already, miss." Cirie turned her back around. "Now sit still so I can pin up yer hair. Ye don't want to be late for the evenin' meal."

****

The dining table was exquisite, set in a blue pattern. Sunny realized her aunt favored the serenity such a shade captured, as many fabrics, the wallpaper, and carpets throughout the mansion were similar in color and trim.

The floral china, in calming tones of blue and white was set in matching service to the lace tablecloth, obviously handmade. The combination brought an elegant touch to the meal they would share.

The pitcher, teacups, saucers, and platters with swirling flowers of blue complemented the flatware and flute-stemmed glassware, also of a deep blue scheme.

Her aunt sat at the head of the table, pale curls laced with silver strands of hair were now arranged neatly atop her head. She wore a yellow dress with a modest neckline, the sleeves and collar trimmed in peach lace.

Gabriel sat to her right, his shoulder-length hair slicked back and fastened with a cord. In a clean white shirt and black vest to match his trousers, he looked every bit the part of an Englishman.

Rafe was seated at the other end of the table, but stood politely when she entered the dining room and held out the chair to the left of Kaylena for her to sit upon. His hair, also combed neatly away from his face, pronounced strong yet handsome features. A wisp of ebony curls hung down his forehead. He wore a black shirt, a waistcoat, and black trousers.

"Well, you all clean up quite nicely," Kaylena commented.

"Where is Margaret?" Sunny asked, missing the elder woman from the table.

"Taking her meal in the kitchen, along with the other help, where she belongs," Kaylena said. She reached for one of the flute-stemmed glasses filled with wine and took a sip. "It's best not to, under any circumstances, allow the help an opportunity to stray from their station in life."

She shared a look of annoyance with Gabriel. He knew firsthand how it felt to do a hard day's work and still be looked down upon. In America, their Apache heritage was considered a lower class of people, as Margaret and the other servants were thought of here in England.

Their disdain for Kaylena's attitude did not go unnoticed by Rafe. He cleared his throat and changed the subject. "Before dinner, Gabriel and I spoke in the den about the dangerous condition of Bentwood's entrance road."

"It's only dangerous in a storm," Kaylena snapped, taking another gulp of the wine.

"I think I can remedy the problem, if you would allow," Gabriel offered.

"And how would you go about doing that?" Kaylena asked.

"I believe I can widen the road by chopping down the line of trees on the one side, then with the wood I can fashion a fence along the cliff side. The barrier will safeguard against anyone," he looked at Sunny for a brief moment, "or anything from going over the side."

"Sounds like a lot of work to undertake," Kaylena said.

Gabriel nodded. "But it is necessary. If I could use the carriage to go into town, to buy the supplies I would need, I could also ask around as to who needs work. There are always men wanting employment."

Kaylena chuckled. "Aye, derelicts hoping to get close enough to snoop around the mansion and steal the silverware."

Sunny glanced at Rafe and arched a brow. "It seems to me you folks are quite protective of your eating utensils."

Rafe ignored her remark, acting much more interested in the conversation between Gabriel and Kaylena.

"I would keep a close eye on all who agreed to sign on for the job," Gabriel said. "And I see no reason why anyone would have to enter the mansion at all. I have lived out of doors while working, the men I hire can do the same."

"The climate here is not that of Arizona," Kaylena explained. "Sleeping out of doors around a fire in Brighton is much different. But there is an old bunker behind the mansion with a wood burning stove; perhaps you could restore that for your use."

"It would be all that is needed," Gabriel agreed. Then he turned his attention toward Rafe. "You would be a huge asset in this venture, knowing the ways of the folks. Could I count on your help to get this all started?"

Rafe hesitated a moment before answering, as if he were weighing an issue much more complicated than helping Gabriel. His brief silence agitated Sunny, as she got the distinct notion his pause had something to do with her.

"I fear anyone could go over that cliff," Gabriel said, looking again at Sunny.

She locked eyes with her brother, the flesh of her cheeks heating and her stomach clenching. How dare he single her out as the reason the road to Bentwood was so dangerous. Obviously, since the driver of the carriage that brought them to Bentwood, decided not to try navigating on the road himself, her accident was not the first. Perturbed, she sent her brother an angry stare and reached for a glass of water.

Without her gaze wavering from Gabriel's, she sensed Rafe's eyes observing her as he responded with clarity. "I would indeed oblige you in your request, as I agree to your concerns."

She pinched her lips together. Did they all perceive her as a clumsy child?

"Come the morning, I'll accompany you to town, with Margaret along as well." Rafe went on, "Once I have Margaret seated safely aboard a train heading back to London and my waiting mother, I'll stay on a few days here to lend a hand."

Gabriel broke from her glance to look at Rafe. "*Ashoge*, thank you, I am most grateful." Then he brought his attention to Kaylena. "Are you in agreement to this, Aunt?"

Kaylena, now finishing a third glass of wine, nodded in accordance before adding, "I have set up an account for you and Sunny and will deposit a fair sum in each every month. To your account, I will add a bit more, Gabriel. In this way, you can purchase whatever you need for the road work." She arched a brow. "I trust you will keep all receipts on everything purchased as well as the workers' salaries for my records?"

"Of course, Aunt," Gabriel said.

"Then I give you the freedom to handle Bentwood's affairs and that of your own account. However," she said, glancing at Sunny, "until your début you will be accountable to me for whatever you need."

"My début?" She frowned. "And what might that be?"

"It is *the* event every young woman of means strives for in life, as it is her opportunity to be presented to society. You will need a tutor and a governess to help you learn the necessities, of course. That's why I've hired Flossy and Helga Grant. The two sisters will be arriving in a day or two." Kaylena sighed. "We haven't a lot of time left before the grand ball and your formal presentation to the queen, so I ask that you cooperate with both of these women. They're strict, but very skilled in turning young women into proper young ladies."

The heat again rose to her face. "I am already a proper young lady."

Kaylena wrinkled her nose. "You are far from England's standards, my dear. Growing up as you have has been a positively atrocious injustice. I should have insisted your mother return with me when I had the opportunity."

Sunny was glad her mother stood her ground and remained with Proud Eagle and his people. In fact, she suddenly understood why her grandmother, Amelia, left Bentwood for a life somewhere else.

Just as she was about to defend her parents and their honorable ways, Gabriel spoke. "Both my mother and father are good and proud people, as are all those of my tribe. My sisters and I have been brought up to be just as honorable and courteous as any of you English folks. Our women, my sisters, are proper ladies and deserve respect."

"We play by different rules here, Gabriel," Kaylena snapped. "Do you want your sister shunned, accused of unspeakable actions?"

Gabriel frowned. "She will not be accused or shunned when she has done nothing wrong."

"Tongues wag for no reason, and then a person's reputation is ruined," Kaylena said. "I will not allow this sort of thing to begin. Sunny must have her début, be presented to society."

Her pulse quickened. "What if I choose not to be presented to society?"

Kaylena waved a hand over her head. "Well, that's just an absurd notion that you must wipe from your thoughts immediately. You now are in line for more than my estate and must act accordingly."

"You have had word from Lady Collins?" she asked.

"Aye." Kaylena pulled a letter from her pocket. "This arrived from Lucinda only yesterday." She sighed. "And I suppose it is only right I send word to America about your arrival."

"Reverend Holmes has already taken care of that," Gabriel was quick to offer.

Sunny took the envelope Kaylena handed her, noticing the red shield and crest insignia of Collins Stead in the corner. She read the letter enclosed.

"As you see, Lady Collins will sponsor you, but it is my responsibility to make you ready," Kaylena said.

She looked up from the letter. "Ready in what way?"

"It is important for you to learn to speak a second language," Kaylena began.

"I already know a second language, Apache," she said.

Kaylena's sardonic chuckle grated on Sunny's nerves. "Such a tongue would hardly be considered suitable. Nay, you will learn French as well as how to hold your posture correctly while walking and sitting. You'll be taught how to curtsy with grace, the proper utensils to use at dinner, as well as how to sew a sampler. But the first plan of action is to see to it you have a new pair of shoes and are fashionably dressed." She eyed Sunny's clothing. "That will never do, so when the Grant sisters arrive you will be taken to town for a shopping spree."

"What is wrong with what I already have?" she asked, smoothing the skirt of her dress. All this time she believed she looked quite grown-up and elegant in the garments Sylvie Newcomb purchased for her to wear. She cast a glance at Gabriel. This time he held his tongue, but the muscles at his jaw throbbed, indicating his disturbance with what was being said. Even though he was displeased, she really did not expect him to come to her defense in this matter. Gabriel would not allow another to look down upon their character, and he thought ill of those who treated others cruelly, but he had no problem conforming to the way of dress suited for the times. He doffed the traditional Apache garb years ago, wearing only the white man's clothing. It was how he fit in, made a living, and helped to support the family. Because of what he had to do in his own life to survive, he would not think wearing England's latest fashions was such a horrible thing for her to do.

Her aunt held up a finger, silencing any further protests. "I will discuss nothing further on this matter or any other right now. It is time to eat." Kaylena clapped her hands, and Bertha emerged from the kitchen with the first tray.

Sunny hardly had an appetite now, but Bertha smiled and filled her dish with such care, that she felt obligated to try everything. She bit into a piece of bread stuffed with cream. A vanilla flavor pleased her taste buds, and something more. "What is in the bread, Bertha?"

"That would be lavender, miss, that yer tastin'," Bertha said.

"Lavender?" she said, taking another bite.

"Aye, it's often substituted for rosemary in bread," Kaylena chimed in. "The lavender brings out an earthy accent to plain flat bread and crackers."

"Then it's topped with goat cheese soaked in honey," Bertha added.

"Turning an ordinary loaf of bread into a delicious pastry," Kaylena concluded. "And not only does lavender smell and taste heavenly, it's a plant hearty enough to continually survive winter."

"Well, I really like the taste," she said, reaching for another piece of bread.

Kaylena slapped her knuckles gently. "Nay, child, you've had enough. Leave room for the main course."

Humiliated, she raised a defiant chin. "I will be

able to eat my meal if I take another piece of bread."

"If a lady overeats it is looked upon as ill-mannered," Kaylena explained.

She felt the hairs stand on end at the nape of her neck. "I fail to see the connection."

"Well, that is what Flossy and Helga's part is for, to help you connect with our ways," Kaylena said. "Just give yourself time to learn everything your tutor has to offer, behave at all costs like a proper lady, do as you're told, and you and I will get along famously. Whether you like it or not, you are now my responsibility, Sunny." Her aunt forced a smile. "It will be as though *you* are my daughter now, the one I never had but always wanted."

Chapter Twenty-One

After his dual with Howard Cross, Deandra's fiancé, Rafe chose to live his life unconcerned about what happened to others, but as he spent time with Gabriel and Sunny he'd begun to see his perspectives were wrongly boxed. He had to admit he took the servants for granted, and rarely considered them as sharing the same wants and needs as those of means. In a strange sense, he believed they should be grateful for their servitude, as it kept them from starving in the streets. When in truth, the price they paid to survive was the freedom to live their life as they desired.

It was the same way women were treated. The double standard was something he'd never dwelled upon. He'd been brought up to believe it was a woman's lot in life to submit to her husband, have his children, and care for his home. As long as her husband supplied for her needs, her own wants and wishes were of little importance. It was how things were in the world he'd known, but now as he questioned the status quo, he realized it was only a fair world for the male persuasion, and a rich man at that.

After watching his brother, Simon and fiancée Fiona, he'd begun to see a different side of the union between a man and his woman. And although he still burned with Deandra's betrayal, he liked the way Simon considered Fiona in all instances, in every manner. He cared not for such a relationship himself, but since he met the Eagles his eyes had been opened, his opinion of women changing. Not only had his thoughts secretly marveled over Sunny's splendor, but of her substance as well. She was refreshing and had a caring heart, not at all like Deandra. Being around her woke something in him he never knew existed. He admired her spirit, intelligence, and strength. She was clever and resourceful, yet she was feminine and had an air of innocence he felt he needed to protect. He didn't want to see her individuality destroyed, the person she was crushed just to fit the usual mold. He certainly wouldn't relish living a life of servitude or submission just to survive, so how could he expect that from her...from anyone?

Throughout dinner and after, as they all sat around the fireplace in the parlor sipping brandy and tea, Kaylena continued to harangue her niece on the protocol she'd be expected to follow. He watched Sunny fight back the tears welling in her large, sapphire eyes, and his urge to strike Kaylena's mouth shut grew stronger by the moment. But the brandy and wine she'd heavily consumed all evening finally stilled her tongue. She ended up falling asleep in her chair. As Gabriel carried his aunt up the stairs and to her room, Sunny followed. In spite of Kaylena's harsh demeanor toward her, Sunny willingly offered to help Cirie and Gerta ready the elder woman for bed.

"Your sister is a kind and caring woman," Rafe said to Gabriel when he returned downstairs.

Gabriel arched a brow. "You should see all the wounded animals she brought home to mend." He shook his head in disbelief and smiled. "I believe at one time, her tiny hospital consisted of a doe, a robin, a rabbit, two squirrels, and a very nervous mole."

He could picture her in his mind's eye, caring for the critters, then setting them free to live out their lives. Tender administrations from small, gentle hands...aye, the whole scene came to him clearly. "She doesn't deserve your aunt's harassment." He laughed sardonically. "If anyone treated me as Kaylena treated Sunny this evening, I wouldn't care where they slept." He frowned. "Anyone drinking as much as that woman did all evening deserves whatever consequences that befall them." Now it was his turn to shake his head. "And she has the nerve to preach about protocol."

Gabriel sighed and made his way to the window, looking out into the dark of night. "I was the same once."

The other man's remark now reminded him of a confidence Sunny had shared aboard the *Entrenous*. Gabriel left the ship to visit an ale house, causing Raven to search for him when he failed to promptly return. Thus the reason she became separated from the two of them.

"I filled my body with the white man's spirits," Gabriel continued. "Firewater, my people call it. I drank all I could whenever I got the chance." He turned to look at Rafe. "It was how I dealt with the emptiness left in my heart after my wife and son's death."

Rafe's own betrayal was heartache enough, he didn't even want to imagine such grief; glad one hundred times over his love was now for the sea and not a woman. "I'm so sorry for your loss."

"It goes way beyond loss, Captain," Gabriel said. "Such devastation has made it hurt to even breathe." Then appearing ashamed at revealing so much about his personal life, Gabriel changed the subject. "When we go into town tomorrow, would you help me find someone?"

"Aye, if I can," he said, glad for the change of topic. "Who is it you're looking for?"

"A man...a painter your father talked about. Elwood Hunter is his name," Gabriel said. "Do you know him?"

"Aye, he has a small gallery and art school in town."

"Your father said he gives private lessons as well," Gabriel said.

"Aye, I've heard the same." He smiled. "I had no idea you were an artist."

"I am not, but Sunny is. And quite a talented one at that," Gabriel said. "I want her to be able to pursue something she is good at, that she enjoys."

"Hoping it will help her over the changes to come?" he said.

Gabriel nodded. "All I want for both of my sisters is their safety and for them to be happy. I have no control over Raven's life right now, but I can be here for Sunny. I will not allow her to be hurt, by anyone or anything." He arched a brow, locking his gaze with Rafe's. "Have I made myself clear, Captain?"

Gabriel Eagle had nothing whatsoever to worry about on his account. The last thing Rafe wanted was to be tied to a woman. But he wasn't about to share his personal feelings tonight. Instead, he nodded in agreement and inclined his head politely.

"Perfectly clear."

Chapter Twenty-Two

Sunny helped Cirie and Gerta strip her aunt of her clothes and wash her body with a warm, moist cloth. Kaylena's flesh was so fair it appeared transparent in some areas, the blue veins visible. Though not as handsome in her bones as Golden Lady, Kaylena still held onto some measure of beauty, resembling in many ways her younger counterpart. Now showing the signs of aging, her aunt's ample breasts sagged, as well as the flesh beneath her arms. Kaylena's neck, stomach, and thighs were wrinkled, as was the area of the brow and around her mouth. Without the high-layered neckline and generous material of a full skirt, the elder woman's frame was slim, almost gaunt.

"Does she not eat well?"Sunny asked, helping Gerta pull a nightgown over Kaylena's head.

Gerta's delicate hands smoothed the nightwear down as far as Kaylena's hips. "Not as of late, miss."

She frowned. "There is more than enough of the nightdress to cover her to the ankles, why have you left it to her waist?"

"Leaving it raised keeps it from becomin' soiled when Mum sleeps through a nature call." Gerta lifted Kaylena's hips from the mattress while Cirie placed several folded towels beneath her backside. "That's why we put down the towels. They are much easier to clean than the beddin' every mornin'."

"And then on some nights she tosses and turns, calls out names in her sleep and cries," Cirie said. "The only way to calm her is with a cool cloth to the forehead."

Sunny's frown deepened. "So then someone has to stay with her throughout the night?"

"Aye, miss," Cirie said, making sure the towels were in place before covering Kaylena with the quilt. "Sometimes I wish we could put her in a nappy, but it would be difficult to find one large enough."

"Besides," Gerta added. "If Mum woke to find herself clothed like a babe and needin' a change, she'd have our heads for sure."

"This is a very disturbing situation," Sunny said, taking a seat on the lounge beside the fireplace. "I am shamed for her."

"I am as well, miss, but 'tis how things must be if Mum won't stop the drinkin'," Gerta said. "She's been doin' this ever since that letter coom."

"What letter are you talking about, Gerta?"

"There was a letter that coom about six months ago, special delivery. After readin' it, Mum threw it into the fire, then she locked 'erself in 'er room and cried for days. We were all so worried."

"Aye, worried straight through to our bones," Cirie added. "Eventually we had to call the Reverend Holmes for 'elp. Only way to get to Mum was for 'im to take the door down."

"We found 'er on the floor, curled like a babe just out o' its mama's womb, and just starin' at nothin'," Gerta said.

"We fetched the doctor at once, and he thought she'd 'ad an emotional breakdown as she appeared to be sufferin' from a shock o' some sort," Cirie said.

"And ever since that time, Mum's been takin' part in drinkin' the spirits, brandy, wine, ale, whatever she can find," Gerta said.

"Almost like she's tryin' to forget somethin'," Cirie reflected.

"Aye, that's just how it seems, miss. Mum wants to forget whatever she read in that letter," Gerta concluded.

Sunny stood and made her way to stand beside the bed. Looking down at her aunt, she took her hand. Gabriel, when he lost his wife and baby, used the firewater to drown his sorrows.

But what could Kaylena be trying to drown?

If she could only find out, perhaps she could help her aunt.

Gerta sighed. "I'll take the first watch, Cirie. You go on and get a bit o' rest."

Cirie nodded and left the room.

"I will stay with my aunt, Gerta," she said. "You go on to bed as well."

"Are ye sure yer not mindin', miss?"

"I am sure," she said, sitting at the edge of the bed.

"I'll be relievin' ye coom midnight," Gerta promised before she left the bedchamber.

She again took her aunt's hand in hers, "All will be well, Aunt Kaylena. I am here now, and I will help you get through whatever it is that troubles you. On that, you have my word."

Within an hour into her watch Kaylena began to mumble in her sleep. Kicking off the quilt, the elder woman rocked from side to side.

"You had no right to keep it from me," she groaned. "He was mine!"

Sunny reached for the cloth on the bedside table and dipped it into the filled wash basin. "All is well," she said as she dampened her aunt's forehead.

"I'm sorry, I didn't know. Please don't hate me. Please forgive me," Kaylena cried.

"All is well, my aunt," Sunny repeated in a soothing tone.

"He hates me, will want revenge," Kaylena carried on.

"Shush, all is well," she said a third time. "I am here and I will not let anyone hurt you."

Gerta had come, to her relief, earlier than

promised. Wearily Sunny made her way to her own bedchamber, the causeway to her quarters dimly lit and quiet, except for the chime of the grandfather clock striking midnight. Now she longed to undress and stretch upon the bed. But once resting snug between the freshly washed linens, her mind raced, reflecting back to the evening's events.

Irritable and unhappy with the entire outcome, she tossed and turned. Gabriel was allowed privacy and trusted to make the right decisions for himself, but she was expected at all times to be accountable to her aunt...like a child. After learning how unstable Kaylena really was, she would be much better off running her own affairs.

Then she would also be subjected to whatever Flossy and Helga Grant deemed proper, as the two sisters arrived in a few days to tutor and govern her every move. Told what to wear, how to speak and eat, Sunny could not see happiness any time soon coming her way.

Oh, Raven, I miss you so much, was her heartfelt cry.

It was not only her sister she missed, but her parents and friends. As the tears slipped from her eyes, wetting the linen pillowcase, she thought of her home in Arizona; the comfort her folks gave her, sharing good and bad times together. Being so far from them all left a hole in her heart.

But Gabriel is with me...I still have my brother. Raven has no one.

And with that thought in mind, Sunny realized she was far more blessed than her sister. In spite of all that was to come her way, she was not alone. Taking a calming breath, she wiped her eyes with the backs of her hands, squeezed her lids shut, and forced sleep to come.

****

It was nearing noon when Cirie entered Sunny's

chamber with a brunch tray.

"Why did you allow me to sleep so long," she chastised, her stomach rumbling with hunger.

"I explained to yer brother, miss, o' yer duty to Mum, and 'e insisted ye be left to sleep as long as ye liked," Cirie said.

She took a bite of the hot, buttered scone, her taste buds savoring its sweet and creamy flavor. "Has my brother left yet for the city?"

"Aye, miss, quite a while ago, and 'e took Margaret and the captain with 'im."

She would miss Margaret, a small pang of regret assailing her at the thought of not bidding the woman goodbye. "And my aunt, has she risen?"

"She is awake, miss, but like ye takes 'er fast while sittin' in 'er bed," Cirie explained.

"You said you talked to my brother?"

Cirie nodded.

"What exactly did you tell him?"

"I shared the true extent of Mum's problem with the drinkin', thought it only right 'e know, being 'e's the man o' the household now. Then I told 'im ye spent most o' the night by 'er side," Cirie said. "That's when 'e said to let ye alone, give ye a chance to catch up on yer rest. Then 'e said to tell ye the two o' ye needed to talk when 'e returned."

She took a sip of the tea, the warm liquid coating the back of her throat. "I imagine we will." She sighed. "It will be necessary for us to take some sort of steps to help Kaylena, Cirie."

"Aye, miss, 'tis what family does for each other." Cirie smiled. "Glad I am that the two o' ye are 'ere now, so ye can do just that."

She frowned. "Problem is, I hardly know where or how to begin."

"Ye might start with talkin' to the Reverend Holmes. In truth, 'e knows the Mum better than any o' us. Mayhap 'e'd be able to guide ye down the right path," Cirie suggested.

She smiled. "That is a splendid idea, Cirie. As soon as he returns from London, I will certainly seek his advice."

"Oh, 'e's here now, miss, takin' 'is tea in the library," Cirie said.

She pushed aside her meal tray and hopped out of bed. "Then I must hurry and get dressed, Cirie, before he leaves."

"The reverend's not goin' anywhere soon, 'tis 'is day to do Bible study with Mum. Ever since the letter coom, she won't leave the house to go to church." Cirie frowned. "Won't leave to do anythin', truth be told. Almost like she's afraid someone's going to 'urt 'er," Cirie frowned. "But who would want to 'urt Mum?"

She thought back to Kaylena's nighttime ranting. "In her sleep, my aunt apologized, sought forgiveness from a man she said was hers. She even felt he would hurt her, take his revenge for whatever she has done wrong to him. Would you know of any such incident, Cirie?"

"Nay, miss, but I wouldn't worry so over the rantin' o' someone full o' the spirits."

She slipped off her nightgown and accepted the chemise Cirie held out for her to wear. "My brother always says a drunk speaks the truth, Cirie."

Cirie frowned. "If Mum 'urt a real bloke, it was long before my time, 'cause I've never set eyes on 'im."

"Well, obviously he is real to Aunt Kaylena and has upset her something fierce."

Cirie gasped. "Do ye think 'e's the one who sent Mum the letter?"

She stepped into bloomers and petticoat. "I cannot say for certain, Cirie. But from this point on, I definitely plan on finding out."

Chapter Twenty-Three

Rafe accompanied Gabriel into town, sitting opposite him in the carriage. "Brighton in itself isn't as seedy and crowded as London or even Liverpool, but still in all one has to be cautious as to who you converse with...and especially whom you hire. There are misfortunate folks struggling to maintain a living, thankful for the opportunity to earn an honest wage, and then there are those who lead you to believe they're just down on their luck. In truth, the latter type would rob you blind. These con-artists have no intention of putting in a hard day's labor, but instead be the sort to rob the silver." He remembered Sunny's remark at last night's dinner table concerning the silverware and stifled a smile. "The very sort Kaylena Bentley is worried about, and with good cause," he added.

"I have learned people are just people, no matter where they live," Gabriel said, gazing out the carriage window at those milling along the town streets. He turned to look at Rafe. "It took a few swindlers, trouble-makers, and outlaws to come my way before I came to this conclusion, of course."

"Then why would you think you needed my help?"

"Because you would be listened to a lot better, being I am a stranger to these parts and all." Gabriel frowned. "Most do not take well to a...a..."

"Outlander," he supplied.

Gabriel nodded in agreement. "Yes, outlander...good word."

"Ah, well, they're a crafty lot, these

Englishmen."

Gabriel chuckled. "And does that statement include you as well?"

"Indubitably not, I am as honest as the day is long."

Gabriel chuckled again. "Well, at this point I have no choice but to trust you...with the business at hand, that is."

He arched a brow. "I assure you, this is the only business I care to have a hand in."

Fritz found a place to park the carriage a block away from The Red Boar Pub. They each ordered a mug of ale, and downed it to quench their thirst. When they ordered the second draught, Rafe was a bit concerned Gabriel's past problems with drinking would hamper their goal. He didn't care to play nursemaid to a drunk. But the other man sipped slowly at the second mug while he glanced around the pub.

"Certainly enough men in here to pick from," Gabriel commented. "Let's hope they want to work."

"Only one way to find out," Rafe said, turning to face the other patrons. With a sharp whistle and a clap of his hands, he managed to get their attention. Rafe gestured to Gabriel. "I have with me here, gentlemen, Gabriel Golden Eagle, the legal heir of London's Glenshire Sussex Collins Stead and Brighton's Bentwood Manor."

A fair-haired fellow sitting at a table a few feet away quickly raised his gaze from his mug to impale Gabriel with amber eyes. For a reason Rafe couldn't explain, the man's facial expression left him feeling uneasy.

"Aye, and so what o' it," another man sitting at a corner table grumbled.

"Mr. Eagle has gainful employment for any man who is interested in making an honest wage," he went on.

"Who says any o' us is interested in an 'onest day's wage?" the grumbler commented.

Laughter went all around the smoke-filled pub, sweat and the stench of unclean flesh filling the room.

"Speak for yerself, Breckinridge," another man shouted.

The blondish man's eyes bore into Gabriel's. "What's the job?"

Gabriel matched the stare. "Cutting trees to widen a path, then building a barrier along the cliff's edge."

"And what's the pay?" the man said, his tawny orbs round and severe.

"A daily wage plus food and lodging," Gabriel said.

The man nodded in agreement, then stood and made his way to the bar, his gait slow and confident. Another unexpected warning signal flared in Rafe. There was something about the guy that he didn't like, though he couldn't put his finger on what. Gabriel must have had the same inclination, as he hesitated when the man extended a hand and introduced himself as Cody Denton.

Gabriel placed the man's accent the moment he opened his mouth. "What part of America are you from, Mr. Denton?"

"Texas," Cody drawled.

"And what brings you to England?" Gabriel inquired.

Cody hesitated a moment with his answer. "I've learned I've got family here in Brighton, came to meet with them and claim an inheritance."

"I am from the West and coming to know my English family, as well," Gabriel admitted.

Cody's amber eyes searched Gabriel's face. "Then we're alike."

"I know many in this area. My uncle is pastor in

Brighton and I'm London born. Perhaps I can help you in your search?" Rafe offered.

Cody's tawny gaze shifted to his. "I've already located the family; now I'm just trying to figure out a way to—" he paused, casting his glance back to Gabriel—"go about meeting them. But in the meantime, I've run out of cash and would prefer to call upon them when I've got my own source of funds. So that job you're offering sounds right perfect, since I'm a logger by trade."

Gabriel gave a taut nod. "Then cutting down a few trees is not a problem for you."

"No sir. I've done my share of chopping and cutting, building, and even some demolition. To me it's all in a day's work," Cody bragged, hands shoved deep into his pockets.

Gabriel arched a brow. "Then I would say you are just the type of man I am looking for."

"Reckon I am, sir," Cody agreed, his lips curling with a smirk.

"Calling me Gabriel will do," Gabriel said.

Cody nodded. "When can I begin?"

"Immediately," Gabriel said, then looked around the pub. "Any other takers?"

By the time they left The Red Boar a total of seven men had been hired and were set to arrive at Bentwood Manor in the morning.

"Now, with that accomplished I have one more stop before we return to Bentwood Manor," Gabriel said, as the two made their way to the carriage.

Rafe inclined his head in a polite manner. "Aye, and that would be to see Elwood Hunter."

Gabriel nodded. "All I want is to have my sisters safe and happy so I can return to my people," Gabriel said. "And I have a feeling Elwood Hunter and his art classes will make Sunny a very pleased young woman."

Rafe frowned; annoyed with the thought of that

notion.

"What troubles you, Captain?" Gabriel said, noticing the furrowed brows.

He cleared his throat and lied. "Just concerned about the weather holding when there's so much work to be done."

Gabriel nodded in agreement. "I share your concern. But I believe hiring someone like Cody Denton will help us meet the deadline."

Rafe frowned. "How is that?"

"Someone with his skill can get the work done in a short amount of time." Gabriel looked up at the sky, well traveled with large, white clouds. "And with winter upon us soon, the faster the work is done, the better." Gabriel opened the carriage door. "Now, let us be on our way to meet Mr. Hunter."

Rafe nodded and shouted the directions to Elwood's art school out to Fritz, as he climbed into the carriage beside Gabriel.

Elwood Hunter's establishment was at the far end of town, a small gray-stone building set back and apart from the others by the bright blue shingle with the words, *School of Art & Galleria*, written across it in white lettering.

It had been almost ten years since a young, shy, Elwood Hunter, with thick brown curls framing a sensitive face, came to Cavenworth to paint the Cavendish family portrait. Rafe hadn't been all that worldly himself at the time. When his gaze locked with Elwood's large dark eyes, the time he sat for the portrait flooded his thoughts. How many days was he made to sit, staring straight into the young artist's eyes, while he captured Rafe's true essence on canvas?

"Raphael Cavendish," Elwood said, extending a hand in welcome. "What a surprise."

"You remember me, sir?" he said, accepting the greeting.

"Aye, I never forget a subject," Elwood admitted, giving Rafe a quick reprisal with a glance. "You are looking well."

"As are you," he countered, doing a bit of surveying himself. It was evident Elwood had been doing something other than wielding a paint brush, because his shoulders were broad and his arms bulged beneath his jacket sleeves.

"And what brings you to me on this day," Elwood probed, casting a curious glance Gabriel's way.

Rafe proceeded to introduce the two, and as the other men talked about Sunny's drawings, he browsed the small gallery. Now and then he was able to catch a few words of the conversation, his chest tightening when Elwood agreed with vigor to tutor Sunny.

What does it matter how exuberant he is to meet Sunny? The woman means nothing to me. I've my own life to get on with.

They left the art school, and Gabriel, gave him a friendly pat on the back, thanking him for his time and said, "I am sure you will be pleased to get back to London come morning."

Rafe had mixed feelings about leaving.

"I don't mind staying on a bit at Bentwood Manor, just to make sure the blokes you hired are serious workers," he offered.

"I thank you again for all you have done, but it is not right to keep you any longer from your own business, captain," Gabriel said. "My sister and I have troubled you enough."

If you only knew how much your sister troubled me, you'd escort me yourself out of town.

Rafe turned back to look at the art school, where Elwood stood on the stoop watching them leave. He knew some women were very taken with a man who had a moody gaze—that gifted mix of creativity, sensitivity, and seduction. Elwood Hunter was just such a man. Would Sunny be taken by the young artist as well?

With such thoughts crossing his mind, Rafe's own reply surprised even him. "It's no trouble at all. Besides," he said, looking back once more to where Elwood stood. "I'd truly feel better if there were a second pair of eyes on all those you hired today."

Gabriel nodded. "It would not hurt, I suppose."

He arched a brow. "Aye, it can't at that."

Chapter Twenty-Four

Sunny put the final touch on her outfit, the brooch Collette Halston had gifted her while aboard the ship. After clasping it to the neckline of the pale green day dress, she took the stairs two at a time, stopping only a moment at the library's door to collect her thoughts. Her aunt really needed help, and the only way that would happen was if Sunny took control of the situation. But she needed to approach the problem with caution and a clear head. Hopefully her talk with Reverend Holmes would guide her and set her on the correct path.

The library at Bentwood Manor was situated at the front of the mansion. Every wall, covered with shelves, held books of all shapes and sizes. The gold flowered wall paper complimented the dark wood trim and hardwood floors. A fire, burning in the large brick fireplace, added cozy warmth to the sparsely furnished room.

A large maple-wood desk placed by a pair of large windows caught the morning sun filtering through the sheer drapery, a splash of light exposing the well-worn finish.

Joshua Holmes sat in a dark brown stuffed chair, his back to her. Salt and pepper curls graced the collar of his black jacket, his shoulders broad and straight. Upon hearing her footsteps on the wooden floor, he turned away from the book he read, and smiled. His specs rested mid-way on the bridge of a straight and well-proportioned nose, deep blue eyes meeting hers.

He placed the book on a nearby table and stood,

removing his glasses. After folding them to fit into his vest pocket, he extended both his hands. "Good morning, Sunny. I trust you're making yourself right at home here?"

She nodded and returned the smile, accepting his greeting by placing both her hands in his. They were smooth and warm, long fingers giving hers a quick, affectionate squeeze before motioning for her to join him.

She took the seat opposite his, watching as he made his way to a serving tray and filled a cup with tea from a china pot. He handed her the china mug and saucer, then reclaimed his own seat.

She took a sip of the tea, placed it aside, and leveled her gaze to match his. "I need your help, Reverend, if I am to care for my aunt." She smoothed out the material of her skirt. "I believe she is quite a drunk."

He cleared his throat. "You waste no time in coming to the point."

"As I see it, too much time has been wasted already." She sat forward in her seat. "Do you know anything about the letter that arrived that disturbed Kaylena so?"

"Nay, not a thing," he said. "She tore it up and threw it into the fire before I had a chance to examine it. Then when I approached her on its contents she wouldn't say a word."

"I sat with her through a portion of the night and heard her ramblings. She fears a man…someone she believes belonged to her, will seek his revenge for something she has done to him. Does this make any sense to you?"

Josh sighed. "Nay, not a word of it. I would say you know more at this point than I do, Sunny." He frowned. "But whatever is going on, it has taken a toll on Kaylena's health. Her condition isn't getting better. In fact, I fear it will only get worse unless she refrains from drinking the spirits."

She raised a defiant chin. "Then if need be, I shall remove every ounce of firewater from the house. In that way, she'll have no choice but to stop with this sort of behavior."

His deep, sardonic laugh filled the room. "I can see then, you don't mind receiving a good birching."

She frowned. "A what?"

"A birching...having your bared bum reddened with a wet birching rod," he explained.

Sunny's face heated, the thought of her aunt administering such a punishment humiliated her to the core of her bones. "Surely you cannot believe...I mean to say certainly I am too old for her to take such measures."

He arched a brow. "I wouldn't count on that mind set. Kaylena was brought up by the old, strict ways of high society, and there is no doubt in my mind she was still birched at your age, if not by her father, then by the governess in charge. I have heard stories from the staff as well, to the nature of Wilson Bentley even taking a switch to his servants at times."

"My great-grandfather sounds like he was a most dreadful and horrible man."

"I believe it was more about being disciplined and proper, at least by society's standards." He narrowed his eyes. "Don't you recall what Lucinda Collins said? Your own grandmother was beaten when she expressed a desire to travel to America to teach."

She gasped. Bad enough she witnessed little Clarissa Jones's discipline, but to imagine her grandmother receiving the same at an older age was unthinkable. "But I am not Kaylena's daughter. She has no right to—"

"She has every right," he interrupted. "Kaylena Bentley is now your legal guardian. You will live beneath her roof until you are wed, that makes you her responsibility. Therefore you must at all times obey her rules, and if you don't, she has every right to take you to task in any way she deems fit."

Sunny was beginning to like the ogre idea more and more. "The woman, at this point cannot even take care of herself, how she would be able to...to—"

Again, he interrupted. "That is why Flossy and Helga Grant have been sent for. They will become the watchful eyes your aunt no longer possesses, and the guiding hand you will obey."

She gasped again. "And do you also believe in such measures, Reverend?"

"Nay, my family was not as rigid in their ideas as the Bentleys. I was brought up on words of wisdom, encouragement, prayer, and explanations instead of the rod."

She chewed on her bottom lip. "Learning of this is most disturbing to me."

He reached forward to pat her hand. "If you remember your place at all times you'll have nothing to fear." His blue eyes twinkled along with his teasing words. "But if you are anything like your mother, whom I dare say was not corrected much in any form once your grandmother passed away, you'd better get used to sitting upon a pillow."

She shifted in her seat. "I think I should very much like to get back to the subject at hand." Sunny frowned. "Since you have strongly pointed out it would be very unwise for me to rid Aunt Kaylena of her firewater, perhaps you could do the deed for me."

"Nay, that would be another unwise idea."

"Why so? She dare not thrash your bottom."

He threw his head back and laughed. "Aye, she dare not, but she could have me thrown in confinement for robbery."

Her eyes widened. "She would not do such a thing to a dear friend as you!"

"Aye, she would, my dear. Someone who depends on the drink, like Kaylena now does, would not think twice about calling the authorities, even on an old friend." He shook his head. "I'm afraid only the head of the house could make such a move and get away with it."

"Gabriel...Gabriel is the head of the household now. I heard Aunt Kaylena claim him so last night at dinner," she said, new hope rising in her heart at a way to help her aunt. "She said he was the next heir to Bentwood Manor and the new head of the household. She has already decided to move money into an account for him, so he can handle all the manor's affairs."

"Aye, then Gabriel is well within his legal right to confiscate the spirits and not allow more to be purchased," he agreed. "But could he be counted on?"

"Yes, if anyone knows the consequences of drinking the firewater it is Gabriel. I have no doubt he will help me on this matter." She smiled and relaxed back in her chair. "Then all I will have to do is be there to care for my aunt during the times she is not allowed a drop to drink."

"Which will not be easy," he warned.

She had seen the outcome in her tribe of those addicted to spirits. "I am well aware of the course, Reverend."

He searched her face, taking in each one of her features with adoring eyes. "You remind me so much of Amanda...smart, willful...and..." the rest of the sentence died on his tongue.

"All these years and she is still so vivid in your thoughts?"

His tone softened. "Aye, that she is."

"Were you in love with my mother, Reverend?" she whispered.

There was a long pause. Josh opened his mouth to speak, but turned away instead, stood, and walked to the window. He gazed out at the front lawn. "I suppose, since you are so much like her, only an honest answer will suffice."

"On that you are correct."

"I should not admit this to you, being Amanda's daughter by your father's seed, but I see no further point in denying it." He sighed. "Aye, I was very much in love with your mother at one time."

"And are you still?"

He turned her way, his blue gaze locking with hers. An awkward silence lasted only a moment, yet it seemed like an eternity as she waited for his reply. But she was not about to hear that answer, for just as Josh opened his mouth to speak, Kaylena Bentley entered the room.

****

Before Sunny was dismissed from the library, by a sharp clap of her aunt's hands as though she were a small child, Kaylena shared news of Olga and Flossy Grant. It seemed the two sisters would not be arriving as planned, due to a family crisis. Though she never wished ill on anyone, she was very thankful for the delay and shared a look of relief with the reverend. Without the harsh and watchful eyes of a strict governess and tutor, she would be able to help her aunt eliminate the drinking habit much better, especially when Gabriel was too busy to be around. And with his project to make Bentwood's entrance safer to travel, there was not a doubt in her mind she would be the main person by Kaylena's side.

When Gabriel and Rafe returned from town, she met them in the foyer. They looked tired, dusty, hungry, and thirsty from their day-long trip, yet she dared not wait a moment longer to explain her plan. "Please, will you both join me a moment in the parlor? I have a family matter I wish to discuss."

Rafe's corn-flower blue eyes deepened with his

frown. "I am sure, Sunny Beth, this personal matter should only be conferred upon between you and your brother."

"No, I wish you to hear what I have to say as well," she said, and not waiting for him to protest, she reached for Gabriel's hand and led him into the parlor.

Gabriel plopped down exhausted upon a chair. "And this truly cannot wait until I have cleaned up and had something to drink?"

She narrowed her eyes. "And just what kind of drink were you expecting?"

He looked at her as if she had gone mad. "What are you up to now, *dayden*?"

She sighed, hating being called a little girl and hoped Rafe did not remember the translation of the Apache word. "Aunt Kaylena is never going to stop drinking the firewater if it is freely about the place."

Gabriel chuckled. "I can hardly wait to hear how you will remedy this problem."

"Oh, not I, but you," she said.

"And how will I remedy the problem?" Gabriel countered.

"You will remove every ounce of the firewater from the house."

He frowned. "I do not like that idea so much, Sunny Beth."

"Yes, well, that is too bad, my brother," she snapped, glancing briefly at Rafe. He stifled a smile and turned his gaze out the window. Looking back at her brother, whose brows now arched with defiance, she continued. "If we are to help Aunt Kaylena, this is the only way I see it happening." She shrugged. "If there is nothing for her to drink, then she cannot get drunk."

Rafe, still looking out the window, cleared his throat. "She has a point."

"Then she can rid the place of the spirits,"

Gabriel said, stretching his legs out before him and clasping his hands behind his head.

"No, I cannot," she snapped again.

"And why not?" her brother probed.

"Because Aunt Kaylena can...she will..." Her face heated. How could she share the real reason she could not do the job without embarrassing herself in front of both men? And she was sure Gabriel would love the opportunity to tease her in some humiliating way, since he threatened at times to give her a sound paddling himself.

It was then the captain turned her way, coming to her rescue yet another time. In his gaze there was an immediate understanding of her dilemma. "You are the head of the household, Gabriel. The task must be done by you."

She sighed, relieved for the reprieve. "He is right, my brother. And you also need to make sure no further purchase of the spirits is made until Aunt Kaylena has this problem under control."

Gabriel nodded in agreement and stood. "Then I had better get to ordering the clean up before dinner, which is when she drinks the most."

She bit her bottom lip. "This is not going to be a pleasant evening, is it?"

"I have a feeling it will be the first of many unpleasant evenings," Gabriel mumbled on his way out the door.

She turned her attention to Rafe, still standing by the window. "*Ashoge*, thank you once again for your help."

His expressive face was almost somber. "Will you promise me one thing, Sunny Beth?"

"It depends on what that one thing is, Captain." He walked to her, and she breathed him in, citrus and wool filling her senses. Drawn now into the rich blue of his eyes, she was compelled to place the palm of her hand upon his chest. Beneath his jacket hard muscle met her tender touch, the beat of his heart quickening as his glance came to rest upon her lips.

His voice shook. "Promise me if anyone should lay so much as a finger upon your person, you will tell me."

Sunny, now unable to say a word, managed a nod.

"I don't care why or what the reason, just that you tell me," he repeated. Then he added, "I want to know."

"Why, Captain, why do you want to know?" she whispered, her heart racing now as fast as his.

"Because I shall then have to kill them," he said, with a spark of some indefinable emotion in his eyes. Taking an abrupt step back, he turned on his heels and left the room.

Chapter Twenty-Five

Well, now Rafe had really done it, frightened the poor woman out of her wits. After his declaration of murder, Sunny's seductive young body stiffened, sapphire eyes widening with astonishment.

What the bloody hell did I think would happen?

Combing a hand through his hair, he made his way to the gardens, running the length of the lawn and not stopping until he reached an overgrown glade of bushes. There he leaned against a tree to catch his breath, inhaling the crisp, fall air.

What possessed him?

She's possessed me, has from the moment I set eyes on her, with the tilt of her head, the pout of her mouth, now the hand upon my chest. Good God he still felt it there, the heat of her tender palm searing him to the very core of his being.

But, in spite of regretting the fear he caused her, Rafe meant every word of what he said. He would kill anyone that touched her, whether to harm her or not. And realizing this now scared the hell out of him; because it wasn't supposed to be this way. It was what he did to protect Deandra and it all blew up in his face. Now he wanted none of this sort of thing again, not one shred of any woman owning his heart and soul to the degree that he no longer had his own goals in focus. The problem was Sunny Beth Eagle wasn't just any woman. And for that very reason alone he should leave. In fact, he wanted to leave Bentwood Manor and never set foot on Brighton's shores again, but that wasn't going to happen. He'd stick around with the pretext of helping Gabriel, but instead he'd be watching her...protecting her...keep anyone from touching her.

You are a sick bastard, Rafe Cavendish, he silently admonished himself, swallowing hard the distinct feeling it wasn't going to get any better.

****

Sunny's heart raced, her face heated, and her mouth went dry. What was wrong with her? What compelled her to touch him? This was not Arizona, nor her village. The women in England did not touch men so freely or make the first gesture to show an interest. She had heard this from Collette and Lady Abbott, why had it not sunk into her pig head? And why would she want to show Rafe she was interested in him anyway, when clearly she was not? Her brother's warning the captain liked women, many women, and used them for his pleasure, spun to mind. Why on earth would she want such a man? Even worse, why would she encourage such a man to notice her?

She bit her bottom lip, becoming upset over the idea of his many conquests, though it was none of her business. Why did it bother her? Why did she care?

She made her way to a chair and buried her face into her hands, ashamed of herself for the outward display of affection. She wished she could disappear entirely. How would she ever face Rafe at dinner? The memory of the way he stepped away from her made her cringe.

What must he be thinking of me?

Well, it was too late to worry about that now. With a sigh, she rose from her seat and made her way to the dining room. Perhaps with Aunt Kaylena's expected outburst at learning the spirits in the house have been removed, the focus would be off her and the stupid and silly mistake she had made. She must remember to keep her hands to herself, even if that meant sitting on them.

This is England and not Arizona, she mentally reminded herself again, then squared her shoulders to face the evening's ordeal.

And an ordeal it was, with Kaylena ranting and raving at Gabriel. Sunny felt guilty her brother took the brunt for her idea.

"Aunt Kaylena, we are only trying to help you," Gabriel said, attempting to calm the elder woman.

"When I need your help, I shall ask," Kaylena snapped. "Until then I thank you to mind your own business."

"This is my business," Gabriel countered. "As the acting head of the house, everything that goes on beneath its roof directly concerns me."

"I can remedy that, nephew, by simply removing you from your post," Kaylena spat.

"Perhaps that is true, if you were capable of making clear and sound decisions," Gabriel said.

"I am capable of doing both," Kaylena shrieked.

"Not at the present," Gabriel challenged. "Not while you continue to drink. So the position will have to rest on my shoulders."

Kaylena picked up a china figurine from a nearby shelf and threw it across the room. Sunny jumped as the delicate ornament crashed to the floor and shattered into pieces.

Stomping a foot, like a child having a temper tantrum, Kaylena screamed at the top of her lungs. "I am thirsty. I want a drink. I need something to drink, now!"

Gabriel forced his voice to remain calm. "Sunny, go to the kitchen and ask Bertha to bring in a tray of tea."

Kaylena shot an angry glare her way. "You will tell her instead to bring in the wine, Sunny."

She glanced at Gabriel for further direction.

He motioned for her to stay put before confronting their aunt. "I have already explained to you there is not a drop of wine, brandy, or ale anywhere in this house, Aunt Kaylena. I have removed every ounce." He inclined his head politely. "So, if you are in need of something to drink, I will go myself to ask Bertha to bring in a tray of tea."

"But I do not want the tea," Kaylena said through gritted teeth.

"Then I will tell Bertha we are ready for dinner," Gabriel said, the muscles at his jaw throbbing. Their father did the same when trying to control his anger.

"I'm not hungry either," Kaylena said, folding her arms in front of her.

Gabriel combed a hand through his hair. "Then perhaps it would be best for you to go up to your room and rest a while. I will have Greta bring you up a tray later."

"Nay, I shan't rest either," she challenged.

"Ah, but you will, Aunt Kaylena, because I will not have you screaming in my face any longer." Gabriel said, reaching for the elder woman, tossing her over his shoulder like a sack of flour, and making his way to the staircase. "Cirie, Gerta," he called out.

The two women came into the foyer so quickly Sunny knew they must have been nearby and listening. Wringing their hands in front of them, their eyes widened as Kaylena pounded on Gabriel's shoulders and demanded her release.

Gabriel ignored her command, acting unaffected by the abuse upon his back. "I want you to give my aunt a hot bath, help her into her nightwear, and then bring her a dinner tray." He turned toward Sunny. "You are to take your dinner with her as well, and not leave her side until she is asleep."

She nodded, not daring to upset her brother further, and also relieved she would not have to face

Rafe for the rest of the evening.

But just as Gabriel was about to carry Kaylena up the stairs, Rafe came into the foyer. His arched brow and quizzical expression was almost comical. Had it been any other time, she would have easily burst into a giggling fit. Neither of them spoke as she passed him, but she felt his eyes on her as she followed her brother and the other women up the stairs.

Gabriel's booted feet marched down the hallway to Kaylena's room, Gerta running ahead to open the door. Once inside, he placed their aunt upon the bed, looking down at her for a moment before he spoke. "I am doing my best to help you, because that is what family does for each other. Sunny and I are your family, and we are here to get you through whatever troubles you." He sighed. "Now, I ask for you to bathe, eat, and have a good rest, my aunt."

"I will do anything but rest, and it is entirely your fault," she shrieked as he made his way to the door and closed it behind him.

Sunny approached the bed. "Come, Aunt Kaylena, let me help you undress."

"I don't want to undress, I am perfectly happy clothed," Kaylena retorted.

"Please, let me make you more comfortable," she persisted, leaning down to unbutton Kaylena's blouse. "I only want to help you."

"I don't want or need your help," Kaylena spat, then raised a hand and slapped Sunny hard across the face.

Shocked, she stumbled back, her cheek stinging from the blow.

Cirie gasped, running to her aid. "Oh, miss, are ye all right?" She caressed Sunny's burning cheek. "Let me get a cool compress for ye."

By now her eyes watered with the pain, but she swallowed hard and shook her head. "I am fine,

Cirie."

"Sunny, I am so...so very..." Kaylena stammered. With a hand over her heart, the elder woman broke into sobs. "I have hurt my own family, my dear Sunny who only wants to help me. What is wrong with me? What is happening to me?"

Sunny went to her aunt and knelt down beside the bed. "All is well, Aunt," she said, embracing Kaylena's frail body.

"Can you ever forgive me?" Kaylena moaned, bending her head to rest on Sunny's shoulder. "It seems I have hurt yet another."

"There is nothing to forgive." She pulled back to look into her aunt's eyes, they were the same deep sapphire orbs as her mother's, etched now with sorrow and fear. "Let us get you into a hot bath to soak and fill you with nourishment." Sunny forced a smile. "Then suppose you tell me about the letter."

"Aye," Kaylena whispered and allowed Gerta and Cirie to undress her.

Chapter Twenty-Six

Sunny sat at the edge of her aunt's bed. Now calm from her bath and well fed, Kaylena Bentley lay comfortably back against the pillows.

"Are you feeling better, Aunt?"

"Aye," Kaylena said, stifling a yawn. "Though I hate to admit it, your brother prescribed just what I needed." She frowned. "How is it he would know this?"

She sighed, not wanting to divulge Gabriel's personal business, but they were asking just that of her, so all was fair.

Kaylena listened intently as Sunny explained to her the death of her brother's family and his drinking to forget.

Tears filled Kaylena's eyes. "How horrible for him. And I understand such grief, even though Wesley and I were only engaged when he was killed." She sighed and confessed. "Drinking only lets you forget for the moment, and I'm glad Gabriel found that out."

"Do you realize this fact, too, Aunt?"

Kaylena nodded. "But why did he order the bath and food?"

"In our village we have a little hut built by the river we call the sweat bath. Inside the hut there are heated rocks placed in a circle, and when cool water is poured over them, steam fills the hut. Sitting in the steam not only cleanses the flesh, but the spirit as well. All ailments and troubles seem to leave, and a fresh outlook replaces the old. Then a jump into the cold river water clears the senses and strengthens the body. After partaking in a meal, a person is again ready to face what comes their way." She smiled. "I am sure this is what Gabriel had in mind when he ordered a hot bath and a meal for you."

Kaylena cocked her head sideways. "Do you think Gabriel would be able to build such a sweat bath hut here at Bentwood Manor?"

She shrugged. "I do not see it being all that difficult. Why?"

"People come to Brighton from miles around for cleansing treatments. I was just thinking, if Gabriel could build a sweat bath near the water, a hut for the ladies and another for the men, at different ends of the channel to insure privacy, we could offer something unique, have quite a lucrative business."

Sunny's spirits brightened at the hope of her aunt having a new project to keep her busy. "I think Gabriel would love such a venture."

"Would you talk to him for me?" Kaylena asked.

Sunny nodded. "If you would do something for me in return?"

Kaylena chuckled. "Aye."

"Send word to the Grant sisters that their services are no longer needed."

Kaylena frowned. "But who would tutor you for your début? Who would govern you?"

"You, Aunt Kaylena. You can teach me all I need to know and be my guardian."

"Oh, I don't know, Sunny," Kaylena began to protest. "It's been many years since I was a girl readying for my own coming out. After all, I'm hitting sixty in a few years."

She leaned forward and took her aunt's hand. "You said I was like the daughter you never had, am I right?'

Kaylena smiled. "Aye, and I know she'd be just like you."

"Then be there for me. Take me shopping for the right clothes and shoes; teach me how to speak French and all the other things I need to learn. The two of us can work together, like a real mother and daughter. Besides, your age has nothing whatsoever to do with a thing. My people believe a person's age is only the number of years they've lived on earth and nothing at all to do with how their spirit feels."

"You would really like me to teach you, Sunny?"

"Yes, very much," she said. "Will you do it for me?"

A broad smile spread Kaylena's full lips. "I would be honored."

Since they were meeting on common ground, she felt it a good time to approach her aunt about the letter, which had started the drinking in the first place.

"Now, please Aunt Kaylena, tell me about the letter you received that upset you so."

Kaylena's face fell. "It is a long story, my dear."

Sunny slipped off her shoes and climbed in bed beside her aunt; resting her head on her shoulder as she sometimes did with her mother. "I have all the time in the world to listen."

Kaylena sighed. "Very well then, it all begins many years ago, when I journeyed to America to visit your mother."

"After great-grandpa Wilson died?"

"Aye, he would have never allowed me to go if he were alive," she admitted. "After losing Amelia to her travels and my mother to a fever, he kept a tight hold on me. In fact, he treated me like a child. I had to eat when he said, dress the way he said, go to bed when he said, and I was never allowed to be alone in the house."

"But surely he knew you would one day leave him, after all you were engaged to be married."

"Papa never knew of my plans to wed. Wesley

was the gardener's son, my best friend and playmate since I was a child. We shared laughter and tears, and as we grew our moments together turned to stolen kisses and promises of a future together. Papa would have thrown a fit if he knew of my feelings for a commoner, a servant's child. That was the main reason Wesley joined the military. He believed, once he was established in the Royale Navy, he'd return in uniform and ask Papa for my hand. So we secretly got engaged, pledging our love and loyalty to one another, and then he left me to deal with my father until he returned." She inhaled sharply. "And Wilson Bentley's wrath at times was unbearable to endure."

She snuggled closer. "Did he beat you, Aunt Kaylena?"

Her tone was sad, resigned. "Every chance he could get for whatever reason he could find. The punishment he bestowed was degrading, humiliating, and painful."

"And not one person working here at Bentwood put a halt to this abuse?"

"Nay, they all feared him, because Papa beat the help as well." Kaylena covered her face with her hands. "But I do believe if Wesley had known about the beatings and the nature in which they were given, he would have killed my father for his despicable actions."

Sunny's heart went out to her aunt.

She could not imagine having a father as cruel as Wilson Bentley, especially since her own was so loving and kind. Though she was punished and disciplined for bad behavior, neither her father nor mother ever raised a hand to strike her. Both were nurturing and wise in how they reared their children, teaching them all the skills and wisdom they knew.

She rose from the bed and poured her aunt a glass of water from the bedside pitcher, handing it to her. "Drink this."

Kaylena obeyed, then wiped her eyes with the backs of her hands before she continued her story. "We planned on eloping when he returned from his duties, but that never happened because he was killed in action. When I got the news, I couldn't even mourn him properly at the burial for fear of drawing my father's attention."

She climbed back upon the bed. "I am so sorry you had to go through all of this."

"After Papa died, all I had left was my handmaid, Aggie. She and I shared an unusual bond. When I was unable to stand the whippings further, Aggie would take my place."

Sunny gasped. Her great-grandfather was truly a disturbed person.

"The house felt so large and desolate, I rattled about in it," Kaylena went on. "Then the will was read, and I discovered everything was left to my sister, Amelia. Even after Papa heard of her death, he didn't change his affairs to include me, so everything then went to Amelia's daughter, Amanda." She inhaled sharply. "He left me penniless and homeless."

"So, it was then you traveled to visit my mother?"

"Aye, I hadn't a choice after all the wild stories I heard about pioneer America. I was sure this child named Amanda wasn't receiving the proper care. I had no idea what sort of man my sister married, and I didn't want Amanda brought up by a man's hand."

"Like you were, Aunt Kaylena?"

"Aye, so I planned to bring her back to Brighton and educate her in the ways of a suitable lady."

"And perhaps she would let you continue to live at Bentwood," she concluded.

"Aye, that was one reason, but mainly my first thought was to save my sister's child...the only family I had left in the world." Kaylena arranged the quilt over her sagging bosom. "But everything from the start went terribly wrong."

She frowned. "How did things go wrong?"

"I first encountered a problem traveling from England to America due to the war there between the northern and southern states." Kaylena frowned.

Sunny nodded. "You speak of the Civil War."

"Aye, and because of this fighting, British ships couldn't get through the north's blockade of the southern parts. Had I sailed from New York, the war would have prevented me from getting around the southern territory."

She frowned. "So, how did you get through?"

"The only solution was to travel to Holland and sail on a Dutch ship to New Orleans, the one southern area controlled by the North," Kaylena explained further. "Aggie, who accompanied me against her better judgment, and I spent the holidays aboard that dank ship filled with illness. Instead of Christmas cheer and glad tidings for a new year, passengers were crying over their dead as they were thrown overboard. But the last straw was losing Aggie. The poor woman succumbed to pneumonia and was laid to rest in her own watery grave in the middle of the Atlantic Ocean."

She felt her aunt's loss as though it were her own. "How awful for you, Aunt Kaylena."

"If not for the administrations of a young clergyman by the name of Benjamin Newcomb, I would have also become ill," Kaylena whispered.

Sunny arched a brow. "You know our Reverend Ben?"

Kaylena's eyes widened. "You mean he's still in Willow Creek?"

She nodded. "He married Grace's niece, Sylvie, and they have a grown daughter, named Sarah Joy. She is married and the mother of five children. They all live in Montana."

Kaylena smiled. "Then he's done well for himself and is happy?"

"He seems to be, always teasing and hugging Sylvie, played with Sarah Joy lots when she was little. He also smiles and laughs with my people whenever he brings supplies to the village."

Kaylena giggled. "I remember Grace. She was a cantankerous old biddy with a good heart,"

She giggled, too. "That is Grace, for sure. I did not know her for as long as Gabriel because she died when I was seven."

"I shall always be thankful for Ben. He was a Godsend aboard that ship," Kaylena reflected. "He approached me the night Aggie died. I was prostrate with grief, walking the deck of the ship tormented. I was so sheltered, treated like a child all of my life, that I didn't know the first thing about being away from home, let alone on my own. I was so afraid and so grief-stricken, I wasn't able to eat or sleep. Ben stayed by my side to comfort me, coaxing me to take nourishment and holding me when I sobbed. He became a constant companion while we sailed."

"What was Reverend Ben's reason for being on the ship?"

"He was traveling to California to establish a church in one of the bustling boom towns of the gold rush area. I told him, if he was anywhere near Willow Creek, Arizona, to look me up. Surprisingly enough that's just what he did, after his plans in California fell through." Kaylena shook her head. "I knew he took over for Josh, when he decided to chaplain the church in Brighton, but I had no idea he stayed on."

"What happened when you docked?" Sunny probed.

Kaylena took a moment to secure a more comfortable position against the pillows. "I had to catch a wagon train to Arizona." She wrinkled her nose in disdain. "Most uncomfortable things, those wagons, with only wooden planks for seats," she remembered. "I couldn't help but believe Americans had a lot to learn about travel. Were I in England, riding in style in my own coach, my lower posterior would be well cushioned upon a plush seat, and I would be journeying over cobblestone streets instead of the abominable, choppy land that loomed ahead." She sighed. "I remember thinking my poor sister, Amelia succumbed to a fever in this God-forsaken country. Then I prayed I arrived in time to save her daughter."

Sunny tried to stifle a yawn, but her aunt noticed.

"It grows late; perhaps we could finish our talk tomorrow?" Kaylena suggested.

Afraid her aunt's willingness to explain about the letter would fade if prolonged, Sunny lied. "I am fine, Aunt Kaylena, if you are."

Kaylena nodded in agreement and continued to speak. "I watched the young, handsome lieutenant as he supervised the loading of my baggage. Against my better judgment, I had been convinced to leave a trunk behind. Ryan Duffy spared me nary a gruesome detail when he explained the essential need to travel light over the untamed land we were to embark upon. In fact, I believe he rather enjoyed watching my horror-stricken expression as he boasted he 'always got his man'."

Sunny knew Lieutenant Ryan Duffy's name well. He was the white lawman who had almost hung Proud Eagle, and would have succeeded if it were not for the courage of her mother and Reverend Holmes. "He did not get my father."

Kaylena arched a brow. "Ah, I see you know of the man and his tactics concerning Indians."

"My parents have told the story to us all, but I

wish you to continue yours."

"I watched him intently that first day of travel, riding ahead of the wagon train." Kaylena's cheeks flushed. "And I must admit Ryan Duffy fascinated me. The mischievous twinkle in his amber eyes made him dashingly handsome as well."

"He was a rogue," Sunny said.

"Aye, his mannerisms were crude, but I supposed one had to be unconventional to cope with the Indians, to fight and win against such savages."

She bit her bottom lip to remain silent. *Not all of them were savages.* She lowered her gaze. "It is hard hearing of Ryan Duffy's attributes when I know of the hatred he held for my father and his people."

Kaylena lifted her chin with a finger. "Then I think it would be best we stop here for now."

She began to protest, but the elder woman raised a hand for her silence.

"However, I do have something I think you should read." Kaylena reached over and opened the night table drawer, pulling out a journal. She handed the worn, leather covered volume to Sunny. "Read what I wrote of that time and on the morrow I will explain what it all has to do with the letter I received months ago."

She frowned. "But my brother asked that I stay with you till you fell asleep."

"Gerta will stay with me." Kaylena tapped the journal's cover with the tip of a finger. "You go now to your room and read this...every last page. Then, I promise, we'll talk further in the morning."

Sunny finally agreed, giving her aunt a kiss upon the forehead and making her way to the door.

"Oh, and Sunny," Kaylena called after her.

She turned, locking eyes with her aunt.

"There is one thing I might ask of you?"

She nodded. "I am listening."

"Please, after you've read my words, I would ask

that...that you..." Kaylena hesitated.

"Yes, yes, go on," she encouraged.

Kaylena sighed. "That you not judge me too harshly."

Chapter Twenty-Seven

Sunny ran to her room, lit a lantern, and stoked the fire before she undressed and climbed into bed. With pillows stacked at her back and legs bent beneath the quilt, she began to read her aunt's journal that was now balanced upon her knees.

Winter, 1864:

I sat as proper and straight in my traveling suit, as any lady could upon that hard wooden plank of a seat, all the while my bum aching for the plush comforts of an English coach. And while I thought of home, I watched the handsome Lieutenant Duffy supervise the loading of the wagons.

The younger soldier, Private Alexander Thomas, introduced himself to me earlier. Timid and shy, his sun burnt, freckled face almost as red as the flaming locks upon his head, was not as confident as the lieutenant. But I found his boyish charm refreshing.

Mounting his horse, Ryan Duffy rode up beside my wagon, doffed his hat in greeting, smiled, and spoke with a twang. "We're about ready to roll, ma'am...just waiting on Abe Hollister. He'll be driving your wagon and should be along shortly."

I smiled and thanked him, then I watched him ride to the head of the wagon train, broad shoulders filling the dark blue shirt of his uniform, torso tapering to a slim waist, tight breeches clinging to muscular thighs, and my heart quivered. Sheltered as I was in this life, I had no idea how the elements of such a man could drive my insides to havoc.

Sunny inhaled sharply as her own heart raced. She was guilty of the same thoughts. Noticing Rafe in such a way gave her the same unexplained pleasure. Clearing her throat, she continued reading.

Private Thomas rode up beside me just then, and grateful for the interruption, I gladly accepted the flask he handed me.

His western drawl was much cruder than the lieutenant's. "Here ya go, ma'am, a canteen of water in case ya get thirsty."

When I smiled and thanked him for his kindness, he cast his green eyes to the ground. Good heavens, he couldn't be more than seventeen if he was a day. "Your mother must miss you."

His gaze then met mine. "I reckon she does, ma'am."

"Do you write her?" I probed.

He wrinkled his freckled nose into a childish squint. "I'm not much for writin', bein' a poor speller and all." He shrugged. "Don't make no difference, since Ma can't read none anyhow."

The thought of not being able to read and write was appalling to me, but I kept my opinion to myself, and politely inclined my head when he tipped his hat and rode ahead, taking his place beside Lieutenant Duffy.

A moment later I almost tumbled off the seat when Abe Hollister's large, bulky frame plopped down beside me. I gripped the edge of the wagon to keep my balance.

Abe tipped his sweat-stained cowboy's hat and smiled. "Howdy, ma'am.

I nodded. "Good day, Mr. Hollister."

His smile broadened. "Shucks, ma'am, there ain't no call for ya to be standin' on formality with me. I'm just an ornery cuss drivin' a wagon." He chuckled. "If I get too ornery, ya just feel free to put me in my place. Deal?"

I nodded. "Aye, sir."

"And none of this sir stuff either, just Abe will do," he said, taking the reins.

I nodded again, arranging the brim of the bonnet I wore to keep the sun off my face.

Ryan Duffy shouted, "Wagons, ho," from his position at the front of the line, and we were off...my backside bouncing on the wooden seat. Within an hour's time my entire body ached.

The pain must have shown upon my face because Abe pulled the wagon to a stop, demanding I climb to the back of it and lay down. But the lack of ventilation caused the perspiration to trickle between my breasts, leaving my flesh moist and sticky.

I slipped off the enormous weight of my petticoat, as well as the jacket, and after unfastening the first three buttons on my blouse and rolling up the sleeves, the ride became bearable. I was able to lie down and fall asleep, but woke with a start several hours later to the smell of coffee and the sound of men's laughter.

Nightfall chilled the wagon, and I shivered as I fixed my blouse and donned my jacket. The bite of the night air slapped me in the face when I opened the back flap and climbed down from the wagon.

I walked the length of two wagons, following the smell of wood smoke, before I came to the campfire and the men gathered around it, laughing and talking over coffee. They stopped their playful banter when I approached, their silence making my entry all the more awkward.

I buttoned my jacket. "My wagon has taken on quite a chill." Then I motioned to the fire. "If you gentlemen don't mind, I'll just warm myself for a bit before I return."

Private Thomas then stood and offered me the crate he was seated upon. I smiled and thanked him. Again he cast a shy glance at his feet and mumbled, "My pleasure, ma'am."

Sunny smiled as her mind's eye pictured Private

Thomas and his shy, timid ways. Her mother had told her about the young soldier, and how she and Grace tricked him into helping Proud Eagle. Rolling onto her side, she placed a hand beneath her cheek, and read further.

Abe Hollister stood and went to a pot hanging over the fire. He filled a bowl with stew, grabbed a piece of bread, and brought the meal to me. "I saved ya some grub, ma'am," he drawled. "It ain't nothin' more than a potato stew, but it'll stick to ya ribs and take the chill from ya bones."

I accepted the man's generosity with a warm smile and thanked him, as I was quite famished at that. As I balanced the bowl upon my knees, I glanced around for utensils.

"Whatcha lookin' for, ma'am?" Abe asked, pouring himself another cup of coffee.

"Just wondering where there might be a spoon I could use, Abe."

The other men broke into hearty laughter at my request and I felt the heat rise to my face.

"I find nothing amusing in the lady's question," snapped a voice from behind.

I turned to see Lieutenant Duffy standing relaxed against a wagon, void of his uniform jacket, shirt unbuttoned to the waist and sleeves rolled to his forearm. His hair was wet and slicked back, the honey colored strands ending in a row of curls at his nape, and his face freshly shaved.

He knelt down beside me, my senses filling with his clean, spicy scent, and took the bread from my hand. "May I, ma'am?"

I nodded, not quite knowing what I agreed to.

He then broke a piece and dipped it into the bowl. "You use the bread to scoop the stew," he explained, securing a potato. "And eat it like this," he concluded, popping it into my mouth. Sitting back on his haunches, he smiled. "That's all there is to it, ma'am."

I looked at the bread and the bowl of stew, then glanced around to all the eyes staring at me, waiting for me to try.

Lieutenant Duffy broke another piece of bread and handed it to me. "As crude as it is, Miss Bentley, you'd better learn or else you're gonna starve while we're out here." His amber eyes gleamed with a devilish glint. "I may not always be around to feed you."

The other men chuckled at that last remark.

An unwelcome blush crept into my cheeks, not to mention the pang of hunger piercing my stomach. It was then I nodded, took a deep breath, and accepted the broken piece of bread the lieutenant held. Dipping it into the gravy, as he'd shown me, I captured a potato and brought it to my mouth. It slipped off the bread, dropping back into the bowl and splashing gravy onto my skirt.

"Get a little more of a twistin' action goin' on with ya wrist, Miss Kaylena," Alexander suggested.

"And be quicker with bringin' it up to ya mouth," Abe added.

I nodded, squared my shoulders and dipped the bread once again into the bowl, securing a potato. Determined this time to get it all the way to my mouth, I lowered my head to meet my hand, then popped the food passed my lips. As I chewed triumphantly, all the men cheered.

After a cup of coffee the consistency of mud, the men passed around something stronger to drink. I politely declined, and knew I had overstepped my welcome when they began to sing bawdy songs. Excusing myself, I stood to leave and accepted the lieutenant's offer to walk me back to my own wagon. It was then he asked me to call him Ryan. I agreed and asked him where I might bathe, since I could feel the grit forming on my flesh.

He gestured to a clump of trees. "Yonder, in the creek, but you must wait until nightfall." A slow, easy smile spread his lips, amber eyes locking with mine. He was handsome in a rugged sort of way, and I felt my pulse quicken. "Sorry to say there isn't a maid out here to draw you a hot bath."

I questioned his advice. "Isn't night bathing rather dangerous, with the hostiles roaming about and all? One never knows if one could be lurking."

"Exactly, it's what Injuns do best…lurk. But they won't attack at night." He leaned a shoulder against my wagon. "And I'd never allow you to go off alone." I gasped and he chuckled. "You ain't got anything I haven't already seen before."

I folded my arms across my chest, annoyed. "I'm sure that's true, Lieutenant, however…"

He moved closer. "Call me Ryan, ma'am," he interrupted.

I fought to keep my composure. "However, Ryan," I continued, "I must insist we find a more appropriate solution."

He leaned forward, pushing aside a wisp of hair that fell across my forehead, and looping it behind my ear. "You listen to me good, little lady. I've been assigned to see that your pretty hide gets to Willow Creek safe and sound, and that's what I'm gonna do. So, appropriate or not, if you need to bathe, you do it with me and my rifle standing guard." He arched a brow. "And that's an order."

My voice shook with frustration. "You are an abominable man, Lieutenant."

He stepped back. "Ryan, ma'am, call me Ryan." Then he smiled. "And let me give you one more word of advice before I leave you." He glanced down at my feet, then back up to my eyes. "I wouldn't stay out here too long if I were you."

Exasperated, I sighed. "And why is that, Ryan?"

"Snakes, ma'am…these parts are noted for

them."

I shrieked and climbed into the wagon, sitting in the dark and fuming as I heard him laughing all the way back to the campfire.

There was a break in the writing at this point; several ink-drawings filling the pages that followed. Sunny admired the mini-portraits of Alexander Thomas, Abe Hollister, and Ryan Duffy. Kaylena's artwork was exceptional, and even though Sunny had no idea if each subject was drawn precisely, the pictures were still life-like. She smiled, realizing it was her aunt's talent she inherited.

As she turned each page, she lingered on the lieutenant's likeness, absorbing each and every feature, and looking deep into eyes that could not look back. Her aunt's assessment of the man was correct, he was ruggedly handsome. But after all the stories she had been told, she knew Ryan Duffy was deadly frightening as well...and putting a face to the name of the man that whipped her father, leaving permanent welts upon his back, and almost killed him made her shiver. She snuggled down deeper beneath the quilt and read on.

Ryan Duffy rode out daily to scout for Indians. One night he returned to camp and began securing boxes of supplies into a barrier around the wagons. I walked up behind him as he was placing the last crate in line, hoping to approach him about going to the creek to bathe. I wasn't at all satisfied with the way things were left a few nights previous, but by now my skin itched. Sensing a presence, he drew his gun and spun around to face me.

I shrieked and stepped back.

"Never, ever sneak up behind a soldier like that," he scolded. *"Or else you're sure to get your head blown off,"* he warned.

I took in the barricade. "What is the meaning of this?"

He replaced his weapon in the hip holster. "It's just a precaution."

Fear, raw and stark, filled every fiber of my being. "A precaution against what?"

"Indians."

I looked around. "Where?"

"In the canyon. I spotted a small band this morning, and I'm making sure they can't get any closer."

My voice climbed an octave. "And you believe this pitiful wall of supplies will keep them away?"

"It will add some protection."

My eyes widened with horror. "And what will add the rest?"

"I will."

When I opened my mouth to protest, he held up a hand.

"Now just calm yourself, ma'am. I've got everything under control, so there's no need for you to fret none. I know what I'm doing, trust me."

My frustration and fear mounted. "It appears I have no choice, Lieutenant."

"Call me Ryan," he again reminded me with a devilish grin. "Now, is there a reason you've come looking for me?"

I bit my bottom lip and looked down at the bar of soap and towel I held in my hand, hesitating with an answer. There was nothing more I wanted but to scrub the grit from my scalp and the dust encrusted on my flesh, but clearly the man had more pending things at hand than to take me to bathe. I sighed and raised my gaze to his. "Abe told me while we're traveling through Louisiana and Eastern Texas, there'd be places to bathe, but once we approach the Arizona territory that could change."

Ryan nodded in agreement. "Watering holes are less plentiful."

"Then I should probably bathe now, while I have

the chance." I eyed the barricade again. "However, I see this is not a good time to ask you for that escort."

His mischievous smile broadened. "Fact is, I've done all I can do for now, and I'd be right pleased to accompany you to your bath."

I had no doubts about that, but held my tongue and returned his smile with a timid one of my own.

He held out an elbow in gentlemanly fashion. "Shall we, ma'am?"

I inclined my head. "If that's how it has to be, then lead on."

Sunny's face heated. She still had trouble allowing Cirie to help her wash and dress; let alone tolerating a man watching her bathe.

The moon's reflection danced in the water, a light breeze rustled the treetops, and a lone owl hooted his song in the distance.

Sunny frowned...owls were bad omens.

Ryan walked me to the edge of the bank and then took a seat a few feet away, on a nearby rock with his rifle draped across his lap. I set the soap and towel aside and turned my back, humiliated to the roots of my hair, as I removed my jacket, blouse and skirt. I felt his eyes bore through me, and my flesh heated with embarrassment as I slipped off shoes, stockings, and petticoat. Quickly I reached for the soap and ran into the water, clad only in my chemise, thankful for the darkness.

I submerged myself completely, the shock of cold water making me shiver. My fingers trembled as I lathered my hands with the soap and scrubbed my scalp. The Jasmine scent transported me to the luxurious memory of soaking in a steamy tub, void of watchful eyes.

When I glanced his way, I noticed he hadn't twitched so much as a muscle, eyes riveted on my every move. After lathering my flesh, I dove beneath the water to rinse myself clean, and then emerged with a gasp. I pushed aside the long strands of hair clinging to my face and keeping a tight grasp on the slippery bar of soap, I ran to the riverbank where I'd left the towel.

He watched as I dried myself, a slow smile spreading across his handsome visage. "That garment clings to your every curve."

I looked down at myself and gasped. My cotton chemise had become transparent.

"Thanks to the light of the moon, your tiny waist is silhouetted, outlining your rounded hips and ample breast, teats ever so erect and tantalizing," he said in a seductive tone. "And it's all affording me a magnificent display of your womanly splendor."

I raised my eyes to lock with his. He wet his lips, put aside his rifle and stood. With a hand, he adjusted himself in his trousers.

"It's been a long time...too long, since my eyes feasted on a woman as fine as you." I covered myself with the towel, but in one fluid motion he was in front of me, taking it from my hands. "Don't cover such beauty."

My heart raced, my voice shook. "Please Ryan, I ask that you remember your place."

He set each of his hands on my shoulders, moving them to caress the expanse of my neck and cupping my chin. "I look at you, your body so beautifully exposed, and I can't help but believe this is my place."

Then he lowered his face and crushed my lips with his own, his tongue swirling and playing with the soft folds of my mouth. A whimper escaped my throat, and I attempted to break his hold. But he pulled me close, his embrace all encompassing, his kiss intensifying. I melted against him as he lowered me to the ground. When he removed my chemise, I don't know...nor when he rid himself of his own clothes. All I do remember is our nakedness, two bodies entwined, exploring and experiencing sensations I never dreamed possible. And it was there he took my maidenhood, or was it I who offered it willingly to him? It's hard to say now. All I do know is I had a great need for his arms to be around me, to feel his warmth, his touch, his body filling my own.

Later, as I took refuge in the wagon beneath a worn, scratchy blanket, head resting against my baggage, I remembered what Ryan had said, "I blame it on the wilderness. This vast, untamed land does strange things to a person's mind and soul, has a way of making you feel empty and small and so very alone." I knew the empty and alone feeling well, lived it daily for years after the loss of my fiancé, Wesley Hughes. But was that a reason to be immoral? Or was it just the wonderful sensations Ryan Duffy stirred within me that left me powerless to object? Although I loved Wesley, not even his kisses flamed my passion as Ryan's did.

I squeezed my eyes shut, ashamed of my behavior. How could I have permitted him to do what he did? My thoughts left me no peace, replaying the places I allowed him to touch with his hands, his fingers, his tongue and his..."Oh sweet heaven, I acted wanton," I whispered to myself. How was I ever to show my face come the morning? I pulled the blanket over my head, feeling scared, disappointed, and tired from the tragedy I'd endured on this journey, and wished I could dissolve and reappear in England. Curling myself into a ball on the floor of the wagon, tears slipped down my cold cheeks, wetting the blanket. I missed Aggie, I missed Brighton, and I missed my own bed.

There was no more written after that last entry. Sunny closed the diary and placed it on the bedside table, then reached over and turned down the lantern. In the darkness, her thoughts replayed all her aunt endured on her journey west. But what did any of it have to do with now? She knew Ryan Duffy was dead, and certainly Abe Hollister or Alexander Thomas would have no reason to send her aunt a threatening letter. She rolled onto her side, snuggling beneath the quilt...wishing for the morning to come so she could find out the rest of this mystery. Who was the man her aunt felt remorse over and why did she beg for his forgiveness?

Chapter Twenty-Eight

Sunny was up and partially dressed before Cirie arrived to assist in the usual morning routine. Anxious to learn the rest of her aunt's secret, she hardly slept a wink. Yawning, she washed and tied her hair back into the *nah-leen*, then slipped on stockings and shoes. Cirie entered just in time to button the back of the pale green day dress she chose.

"Yer nearly all dressed, miss," Cirie said as she fastened the last button.

She turned to face the other woman. "Is my aunt awake?"

"Aye, she is." Cirie frowned. "Gerta said she tossed most o' the night."

"That makes two of us."

Cirie's frown deepened. "I'm not sure 'ow pleasant she's going to be, miss."

"I will take my chances." Sunny reached for the journal and made her way toward the door. "Please have my breakfast tray brought to my aunt's room."

On her way to Kaylena's chamber she bumped into Gabriel. With both hands upon her shoulders he steadied her. "Whoa, *dayden*, where are you going in such a rush?"

She took a moment to catch her breath, and briefly explained about the journal.

Gabriel frowned as he took the old diary from her and leafed through the pages. His frowned deepened when he came upon the drawing of Ryan Duffy. "His face is strangely familiar to me."

She shrugged. "You know that is not possible,

my brother. He died long before you were even born."

He nodded. "Must be all the stories I've heard playing tricks on my eyes." He sighed. "I find it hard to gaze upon his face." He looked up at Sunny, the muscles at his jaw throbbing. "If he won his way, our father would be dead."

"I know, I thought of that as well."

He handed her back the journal. "I do not need a drawing to remind me of his existence, Sunny. The scars across father's back are enough of a reminder."

"I agree," she said, running a finger over the worn cover. "But as much as we would like to put all this behind us, what is written in this journal long ago has something directly to do with what is happening now." It was her time to sigh. "And that is what I am on my way to find out."

He nodded. "And you will come for me; tell me what you discover?"

"Yes, you have my word."

Gabriel nodded again and started for the staircase.

"Gabriel," she called after him.

He turned to look at her.

"I explained to Aunt Kaylena about the sweat bath in our village, and she would like you to build two for her, here at Bentwood."

He frowned. "Why?"

"She wants to open a health resort and believes folks will come to be cleansed. One dwelling she would like built by the water for the men and another, spaced far enough apart to ensure privacy, for the women. I figured after you cut down the trees and made the guard rail for the cliff, there might be some lumber left over to build the sweat baths."

His face brightened. "There will be more than enough wood." Then he neared her, picking her up, and swirling her around. "To build sweat baths is an excellent idea."

She giggled, wrapping an arm around his neck. "Why are you so pleased?"

He set her down and looked into her eyes. "Because I believe such a business venture will work here in Brighton. And not only will I build the bath huts, but I can fix up the east wing of the mansion for guests who wish to stay on a few days. We will have to hire more staff to assist them, but with the fee we will charge for the service we provide, there will be enough funds to pay for the extra help. Perhaps we can offer healthier foods, serve some of the dishes our people favor."

"And since I have a knowledge of herbal remedies, I can provide them with the resources to continue being well." She stood on tiptoe and planted a kiss upon her brother's cheek. "This will be so good for Aunt Kaylena. With a new project, a new outlook on life, she will be well again herself."

"And think how we will all prosper, Sunny. In no time I will have enough resources to return to America and help our people."

She seemed to float with anticipation and joy as she made her way to her aunt's chamber. Finding Kaylena sitting in a chair by the fireplace, dressed and looking better than she had in days, added to her happy mood.

Kaylena's brow creased with a worried frown when Sunny sat in the chair adjacent to her own. "Have you read everything?"

She nodded. "Every last page."

Kaylena glanced down at her hands clasped together in her lap. "What you must think of me."

"I think you are a brave woman, lonely and scared, but nevertheless, brave."

Kaylena raised her gaze to meet Sunny's. "I am ashamed of my behavior."

"I would ask that you no longer allow these memories to pain you, Aunt Kaylena. It was a very long time ago. What is done is done, and no one else needs to know."

"But that isn't true, Sunny. Soon everyone will know what I've done, what I am."

She frowned. "How can that be if Gabriel and I keep silent?" Then her frown deepened. "The letter...the one that has scared you so, was it by a man from your past?"

"Nay, not directly," Kaylena admitted.

"I do not understand, Aunt Kaylena."

Kaylena sighed. "The letter was from Sister Carmelito Sisko, or should I say her assistant Maria, who wrote down the words while the sister lay confessing on her death bed."

"And how is it a dying woman's last words have upset you?"

Kaylena stood and made her way to the window. For a long moment, she just gazed down at the ground, then lifted her eyes to the sky before turning around to look at Sunny. "After Ryan Duffy sent a message to the parsonage that he hung your father, your mother didn't believe Proud Eagle was dead."

She nodded. "As I heard it told, she needed proof, so she went looking for where the lieutenant said my father's body would be."

"Aye, and when we discovered her gone, Josh went after her."

"It was from their efforts alone that my father lives."

Kaylena reclaimed her seat. "I decided to stay on, wait for Josh to return and hear the outcome. If Amanda had come back with the reverend, and indeed she was widowed, I wanted her to return with me to Brighton."

"But Josh returned without her, because my father was not dead, they rescued him."

"Aye, but by that time several weeks had passed, and it had been over two months since Ryan

Duffy escorted me to my bath." Kaylena cast her glance again at her folded hands. "Though you are still young, you are not a stupid girl. I'm sure your mother has explained the nature of life to you."

She nodded.

"Then, if you indeed read the journal to the very end, you must realize by now that I...that we—" Kaylena clipped her sentence short and cleared her throat.

"Yes, I have drawn conclusions as to what took place on the river bank that night."

Kaylena inhaled sharply. "Well, that night left me with child."

Chapter Twenty-Nine

Sunny gasped. "You have a child?"

Kaylena held up a finger to silence her. "Wait, lest you get ahead of yourself."

She nodded and waited with anticipation for her aunt to explain.

"When Josh returned to the parsonage without Amanda, I knew there was no reason for me to stay on any longer, but I feared traveling alone overseas, carrying a child within me. My reluctance at an immediate departure must have shown upon my face, because Josh insisted I stay on for a few months. During that time I talked him into returning to England to chaplain a small congregation in Brighton. He finally agreed, under the condition it would be after your mother had her baby. He cared immensely for her welfare and wanted to make sure all went well during the birth."

"He was in love with my mother, was he not?"

"Aye, in many ways I believe he still is," Kaylena admitted.

"I do as well, but back to your story," Sunny said.

"Reverend Holmes' delay also afforded him the time to school Benjamin Newcomb in his new duties so he'd be able to take over when Josh left America."

"But staying on would mean all would know of your own condition," Sunny concluded.

"Aye, and I couldn't have that, either. I knew I had to leave before my condition began to show. "

"So what did you do?"

"On one of my walks with Grace to the general

store, I overheard a woman talking to another about the Holy Sisters of Our Lady of Christ's mission in Texas. These nuns took in unwed mothers, finding the babies homes and helping the women to start a new life. So, I stored that bit of information away, and around the middle of March sometime, I made up a story to Josh, Ben, and Grace about going to visit friends in France." She laughed sardonically. "Imagine me with friends in France. I hadn't friends anywhere. " She sighed. "My father saw to that."

Sunny placed a hand on her aunt's arm. "He has long been gone and can hurt you no more."

"And yet his wrath sometimes is still very much alive." Kaylena shook her head and continued on. "Josh's plan to stay on until Amanda's baby was born fit right into my plans. All the while thinking I was in France, no one at the parsonage became the wiser I was really traveling to Texas to have my own baby. Once at the mission I told the sisters I was a widow, said my husband died of an illness aboard the ship we sailed upon. Since many did die on that voyage, including my dear Aggie, the nuns believed my story."

"Did they not question why you came to the mission house to have your child?"

Kaylena nodded. "But I told them it was business I accompanied my husband on, and had no family once I landed in America. Too afraid for the baby's health to travel back before I gave birth, I decided to wait out the event. Upon hearing this, they agreed to let me stay." She sighed. "I had a rough time of it, though. My feet swelled to enormous proportions, and I was unable to wear shoes of any kind. Then I felt nauseous most days and could barely hold down enough food to gain a substantial amount of energy. So, I became very weak, bedridden, and fully dependent upon the nuns for my daily care."

"And did they treat you well?"

"Aye, they did, all of them are extremely dedicated to helping others. Never was I left long alone in my small room, and every need I had was taken care of. During those months I was in many ways just like a babe, unable to do anything for myself," Kaylena reflected. "My labor was hard and long, taking from me what little strength I had left. I nearly bled to death and then developed a fever that left me delirious for many days." She cleared her throat as tears welled in her eyes. "When I was able to comprehend my surroundings again, I was told my son was stillborn."

Sunny's own eyes grew moist. "I am so sorry, my aunt."

"It took me a month to be able to function on my own again, both physically and emotionally. Throughout my delirium I heard a baby crying. Afterward, I had nightmares of the same nature and would wake up drenched with perspiration." Kaylena pressed her fingers to her temples. "I thought I was going mad, because I believed the cries were that of my son…my dead baby."

"Immense grief plays tricks on us. After Fire Star, Gabriel's wife, died, he swore he saw her walking by the river one night," she said.

"Aye, well I heard my son's cries more than just for a night, and I began to question the nuns. My interrogations upset the household, and it wasn't long before it was suggested I leave."

She gasped. "They would dare to send a sick and saddened woman away?"

"By that time, I had gained back most of my physical strength and was able to care for my own needs, just the nightmares plagued me. Sister Carmelito concluded my agony stemmed from remaining where my son was born and had died. She advised I leave for England immediately and seeing her suggestion as valid, I left for my home three days later."

"If your son had lived, how did you plan on explaining him once you returned?"

"As I lay many a day and night in bed I concocted a plausible story, much like the one I told the nuns," Kaylena admitted. "I would simply say I met a man while aboard the ship. His kindness toward me after Aggie's death warmed my heart, and we fell in love. But his duties led him to Texas, and mine to Arizona. However, once I learned my niece wished to remain in her own land, I traveled to Texas, and the two of us reconnected. Upon my arrival he proposed marriage, as we wished never to be apart again, and a few days later we wed. Soon I was with child. But before my baby's birth, he became ill and died. Without him around to care for me, and unable at that point to travel overseas, I went to stay at the mission. There my child was born. Since there was no further reason to stay in America, once I was able, I journeyed back to England with my tiny baby, now the only reminder of my good and loving husband."

"Hmm, a well thought out tale and very believable," Sunny agreed.

"I thought it would work, and there'd be no reason for anyone to point a finger at me or my child," she concluded. "I'd be accepted as a widowed mother and be able to raise my child with dignity." Kaylena's face saddened. "But then my son was born dead, and there wasn't a reason to breathe a word he ever lived."

"And so you kept this whole situation a secret," she concluded.

Kaylena sighed again. "Aye, until now. Sister Carmelito's letter changed everything."

"And how did that happen, my aunt?"

"As it turns out Sister Carmelito was not as

pious as her vows requested. She told a lie, Sunny. My son wasn't stillborn. And the baby I heard crying all those days after I delivered, was not my imagination gone mad."

She frowned. "I do not understand. Why would she do such a thing?"

"The mission stayed intact through the donations of wealthy people. And there were many well-to-do women who were barren, having no one to carry on the family name. Desperate for an heir, and in the hopes their husband's attentions did not wander, they would secretly come to the mission to adopt a newborn. Therefore male, Caucasian babies were in great demand."

"How is it their husbands did not know?"

"Many of these rich families spent little time together; a husband off on business for six months to a year at a time, a wife visiting her family. All it took was a night in bed together before either left, and the rest was easy." Kaylena clarified.

"Ah, then the woman would claim she became with child, but instead adopt one from the mission for a large sum. And then by the time the two are rejoined, they are a family," Sunny countered.

"Aye, that was the way of it, and again the reason a white male child was in such demand," Kaylena explained. "It seems, from Sister Carmelito's death bed confession, she switched a dead white male infant she had already accepted payment for, with my son. Now, after all these years, and with a desire to enter heaven after death, she has confessed to the wrong doing."

Sunny's face brightened, and she clapped her hands in delight. "Then somewhere you have a son."

"Aye, but I am hardly as exuberant over the situation as you are," Kaylena muttered.

She bit her bottom lip. "You are worried now about your reputation and a scandal."

"That and repercussions from my now adult son," Kaylena admitted.

"He knows about you as well?"

Kaylena nodded. "It also seems Sister Carmelito needed to purge all of her sins from her soul, and contacted the adopting family. Since the woman and her husband are dead, Sister Carmelito's assistant talked with my son and learned his life was not a happy one. He was badly abused at the hands of his father and disinherited. Now that he knows of a blood mother, and one of considerable financial means at that, he resents the life he was made to live. He is anxious, angry, and has decided to contact me."

"Was it not explained to him by Sister Carmelito you thought he was stillborn?"

Kaylena shrugged. "I'm not sure Sister Carmelito, or her assistant, decided to divulge that bit of information. Nor have they told me his name. But it stands to reason, since he resents me so much, he doesn't know the full truth."

"How is it Sister Carmelito was able to find you?"

"When I returned home I wrote a long and grateful letter to her, enclosing a handsome sum of money to help sustain the mission and the good work the nuns did for other women. Of course, my family crest and home address were on the envelope. Sister must have saved it all these years."

"And so now your son is coming to meet you?"

"Aye, that he is. Sister Carmelito's letter was not only a confession and an apology, but a warning as well."

She frowned. "When did she say he would arrive?"

Kaylena shrugged. "That part of the sister's letter was not clear, but since much time has passed since I first received her post, I have nay a doubt it will be soon."

Sunny watched her aunt. "How soon are you thinking?"

Kaylena took an audible breath. "In the very, very near future."

Chapter Thirty

The next few weeks were chaotic at Bentwood Manor. Sunny was pleased her aunt had other things to focus on and bide her time with, instead of worrying and drinking. Already Kaylena thrived, putting on a bit of flesh upon her bones, her complexion becoming of a healthy pallor. She laughed more, listened better, but most of all, she began to mellow a bit.

Excitement increased with the arrival of Elwood Hunter, a soft spoken, well-built young man who had a passion for colors and shapes. When he burst upon the scene, he completely swept both women into a drawing frenzy, teaching them to notice and appreciate every object in sight. Kaylena immediately enrolled Sunny in art lessons, and sat in on each class, her own sketch pad upon her lap.

Elwood's style and tutelage was one she picked up quickly and soon her own work became miniature masterpieces in themselves.

"I have never enjoyed teaching a student as much as I have your niece, Miss Kaylena. She has brilliantly mastered many techniques in such a short time," Elwood admitted one afternoon.

Sunny blushed at his complement, trying to keep her attention on the vase of flowers she was transforming into oils.

"I'd like to show her work in my gallery," he said, moving to sit beside Kaylena.

"That is up to Sunny," Kaylena responded.

Inwardly, she smiled. Since Sunny first came to Bentwood Manor Kaylena had made a big change in her attitude toward her niece. As of late, the elder woman refrained from treating her like a child to control and discipline. They were slowly becoming family, the three of them...with Gabriel taking over the manor's affairs and Sunny caring for her aunt's well being.

Elwood neared Sunny now. "Would you, miss?"

She turned from her work and released the smile growing within. "I would be honored, but I have an idea that just might be the most interesting and unique paintings of all."

Elwood cocked his head sideways. "I'm excited to hear your proposal."

"I would like to work with material," she began.

He frowned. "You mean textiles?"

"I mean samplers and wood," she clarified.

His frown deepened. "I'm afraid you've lost me, miss."

"As you know my brother has hired men to cut down the trees along the mansion's entrance to build a barrier along the cliff's edge."

He nodded. "He has accomplished much in a matter of weeks."

"Well, when he is finished he is going to also build a few sweat baths and expand Bentwood Manor to house a health retreat."

Elwood smiled. "What a fabulous idea."

"How would your artistic idea coincide with the health resort, my dear?" Kaylena asked.

She could feel the excitement welling in her chest. After placing the paint brush aside and wiping her hands upon a cloth, she made her way to sit beside her aunt. "You know how you have been teaching me to sew samplers?"

"Aye," Kaylena said, reaching over to push a wayward tendril of hair from Sunny's forehead. The endearing and motherly way Kaylena touched her made her heart burst with affection and respect for the elder woman.

"I would like to draw on the material, create my own samplers to sew. Then I would like to frame them after they have been colored with the thread, but stuff others to make cushions and pillows. Gabriel knows how to work with wood. He can make stools, chairs, ottomans, tables and the like. I would wish to use my cushion creations for the seats, or paint scenes upon the tables. Then sell them in a tiny shop at the health resort."

"And what sort of scenes would you paint?" Elwood said, sitting in a chair adjacent to Kaylena's.

She turned her gaze his way. "Some could be of Bentwood Manor, so the guests would have something to remind them of their stay."

"A souvenir shop, then," Elwood probed.

"Not entirely, as I would also like to offer serious pieces," she said. "So, perhaps a gift shop would be more to my liking."

"I think that's a capital idea, Sunny," Kaylena said, squeezing her arm affectionately. "But I would ask you to wait a tad, till after your début. There is much for you to learn if you are to be presented to the Queen in the spring."

"That will be fine, my aunt. Gabriel will want the sweat bath's built and the mansion converted before he can help me supply a shop with sale items, anyway."

"I know a lot about refinishing furniture myself," Elwood offered. "If your brother will do the building, and you will paint the scenes, then I can do the refinishing."

Kaylena smiled. "How wonderful, this will be our own little business."

Elwood returned the smile with a large one of his own. "And one I have no doubt will flourish in time."

****

Rafe hated the days Sunny took her art lessons. One afternoon, he happened by the solarium and his fists clenched at how close Elwood Hunter stood beside her. With their heads touching they talked, Sunny's giggle lilting through the room.

He combed a hand through his hair and stalked away, heading for the open air where he could breathe. As soon as he finished helping Gabriel and the men with the cliff's barrier he needed to distance himself from Bentwood Manor and Sunny Beth Eagle. His fixation on the woman had completely gotten out of control. There hadn't been a night yet that he didn't have some exotic dream of the two of them engaged in passionate escapades. God help him, he woke with her scent in his nostrils, her touch upon his flesh...and his inner thighs wet.

Making his way to a cluster of trees, he removed his jacket and picked up the axe embedded in a trunk. With one hand, he released the blade and began to chop at a nearby standing tree. With each swipe he expelled the disgust he had for his situation.

I will remain free of all binds.

He hit the trunk again.

I will leave here and go on to a life at sea.

Another strike hit the tree.

I do not want to love or be loved.

Though the fall day was cool, he became heated with the exertion. Sweat dripped from his brow, into his eyes. Wiping it away with the sleeve of his shirt, he took a deep breath, filling his lungs with Brighton's crisp air. Placing the axe aside for a moment, he drew off his shirt, then took up his stance again. As he whacked away at the tree's trunk he mentally repeated his affirmations.

I'm a man of the sea, no woman shall bind my hands, no woman shall own my heart, no woman shall...

He stiffened beneath the gentle finger that traced the scar across his back.

"How did you get this?" a voice laced with concern said from behind.

Rafe spun around to find Sunny standing with a flask of water in her hand and a most endearing look upon her beautiful face. "Don't look at me like that."

She neared him. "Like what?"

Frustration coursed through his body. "Like that...the way you are now, as if I were an injured animal in need of rescue."

She gasped. "How do you know about my animals?"

"It doesn't matter how." He scowled. "I'd also advise you not to go sneaking up behind a man wielding an axe. It could be disastrous."

"I did not sneak up. In fact, I called out your name twice," she defended.

Frustration mounted to rage. "And so you thought touching me would be better?"

She ignored his anger. "How did you get that scar?"

He frowned at her audacity. "That's none of your business."

"Why?"

He wiped the sweat from his brow with an arm. "Why, what?"

"Why is it not my business?"

"Because it isn't," he retorted. "Nothing I do has any bearing on you at all."

"How can you say that?" she argued. "We are friends, are we not? You are staying in my aunt's home, helping my brother, you have saved me from my doom twice already...and you even know about my rescued animals. Why am I not part of your life as you are of mine...why can I not ask you a simple question?"

Her bold assessment to the rights of his privacy

took him totally by surprise. He arched a brow. "You can ask any question you wish, it doesn't mean I will answer."

"Why are you so grumpy all the time?" She flung at him. "I can honestly say I have never met such a man, so out of sorts all the time, as you."

"Why are you here bothering me while I'm working?" he spat, his rage impossible to control.

"I peered out the window and saw you looking tired and warm, so I brought you a flask of water," she said, holding out the container for him to take. "In my village, when a man works hard a woman brings him something to drink."

"Well, you're not in your village anymore," he snapped, refusing to take the flask in spite of his growing thirst. "And it's best you begin to realize it. You are in England, not Arizona. Women here do not touch men that are not their husbands unless they want to offer them something more than a flask of water." He frowned. "Do you see, Miss Eagle?"

"What I see is that you are an ass, Captain Cavendish," she replied curtly, pushing the flask into his hand and stalking away.

He threw the flagon to the ground and marched after her, turning her around by the shoulders. "You are bound and determined to get yourself caught into something you will definitely regret."

"What I regret is ever trying to be nice to you," she snapped. "You are a mean, bitter, and confusing man and I..."

He could listen to no more, especially when the words were sprouting forth from the most desirable and tantalizing set of full lips he ever yearned to taste. And then the scent of her, the feel of her shoulders beneath his hands, the heat coursing through his flesh and filling his loins, was just too much for a man to ignore. He pulled her to him and lowered his mouth to hers, smothering her lips with demanding mastery. He took her with a savage intensity, crushing her to him.

To his pleasure, she returned the kiss with reckless abandon, succumbing to the forceful domination of his lips. Rafe's entire body burned with the smoldering heat that joins metals as her body quivered with fervor within his grasp. His emotions, roused by her passion, made his thoughts spin and his senses whirled and skidded.

She gasped lightly between his parted lips, her warm, sweet breath causing the blood to pound in his brain. He wanted to punish her for infiltrating his thoughts, for wreaking havoc upon his life, for confusing him and unnerving him, and for whatever else she caused him to endure. But all he could do was ravish her mouth, explore the recesses and soft folds, his lips hard and searching.

She returned his kiss with a hunger, an urgency he didn't expect. Wrapping her arms around his neck, her lips were more yielding and persuasive than he cared to admit. He moved his arms to embrace her midriff, her soft curves molding to the contours of his body.

Stop...release her now, before it's too late. She will poison the future, ruin everything.

His thoughts swam, his heart hammered foolishly and the pit of his stomach churned. This was not how he wanted it; this was not how it was suppose to be. She upset the balance of his life, made him question the dreams and goals he set out to accomplish.

But in the end it wasn't he who parted their intimacy. She was the one to pull back, lifting her sapphire gaze to his and whispering, "Next time, Captain, kiss me gently."

With that said she casually turned upon her heels and left him to stand alone, mouth agape, and Brighton's autumn breeze cooling his shirtless back.

Chapter Thirty-One

Sunny walked calmly to the mansion, in spite of her racing heart. Once she reached the front steps, out of Rafe's sight, her wobbly knees forced her to sit. With all serenity disturbed, quakes of nausea clenched her insides. Now, would her stupid remark actually cause her to be sick...right here on the front stoop? She rolled her eyes and moaned, swallowing hard as she rehashed her words.

Next time kiss me gently, she had whispered to him. What in God's name possessed her to say such a remark?

"He possessed me," she mumbled, placing her head in her hands. The truth was, Captain Rafe Cavendish had taken over her thoughts more than once, and lately quite often. His handsome looks and heroic deeds made him quite an adamant player in her dreams. And his bitterness, the restless anger that consumed him had made him a mystery, a curiosity that plagued her when she was awake. Either way she looked at the situation, his very existence controlled her thoughts, took up every minute, and now...after the first and most wonderful kiss of her entire life, he would forever be etched in her brain.

"Not just my brain, but my heart as well," she muttered miserably, touching her lips and still feeling the warmth of his kiss upon them. Sighing she stood, making her way into the mansion.

Cirie met her in the foyer. "Ah, there ye are, miss. I've been lookin' all over for ye."

Sunny frowned. "Is everything all right with my

aunt?"

"Oh, aye, Mum is fine, takin' a nap in the solarium," Cirie informed her. "It's the gentleman caller in the parlor that's waitin' on ye, miss."

Sunny's frown deepened. "I have a gentleman caller?"

"Aye, miss. His name is Steven Bates and 'e's Lord Wade's assistant…says 'e's got a letter for ye from yer sister."

She ran to the parlor as if her feet had sprouted wings and burst with excitement through the doors.

Steven Bates, sitting in a soft armchair by the fireplace, jumped to his feet upon her entrance and bowed politely from the waist. "Good day to you, miss. My name is Steven Bates, and I am Lord Morgan Wade's assistant."

She neared the man, tiny in stature, with small beady eyes, and a rat-like appearance. "And a good day to you as well, Mr. Bates."

He pulled from his vest pocket an envelope. "I've been instructed to make sure this goes to the hand of Sunny Beth Eagle." He arched a thin brow. "Am I correct in assuming you are she?"

Sunny nodded.

"Then I present this correspondence to you, and will return promptly the same time tomorrow for your response."

She took the envelope from his bony fingers. "*Ashoge*, thank you, Mr. Bates." In spite of her growing anticipation to dive into Raven's letter, she did not forget her manners. "And can I offer you something to eat or drink?"

"Nay, Miss Eagle, I must be on my way, but I thank you for your hospitality." He bowed again and made his way out the door.

She fled from the parlor, taking the stairs to her chamber two at a time. Once in the privacy of her own room, she took a seat by the window, ripped open the envelope and began to read Raven's letter. Her sister's familiar handwriting brought tears to her eyes before she was able to comprehend a word. How she missed Raven and needed her advice to help sort out all the strange and frightening emotions surrounding her heart. Swallowing hard the lump growing in her throat, she wiped her eyes with the back of a hand and settled down to read the letter.

My Dearest Sister,

I cannot tell you how pleased I was to receive a letter from you through Lord Wade. Such a splendid man he is, and I am so grateful for his efforts in bringing us back together, even if it is only with our words.

I miss you and Gabriel so much, but rest assured I am treated well by my new husband. I lack for no necessity, as he is kind, generous, and always tries to please me. Because of this, I have a special request. I wish to give Braiton a glimpse of the life we all left behind in Arizona. The only way I can accomplish this is if you would share your drawing talent.

In your letter, I read you were to take art lessons. I thought the sketch you did of me just before we left the reservation, the one where I stood with one foot upon a rock, a spear in one hand, the other on my hip and dressed in Apache garb, would make a lovely painting, and one I could give my husband as a gift on Christmas. I know there are many months yet before the holidays, but I have no idea how long you need for such a grand project as this, to be complete; or how long it would take for me to receive, once the painting is sent. And I also wanted you to have enough time to make a change, as there is just one I need done. Since I am now married, it is no longer appropriate for me to wear my hair as a maiden. Please, when doing the painting, remove the nah-leen, allowing my hair to fall freely, as you know is the custom of the married women in our tribe.

Enclosed is a bit of money I saved from my own wifely allowance. Please purchase whatever supplies you will need as well as a gold frame. There should also be enough to use for the shipping cost.

My heart is with you always. Do not forget me.

My Love,

Raven

Forget her...how could Sunny ever forget her beloved sister? She choked on her emotions, the ache in her heart from missing Raven so acute it pained her. Closing her eyes she inhaled sharply, recalling her sister's face, the sound of her voice, the way she smiled.

No, my sister, I could never forget you.

Clutching the letter to her heart, she made her way to the writing desk. She composed a return letter and agreed wholeheartedly to paint the portrait as Raven requested. Raven's picture would be the perfect project for her tutor to instruct her on. Not to mention working to complete such a venture on time would take her mind off Rafe Cavendish...and his kiss.

To Sunny's relief, Rafe did not join them that evening for dinner. He decided instead to eat with the other workers. This did not surprise her, though it left her both sad and angry, spoiling her appetite.

Come the morning, she was ravaged with hunger, caring little if the captain ate the first meal of the day with her or not. But when she came down for breakfast she was informed he would eat no further meals at her table. In fact, she would no longer have to put up with his anger or bitterness or sharp remarks.

Captain Raphael Cavendish had gone back to London.

Chapter Thirty-Two

A début for a young woman in 1892 England was a very big event, and Sunny soon discovered the rigorous preparation involved. Her first lesson was in figure training.

Kaylena's old backboard was fetched from the attic, and Sunny was soon enslaved in the uncomfortable contraption. The unyielding block of wood, worn above clothing, was strapped flat against the back of her waist and extended up the spine. A steel ring, covered with leather, projected to the front and encircled the throat. It held her upright, like the Buckingham Palace guards depicted in the painting that hung in the library.

"If you stop wiggling it will be easier to bear," Kaylena warned.

"How long must I stay in this thing?" she protested.

"Every day till bedtime, when the board will be removed, but the leather ring will remain on your neck so the backboard can easily be fastened in place the next day."

She gasped. "Certainly there must be an easier way?"

"Not if you want to be the prettiest and most graceful young woman at your coming out," Kaylena advised.

"I do not care if I am the prettiest or the most graceful. In fact, I do not want to go to this *coming out* at all," she countered.

"As a young woman of good standing, it is required. I will not allow you to shame us all,"

Kaylena snapped. "Besides, no gentleman wants to court a lady with slouched shoulders."

"I do not have slouched shoulders, and if that is all a man looks for in his woman, then I want no part of him," she grumbled.

"You should be happy I am much more patient with you than my own tutor was with me. If I protested like this, I'd have found myself bent over a chair, skirt flipped up over my head and bloomers lowered to my ankles, receiving a birching to remember. And then another before bed, this time given by either the governess or Father, my punishment for troubling the tutor."

Sunny was thankful, when she heard snippets of the abuse her aunt endured, that she was brought up in an Apache village instead of England. In spite of the white man's intrusion, her family life was happy and filled with much love. Her parents would never inflict upon her such a humiliating punishment.

Kaylena cleared her throat with authority. "Now, arms out, chin held high and eyes straight ahead." She placed a book upon Sunny's head. "Try your best not to let it slip off while you walk." She gave Sunny a taut nod. "Now, once around the room you go. As you promenade a few times, you'll get the gist of it. And after we master your walk, you will learn to curtsey to the floor without losing your balance and falling over."

As much as she hated the backboard, she was not a person who gave up or quit something because it was hard. Using the bow and arrow was not easy, neither was warrior fighting, but she learned because it was the way of her people. It was no different now. This was her aunt's way, and Kaylena was family. Besides her brother, her aunt was all the family Sunny had present. So, all afternoon she marched around the solarium, pretending the book was a basket of fresh vegetables just picked for supper and the backboard a cradleboard carrying a friend's baby. And throughout the lesson her aunt watched with hawk-like eyes, instructing, scolding, and occasionally encouraging her efforts.

But when she had to stand to eat dinner, Gabriel put an end to her confines. Reaching for the knife laying beside his plate, he slashed apart the straps, broke the board over his knee, and removed the steel collar.

"I would not tether my horse in such a way," he retorted. Then, pointing to a chair, he demanded she sit and eat. Casting an angry glare Kaylena's way, he demanded she never place his sister in such a device again.

Kaylena nodded in agreement, eating the rest of her meal in silence.

Sunny may have won that round, but there was more ahead. French lessons occupied the mornings that followed. When she did not pronounce a word correctly, Kaylena would squeeze her cheeks together, puckering her lips, and causing her back teeth to dig into the soft inner flesh of her mouth.

"French is a romantic language," Kaylena explained. "Speak it as you would sing the lyrics to a beautiful love song, let it flow and linger. Roll your tongue, accentuate the syllables, and pronounce each word with feeling, like a poet creating prose."

Learning what utensil to use with each meal course took up the afternoons, as there were several to know. There was a special spoon for eating soup, a fork for eating oysters, a different fork and knife for eating fish, as well as a butter knife and a dessert spoon. She could not understand what all the fuss was about. As long as you had a substantial utensil at your disposal, what did it matter which one it was? Her people never starved for the lack of a proper fork, only from not enough food.

Between her lessons and working on Raven's portrait, Sunny kept busy...too busy to think about Rafe Cavendish. But at night, alone in her room and beneath the warmth of the quilt, her thoughts turned to *the kiss*. And she found herself yearning for his lips to smother hers again, to pull her close to his hard chest and make her melt in his embrace. Every inch of her body cried out for his touch, longed for him, wanted his kiss upon her lips again.

Where are you now, Rafe Cavendish?

****

Sunny's last words continued to plague him, echoing in Rafe's thoughts throughout his journey home, *"Next time kiss me gently."*

"Next time my ass. There won't be a next time," he mumbled as he departed from the train.

He sat gazing now out the window of the carriage he rented, rehashing for the millionth time the moments their lips locked. Those moments set every fiber of his being on fire with passion, brought him extreme pleasure, and fueled a desire he'd never tasted. He shook his head to clear it. The whole episode infuriated him to no end. How could he have lost control? How could he have allowed himself to make such a paramount blunder?

His mood hadn't changed by the time the carriage stopped in front of Simon's flat. He stalked up the stairway, silently chastising himself for his weakness, and banged upon his brother's door.

"What the devil..." Simon bellowed, swinging the heavy entrance open. His temper cooled the minute he set eyes on Rafe. "Well, the prodigal son has returned."

He pushed passed his brother with a scowl and entered the modest parlor. "I never left, just was slightly detained."

Simon chuckled. "And a good day to you, too."

Sitting upon one of the only two stuffed chairs in

the room, he lounged back and crossed his leg over the other. "I am in no mood for your antics, Simon."

Simon chuckled again. "My antics, is it? I'd say your mood was foul way before I opened my mouth." He took a seat opposite Rafe's. "Care to tell me why?"

"Nay," he grumbled.

Simon slapped his hands on his knees and stood. "Well, then with that all straightened out, how about a mug of ale?"

"Aye, that's the best offer I've had all day," he retorted, standing to remove his jacket.

When Simon returned with the beverages, he handed a mug to Rafe, then reclaimed his seat to sip at his own drink. "I was beginning to worry."

He arched a brow. "Worry over what?"

"Your whereabouts," Simon countered.

Rafe took a swig of the cold mead, letting it refresh his dry throat. "Didn't Uncle Josh tell you I escorted the Eagles to their aunt's estate in Brighton?"

"Aye, but that was weeks ago."

He downed the last of his ale, and placed the mug on a nearby table. "Ah, well I got involved with helping Gabriel erect a barrier along the cliff's edge. When we arrived, his sister nearly killed herself when she lost her footing."

Simon arched a brow. "And of course you, being who you are, came to her rescue."

He frowned, knowing Simon referred to the *Deandra incident*, as that situation was called. "What was I to do, let the woman plunge to her death?"

"Hmm, answering a question with a question. Always a good defense mechanism."

His frown deepened. "And what exactly am I defending?"

"Why, your feelings for Miss Eagle, of course,"

Simon teased.

Rafe waved a hand over his head. "Your assumption is preposterous."

It was Simon's turn to frown. "Methinks not, little brother."

"And what makes you so sure?" he challenged.

"The look upon your face," Simon admitted. "Only a man totally disturbed by a woman and completely denying the fact could have such a foul expression as yours."

"Fact is, I am disturbed...disturbed I've wasted my time helping those *Colonists*," he spat with sarcasm.

Simon chuckled. "Well now, the ole boy sounds genuinely miffed."

"What was your first clue?"

"Your tongue-in-cheek term for the Yanks," Simon countered.

Rafe nodded. "Well, I tell you here and now, miffed is putting it lightly. Having to help them settle in Brighton, instead of being in London working at the new post Lord Wade hired me for, has me a hell of a lot more inconvenienced than you could ever imagine."

"Nay, I think your foul mood goes much deeper than being inconvenienced," Simon argued.

"Well, don't think so hard, it doesn't become you."

Simon threw his head back and laughed before downing his own mug of ale.

"I fail to see anything amusing, Simon."

"That's because it's happening to you."

He arched a brow. "And what is it that you think is happening to me?"

"Why, you're falling in love, little brother."

"I most certainly am not!"

Simon locked his gaze on Rafe's. "Not every woman is like Deandra, Rafe."

"I don't need to hear one of your lectures, Simon." He scowled unwilling to listen, yet knew it was coming.

"But that's exactly what you're going to hear, little brother, because you've allowed Deandra and her selfish attitude to poison you from ever sharing your heart with another woman."

"Deandra is far from the problem, Simon. I just know loving the sea and loving a woman doesn't mix well...months of being apart, the danger. I'm not about to put something like that on a woman."

"You're skirting the issue, Rafe."

"It is the issue," he challenged.

"Nay, it doesn't have to be."

His lips thinned. "Not all of us are lucky enough to find a woman with the mindset of Fiona Wade. She's seen her father go off on voyages since she was a mite, surely she'll endure such from a husband."

"I believe a woman and a man, when they truly love one another, learn how to make their relationship work." Simon frowned. "But you'll never know what love holds for you because you're too scared to find out."

"I will deny that to the death," he snapped, folding his arms across his chest.

"Then your denial will kill you," Simon countered.

Rafe combed his fingers through his hair. "What do you expect me to do, Simon?"

"If you've fallen in love with Sunny Eagle, you must tell her, give her a chance and a choice to love you back. If you don't, you will regret it for the rest of your life."

He took an audible breath, his brother's words ringing true.

Simon reached for his mug and stood, giving Rafe a pat on his shoulder as he neared his chair. "Care for another, old boy?"

He handed his brother the empty mug. "Aye, keep them coming."

****

The cold night and cool dawn required the thoughtful Cirie to stoke the fire in Sunny's chamber many times throughout the night. "You must be exhausted, my friend, keeping watch over the fire all night," she said, placing a hand on Cirie's.

In spite of the lines of fatigue around her eyes, Cirie spoke with a cheery tone. "I'm fine, miss, and quite used to sleepin' light."

"I can stoke my own fire, I do it all the time at home," she offered. The village where her parents now dwelled without her came to mind.

"Nay, miss, 'tis not necessary for ye to be troublin' yerself when 'tis my duty," Cirie said, fastening the back buttons of a lime green day dress Sunny chose to wear.

At that moment a knock came at the door, and Gerta called through. "Excuse me, miss."

"Yes, enter Gerta," she returned.

Gerta stuck her head into the room. "Ye 'ave a gentleman caller, miss."

Sunny's heart leaped. "Rafe's come back?"

Gerta frowned. "Nay, miss."

Her spirits fell, the disappointment obviously evident on her face because Gerta's eyes softened. "I'm sorry, miss."

She nodded and forced a smile. "Did this gentleman give a name, Gerta?"

"Aye, miss...said 'is name's Count Ivan Sontag and 'e waits for ye now in the parlor."

Ivan greeted her with a gentle kiss across her knuckles. "I told you I vould find you."

"Yes, you certainly did," she said, not feeling quite as enthused over the prospect as he.

He flashed a charming smile. "And now I vill have the time to get to know you as I vished I could aboard the ship." His smile broadened as he continued to tease her with playful banter. "Thankfully that menacing Rafe Cavendish will not bother us again."

She sighed. "No, you need not concern yourself about him; he is nowhere to be found."

****

During his weeklong visit, Count Ivan Sontag did his best to charm Sunny, attentive to her every word and looking deep into her eyes. His hands were warm and smooth, his voice calm and soft. He definitely won over her aunt, who could not sing his praises loud or long enough. Ivan even managed to find a common ground with Gabriel. In spite of the fact he was a perfect houseguest and the most charismatic individual she ever met, Sunny could not wait for him to leave.

"Such a handsome man," Kaylena said one afternoon when just the two of them sipped tea in the solarium. "I believe his notion is to ask for your hand in marriage."

She gasped. "Marriage!"

"Aye, my dear, marriage. I'm sure you have knowledge of the concept," Kaylena teased.

"It would be a dreadful idea," she retorted.

Kaylena giggled like a schoolgirl with a secret. "I think it's an absolutely wonderful idea. And you have my complete blessings." She placed a hand on her heart. "My word, between your début and planning a wedding, I won't know where to begin."

"You might as well keep your blessings because I have no intentions of marrying the count, so you need not worry about planning a thing," she said, placing the delicate tea cup aside before her trembling hands dropped it. "Besides, Gabriel would forbid it."

"He may be the head of the manor's affairs, but he has no bearings on guiding you, that's my domain, as is the dowry set aside for such a time."

"But I do not choose him."

"But I have, and that's all that matters," Kaylena's voice sharpened. "He's handsome, rich, and totally taken with you. What more can a woman ask for?"

"How about love?" With that said she thought of Raven. How was she faring married to a stranger? Sunny shivered inside.

"It won't be hard to fall in love once you're married. After all, the count is an exceptionally attractive man," Kaylena said.

"The idea is to fall in love with a man before marriage, Aunt Kaylena, not after."

"It's not always necessary, Sunny Beth." Kaylena held a hand up to silence further protests. "We'll speak no more about this, now. I am your guardian, and I know what's best for you." In a flash the old, demanding and controlling Kaylena returned. "You will obey my decision or suffer the consequences for your dreadful behavior. Am I clear?"

She bit back the tears stinging her throat and reached for the tea cup, swallowing the warm liquid past the lump of heartache and disappointment that assailed her. She knew it would do no good to argue. Though Kaylena had warmed up to Sunny in the weeks since her arrival, she was still a woman of England. A product of a strict upbringing with certain beliefs and convictions, not hesitating in the least to act on them.

In spite of Kaylena's hate for the abuse she suffered at the hands of her own father, she would not see the injustice of administering a birching to keep Sunny in line. Even though Gabriel would not tolerate such harsh treatment toward his sister, he was not always around to see what went on in the mansion. His duty to complete the cliff barrier and sweat baths took him away from dawn till dusk and he knew little of the daily activities going on inside the manor house. By the time he discovered she had been disciplined in such a manner, it would already be too late.

Enduring such humiliation was the last thing she wanted. She fought to control the tears welling in her eyes as she realized she could never live down such a degrading punishment, her pride and spirit crushed to such a degree, she doubted seriously she could ever look her aunt in the eyes again. Nor anyone in the house, for that matter, knowing they would all be aware of her sentence.

Complying with Kaylena's wishes was her only choice. Clearing her throat she forced a smile. "Yes, my aunt, you are very clear. I will do whatever you see fit."

"That's my dear girl," Kaylena cooed. "Now you leave everything up to me."

She nodded, the sadness seeping into the very marrow of her bones.

How, in good conscience, can I vow my life and loyalty to one man when my heart is wholeheartedly in love with another?

Chapter Thirty-Three

Her aunt's insistence to accept Ivan's proposal, should there be one forthcoming, doomed Sunny to a loveless marriage. A life with a mate not of your own choosing was not her tradition. The women in her tribe were the ones who chose the men they wanted to wed. And only if the decision was mutual, did a union take place. In view of this, it was hard to see relationships blooming everywhere she turned. She was bombarded by love sick couples. The joys of romance seemed to be in the air and thriving at Bentwood Manor.

Elwood Hunter, her handsome and tender tutor, when finished giving her an art lesson, spent the rest of the afternoon talking in the kitchen with Gerta over tea. The young servant girl reveled in his attention, her pretty face glowing with happiness.

Cirie had found herself an admirer as well. Cody Denton, one of the men hired by Gabriel to help with the renovations, came to the back door frequently for fresh buckets of water. Cirie made every attempt to be the one to accommodate him, and Cody did not seem to mind in the least.

She envied the dreamy looks and sweet words she overheard each woman receive from the attention of these men. Gerta sang as she worked, Cirie smiled a lot. Both couples seemed completely and happily in love.

And if that were not bad enough, Gabriel received a letter from Collette Halston, inviting him to spend a few days with her in London. He appointed Cody Denton as his foreman, being the man had the most experience in such matters, left instructions on what needed completion, and departed two days later on the morning train.

Now all she was left with were her nightly dreams, fantasies her loneliness conjured up of her and Rafe together. Deep within her heart, she experienced his kiss again and again, feeling the warmth of his lips upon hers, and the touch of his caress.

I lay here pining for a man who feels nothing but anger toward me.

Yet his embrace, his kiss said something very different.

Oh, what does it matter now anyway? He is gone, and I will end up marrying Ivan.

And with that stark and final realization, a floodgate of tears spilt her sorrow.

****

England did not celebrate Thanksgiving. With Gabriel gone to London, Raven in Ireland, and the rest of Sunny's family and friends in America, there really was not a reason to worry about keeping the holiday, except for her own sanity. So much had changed for her and many things she held dear taken away, that if she did not make an attempt to hold on to this one tradition, she would truly crumble.

Cody Denton came to her rescue. Being an American himself, he honored the same holiday. Up to that point she had not felt comfortable around the man. Perhaps it was his amber hued eyes, which reminded her of an owl's. Her people believed animals taught lessons in folklore. The coyote was a trickster, the fox clever and conniving, and the owl would rob your soul. Though she knew Cody was not out to get her soul, he strangely enough reminded her of someone that disturbed her serenity...yet she could not place exactly who that person was. But she put all uncomfortable feelings aside when Cody brought several Cornish hens for Bertha to cook. The gravy and stuffing were not what she was accustomed to, but it was still delicious. Besides, the fact that she could gather around a table with good folks helped for a while to quiet the sadness she felt.

Aunt Kaylena, common folk not being her kind, claimed a headache early in the day and took to her bed. So Sunny decided to set up the feast in the bunker house, where it was less formal and whereby all the workers could enjoy a warm meal as well.

She explained to all present the Thanksgiving story, and when Joshua Holmes joined them, he told of his first Thanksgiving in America and the kindness of Amelia and Ethan Gregory. Then he told the story of the first Thanksgiving the Apache's celebrated, inviting him as their honored guest. As he spoke, fond memories of home engulfed her and she found herself wiping away the tears.

"I know this is hard for you, Sunny," Josh sympathized.

"I miss my family so much," she confessed. "I wish I could be home."

He pulled her into a fatherly embrace. "I've learned, as a man of God, home is wherever He is...and He is everywhere. So, you are never alone, you are never forgotten, if you believe in Him."

In the weeks that followed, she threw herself into finishing Raven's portrait, sending it out in the nick of time. She was almost sad to see it go. Being able to look into her sister's eyes had been a comfort. Seeing it off was almost like she had lost Raven all over again.

Oh, how I wish I were able to become very small, climb into a corner of the frame, and journey to Ireland as well.

****

Bentwood Manor was decorated for Christmas

far more elaborately than anything Sunny had ever seen. Wreaths arrayed in ribbons, colorful buttons, feathers, and flowers adorned the interior. The satin, crystal, and porcelain balls that hung from the large tree in the parlor were like miniature artwork. Bertha filled the mansion with the aroma of roast beef and goose cooking in the kitchen, as well as plum pudding, mincemeat pie, shrimp, and oysters.

Sunny's favorite was the fruitcake. One bite into the dessert filled with dried fruit soaked in a rum-based sauce for weeks ahead to allow it to age, and her taste buds tingled with pleasure. But that was the only pleasure the holiday brought.

Kaylena's invited guests were a bunch of stuffy, stiff-lipped society snobs who were boring and talked in a condescending fashion. As she was kept under her aunt's wing most of the day, Sunny felt more and more like she was losing herself. If she stayed the ever obedient and doting niece, she would eventually end up with no life of her own. Kaylena was doing to her exactly what Wilson Bentley had done to his daughter. Did her aunt even realize the similarities, how she sounded every time she demanded and commanded Sunny, rephrased her words or spoke for her?

A few times she glanced Gabriel's way, noticing the tight-lipped and agitated expression he wore. Would he put an end to Kaylena's over-bearing attitude, or would her aunt be the victor? If Gabriel truly had no further jurisdiction where Sunny's welfare was concerned, as Kaylena informed her, then she would gain little alliance from him.

Ivan arrived on Christmas Eve, and though he had ample time to take her aside and propose, he never did. She was relieved, actually believed she was given a reprieve. Perhaps all her worrying was for naught.

On Christmas Day, just as dessert was being

served, Ivan announced his intentions to marry her. Congratulations went all around the table. Every face, especially Kaylena's, was of good cheer.

But then Gabriel put his tea cup down a little harder than usual and stood. "I did not hear if my sister accepted."

Ivan's fair complexion reddened. "I asked your aunt for *Fraulien* Eagle's hand this morning and vas given *her* blessings."

"But did my sister accept?" Gabriel pressed, the muscles at his jaw throbbing.

Ivan swallowed hard. "I did not ask your sister."

Gabriel arched a brow. "Is that not customary to do here in England?"

"Nay, it is not necessary, Gabriel, I have already given my permission," Kaylena interjected, her smile now frozen across her face.

Gabriel ignored Kaylena's words and made his way to Ivan's chair. "I would like to see you, Count, for a moment...privately." He motioned to the library door. "Shall we?"

Ivan gave a taut nod, his face so red it almost appeared purple, and stood.

The two men left the room together and not a sound could be heard amongst the other guests. The awkward silence seemed to last an eternity. Sunny was sure everything she had just eaten would soon come back up.

"You must excuse my nephew," Kaylena apologized. "He is not accustomed to our ways."

Sunny's temper rose, wishing she were able to slap every smug face that turned her way, especially her Aunt Kaylena's.

When the front door slammed, everyone jumped. Soon Gabriel returned to the dining room. His eyes were wide, hands clenched to his side. "Unfortunately the count had to leave," he said as he made his way to his chair.

287

Kaylena stood and gripped his arm. "What have you done?"

He looked down at her hand, calmly removed her grip from his arm and continued toward his chair. "If the count wishes to marry my sister, he must first ask her, and if she agrees then I will give *my* blessings, as it is my right to do, as her brother and head of the household." He pulled the chair from the table and sat. "Until then the proposal is denied."

"Don't you realize what you've done, you foolish man," Kaylena snapped.

Gabriel did not answer.

Silence enveloped the room like a blanket. Then, one by one each guest stood, left the dining hall and made their way out the front door.

"There, you see," Kaylena said, gesturing to the empty seats around the dining table. "Because of you and your sister, I will be the laughing stock throughout all of Brighton...probably London as well."

"You were a laughing stock way before we arrived," Gabriel retorted. "Before my sister came to your aid, helped you to stop drinking, you were falling on your face, slurring your words, and pissing in your bed."

Kaylena gasped. "How dare you speak to me with such disrespect."

Gabriel stood and in two strides met her head on. "How dare you treat Sunny like she had no feelings or brains! You have been demeaning my sister since the moment we arrived, doing to her just what your own father did to you."

"You have no idea what I endured at the hands of my father," Kaylena choked out, wringing her hands in front of her.

"I know he whipped your naked ass," Gabriel bellowed.

Kaylena's eyes widened with disbelief.

"Ah, yes, I am aware of all that goes on and that has gone on here at Bentwood Manor, in spite of the fact I am gone from it most of the day. That is what the head of a household does, stays alert to the goings on no matter where he is." He frowned. "Your father was a brutal parent and dealt with his children in a shameful way. And you will not get away with humiliating and degrading my sister in the same manner Wilson Bentley did to you."

"It would all be for her own good," Kaylena's voice broke slightly.

"What good did it do for you, Aunt Kaylena?" Gabriel challenged. "Wilson Bentley stripped you of your true spirit, broke your heart, and left you a mean, bitter woman."

Kaylena turned away, walked to the window and gazed out. "If it weren't for Wilson Bentley's money you and your sister's would be taunted and terrorized by the white agents who have taken over your home."

Gabriel neared Kaylena. "You speak the truth, and when we accepted your help it was because we believed Raven and Sunny would be safe here in England, treated kindly and given opportunities to live a better life."

Kaylena turned sharply to look at Gabriel. "And that was what I was trying to do."

He arched a brow. "By forcing Sunny to marry a man she did not love, taking her dignity, threatening to shame her and beat her into submission if she refused?"

Kaylena raised a defiant chin. "If you don't like abiding by my rules, then you can leave my home…until I die it still belongs to me, and I will do in it what I see fit."

"Sunny and I do not want your home; leave it to charity for all we care. Come the morning, we will be on the first train bound for London. While I was there visiting Collette Halston, I had the good sense to stop by Collins Stead. Lady Collins and I had a long talk. When I confided in her my concern for Sunny's welfare here, she jumped at the chance to be of help. She is more than happy to have us live there, as having family to love and heirs to her estate mean everything to her. And her generosity does not have unreasonable rules attached." He walked over to Sunny and took her by the hand. "Come, my sister, and pack your things for our journey tomorrow."

"There is nothing for you to pack, as all you own I have purchased," Kaylena snapped.

Gabriel's jaw clamped as he turned around to face their aunt. "I have worked for over a month on the sweat baths you requested without a wage for my labor. In place of money, my sister and I will be taking the clothes we arrived with and for my trouble, a ride to the train station."

"And so that's it then?" Kaylena snapped.

Gabriel forced a smile. "How thoughtless of me to forget...Merry Christmas, Aunt Kaylena."

Chapter Thirty-Four

"I'm cooming with ye, miss," Cirie said as she helped Sunny pack her clothes and the maid of honor gown she was to wear in Fiona Wade's wedding. The nuptials were only a few weeks away, and in truth she would be leaving for London soon anyway. It just saddened her to be leaving under troublesome conditions.

As stubborn and strict as Kaylena was, Sunny felt her aunt had basically a kind and generous heart. The elder woman, at Proud Eagle's request, did not hesitate in the least to send them the funds to travel to England, as well as immediately trusting Gabriel, appointing him the head of the household. Sunny also feared leaving her aunt alone at a time when a long, lost son was soon to pay a vengeful visit. Would Kaylena turn to drinking again?

"My aunt will need you here, Cirie."

"I don't care if she needs me," Cirie said.

"But you and Gerta will be the only ones left to see she does not start the drinking again."

"Gerta will 'ave to watch out for Mum herself," Cirie went on. "Since I won't stay 'ere when ye are gone, I just might as well go with ye."

"But I have no funds in which to pay for your services," she explained.

"All the same, I refuse to stay 'ere," Cirie said, her bottom lip puckering like a child ready to cry.

"What about Cody Denton? I thought you two were sweet on each other?"

Cirie shrugged away the tears welling in her eyes. "I thought the same, but now it looks like we both were wrong on that account. Cody left late last night."

She hugged the young woman. "I am so sorry, Cirie." Sighing, she forced a smile. "I am sure Lady Collins plans on hiring someone to assist me, as I have learned it is the privilege of a woman of means, so I see no reason why it cannot be you. Besides, my dear brother would probably feel more at ease if I had a companion with me while riding in the ladies compartment on the train."

"Thank ye, miss," Cirie said. "As soon as I'm done 'ere, I'll pack what little I own and meet ye at the carriage."

****

Glenshire Sussex was not the fast paced, bustling town that London was, or as airy and bright as Brighton. Collins Stead set back from the main area, nestled within the trees and even by day the gargoyles atop the roof and the Victorian architecture of the mansion gave the place a frightening appearance. Inside, however, a warm fire burned within each fireplace of each room, lending a bit of coziness to the tasteful decor.

Sunny's bedchamber was especially pleasant. Light blue walls framed by white trimmed panels and bordered in a sculpted rose design gave way to a romantic appeal. The furniture was also white, with scallops of gold framing the armoire's doors and drawers. The vanity table's skirt matched the bed's canopy, coverlet and drapery, and a large oval mirror hung above it on the wall. The bed itself was joined on both sides by white, gold trimmed tables. Two upholstered chairs, set on each side of the fireplace, were designed in fabric that was in accord with the rest of the room.

"Oh, miss," Cirie purred. "Such a nice room to shelter yer dreams in."

Her dreams were anything but of a sheltered

292

nature, and as of late were replays of Rafe Cavendish's passionate kiss. The fantasy left her wanton, and just thinking of it brought an unwelcome blush to her cheeks. Clearing her throat, she nodded in agreement and busied herself in lending Cirie a hand to put away the rest of her clothes.

Lady Lucinda Collins, in Sunny's estimation, would have fared well dwelling amongst those of the western plains. Though several years Kaylena's senior, Lucinda had a hearty attitude. No doubt, in her younger days, Lady Collins took on things the more conventional British woman would have shied away from due to protocol and tradition.

"Why did you not journey with my grandmother to America?" she asked Lucinda over tea that evening.

Lucinda narrowed her blue eyes. "I thought seriously of it, I can tell you that, but at the time I also thought I was in love with a young barrister by the name of Dennis Ingram. I fancied he was in love with me as well, until his wife cleared that bit of folly from my mind." She sighed. "Live and learn, is what I always say. And by the time I learned there was no reason to wait on Mr. Ingram, my dear friend, Amelia had long set sail for her new world, and I was stuck alone in the old one."

"You are so different from my Aunt Kaylena," she admitted.

"Well, mind you now I don't stand for foolery, Riley can vouch for that," Lucinda said.

Sunny cast a glance Riley's way and caught the beautiful young woman smiling as she took a sip of tea.

"Auntie Cinda has a bark bigger than her bite."

Lucinda giggled. "Hush now, love, don't be telling all my secrets."

Sunny smiled in return. "I hear much affection

in both your words for each other."

"Ah, what is life without it?" Lucinda said.

"I truly wonder if Aunt Kaylena knows what it is," she reflected.

"You can't know something you were never taught, Sunny," Lucinda said. "From all outward angles Wilson Bentley appeared to be a proper father and husband. My own dear father, who gave to me a loving childhood, thought Wilson to be a fair and honorable man. But I can tell you I learned firsthand from Amelia what he was capable of behind closed doors. And I also believe Kaylena got the brunt of it all. In later years, with his wife dead and his oldest daughter gone to America, Wilson took his frustrations and grief out on his youngest daughter."

"I pity my aunt, as I also had a loving childhood."

"That's because the same blood runs in your father's veins as does in my father's. All of them are good men, and I see it now in Gabriel."

"And what of the women, my lady?"

"They're the nurturers with a strong will and smart brains, Sunny."

"And where are such women appreciated," she mused aloud.

"Here, in my home, Sunny, that's precisely why I would like you to remain at Collins Stead, living with me, even if you and Kaylena make amends with each other," Lucinda said. "I don't believe Kaylena's past can ever release her enough to guide and teach another with cordiality. She will always believe a severe hand must be dealt."

"And you do not?"

"Nay, I believe in a firm hand not a severe one, and never would I demean. Riley can tell you, though she was disciplined as a child and made to do the proper thing, she was not treated disrespectfully, anguished or humiliated in the process. I did not need to wound her pride and strip her of her dignity to make her obey."

"Auntie Cinda speaks the truth. I was always dealt with fairly and because of my love for her, and the respect she bestowed upon me, I didn't have to be asked twice to obey her rules...which were not hard to obey in the first place," Riley added.

"And now that Riley is a young woman, as you are, the tactics Kaylena still believes are useful, are most inappropriate and completely unnecessary."

"What is expected of me here?" she probed.

"I would ask you make your début, not because I fear scandal, but because it is a beautiful rite of passage for a young woman, and I want you to experience the excitement and fun. You deserve the respect and honor just as any Collins woman, and I want so much for you to have that."

Riley nodded in agreement. "I felt so special throughout the entire evening, getting all dressed up and being received by Queen Victoria." Her beautiful face broke with a smile. "I was escorted to the ball room, my hand delicately upon the arm of my escort, in the proper lady's fashion. At the entrance, I waited for the courtier to call out each girl's name. When it was my turn to be announced, I proceeded to walk with trembling knees down a long red carpet. My heart raced, my throat went dry as I was presented to Her Majesty, Queen Victoria."

Sunny gasped. "What was she like?"

"She was very regal, wearing a crown encrusted with gems. They sparkled as she sat stiff, a solemn expression on her round, plump face," Riley reflected. "I called upon all my instructions and was able to curtsey to the floor without losing my balance or falling over. Once bowed low, the Queen tapped me upon the shoulders, indicating I could rise and take my place off to the side with the other girls. All of them had now become women."

"And where did all this take place?" Sunny probed.

"St. James Palace, a breath taking place, once the residence of kings and queens for over 300 years," Riley explained. "It was built by King Henry VIII on the site of the Hospital of St. James, Westminster, and used only for England's most important events. Now the queen resides in Buckingham Palace, but the red brick bastion is still an exquisite dwelling. It consists of four courts," Riley continued. "A Chapel Royal, a gatehouse, some turrets, a few Tudor rooms and a state room. Along St. James' long corridors royal portraits, those of military and naval heroes, as well as important battles, join displays of arms and armor hanging on the walls."

Lucinda cleared her throat, bringing them all back to the situation at hand. "I will continue to sponsor you, and Riley, who you have heard for yourself, is somewhat of an expert, can help you with your preparations."

Sunny frowned. "I will not wear the backboard again."

Lucinda arched a brow. "Good heavens, child, Kaylena inflicted you with that horrible device?"

She nodded. "And my brother broke it in half."

Lucinda laughed. "Good for Gabriel."

Riley's tone was soft. "He is a good brother, looking out for you."

She turned to catch Riley's eyes softening as much as her voice. "He is a good man who looks out for a lot of folks."

Riley sighed. "I had a feeling he is just as you say."

Lucinda cleared her throat again and brought the conversation once more back on track. "I will not allow you to travel about without benefit of a chaperone, so at all times either I or Cirie will accompany you out and be present if you have a gentleman caller."

"And am I allowed to choose the man I will wed?"

Lucinda stifled a smile. "If he is of good standing, has an ample way of supporting a household, vows to love and care for you appropriately, and you feel love for him, then aye, you will have my blessings."

She nodded in agreement. "Then I should very much like to live here."

Riley reached over and gave her arm an affectionate squeeze. "I am so very pleased to hear that, Sunny."

"I am in agreement with Riley," Lucinda said, taking a sip of her tea.

****

In only a matter of days, Sunny fit into the Collins' household. Gabriel appeared to feel the same because over breakfast one morning he asked Lucinda if she would like to have horses again at Collins Stead. When she responded with delight, he set the wheels in motion to rebuild the stables. Once again men were hired to help erect the new structure.

Cirie made it a point to bring refreshments out to the working men on the first day, but returned disappointed when Cody Denton was not amongst them.

Sunny's heart went out to Cirie, and to Riley, who had the same look a few days later when she learned Gabriel had gone off to ring in the new year with Collette Halston.

"Then he is betrothed to this Halston woman?" Riley probed at dinner that evening.

Lady Lucinda, tired from all the excitement cast upon her homestead, took her evening meal in her room, leaving Sunny and Riley to dine alone together.

"No, not hardly," she said, fingering the amber brooch pinned to her collar that Collette gave her while aboard the ship. "Collette is not the marrying sort."

Riley frowned. "I don't understand."

"Collette Halston is not interested in marriage, to my brother or any other man. She wants to remain free, to do as she wishes when she pleases and not be accountable to anyone."

Riley's frown deepened. "And this is the sort of woman Gabriel wants?"

She took an audible breath. "No, I do not believe it is."

"Then why does he continue to see her?" Riley probed. Then she cleared her throat nervously. "I'm sorry for being so nosy; I have no right to question Gabriel's encounters." She sighed. "It's perfectly acceptable for men to have them."

Not wanting Riley to get the wrong impression of her brother, she explained Gabriel's grief, the death of his wife and newborn son. As she spoke the other woman's eyes filled with tears.

"So, I believe, since Collette was the first woman to spark hope and a sense of belonging in Gabriel, he naturally feels she is the one he will make a new life with."

"But if it isn't what Collette wants then Gabriel will be hurt again," Riley said.

"I had the same thought and shared my feelings with Gabriel," she said.

Riley leaned forward in her seat. "What was his reaction?"

"After he called me a selfish and willful trouble maker, he said he believed, in time, he could change Collette's way of thinking."

Riley's eyes became dreamy. "If any man could

change a woman's mind, it would be Gabriel. He is so handsome and smart, polite and caring. Any woman would be glad to have his love."

Sunny stifled a smile. "And are you one of those who would be glad to have his love, Riley?" she teased.

Riley cleared her throat again, her face turning as crimson as the red locks upon her head. "I was merely speculating."

"Ah, yes, strange thing to speculate," she said, knowing full well how much time she spent wondering about Rafe Cavendish.

Chapter Thirty-Five

If Sunny thought the Cavendish's home, known to all as Cavenworth, was impressive; and the Abbot's estate, referred to as Abbotsford, remarkable; Bentwood Manor astounding; and Collins Stead astonishing; then Wade's Landing was absolutely, enormously exquisite. Never had she seen such a large mansion, so many windows in one room or spiral staircases. Nor did she ever believe she would know and be friends with the occupants who dwelled in such magnificence.

She arrived at the Wade mansion early in the afternoon, accompanied by Cirie, Riley, and Riley's attendant Jane, who was a cheery blonde with a stocky build and a great sense of humor. She thought her father's people, who were fun loving and enjoyed laughter, would appreciate Jane. In a sense, Jane balanced Riley's personality, which at times was too serious and straightforward. With Jane around, Riley relaxed and had fun.

When Sunny suggested Riley need not take everything so seriously, Riley's response was, "I think, since I was the only one to take care of my mother until her death, I somehow bypassed childhood. When you are the one who has to be accountable for another and their wellbeing, it is hard to be anything else but serious."

Hugging her newfound friend, she reassured her with a tender smile. "Well, now you are not alone, and need not be the one to do all the work and worry over all the decisions. So, enjoy the good things you have and those who love you."

Riley sighed. "I will try."

Strangely enough, when they all arrived at Wade's Landing, they found Fiona fretful and stressed over her coming nuptials. Lady Wade was in such a state, that Riley's take-charge attitude actually became a calming balm for the bride-to-be.

Maura, Fiona's attendant, turned out to be Jane's old next door neighbor and childhood friend. The two had not seen each other in years, and the reunion was one of hugs, tears, and giggles. With so much excitement and so many women chattering, Sunny's thoughts momentarily strayed from Rafe Cavendish, until Fiona mentioned his name.

"I am so blessed it is Simon I am marrying and not Rafe," Fiona gushed.

Riley sighed. "Both the Cavendish men are handsome enough."

"Aye, that they are, but Rafe hasn't the heart of Simon," Fiona countered.

"Rafe is a good and kind man," Sunny defended, remembering the time he put her heart at peace over Raven's plight, and the few heroic moves to save her life.

"Oh, all the Cavendish's are good and kind people," Fiona said. "All I mean is Rafe is not sincere in matters of love and loyalty, as is Simon."

Sunny frowned. "You do not think he can change, fall in love if the right woman comes along?"

Fiona hesitated a moment with an answer. "Perhaps, but Rafe views all women as conquests. I doubt, with such clouded judgment, he'd know the right woman when he saw her."

A few days later, Fiona's words still rang fresh in Sunny's mind. And when the handsome young captain, wearing a dark suit that accentuated his broad shoulders and muscular chest, stood at the bottom of the main staircase waiting to escort her into the large room where Simon and Fiona would take their vows, she fought desperately the yearning that rose to her lips for another kiss.

****

Rafe had never seen such loveliness. The deep green dress Sunny wore, draping every curve of her young, sensuous body, complemented the golden curls piled atop her head. As she descended the stairs, his eyes rested on the scooped neckline. A dizzying current rushed through him as the fleshy mounds of her full bosom came nearer for his viewing pleasure.

Taking her warm, delicate hand into his caused his pulse to become as erratic as a summer storm. He ached to touch her, take her fully into his embrace, and smother her with searing kisses. What her tanned, naked body looked like void of the dress and all that she wore beneath, brought his thoughts into blissful wonder.

And oh, if only that blissful wonder was mine to love.

His secret declaration stunned even him, but alas it was the truth. He had fallen in love with Sunny Beth Eagle and wished to make her his wife. Simon was right; there was no use to deny it further. The woman had taken up residence within the very marrow of his bones, and there'd be no getting away from her. In all honesty, he didn't want to get away from her. Not anymore. Not ever again.

The time was now to announce his intentions to her, lest another sweep her away. When he learned from Gabriel that morning of the German's proposal, his stomach clenched with jealousy and then was consumed by rage. If Sunny belonged anywhere, it was by his side, and no others.

"You and your beauty honor me this day, Sunny Beth," he whispered.

Her sapphire eyes locked with his. "I have missed you way too much, Captain."

The woman was always forthright, open with her feelings. From this day forward he would be the same in return. "As I have, you."

She leaned lightly into him, a small smile of enchantment touching her lips. "Can I count on *not* missing you again?"

He rewarded her with a larger smile of his own, squeezing her hand affectionately. "Aye, never again."

The rest of the day seemed to pass in a slow haze, his excitement to claim her pressing against his chest. And for the remainder of the evening he tried his best to stay close to her, in spite of his obligation to his brother. As the best man, he took his post seriously, even if not wholeheartedly, and received the guests he was expected to be polite to, tolerating the boring small talk.

Each time someone handed Sunny a goblet of wine, his concern for her mounted. She wasn't use to consuming so much of the spirits, and after the fourth glass, her steps faltered. Taking her arm, he led her out onto the veranda for a bit of air.

"You must have something more to eat," he suggested, removing his jacket and placing it over her shoulders.

"I have already cleaned my dinner plate," she said, slightly slurring her words.

He stifled a smile, remembering her hearty appetite. "Then slow down on the wine."

"I did not want to hurt the feelings of all those nice men offering."

He laughed. "They are paid to walk around and offer, Sunny. But they won't feel bad if you refuse."

"I did not want to chance it; they are trying so hard to please everyone."

Her response was typical. Sunny Eagle was a woman who cared for others, didn't want to hurt a soul and accepted whatever circumstance arose. A protectiveness for her welled deep within him, and he reached over to push a wayward tendril from her brow. "If you don't refuse, you'll end up falling flat on your face."

"Not to worry," she said, raising the skirt of her gown to well above her knees. "See, I have very strong legs."

Happily he took a long look at the shapely limbs, enjoying every inch of what he saw. "Aye, I agree."

"They got that way from running and climbing trees. I am the best in my village."

He arched an amused brow. "Tell me more about village life."

"Everyone loves to dance, and there are several dances for different occasions," she began.

"Like what occasions?" he probed.

"There is a dance to call the rain, one for healing, one to ready the warriors for war, one done before a hunt," she explained. "But my favorite is the mating dance."

He frowned. "Your people mate while dancing? Openly?"

She giggled and wrinkled her cute nose. "Oh heavens no, they do not actually mate. The dance is more of a courting ceremony, like an admission or announcement of one's intentions."

"Ah, I see." He cast a mischievous smile. "And how does one go about it?"

She hiked her skirt higher, revealing pantaloon covered thighs in perfect proportion to the rest of the shapely limbs. Then she began to bend her knees, first one, and then the other. Her hips swayed, her back arched, and every inch of her body seduced him in a way no other woman had ever done.

"Blimey," he whispered, his eyes mesmerized by her movements.

"Of course it is much easier to dance without all these clothes and with the rhythm of a drum," she said, her luscious bum moving back and forth.

His loins thickened beneath his breeches, his throat went dry. Wetting his lips he reached to stop her. *God save me, if she doesn't quit this soon, I'll have her stripped and bedded right here on the veranda floor.*

Unaware of what she was doing to him, she fell into his arms. "Then, since the woman is the one who chooses, she makes her way to the man she loves, and taps him gently on the cheek." Raising a hand, she softly touched his face, giving his cheek a tender pat.

Her scent engulfed him; her touch set him on fire. He enclosed his fingers around her tiny wrist and pulled her closer. "And then what does the man do?"

"If he is agreeable to her decision, he gives her a nod," she whispered, her lips so very tempting…so very close to his.

Her warm, sweet breath intoxicated him. "Or perhaps a kiss?" he offered, lowering his mouth to hers.

"Oh yes," she breathed against his lips.

His day had been interrupted constantly by the anticipation of her, and now that she was in his arms, her lips fused with his, the expectation was even greater than he could have ever imagined. His hands explored the hollows of her back; her arms encircled his neck, deepening the kiss. He felt her submit freely to the passion igniting their bodies, as he recaptured her mouth, more demanding this time.

"Your kiss sings through my heart," she whispered against his mouth.

Her words severed all control, and he reached for her hand. "Let's go somewhere more private where I can—"

She pulled away from him. "Where you can

what? Have me like your other women?" she interrupted. Her eyes filled with tears. "Do you not see...do you not realize by now I am not like those others?"

Her remark slapped him in the face, the blood freezing in his veins. "Nay, you misunderstand."

"I understand perfectly," she sobbed. "Oh, I did not want to believe the things that were said about you, hoping with all my heart the others were wrong. I really believed I felt something more, something genuine within your kiss, but I was wrong."

The hurt in her eyes crushed him, tore him to shreds. He extended a hand to her and again tried to explain, but she widened the distance between them.

"There is more, Sunny. With you it is—"

"It is what it is, Captain," she interrupted again. Then she removed his jacket from her shoulders and threw it at his feet. "And there is no one sorrier than I," she choked out before running from the veranda.

"Wait," he called out, taking off after her.

But Rafe was stopped at the door by his brother. "Ah, there you are, old chap," Simon teased. "It's time for you to give the parting toast. And I do wish you'd make it a fast one." He smiled mischievously. "I'm anxious to whisk my wife off to the hotel and the romantic honeymoon suite that awaits us there."

Forced into obligation once more on this day, he reluctantly followed his brother into the ballroom. As he gave the toast, his mind and heart wasn't centered on the newlywed couple that stood before him, but instead on the beautiful, young woman who had permanently left her touch etched upon his flesh.

****

Sunny ran blindly from the veranda, past the milling guests, and out through a side door. Over the landscaped lawn, down a wooded path, and out to

306

the main street her feet carried her. She cared not that she shivered from England's winter chill, or that her beautiful shoes and the hem of her gown were damp and muddy. All she wanted was to get far away from Wade's Landing and Rafe Cavendish.

She leaned against a brick wall to catch her breath, rehashing her time with him on the veranda. They were beautiful moments...tender moments...and then it all turned so horrible. All he wanted was to bed her, to make her just another one of his conquests. She had heard of his ways, why did she think he would treat her differently?

I have no right to accuse Gabriel of being a fool for Collette when I have been an even bigger one for Rafe.

The pain in her head mounted, and she squeezed her temples to relieve the throbbing, but to no avail. Her torment continued, consuming her entire body.

Why does love have to hurt so much?

She had seen the damage it did to Cirie when Cody Denton left, and in Riley's gaze as she watched Gabriel dance with Collette tonight. And she had no doubt, when Collette finished with her brother, she would see him hurting as well. Now she joined the ranks, heartsick and broken over a man who thought nothing more of her than a night of pleasure.

Her stomach lurched, and the bile rose to choke her. Leaning forward, she emptied the contents of her stomach, retching loudly.

Then she felt a presence behind her, the sound of his voice familiar, yet strange. "I've got you now."

But before she had the chance to turn and face him, see who it was that crept upon her as he did, his hand covered her nose with a cloth. The odor stung her eyes, she gasped and called out for help, but her words seemed to evaporate in the sound of the wind. She tried to push him away, but her arms went numb and her knees weakened. As limp as a rag doll she flopped helpless in his embrace.

"It will all be over soon," he whispered in her ear.

His frightening words were the last thing she heard before everything went black.

Chapter Thirty-Six

Rafe looked everywhere for Sunny, but had no luck in finding her. All he could think was she escaped to the bedchamber she occupied while at Wade's Landing, and hid there. He would go up himself to speak with her, but with so many watchful eyes he didn't want anyone to misunderstand his actions. England's tongues wagged and an inappropriate advance upon Miss Eagle's privacy could have all sorts of unkind and damaging rumors making the rounds.

He sought out Cirie, hoping she would go to Sunny on his behalf, but the other woman was also nowhere to be found. With head in hands, he sat alone in Lord Wade's den, wondering what his next move should be.

"Under the weather, are you, nephew," Josh Holmes commented as he walked through the door. "Or did you just have too much wine?"

He raised his gaze to his uncle. "Neither, I was just trying to think of a way to repair a misunderstanding."

Josh took a seat opposite him. "Sometimes two heads are better than one. Perhaps I can shed some light on the problem."

He stood, made his way to the window and gazed out while he explained his awakened feelings for Sunny Eagle and what conclusion she arrived at on the terrace.

"Hmm, that is more than a misunderstanding," Josh admitted.

He turned to face the elder man. "What can I do

to make her see my intentions are honorable?"

"You must go immediately to her and flawlessly deliver your heartfelt emotions," Josh advised. "And spare her no detail on where you stand and what life you hope for the two of you, Raphael," he warned. "To lose the woman you love is a terrible thing...a most heart wrenching ache that never fades."

"It sounds like you know all about such things firsthand," he said.

"I do," Josh confessed.

Before he could ask his uncle further questions Gabriel came into the room, his face flushed. "Sorry to interrupt, but I am looking for my sister. I have not been able to find her for quite some time, and I am becoming concerned."

He took an audible breath. "I'm afraid her disappearance is my fault."

Gabriel frowned. "And how is that, Captain?"

Knowing it would be unwise to go into detail, he only admitted there was a misunderstanding between them. "I believe she must be taking refuge in her chamber."

"I have already been to her room and found it empty," Gabriel said, his frown increasing.

"Well, certainly she can't have gone far," Josh said. He stood and neared the door. "If we split up, I'm sure we'll run into her somewhere."

Who they ran into was Cirie, out of breath and near to tears. "Thank God I found ye, Master Gabriel. They've taken Miss Sunny. I saw 'em, there was two o' 'em, and they took 'er away," Cirie rattled on.

Gabriel placed a hand squarely upon each of the young girl's shoulders and talked to her in a calming tone. "You must pull yourself together, Cirie."

She inhaled sharply. "Aye, sir."

"Now, tell me exactly what you saw and where," Gabriel probed.

"I saw Miss Sunny run from the veranda. She was in tears, didn't even stop when I called out 'er name. So, I followed 'er, thinkin' she'd need me when she got wherever she was runnin' off to."

"And where was that," Rafe interrupted.

"She stopped at the street, stood against the brick wall, cried, got sick, and just as I was about to 'elp 'er, 'e came up behind 'er," Cirie explained.

"Who came up behind her?" Gabriel questioned further.

"I don't know who 'e was, Master Gabriel. It was too dark to see, and besides 'e 'ad a 'at pulled down low over 'is brow. But 'e reached around Miss Sunny's face with a cloth and capped it over 'er nose. Then she fell limp in 'is arms."

"She was drugged," Rafe concluded. "Perhaps if we hurry we can catch up to this intruder. He couldn't have gotten too far carrying an unconscious woman."

"Oh, 'e weren't carryin' 'er, Captain," Cirie confirmed. "A carriage pulled up and another man 'elped to get Miss Sunny inside."

He combed a hand through his hair. "What's going on here, anyway?"

"My question exactly, Captain," Cirie agreed. "Especially since the carriage which took Miss Sunny was the Mum's own coach."

The muscles at Gabriel's jaws throbbed. "The carriage belonged to my Aunt Kaylena?"

Cirie nodded.

"Are you sure, Cirie?" Rafe questioned.

"Aye, Captain. I know it as well as my own 'and," Cirie said.

He frowned. "But why would Kaylena go to such lengths to—"

"Because she is a mean and stubborn old woman," Gabriel interrupted. "And she is hell bent on marrying my sister off to Count Sontag."

Rafe could feel his rage mount. "That buffoon is not good enough for Sunny."

"On that we agree," Gabriel said. "Sunny did not want the union, so I stepped in and forbid the marriage, which did not set well with Aunt Kaylena. She told us to obey her rules or leave. So, that is exactly what we did. Now we are living with Lady Collins. But it seems this makes no difference to Kaylena Bentley. She will have her way at all cost."

Josh gasped. "You can't believe she'd have her own niece kidnapped and forced into marriage?"

"I believe that is exactly what she has done," Gabriel said.

"Or the letter 'as somethin' to do with this," Cirie offered. "Ye all know Mum's been pretty scared ever since she got it."

"Either way, we've wasted enough time talking," Rafe said, heading for the stables. "Uncle Josh, find Lord Wade. Tell him I need two of his fastest horses and to meet us in the stables." He turned then to Gabriel. "Come on now, mate, tonight we ride to Brighton."

****

When Sunny opened her eyes, her vision blurred. The pain in her head made her gulp for air, as she sat up and took in her surroundings. It was a familiar room, the very one where her aunt taught her to walk, ram-rod straight, for hours on end. Bentwood Manor's solarium was dark but for a candle on the mantel. No fire burned in the fireplace, setting an even greater chill about the place.

Kaylena sat in a chair on the far side of the room, her eyes wide with terror, staring at Sunny like she was looking right through her.

"He's come, Sunny," she whispered. "My son has come, and he means to kill us all."

Her steps were sluggish as she made her way to her aunt's side, taking the frail elder woman fully into her embrace. "Do you have a knife, a gun, any sort of weapon hidden in this room, Aunt Kaylena?"

"Nay, the rifle is in my chamber," Kaylena said.

She shook her head to clear it and scanned the solarium, spotting the fireplace poker standing in a corner. It was not the best defense, but better than none at all. Standing slowly, she neared the cast iron rod, and picked it up, feeling its weight in her palm. From hand to hand she tossed it, getting a feel for its size.

"What are you doing?" Kaylena choked out.

"I think I can use this poker like a spear. It is not as light, but if I thrust it just so," she said, gripping the poker at its center and raising her arm. But such an action made her head swim, and she leaned against the wall to keep her balance.

"Are you dizzy?" Kaylena asked.

Sunny nodded.

Kaylena stood, coming to her niece's aide. With an arm around her shoulders, Kaylena helped her to a chair. "It's the after effect of the drug used to subdue us. I felt the same at first." The elder woman went to the serving tray placed on a nearby table and poured water from the pitcher, into a glass. Handing the goblet to Sunny, she searched her face with motherly concern. "I am so sorry to have dragged you into all this."

"Did your son come alone?"

"Nay, he brought another along."

"And where are they now?"

Kaylena sighed and closed her eyes in agony. "Dealing with the rest of those in the household." Upon opening her eyes, her gaze was terror-filled as she whispered. "We are to be last."

Sunny took a sip of the water and inhaled a cleansing breath. "The dizziness has passed. I think the drug is wearing off." She looked down at the poker she still clutched in her other hand. "We have to find a way to fight them."

"Save yourself, Sunny," Kaylena whispered again.

"I will fight for both of us," she said.

Tears welled in her aunt's eyes. "I have been so dreadful to you, treating you as my father did me. And I am ashamed of myself for such behavior." She knelt down at Sunny's knees and clutched her arm. "Can you ever forgive me for my actions?"

She placed the glass aside and wrapped an arm around her aunt's neck, laying a cheek upon the elder woman's head. "All is forgiven, but now we must set our sight on fighting these men. A good warrior has to clear his mind of all things, focusing only on his enemy."

Kaylena pulled back to gaze into her eyes. "You can't plan to fight these men?"

"I will not just sit here and allow them to kill us," she countered.

Kaylena stood; mouth puckered and looked around the room. Her eyes rested on the heavy paperweight sitting on a writing table. She picked it up, clutched it in her hand, and raised her arm, pretending to throw it. "I don't know how much good I will be, but I will do my best to help. Just tell me what you want me to do."

"First we need to light more candles. Being able to see the enemy is always better than not. Then we must fight to the end."

****

Rafe hadn't ridden in years, and being bogged down with warmer clothing, while carrying a weapon other than the dirk he usually hid in his boot, didn't help the situation. But as soon as he sat in the saddle and urged the horse forward, it all came back to him. Gabriel was an excellent horseman. His body became one with the animal he straddled, and he took the road with speed only a confident rider dared.

Lord Wade led the way. A seasoned equestrian himself, he knew a route to Bentwood Manor through back roads and forest paths. By train Brighton was a two hour trek, by horseback the journey tripled. Even then the horses would have to be pushed beyond reasonable expectancy. Most definitely the short cuts would slash their traveling time and give them an advantage, since the kidnappers had their mounts hitched to a carriage and only about an hour's head start. With the carriage, they would most likely stick to the main roads. At any rate, they went after the scoundrels with clear heads about them, the three of them armed and ready for a fight.

I haven't had a good brawl in years, perhaps I'm due.

Rafe vowed as he rode that he wouldn't let any harm come to Sunny, whatever the cost. Even if saving her meant he lost his own life.

Love, this is what it does to a man.

He had to smile, thinking back to how Simon tried to warn him. And he was grateful his brother swept his new bride off to their honeymoon suite before Sunny's disappearance was discovered. Otherwise Simon, also loving a good brawl, would have joined them. Realizing the consequences ahead, he shook his head to clear it. The possibility someone might not be coming back from this battle tonight haunted him. But at least Simon was safe, and Fiona wouldn't be trading her wedding gown for a widow's dress any time too soon.

When the trio pulled up to the path leading to Bentwood Manor, Gabriel raised a hand for the riders to halt and dismount. "We are better off to go the rest of the way on foot. The intruders will not hear us coming that way." He gazed heavenward. "We are in luck. The full moon will light our way."

As they ran with silent steps to the main entrance, they spotted Kaylena's carriage, still hitched to the horse and ready for a fast getaway. From a nearby bush a man stepped out, creeping around to the back of the manor. In one fluid motion Gabriel was on him, tackling the other man to the ground. Rafe couldn't help but remember his own skirmish with Gabriel aboard the ship. The man was incredibly fast and strong. With quiet force, he dragged the man to where Rafe and Lord Wade stood watching.

Cody Denton stumbled and balked. "What in blue blazes are you doing?"

Smashing Cody against a tree Gabriel gritted his teeth and eyed the other man with a new awareness. "Now I know where I have seen the picture my aunt drew of Ryan Duffy...on you! It is his face you wear."

Cody stiffened. "Why would your aunt draw a picture of my uncle?"

Gabriel frowned. "Your uncle? Do you not mean your father?"

"No, my father is Calvin Denton," Cody snarled. "Ryan Duffy is my uncle...my mother's brother who died while fighting Indians in the military over twenty-nine years ago."

Gabriel stepped away from Cody. "I do not understand."

Cody raised a defiant chin. "That makes two of us." He folded his arms across his chest. "How does Kaylena Bentley know my Uncle Ryan and why would she draw pictures of him?"

Rafe got in between the two men. "None of this matters right now." He glared at Cody. "Why are you here?"

"I came back for Cirie," he said.

"And why did you walk out on the girl in the first place?" Gabriel probed.

"I didn't walk out on her. I left her a letter explaining I'd only be gone a week to seek out my relatives living here in Brighton. My father's uncle passed away and left a sum of money to our family. My father, being too sick and elderly to travel, sent me in his place. But on my journey I was robbed by two mangy looking thugs. They took all my money, except for a few dollars I hid in my boot. Since I didn't want my new relations to think I was some sort of freeloader, I took the job at Bentwood."

"Who did you leave the letter with?" Gabriel said.

"I gave it to Bertha, with Cirie's name written on the envelope. I thought for sure she'd give it to her," Cody said.

Gabriel arched a brow. "Well that explains why Cirie never got your message, Bertha cannot read."

"So, you are just now returning for Cirie?" Rafe queried.

Cody nodded. "But then I saw these two men carrying Miss Sunny into the house, and I knew something wasn't right. I hid in the bushes and was just about to scope out the back of the manor when Gabriel jumped me."

"There is good reason to believe my aunt and sister are in grave danger," Gabriel said.

"And what about my Cirie? I didn't see her with Miss Sunny." Cody said.

"She is not at Bentwood. We left her in London, at Wade's Landing. She is the one who saw Sunny kidnapped," Rafe explained.

"Did you recognize these men, Cody?" Gabriel said.

"No, never saw the culprits before, but one of them is a big bastard," Cody said.

"Sons of bitches," Rafe snarled. "They better not lay a hand on Sunny."

Gabriel arched a brow. "Ah, so it is that way for

you now, too?"

"Aye," he muttered.

"Well, come on then, let's get the scoundrels," Cody hissed.

"I totally agree with this chap here," Lord Wade added.

"Come, then," Gabriel said. He led the way, followed by Cody, then Lord Wade.

Rafe squared his shoulders and took up the rear.

Chapter Thirty-Seven

The knob on the solarium door jiggled. Sunny hid the poker behind her back and moved to stand near her aunt. Kaylena shielded the paperweight she held as well. The two women, though poorly armed, stood ready to defend themselves.

When she spotted him, her heart leaped with hope. "Thank heaven it is you! We have been taken over by intruders and at any moment they will return."

Kaylena placed a hand on her arm. "Sunny, he is the intruder."

"Now, now, mother," Ivan Sontag drawled, his German accent gone. "Is that a nice way to introduce your long lost son?"

"Count Sontag?" she gasped. "You are her son?"

Ivan bowed. "At your service, only I am not really a count, as you probably have already guessed." He chuckled. "I do believe I put on a rather convincing act though, if I do say so myself. However, if you look closely you can see the resemblance I hold to my darling Mama."

It was true; they shared the same blue eyes and fair complexion, the straight nose and high cheekbones. Before she had a chance to speak, another man entered the solarium. Sunny recognized him as Armond Preston, Ivan's companion from aboard the ship. Her heart raced with fear. "Why are you doing this, Ivan?"

"It's what *she* deserves," he said, casting a glance at Kaylena, "for abandoning me at birth."

"But I've already explained that to you. I

thought you died at birth. The sisters at the mission told me you were stillborn," Kaylena said.

"Why would the nuns lie?" Ivan snapped.

"They survived on donations and money they received from rich, barren women who needed to give their husbands an heir. So, they'd come to the mission to adopt a child. Because of this, white male babies were in high demand. Your mother was set to take home a child, born a day before my own baby. Her baby actually *did* die at birth. Needing the money, the nuns gave her my child instead and told me my baby had died," Kaylena explained.

"Why were you at the mission anyway? Where was my real father?" Ivan demanded.

"He was killed in the Indian wars," Kaylena said. "Since I was an unwed mother, I went to the mission to have my baby in private, figuring I would sail back to England when we were both able to travel." She sighed. "And I had hoped we would have a life together then, but it was not meant to be."

"No, what was meant to be was that I spend a life of hell with the man I called, *Father*. He wanted a burly son, a son who liked to hunt and fish, who was strong and fearless. Not one who admired his mother's lace and the fellow students at the boy's academy." Ivan swallowed hard. "And when he found out my preferences, he beat me within an inch of my life, left me to die, naked and bleeding in the woods."

"Oh, Ivan," Kaylena said, taking a step forward. "You have no idea how much I empathize with you."

Ivan held up a hand to halt her advance. "I doubt that very much, Mother. In fact, I have a feeling things wouldn't have been much different if you had had the chance to rear me. From what I have seen, you would also be ashamed of my lifestyle. Like my adopted father, you would have worried what society thought, feared a scandal, and probably would have also sent me away to live at some horrid and cruel boarding school."

"If what you say is true, why did you want to marry me?" Sunny said.

"To gain the Bentley inheritance, of course, since I've been disinherited by those I thought were my parents. Then, as your husband, I could control your assets." He locked eyes with her. "By and by some drastic tragedy would befall you, my dear, as you would soon come to realize it was not your charms I desired. Next to perish would be my beautiful mother," he said, glancing over at Kaylena. "And last but not least, my dear brother-in-law, Gabriel, who would die at an unfortunately young age. Then Bentwood would belong to me."

"And how do you plan on doing all this now?" Kaylena said.

"Well, sometimes the best laid plans get out of control. When Gabriel set me aside, did not allow my marriage to Sunny, he insured your immediate deaths. I might not have Bentwood Manor and the Bentley fortune, but neither will any of you." Ivan turned to the massive man standing behind him. "Are the servants tied and locked in the kitchen pantry, Armond?"

"All securely bound," Armond said.

"What are you going to do to us?" Sunny said, tightening her grip on the poker she held behind her back.

"After I tie the two of you, I'm going to set the place on fire. It's a pity Gabriel isn't here, so I could get the job done all in one night, but I'll have my chance to hunt him down." Ivan shot a glance at the mantel clock. "Enough with the explanations; I've wasted too much time talking already."

As he neared Sunny, she raised the poker and struck him on the side of the head. He staggered back, blood dripping from his temple. At that moment Kaylena threw the paperweight at Armond Preston, who was advancing on her. The glass globe grazed his shoulder, doing him little harm, before it hit the floor and shattered into pieces.

Sunny heard Kaylena scream, glimpsed her kicking and punching the massive man, but none of her aunt's efforts could stop Armond. He struck Kaylena across the face, the blow knocking her unconscious. The elder woman crumpled to the floor.

During those moments, Ivan regained his composure and plunged at Sunny, throwing her into the table that held the water pitcher and goblets. The poker flew from her hands and everything crashed and shattered, bits of glass cutting her arms.

She struggled to stand, her gown cumbersome and weighty.

Ivan reached for her, but she managed to avoid his grasp. He slipped on the spilt water, and fell to his knees.

She headed for the door, but he rose and caught her by the hem of her gown. As he pulled her toward him, she kicked at his face and chest. But he was stronger than he looked and in no time he was fully upon her, both his hands encircling her throat. She gasped and choked for air, as the pressure increased.

Just as she thought she gulped her last breath, Ivan was ripped away.

Rafe slammed Ivan against the wall. Gabriel and Cody Denton took on Armond, the two punching the large man from every side. She gasped for breath, watching the chaos taking place around her.

Ivan stood and charged Rafe. The two fought with angry fists. Ivan reached for and pulled out a gun he had secured at his waist.

Horror, stark and sharp filled her heart. As fast as her legs would allow, she stood and hurried to stand between the two men, shielding Rafe from

Ivan's aim. The weapon fired, the bullet hit her shoulder. She heard Rafe scream her name as the white heat penetrated her body.

She fell back against a wall, slipping down to sit on the floor. She glanced down at the front of her gown. The forest green material darkened with her blood. The crimson design encircled the amber brooch and spread out across her abdomen.

She thought of her parents, the little wickiup where she slept, ate, and laughed with friends and family.

I miss you all so much...and you, Raven...how I wish I could hear your voice.

The fighting continued around her as her body weakened. Gabriel and Cody had managed to overcome Armond, the two binding the unconscious man's hands and feet with rope. Lord Wade appeared with Gerta and Bertha following close behind.

Rafe continued to brawl with Ivan, wrestling him for the gun. It was then she saw Kaylena crawling to retrieve something from the corner of the room. When she stood she held the poker. Coming up behind Ivan, she buried the sharp edge of the weapon into his back. He weakened, fell limp against Rafe's chest, and dropped to the floor beside Sunny.

Kaylena stood over him; her face pale and drawn, eyes glazed. "Through my body you gained life, by my hand you die," she choked out before collapsing into Lord Wade's arms.

Rafe ran to Sunny, taking her into his embrace. Tears welled in his eyes. "Sunny Beth, my Sunny Beth, stay with me."

She managed to force a smile. "I will be fine," she whispered.

"Gabriel and Fritz have gone for a doctor. You just stay with me," he pleaded.

"All is well, I just need to rest," she reassured him, feeling her strength ebb from her body.

She closed her eyes.

I am just tired...just very...very...tired.

Chapter Thirty-Eight

Rafe paced alongside Gabriel down the hallway outside of Sunny's bedchamber. Cody Denton stood leaning against a wall, Kaylena Bentley sat upon a bench, and Lord Wade perched beside her, an arm around her shoulders.

Inside the bedchamber, the physician, assisted by Gerta, was doing his best to save Sunny's life. The authorities arrived along with the doctor to take Ivan Sontag's body to the morgue and Armond Preston to prison.

As the corridor clock struck midnight, Doctor Barton Yardley, an old friend of the Bentley family, emerged from the room. He wiped his forehead with a handkerchief; his plump face laced with concern, and spoke in a soft tone. "I've done all I can for her at this point."

Gabriel stepped forward. "When can I see her?"

"Let's let her rest some, shall we?" Doctor Yardley suggested.

"Will she be all right?" Gabriel said.

Doctor Yardley cleared his throat. "Well, the good news is the bullet went right through the shoulder."

Rafe neared the doctor now, his voice cracking with emotion. "And what's the bad news."

The doctor sighed. "She's lost a lot of blood, and of course, there's always a chance of infection."

Kaylena let out a choked sob and buried her face beneath Lord Wade's chin.

Doctor Yardley made his way to her, resting a hand upon her arm. "I'm going to stay on, see your niece through the night." He placed a hand across the elder woman's brow. "When was the last time you took any nourishment?"

Kaylena shook her head. "I can't remember."

Doctor Yardley glanced at Lord Wade. "Take her downstairs, my lord. Have Bertha prepare her a bit of food and something to drink."

"Aye," Lord Wade agreed.

"I want to stay, be here in case Sunny needs me," Kaylena protested.

"You will be no good to your niece if you are ill yourself," Doctor Yardley countered. "Now, I insist, Kaylena."

Lord Wade took Kaylena by the hand. "Shall we, my dear?"

Kaylena hesitated a moment before nodding in agreement, then stood with Lord Wade's assistance. The two then made their way downstairs and Doctor Yardley returned to Sunny's side.

"That woman has nerve acting concerned for my sister," Gabriel snarled. "All she did while we lived beneath her roof was disrespect Sunny, and was well prepared to beat her if she didn't marry Sontag."

Rafe frowned, his insides turning. "Did Kaylena place a hand on Sunny?"

Gabriel shook his head. "She did not have the chance. As soon as I realized what was going on, I took Sunny to Collins Stead."

"Speaking of your aunt," Cody drawled. "Why did she draw pictures of my Uncle Ryan?"

Gabriel combed a hand threw his hair. "It is a long story, Denton."

Cody shrugged. "It don't look like any of us is going anywhere fast."

"This isn't the time, mate," Rafe intervened.

Gabriel held up a hand. "Maybe this is exactly the time, Captain." He pointed to Sunny's chamber door. "My sister lies in that room, fighting for her life right now because of the secrets and lies Kaylena Bentley managed." He turned toward Cody. "You said your uncle died in the Indian wars?"

Cody nodded.

"Well, I am an Indian. A half-breed to be exact; part Apache and part white."

Cody's face turned crimson. "Men do what they have to in the face of a battle. Look what we had to do tonight to save your sister and aunt."

"You speak the truth, and it is only because you fought beside me that I will explain everything to you." Gabriel glanced over at Rafe. "It is good for you to hear all I have to say as well."

"All I care about is Sunny, that she lives through the night and heals properly," he said.

"And because your heart now belongs to Sunny, it is your right to know all there is about the family," Gabriel said. He turned again to Cody. "Before I was born my aunt traveled to America. Her reason was to bring her only sister's daughter, which is my mother, back with her to England. Lieutenant Ryan Duffy escorted Kaylena's wagon train to its destination. While on that journey the two came together, both of them lonely people far from home, and as a result Kaylena became with child."

Cody arched a brow. "Well, I'll be doggone."

"When my aunt finally arrived in Willow Creek, she learned my mother had married an Apache," Gabriel continued.

"Bet that didn't set well," Cody sneered.

"No, not by anyone's standards," Gabriel agreed. "To make a long story short," he went on, "Ryan Duffy found out about this *scandalous* union and captured my father; beat him with a whip and sentenced him to hang."

"It was war, Gabriel," Cody reminded him. "And one that long ago has gone."

Gabriel's jaw muscles throbbed. "But my father

still bears those scars across his back, Cody. And the white men still treat us like dogs, taking over our village and compromising our women. That is the very reason we came to England...to keep Sunny and Raven safe. And I have not done right by either of them."

Rafe could see Gabriel was becoming upset and changed the subject. "What happened to Kaylena's child?"

Gabriel explained about the mission, the part the nuns played in Kaylena believing her baby died, and the letter recently received.

"Then we've got her son coming to make trouble as well," Cody said.

"Nay, he's already come...and gone," Kaylena said.

All three turned to find her standing at the top of the stairs.

Gabriel stood. "It was Count Sontag, was it not?"

Kaylena sighed. "Aye, except he never really was a count."

"You mean that piece of shit was our cousin?" Cody snapped.

"Aye," Kaylena said. She neared Gabriel, reclaiming the bench seat she had occupied before. "And I killed him...my own flesh and blood."

"As I see it you had no choice, Miss Kaylena," Cody said. "I believe we all did tonight what we had to do."

"I agree, besides you saved my life," Rafe added.

"No, Sunny saved your life," Kaylena countered, then frowned as she searched Cody's face. "Do I know you?"

"He is one of the men I hired to help build the barrier," Gabriel said. "His name is Cody Denton."

"Nay, I mean, have we met before?" Kaylena clarified.

"Not me, but my uncle," Cody explained.

"And who is your uncle, sir?" Kaylena probed.

"Duffy...Ryan Duffy," Cody said.

Kaylena gasped, covering her face with her hands. "Good heavens, they're coming out of the woodwork to haunt me."

Gabriel looked down at his aunt and placed a hand upon her shoulder. "It is time for all of us to forgive, forget, and move ahead."

"I agree," Cody said. "Many things have happened way before any of us was born. And what's happened now can't be changed."

"And we must all take the time to heal," Rafe added, knowing it was time to let go of the hurt Deandra caused him and start anew—with Sunny. He cast a worried glance at her bedchamber door. "Sunny, most of all."

****

Rafe never left Bentwood Manor, or Sunny's side, when he was allowed into her room. For the most part Cirie, who by now had returned to Brighton, and Gerta tended her. Gabriel sat in a chair beside the bedchamber fireplace throughout the night, watching over his sister with hawk-like eyes. By day, Gabriel worked outside with Cody Denton.

But even with the excellent attention and quality care she was given, Sunny's condition worsened. For days her body was ravaged by fever, her flesh hot and dry to the touch, and it frightened them all.

His Uncle Josh was called in on the third day. Everyone stood around Sunny's bed and joined hands as prayers were said for her healing. He mouthed the pleas, his stomach clenching in fear as he gazed down upon the beautiful young woman who lay so still in the bed.

One afternoon, he found Cirie, as faithful at her post as they all had been, swabbing Sunny's forehead with a cool compress. "It's time to wake now, Miss Sunny, and put the smiles back on all our faces." The young woman looked haggard and worn, but in spite of her own weariness, she kept at her vigil.

"I'll take over, Cirie, you go and get some rest," he offered.

"Nay, I can't leave 'er," Cirie protested.

He leaned down, took the cloth from Cirie's hand and escorted her to the door. "I need some time alone with her." He searched the young woman's face. "Please, do you understand?"

"Aye, Captain, I do," she said, forcing a small smile. "I can't think o' 'er being in better hands."

After closing the door behind Cirie, he made his way back to the bed. Sitting beside Sunny, he remoistened the cloth from a nearby basin and swabbed her forehead, cheeks, neck, and then her arms. Over and over again he repeated the process, hoping his efforts would take down the fever, break her from its grasp.

And while he worked, he talked to her. Told her how much he loved her; how he wanted to make a life with her, have a family and a home, and even a dog.

"You said after we kissed that I made your heart sing. Well, in truth, I feel the same, my love. Not only your kiss, but the color of your eyes, the scent of your flesh, the softness of your hair...as well as your laugh, with its lilting chord, sends happiness to every facet of my being." He gathered her limp, searing body into his embrace. "Come out of this, Sunny Beth. Don't leave me...please, for God's sake, don't leave me."

"I will not allow her to leave any of us," a voice came from behind.

Rafe turned to find Gabriel standing in the doorway with tear-filled eyes.

"And I have had enough of the white man's *izee,* medicine. It does no good," Gabriel snapped.

He sighed, his own fatigue overwhelming, his heart breaking. With a gentle hand he laid Sunny back upon the pillow. "What else is left?"

"The Apache way," Gabriel said.

He stood, facing Gabriel squarely, his voice sharper than he intended. "What nonsense do you speak?"

"It is not nonsense, but truth. I have seen it work in my village." Gabriel gestured toward Sunny. "If she is put into the sweat bath, the fever will leave her body." He reached for a quilt at the foot of the bed and handed it to Rafe. "You wrap her in this and take her down to the beach within an hour's time. I will have everything ready by then."

He frowned. "Is this what you and Cody have been doing these last few days, building a sweat bath?"

Gabriel gave a taut nod. "Bring her within an hour."

"Gabriel, listen—"

"No, Captain, you listen," Gabriel interrupted. "Even the doctor has given up, left Sunny for dead, because he knows he has done everything your people know how to do. So, what can we lose by trying the sweat bath?"

He shook his head, resigned. "Nothing, there's nothing to lose."

"You will bring her, then?"

"Aye, within the hour," he agreed.

****

A parade of people followed Rafe as he carried Sunny, wrapped in the quilt, down to the beach. When he stopped at the door of the little wooden shack, the others encircled it. He glanced around at them all; Kaylena, Lord Wade, his Uncle Josh, Fritz, Bertha, Gerta, Cirie, and Cody, and saw a mixture of hope and fear in their eyes. All of them loved Sunny.

Lord, can you not see what a horrible injustice it would be if you took this woman?

Gabriel emerged from the sweat bath with arms outstretched. "I will take my sister now."

"Nay, I will take her inside," he protested, holding her tight against his chest.

Gabriel nodded and stepped aside. "There was not enough time to build the benches so you will have to sit upon the ground. After you have placed Sunny about a foot from the rocks, you will need to remove your jacket and shirt, as it will get very warm for you otherwise. I will hand you the pitcher of water to throw over the heated stones."

"And what do I do after that?"

"Just sit beside her, watch the steam blanket her flesh," Gabriel said. Then he added, "It also would not hurt for you to pray."

He placed her with loving hands a fair amount of distance from the mound of heated rocks, doffed his upper garments and showered the stones with the cool water Gabriel provided. A fine mist filled the little hut, dampening his hair and chest, seeping into his breeches, making his toes swelter in his boots.

Rafe tended to Sunny, opening wide the blanket she was wrapped in, unfastening the buttons at the neck of her garment, rolling up the sleeves and raising the hem of the nightdress to her knees. It wasn't long after beads of moisture formed on her brow, the tendrils of hair framing her face curled, her breathing eased, as the shroud of fog danced around her.

Listening to Gabriel chant outside the hut, Rafe swallowed hard the lump of grief lodged in his throat. He sat down beside Sunny, turning his back to her and closing his eyes. His head bent in prayer as the vigil went on for almost an hour. But if he had to sit in this haze all night and sweat off every ounce of flesh from his bones, he would if it meant she'd be well again.

He called upon every saint, every Bible passage he could remember, every prayer he was taught, and when he ran the gambit, he began to bargain with God, make deals. Spent of prayers, he wept like a child, hands covering his face, and pleaded for her life.

It was when the vapor thinned that he felt her touch. The tip of her finger traced the line of his scar, as it had done once before. His eyes shot open, his heart raced as the finger was replaced with lips—soft, full lips that now pressed into his flesh and kissed the length of the old wound.

He spun around to face her, eyes blinking to clear them from his tears, and gazed upon the splendor of her beautiful face.

She moistened her lips with the tip of her tongue and smiled. "Well, Captain, are you ever going to tell me how you got that scar?"

Chapter Thirty-Nine

Fall of 1893
Bentwood Manor, Brighton, England

Sunny gazed out her bedchamber window and watched as the rosy dawn was slowly replaced by a brilliant blaze of a full sunrise. It looked like it would be another beautiful autumn day. But today would be gorgeous if the weather decided to cooperate or not. She waited so long for this time to come on two accounts—Rafe had finally returned, just two nights ago, after being months away on an Australian voyage, and today was her wedding day. In just a few hours she would be Rafe Cavendish's wife.

She sighed as she stood from the window seat and made her way to where her bridal gown hung. As she smoothed the lacy skirt she thought of her sister, Raven. By tradition she should have been the next in line to wear their mother and grandmother's wedding dress. But Raven was in Ireland and already wed to Lord Braiton Shannon. Hard to believe the incident had taken place a year ago.

"My, has it been that long already," she whispered to herself.

So much had happened since the day she discovered her sister accidentally boarded the wrong ship. Now, at nineteen, she reflected on all she had endured, as well as accomplished since that time.

She helped her aunt overcome a drinking problem and to embrace a new life with Morgan Wade. Kaylena and Lord Wade were married six months ago and lived at Wade's Landing. They were happy and very much in love. Sunny was so pleased her aunt finally was able to have the life she dreamed, finding a heart of gold in Lord Wade. He was a man who did not hold the past against her aunt, but instead embraced the future.

Bentwood Manor was left to her and Gabriel, and the two of them turned the mansion into a health resort. Her brother's sweat baths, the only such service offered in town, brought in constant business. And Sunny's little gift shop stocked with sampler art and painted furniture and co-owned with her former art teacher, Elwood Hunter, turned a pretty profit as well. Elwood now resided in the east section of Bentley Manor, along with his wife, Gerta. Once employed as Kaylena's handmaiden, Gerta now ran the boutique at the resort, making bonnets, handbags, and other lacy items to sell.

Sunny sat at her dressing table now and pulled a brush through her long golden curls. England had become more a part of her than she ever realized it could be. Her début alone was a day she would never forget. Dressed in an aqua and white lace gown, she rode in a black, highly polished coach. The red plush interior wrapped her in style all the way to St. James Palace. The day enfolded just as Riley had once explained.

"I've come to 'elp ye dress and do yer hair, miss," Cirie said, interrupting her thoughts as she entered the bedchamber. "Can't 'ave ye late for yer own weddin' now, can we?"

"Has my aunt arrived yet?"

"Aye, miss, Lady Wade will be along as soon as she's finished checkin' on the food preparations."

She chuckled. "Always in control, is she not?"

"Aye, miss, that she is," Cirie agreed.

"Well, at this point I am thankful for her help, as I have not a head for a thing."

335

"As it should be, this being yer day and all. And 'tis turnin' out to be a fine one at that," Cirie said.

"As fine as when you married Cody Denton?"

Cirie's face beamed with love for her new husband. "Ah, none could be as fine as that day, miss."

"Have Fiona and Riley awakened yet?"

"I believe so, miss." Cirie giggled. "Not that any o' us could sleep much anyway."

It was not long before Fiona, dressed in a maid of honor gown of gold, and bridesmaid Riley, wearing a burnished shade of orange, joined her. Aunt Kaylena and Marietta Cavendish also made an appearance. Soon the large bedchamber grew smaller by the moment, filled with female giggles and excited chatter.

In spite of her heart bursting with overwhelming joy, a small part of her ached for her parents and sister to be present on this blessed occasion. And though she loved Fiona and was pleased she agreed to stand up for her, the role of maid of honor rightfully belonged to Raven.

"Something old, something new, something borrowed, something blue, I think I've remembered it all for you," Riley said.

"You are most organized, Riley, and I thank you," she said, giving her friend a hug.

Riley's eyes moistened. "Oh, Sunny, you look so beautiful."

"I feel beautiful," she boasted.

"It's every bride's right," Fiona said, straightening the veil upon Sunny's head. Since Sunny's gown was void of a veil, Fiona lent her the one she wore on her wedding day. It was the *something borrowed*.

"My son is a lucky man," Marietta added, bestowing a light kiss upon Sunny's cheek.

Riley sighed. "That I should live to see my own

wedding day."

Kaylena gave the younger woman an affectionate pat on the arm. "And I see no reason why that shouldn't be, child."

Sunny knew why Riley was apprehensive about the future. Her friend was in love with Gabriel. But he was still quite captivated with Collette Halston. She knew from the start Collette was not the woman for her brother, but he had his own mind on the matter and did not welcome her advice. She could only hope that in time Gabriel would come to his senses. One of her nightly prayers was that her brother would see Riley was the right woman for him all along. But for now she would not worry over anyone else's troubles, hopes or dreams, as this was her special day.

Her heart raced when the knock came at the door. It was Gabriel, ready to escort her downstairs to the elaborate, newly constructed gardens. There, beneath the lattice-work gazebo he would give her hand in marriage to Rafe, and they would speak their vows in front of the officiator, Reverend Joshua Holmes. A wedding reception was to immediately follow in the new ballroom.

"Enter," she called out, her heart skipping a beat.

Gabriel, dressed handsomely in a black suit, extended a hand and drew her to him. "You are beyond beautiful, *dayden*."

She smiled up at him. "And will you continue to call me that even though I am soon to be a wife?"

"Especially because of that," he teased, escorting her out of the room. At the top of the stairs he halted. "Are you sure this is what you want, Sunny?"

"Oh, yes Gabriel, with all my heart."

"Then let us not keep the captain wondering," he said, walking her down the stairs to where her groom waited.

****

Rafe didn't know when he'd seen a lovelier vision than Sunny Beth coming forth garbed in her wedding dress. The simplicity of the ivory gown she wore magnified her splendor. As she neared him with angelic beauty, his focus was riveted on her. Their eyes locked, the depth of their love speaking in silent volumes through their gaze.

"My heart is forever in your hands," he whispered in her ear.

She smiled up at him. "As mine is forever in yours."

Taking her small but strong hand in his, he entwined his fingers with hers. It would be his life's blood to stand beside her, care for her, protect her, and love her with every inch of his heart and soul.

He not only spoke the vows but cherished them, tucking them away in his memory to obey and keep throughout his entire life. Never would he do anything to compromise the love and trust they shared.

The day seemed to pass in a blur, as guests congratulated them and all sorts of savory dishes and delicious pastries were served. The wine flowed freely, toasts were made, music played, peopled danced, laughed, and made merry.

And then the time he'd waited for from the first moment he touched his lips to hers, finally arrived. With anticipation, he said his farewells to their family and friends and ushered his young wife into the carriage that stood waiting to take them to their honeymoon suite at the Barcelo Brighton, Old Ship Hotel in town. The next day they'd catch the train to London, and then on to Liverpool, where they'd board a luxury ship to Ireland. Finally his bride would see her beloved sister again. The whole trip was a surprise, his wedding gift to Sunny.

He drew her close and kissed her lips, the blood

in his veins rushing through his body. "At last you are all mine."

She bit her bottom lip and glanced down at their fingers entwined.

"What is it, my love?" he questioned, raising her chin with a finger.

She sighed, meeting his gaze. "I have never...never been with—" she clipped her words and cleared her throat. "I have never known a man, and you have had so many women." Her full bottom lip trembled. "What if I do not please you?"

He cupped her chin and kissed her nose. "Oh, my dear Sunny Beth, you please me already."

She frowned. "By doing what?"

"By just being my wife, vowing to always love me and stand beside me through this life." He chuckled. "Everything else will fall into place, I promise."

She relaxed against him. "Are you sure?"

He kissed the top of her head. "Aye, very."

Chapter Forty

Sunny read aloud the plaque on the wall in the hotel's lobby. "The Barcelo Brighton, Old Ship Hotel, with its breathtaking ocean view, dates back in part to 1559 and is rich in East Indian architecture." She glanced around at the ornate arches, inlayed tile, and artwork on the walls and ceiling. "It does take my breath away."

"Much like you do mine," Rafe whispered, taking her by the hand. The two of them followed the porter carrying their baggage to the reception desk.

After registering, the porter led them to the second floor and the honeymoon suite. Lit candles shed a romantic glow about the room that was secluded from the other guests. To have that extra privacy gave her a rush of relief. She knew what would take place in this room tonight, and though she welcomed the outcome, she did not think others needed to hear their ardor through the walls.

Rafe doffed his jacket and made his way to the small round table that held a bottle of champagne and two long-stemmed crystal goblets. After popping the cork, he poured them each a glass, handing one to her.

"To us," he toasted.

"To us," she repeated, sipping delicately at the bubbly liquid. After setting the goblet aside she eyed the massive bed, covered in brocade and heaped with pillows. A mixture of apprehension and anticipation rushed through her veins. This would be the night she would give herself to her husband, the night when the two would become one. The women in her tribe talked about such a night. Some worried their husbands would not be pleased. Now Sunny knew why, as such fear welled inside of her. Did she dare stall for time?

"I wonder what sort of view of the ocean we have from this level," she said, making her way to one of the large draped windows.

He reached for her hand. "I'd prefer to feast my eyes on the view before me, instead. Besides, I've fancied myself removing your skirts for a reason other than to save your life," he teased.

"Then I must insist, from this day on, it is only *my* skirts you remove," she dared, realizing fully he would not be put off. No, her new husband was ready and anxious for the coupling to begin.

His expression softened. "I have no desire to ever do otherwise."

She bit her bottom lip and turned from him, casting her glance away.

He cupped her chin, turning her eyes to meet his. "I mean it, Sunny. I will remain forever faithful to you. What I did before meant nothing, and I've come to realize it isn't the way I chose to live my life, nor do I want to just roam the sea. Now, I want you, a family, and a home. You must believe me."

"I do believe you; it is just that I am so...so—" she inhaled sharply.

"So, what?" he probed. "Please, my love, tell me what bothers you."

She was always told, by her parents and grandmother, a good marriage harbors no lies or secrets. She would not start out on her nuptial night with a clouded heart. Squaring her shoulders she locked eyes with Rafe. "I am ignorant of what is expected of me. I do not want to disappoint you, but I fear that is exactly what will happen, especially since you are so—"

He pressed the tip of his finger against her lips,

quieting her words. "Hush, my love. All I expect from you is a true heart." He drew her close. "And you are far from ignorant. Innocent, perhaps, but never ignorant."

"And how does innocent set with you?" she whispered.

His face lit with truth. "Amazingly refreshing and ultimately thrilling."

She stepped from his embrace to remove the amber brooch pinned to her collar. "I hope I live up to such expectations." She placed the jewel on the bedside table, fingering for a moment the ornate gold framing. It was so perfect, a bloom of beauty, encased in the amber and never to be touched by time.

He came up behind her and began to unfasten the buttons of her gown. "I have not one doubt you will be anything but incredible."

Sliding the material off her shoulders, he pushed aside the ringlets of curls and kissed the back of her neck. His lips were soft and warm as they trailed a path down her back. Wherever he kissed, her flesh tingled with passion, desire soaring through her veins and heating between her thighs. His touch triggered a million different sensations within her body, foreign yet pleasing. She wondered if it would always be this way. And as he gently turned her to face him, his cornflower blue eyes lit with longing, she silently prayed it would.

Tilting her head upward with the tip of his finger, he whispered, "No longer do I have to wait to feel the warmth of your lips on my own." He captured her mouth, his searing kiss deepening.

His masculine allure fueled even more feverish sensations through her, and she melted in his embrace. He slid the gown off her arms, down passed her hips. It fell in a puddle at her feet. He stepped back a bit to remove the chemise and bloomers. All of her clothes now circled her ankles.

She stood naked before him.

She liked how his eyes caressed her body, lingering in different places, feasting hungrily, roaming the length of her.

He reached out to trace the crescent shaped birthmark over her heart with the tip of a finger. Then he cupped a bared breast in the palm of his hand and caressed it with gentleness. Passion swept her along, and she found herself succumbing willingly to his touch.

Her submission encouraged the foreplay to continue. He teased her nipples, rolling the little buds between the soft pads of his fingertips. He bent his head and drew a hard, pink peak into his mouth. His tongue began a hot dance around the marbleized nub. His attention turned to the other swollen nipple, every muscle in his neck straining and red.

Her own blood rushed through her body, stimulating every fiber of her being. She knew no resistance when it came to this man, and she never wanted to. Forever she would willingly submit to his ardor, compelled, as if under a magic spell, to want nothing more than to constantly be enveloped within his love. That thought now no longer frightened her as it once had. Rafe had proven his heart to her, and no other would ever hold its key. She was free to relish their lovemaking, yearn for it, and enjoy it always, for the rest of her life.

Beautiful, glorious heat spread to the very core of her heart, a slow burning through her body. She swallowed back a moan. In one fluid motion, he lifted her and placed her upon the bed. She pushed aside the pillows, kicked away the coverlet, and lay before him.

His eyes never wavered as he stood looking down at her, hurrying to free himself of his clothes. Boldly, he stood before her in the raw, his erection clear evidence of his manly desires. Her breath caught in her throat as her eyes surveyed the size of his phallus.

"Mercy," she whispered, heat erupting on her cheeks.

A smile twitched at the corners of his mouth. Placing a knee upon the bed, he reached for her hand and brought it to him. She cupped his sac, wrapping her fingers around his stiff yard.

He closed his eyes, and she felt his hot shaft throb in her hand.

"My brother was so right," he whispered. "Your touch is different from the others, gentle, loving, and so wonderfully shy." He opened his eyes and looked deeply into hers. "True love is so different, so absolutely alluring. Never have I felt this way with a woman before."

"Love me now, my *shikaa*."

"The moment I've waited for, anticipated, dreamed of, is now mine. And I will have you, my love...gently, but fully and thoroughly." The love shining in Rafe's eyes filled her heart and freed all her fears.

In one forward motion she was in his arms, feeling his uneven breathing against her cheek as he held her close. Reclaiming her lips, his kiss was slow, thoughtful, sending shivers of desire straight to her toes.

His lips left her mouth and caressed the length of her body, stopping at her navel, his tongue playfully jutting in and out of the small crevice. She marveled in his foreplay, closing her eyes and getting lost in the sensuality he summoned. His hand moved lower, a finger finding the juncture of her thighs. There, he circled the nugget of her passion with featherlike strokes, causing her to become moist and hot. She moaned with pleasure, opening her legs wide, offering herself completely to his touch.

He lowered his face, entering her slick passage with his tongue, taunting the dewy bud. The gentle massage sent currents of desire through her, and she moaned again, calling out his name as her body shattered into glorious spasms.

Instinctively, her body arched toward him, their curves and angles melding as one. As he entered her, parted her with his penetration, a searing heat erupted. She gasped when he broke her virginity, and his body stilled within her.

Rafe held onto her hips, looking deep into her eyes. "It won't always hurt like this," he said softly.

"It is a sweet agony," she murmured.

"Aye, a sweet torture the body craves and the heart yearns for," he said. "I know this will always be the case for me. Never can I live without you now, nor will I be too long apart from you, Sunny. You are the wellspring of my existence, my cornerstone and resting place. Where I thrive and dwell in peace and pleasure...my sanctuary."

"Then it will always be this way between us, this yearning and desire?" she whispered.

"Oh, aye, my love, of that I am certain," he promised her. "Forever I want to be lost deep within the warmth of your body."

Again they found the tempo that bound their bodies together, hers clinging to the helm of his member, tight and hot; breasts rubbing against his chest with the rhythm of their lovemaking. Impatience grew to explosive proportions. Her blood boiled, her pulse hammered within her flesh.

"Never will my heart be separated from yours, and I'd give my life to protect you," he declared in a husky voice. Clearing his throat, he swallowed hard his emotion. "So, this is what it is like, this thing called love...the glorious and complete feeling of belonging to just one woman," he choked, his juices bursting inside of her with a downpour of fiery sensations. "I love you Sunny Beth."

Sunny felt his love flow into her like warm honey, and she lay drowned in the waves of ecstasy that washed over her. As he rolled off of her, she cradled her chin beneath his neck and whispered. "I love you, too, my *shikaa*."

"What is shikaa?" he asked, his hand resting familiarly upon her backside.

"It is the Apache word for husband," she explained, stroking the close-cropped curls of his well manicured beard.

He snuggled closer to her, pulling the quilt around her shoulders. "And what is the word for wife?"

"*Shi'aad* means my wife."

"*Shi'aad*," he repeated.

She smiled. "I like the way Apache sounds on your tongue."

"I hope you will like the surprise I have for you even better," he whispered.

She pulled back to look at him. "You have a surprise for me?"

"Aye, a wedding gift that I think will please you greatly."

She sat up, the quilt falling to her waist. "May I have it now?"

He smiled, a mischievous twinkle glittering in his eyes. "I believe I shall never get tired of seeing you in the glorious state of undress. Nor that delectable birthmark you tote above your heart."

"That is the Collins crest, inherited by my ancestors."

"Then you are a branded woman. Perhaps I should tattoo the Cavendish Coat-of-Arms over your other beautiful breast," he said, surveying her nakedness with hungry eyes.

Her cheeks warmed, and she reached for the

edge of the quilt, bringing it up to conceal her breasts.

He laughed. "Oh, my dear woman, you can no longer hide yourself from me."

She wrinkled her nose playfully. "Let us stick to the subject at hand."

He continued to tease her with a deliberate frown. "Which was?"

She sighed. "My surprise, please."

"Very well," he said, rising from the bed. As he made his way to where he left his jacket, he reached for the wedding gown, still heaped in a pile on the floor, and placed it upon a nearby chair.

She admired his naked backside, the way the muscles in his thighs moved as he bent and walked across the room. She giggled. "I am glad you cannot hide anything from me, either."

He pulled an envelope from his jacket pocket and turned to face her. "Perhaps, since my bride is feeling a bit cheeky"—he held up the envelope—"the surprise can wait."

She reached a hand out to take the packet. "I think bloody not."

He threw his head back and laughed. "Well, I see you've picked up a bit of Brit." Rafe returned to the bed and lay down beside her. "Happy nuptials," he said, handing her the packet.

She ripped the envelope open and discovered two tickets aboard the *Gateway,* a ship bound for Limerick, Ireland. She shrieked with delight and flew into his arms. "We are going to see Raven?"

"Aye," he said, holding her close.

She glanced at the wedding dress draped over the chair. "I will now be able to bring her mother's wedding dress. It rightfully belonged to her first."

"Ah, but you wore it with such splendor," he said, caressing her bared backside.

"Oh, Rafe, *ashoge*, thank you for such a

wonderful gift," she said, bestowing kisses all over his face. "When do we leave?"

"Tomorrow we will catch the train to London, then another going onto Liverpool," he began to explain.

She giggled.

He frowned. "What amuses you?"

"The name of the town."

He arched a brow. "You mean, Liverpool?"

She nodded. "I thought it sounded funny and strange the first time I heard it, and I still do."

He joined her mirth. "Aye, well, to be sure there are many funny and strange people roaming about there." Clearing his throat, he continued. "We will board the *Gateway* from Liverpool and be in Ireland within a few days."

"I love you, my *shikaa*," she whispered.

"As I do you, *shi'aad*," he countered. "With all of my heart."

She smiled. "Ah, yes, you thrill me when you talk Apache."

"Then I shall have to learn more, won't I?"

She nodded. "It is a pure and true love I hold for you, Raphael Joshua Cavendish."

"And do you know what they say about true love, Mrs. Cavendish?"

She beamed with contentment at the sound of her new name. "Please, enlighten me."

He pointed to the brooch upon the bedside table. "True love, like a rose in amber, lasts forever." And with that said, Rafe captured her mouth once again with a searing kiss.

A word about the author...

A Rose in Amber is Roberta C. M. DeCaprio's seventh book to be published. Her love for historical and paranormal romance has made her prolific, writing seven books in four years. A member of Romance Writers of America, Roberta was a former assistant editor and columnist for *A.B.L.E.D. Women* magazine & *Independence Today* newspaper, two publications dedicated to the rights of the disabled. Having a walking impairment herself since birth, Roberta knows first hand the struggles met each day while living with a physical challenge. A mother and grandmother, she lives in upstate New York with her artist husband and many beloved pets.

To browse her site and read excerpts from her books, log on to:
www.robertadecaprio.com.

Thank you for purchasing
this Wild Rose Press publication.
For other wonderful stories of romance,
please visit our on-line bookstore at
www.thewildrosepress.com.

For questions or more information
contact us at
info@thewildrosepress.com.

The Wild Rose Press
www.TheWildRosePress.com

To visit with authors of The Wild Rose Press
join our yahoo loop at
http://groups.yahoo.com/group/thewildrosepress/